The Story Sisters

ALSO BY ALICE HOFFMAN

The Story Sisters

A Novel

ALICE HOFFMAN

BROADWAY PAPERBACKS

NEW YORK

Copyright © 2009 by Alice Hoffman

Reading Group Guide copyright © 2010 by Random House, Inc.

All rights reserved.
Published in the United States by Broadway Paperbacks, an imprint of the
Crown Publishing Group, a division of Random House, Inc., New York.
www.crownpublishing.com

Broadway Paperbacks and its logo, a letter *B* bisected on the diagonal,
are trademarks of Random House, Inc.

Originally published in hardcover in the United States by Shaye Areheart Books,
an imprint of the Crown Publishing Group, a division of Random House, Inc.
New York, in 2009, and subsequently published in paperback in the United
States by Three Rivers Press, an imprint of the Crown Publishing Group,
a division of Random House, Inc., New York, in 2010.

The chapter opener fairy tales "Follow," "Rose," and "Swan" were originally
published in *Post Road Magazine*.

Library of Congress Cataloging-in-Publication Data

Hoffman, Alice.
The story sisters / Alice Hoffman.—1st ed.
p. cm.
1. Sisters—Fiction.   2. Mothers and daughters—Fiction.   3. Loss
(Psychology)—Fiction.   4. Psychological fiction.   I. Title.
PS3558.O3447S76 2009
813'.54—dc22   2008051054

ISBN 978-0-307-40596-8

Printed in the United States of America

10 9 8 7

First Broadway Paperbacks Edition

To Elaine Markson

Part One

Follow

Once a year there was a knock at the door. Two times, then nothing. No one else heard, only me. Even when I was a baby in my cradle. My mother didn't hear. My father didn't hear. My sisters continued sleeping. But the cat looked up.

When I was old enough I opened the door. There she was. A lady wearing a gray coat. She had a branch from a hawthorn tree, the one that grew outside my window. She spoke, but I didn't know her language. A big wind had come up and the door slammed shut. When I opened it again, she was gone.

But I knew what she wanted.

Me.

The one word I'd understood was daughter.

I asked my mother to tell me about the day I was born. She couldn't remember. I asked my father. He had no idea. My sisters were too young to know where I'd come from. When the gray lady next came, I asked

the same question. I could tell from the look on her
face. She knew the answer. She went down to the
marsh, where the tall reeds grew, where the river
began. I ran to keep up. She slipped into the water, all
gray and murky. She waited for me to follow. I didn't
think twice. I took off my boots. The water was cold. I
went under fast.

It was April in New York City and from the window of their room at the Plaza Hotel everything looked bright and green. The Story sisters were sharing a room on the evening of their grandparents' fiftieth anniversary party. Their mother trusted them completely. They were not the sort of teenagers who would steal from the minibar only to wind up drunk in the hallway, sprawled out on the carpet or nodding off in a doorway, embarrassing themselves and their families. They would never hang out the window to wave away cigarette smoke or toss water balloons onto unsuspecting pedestrians below. They were diligent, beautiful girls, well behaved, thoughtful. Most people were charmed to discover that the girls had a private, shared language. It was lovely to hear, musical. When they spoke to each other, they sounded like birds.

The eldest girl was Elisabeth, called Elv, now fifteen. Meg was only a year younger, and Claire had just turned twelve. Each had long dark hair and pale eyes, a startling combination. Elv was a disciplined dancer, the most beautiful in many people's opinions, the one who had invented the Story sisters' secret world. Meg was a great reader and was never without a book; while walking to school she often had one open in her hands, so engrossed she would sometimes trip while navigating familiar streets. Claire was diligent, kindhearted, never one to shirk chores. Her bed was made before her sisters opened their sleepy eyes. She raked the lawn and watered the garden and always went to sleep on time. All were self-reliant and practical, honor students any parents would be proud to claim as their own. But when the girls' mother came upon them chattering away in that language no one else could understand, when she spied maps and graphs that meant nothing to her, that defined another world, her daughters made her think of clouds, something far away and inaccessible.

Annie and the girls' father had divorced four years earlier, the summer of the gypsy moths when all of the trees in their yard were bare, the leaves chewed by caterpillars. You could hear crunching in the night. You could see silvery cocoon webbing in porch rafters and strung across stop signs. People said there were bound to be hard times ahead for the Storys. Alan was a high school principal, his schedule too full for many visits. He'd been the one who'd wanted out of the marriage, and after the split he'd all but disappeared. At the age of forty-seven, he'd become a ladies' man, or maybe it was simply that there weren't many men around at that stage of the game. Suddenly he was in demand. There was another woman in the background during the breakup. She'd quickly been replaced by a second girlfriend the Story sisters had yet to meet. But so far there had been no great disasters despite the divorce and all of the possible minefields that accompanied adolescence. Annie and her daughters still lived in the same house in North Point Harbor, where a big hawthorn tree grew outside the girls' bedroom window. People said it had been there before Long Island was settled and that it was the oldest tree for miles around. In the summertime much of the Storys' yard was taken up with a large garden filled with rows of tomato plants. There was a stone birdbath at the center and a latticework trellis that was heavy with climbing sweet peas and tremulous, prickly cucumber vines. The Story sisters could have had small separate bedrooms on the first floor, but they chose to share the attic. They preferred one another's company to rooms of their own. When Annie heard them behind the closed door, whispering conspiratorially to each other in that secret vocabulary of theirs, she felt left out in some deep, hurtful way. Her oldest girl sat up in the hawthorn tree late at night; she said she was looking at stars, but she was there even on cloudy nights, her black hair even blacker against the sky. Annie was certain that people who said daughters were easy had never had girls of their own.

TODAY THE STORY sisters were all in blue. Teal and azure and sapphire. They liked to wear similar clothes and confuse people as to who was who. Usually they wore jeans and T-shirts, but this was a special occasion. They adored their grandmother Natalia, whom they called Ama, a name Elv had bestowed upon her as a toddler. Their ama was Russian and elegant and wonderful. She'd fallen in love with their grandfather in France. Although the Rosens lived on Eighty-ninth Street, they kept their apartment where Natalia had lived as a young woman in the Marais district of Paris, near the Place du Marché-Sainte-Catherine, and as far as the Story sisters were concerned, it was the most wonderful spot in the world.

Annie and the girls visited once a year. They were infatuated with Paris. They had dreams of long days filled with creamy light and meals that lasted long into the hazy blur of evening. They loved French ice cream and the glasses of blue-white milk. They studied beautiful women and tried to imitate the way they walked, the way they tied their scarves so prettily. They always traveled to France for spring vacation. The chestnut tree in the courtyard was in bloom then, with its scented white flowers.

The Plaza was probably the second-best place in the world. Annie went to the girls' room to find her daughters clustered around the window, gazing at the horse-drawn carriages down below. From a certain point of view the sisters looked like women, tall and beautiful and poised, but they were still children in many ways, the younger girls especially. Meg said that when she got married she wanted to ride in one of those carriages. She would wear a white dress and carry a hundred roses. The girls' secret world was called Arnelle. Arnish for rose was *minta*. It was the single word Annie understood. *Alana me sora minta,* Meg was saying. Roses wherever you looked.

"How can you think about that now?" Elv gestured out the window. She was easily outraged and hated mistreatment of any sort. "Those carriage horses are malnourished," she informed her sister.

Elv had always been an animal fanatic. Years ago she'd found a rabbit, mortally wounded by a lawn mower's blades, left to bleed to death in the velvety grass of the Weinsteins' lawn. She'd tried her best to nurse it to health, but in the end the rabbit had died in a shoebox, covered up with a doll's blanket. Afterward she and Meg and Claire had held a funeral, burying the shoebox beneath the back porch, but Elv had been inconsolable. If we don't take care of the creatures who have no voice, she'd whispered to her sisters, then who will? She tried to do exactly that. She left out seeds for the mourning doves, opened cans of tuna fish for stray cats, set out packets of sugar for the garden moths. She had begged for a dog, but her mother had neither the time nor the patience for a pet. Annie wasn't about to disrupt their home life. She had no desire to add another personality to the mix, not even that of a terrier or a spaniel.

ELV WAS WEARING the darkest of the dresses, a deep sapphire, the one her sisters coveted. They wanted to be everything she was and traipsed after her faithfully. The younger girls were rapt as she ranted on about the carriage horses. "They're made to ride around without food or water all day long. They're worked until they're nothing but skin and bones."

"Skin and bones" was a favorite phrase of Elv's. It got to the brutal point. The secret universe she had created was a faery realm where women had wings and it was possible to read thoughts. Arnelle was everything the human world was not. Speech was unnecessary, treachery out of the question. It was a world where no one could take you by surprise or tell you a mouthful of lies. You could see someone's heart through his chest and know if he was a goblin, a mortal, or a true hero. You could divine a word's essence by a halo of color—red was false, white was true, yellow was the foulest of lies. There were no ropes to tie you, no iron bars, no stale bread, no one to shut and lock the door.

Elv had begun to whisper Arnelle stories to her sisters during the bad summer when she was eleven. It was hot that August; the grass had turned brown. In other years summer had been Elv's favorite season—no school, long days, the bay only a bicycle ride away from their house on Nightingale Lane. But that summer all she'd wanted was to lock herself away with her sisters. They hid in their mother's garden, beneath the trailing pea vines. The tomato plants were veiled by a glinting canopy of bottle-green leaves. The younger girls were eight and ten. They didn't know there were demons on earth, and Elv didn't have the heart to tell them. She brushed the leaves out of her sisters' hair. She would never let anyone hurt them. The worst had already happened, and she was still alive. She couldn't even say the words for what had happened, not even to Claire, who'd been with her that day, who'd managed to get away because Elv had implored her to run.

When she first started to tell her sisters stories, she asked for them to close their eyes and pretend they were in the otherworld. It was easy, she said. Just let go of this world. They'd been stolen by mortals, she whispered, given a false family. They'd been stripped of their magic by the charms humans used against faeries: bread, metal, rope. The younger girls didn't complain when their clothes became dusted with dark earth as they lay in the garden, although Meg, always so tidy, stood in the shower afterward and soaped herself clean. In the real world, Elv confided, there were pins, spindles, beasts, fur, claws. It was a fairy tale in reverse. The good and the kind lived in the otherworld, down twisted lanes, in the woods where trout lilies grew. True evil could be found walking down Nightingale Lane. That's where it happened.

They were coming home from the bay. Meg had been sick, so she'd stayed home. It was just the two of them. When the man in the car told Claire to get in the backseat, she did. She recognized him from school. He was one of the teachers. She was wearing her bathing suit. It was about to rain and she thought he was doing them a favor. But he started driving away before her sister got into the car. Elv ran alongside and banged on the car door, yelling for him to let her sister out. He stopped long enough to grab her and drag her inside, too. He stepped on the gas, still holding on to Elv. "Reunina lee," Elv said. It was the first time she spoke Arnish. The words came to her as if by magic. By magic, Claire understood. *I came to rescue you.*

At the next stop sign, Claire opened the door and ran.

ARNELLE WAS SO deep under the ground you had to descend more than a thousand steps. There were three sisters there, Elv had told Claire. They were beautiful and loyal, with pale eyes and long black hair.

"Like us," Claire always said, delighted.

If they concentrated, if they closed their eyes, they could always find their way back to the otherworld. It was beneath the tall hawthorn tree in the yard, beneath the chestnut tree in Paris. Two doorways no one else could get past. No one could hurt you there or tear you into pieces. No one could put a curse on you or lock you away. Once you went down the underground stairs and went through the gate there were roses even when snow fell in the real world, when the drifts were three feet deep.

MOST PEOPLE WERE seized by the urgency of Elv's stories, and her sisters were no exception. At school, classmates gathered round her at lunchtime. She never spoke about Arnelle to anyone but her dear sisters, but that didn't mean she didn't have stories to tell. For her school friends she had tales of life on earth, stories of demons she didn't want her sisters to hear. A demon usually said three words to put a curse on you. He cut you three times with a knife. Elv could see what the rest of them never could. She had "the sight," she said. She predicted futures for girls in her history and math classes. She scared the hell out of some of them and told others exactly what they wanted to hear. Even in Paris when she went to visit her grandparents, the city was filled with demons.

They prowled the streets and watched you as you slept. They came in through the window like black insects drawn to the light. They put a hand over your mouth, kept your head under water if you screamed. They came to get you if you ever dared tell and turned you to ash with one touch.

Each day, the number of girls who gathered around Elv in the cafeteria increased. They circled around to hear her intoxicating tales, told with utter conviction. Demons wore black coats and thick-soled boots. The worst sort of goblin was the kind that could eat you alive. Just a kiss, miss. Just a bite.

"Don't eat bread," Elv warned these girls, who quickly tossed out their sandwiches. "Stay away from metal," she whispered, and the girls who had mouthfuls of braces went home and begged for them to be taken off. "Be careful of ropes," she warned, and in gym classes there were now troupes of girls who refused to climb the ropes, even if that meant detention or a call home to their mothers.

THAT HOT AUGUST four years ago when Arnelle began, late one inky blue night, the girls went into the garden after their mother went to bed. They drew a blanket over their heads. They cut themselves with a razor blade and held the wounds together so their blood would mix and their word would be true. Ever since, the girls had traded blood in August, including Meg, even though they never told her why they'd begun the ritual. They would creep out through the back door when their mother was asleep. That first time, Claire had cried at the sting of the razor. Elv had given her gumdrops and told her how brave she was, perhaps the bravest of all. Claire knew she wasn't the brave one, but the next time she didn't shed a tear. It had been Meg, always so rational, who suggested they stop cutting themselves and put forth the notion that what they were doing was nonsense. Besides, they might get an infection from this procedure, perhaps even blood poisoning. But she hadn't been there when the demon pulled them into his car. She didn't know what you might be forced to do to save your sister.

"Don't worry," Elv had said. "We'll protect each other."

Now, AT THE window of the Plaza, as they brooded over the fate of the horses, Elv was telling her sisters about love. The Arnish were appalled at mortal love. It was a weak brew compared to true Arnish passion. Your beloved in Arnelle would do anything to save you. He'd be willing to be slashed by knives, tied to trees, torn into a bloody heap.

"What if you're in love like Ama and Grandpa?" Meg asked when the rules of love were recounted. They had the comfortable sort of love where they finished each other's sentences. It was impossible to imagine their grandfather tied to a tree.

"Then you're doomed to be human," Elv said sadly.

"Well, maybe I'd prefer that," Meg offered. She was getting fed up with Arnelle. If she wanted to enter an otherworld, all she had to do was open a novel. "I don't want to be among demons."

Elv shook her head. There were some things her practical middle sister would never understand. Meg had no idea what human beings were really like. Elv hoped she never found out.

As for Claire, she couldn't look away from the street. Now all she could see were the carriage horses' ribs sticking out, the foam around their mouths, the way they limped as they trotted off. There was a spell Elv had taught her one night. Meg was up in their room reading, so it was just the two of them in the garden. Ever since the gypsy moth summer they'd left Meg out of their most intimate plans. The spell Elv taught Claire that night was to call for protection. You were only to use it when it was absolutely necessary. Elv took a trowel from their mother's garden shed, where there were spiders and bags of mulch, and drew the sharp edge across the palm of her hand. She let her blood drip into the soil. "Nom brava gig," she whispered. "Reuna malin."

My brave sister. Rescue me.

All Claire had to do was say that and Elv would be there. Just like that terrible day.

"What if you're too far away to hear me?" Claire had asked.

Their own garden seemed strange at night. There were white moths, and the soil looked black. Claire didn't want to think about the things that lived under the weeds. They'd seen a creepy crawly there once that was as big as her hand. It had a thousand legs.

"I'll hear you." Elv's hand was still bleeding, but it didn't seem to hurt. "I'll find you wherever you are."

STANDING BEHIND HER daughters at the window at the Plaza, Annie had a sinking feeling. They were ten floors off the ground and yet the world was too close. Those horrible horses had captured her girls' attention. She didn't want her children to know sadness; she wanted to protect them as long as she could. She wasn't the sort of woman whose marriage ended in divorce, but that's what had happened. Now here she was, raising three teenaged girls on her own. She'd been especially close to them until this Arnelle nonsense had come up, a few months before the divorce. When the Story sisters were younger, Annie could recognize their forms in the dark. She could identify which one had entered a room, distinguishing them by their scents. Claire smelled like vanilla, Meg like apples. Elv's skin gave off the scent of burning leaves.

It was time for the party. Their grandfather Martin was

ailing with a serious heart condition, and the girls' ama wanted to make him happy by gathering the family together for a joyous occasion. All their friends from New York and Paris were here. Annie and the girls went downstairs. Lately, Annie felt overwhelmed. She longed for the time when her daughters were young. When she was at work in her garden and heard their languid voices drifting out from the house, she wondered how she would manage it all: the household, the children, the art history classes she taught at several local colleges. She felt as if everything she did was in halves: half a mother, half a teacher, half a woman. Annie's garden was her one successful creation, other than her children. She was on the town garden tour and often sold seedlings to people on the committee. This year, there had been a huge influx of ladybugs. That was a good sign. If Annie herself smelled like anything, it was most likely the fresh, bitter scent of tomato vines. Every spring she planted at least five heirloom varieties. This year there were Big Rainbows, yellow streaked with red; Black Krim, from an island in the Black Sea; Cherokee purples, a dusky reddish pink; and Cherokee chocolates, a deep cherry-tinged brown, along with Green Zebras, delicious when fried with butter and bread crumbs. People in the neighborhood asked Annie for her gardening secrets, but she had none. She was lucky, she told them. It was dumb, blind luck.

ON THE WAY DOWN to the ballroom, Annie noticed that Meg and Claire were wearing lipstick. Elv had on mascara and eyeliner as well. The other two girls had blue eyes, but Elv's were a darting, light-filled green flecked with gold.

Elv noticed her mother staring and said, "What?" She sounded petulant and defensive. That was her tone of late. She was moody, and several times had run to her room and slammed the door shut over the most trivial argument. Then she would come out to sit in her mother's lap, her long legs swung over Annie's. The divorce seemed to have affected her more than the other girls. She had contempt for her father—*That nitwit?* Annie had heard her say to her sisters. *We can't depend on him for anything. He doesn't know the first thing about us.*

"You look pretty," Annie told her.

Elv pursed her lips. She didn't believe it.

"Seriously. I mean it. Gorgeous."

Annie could see the remarkably stunning woman Elv would someday become. Even now men looked at her on the street, gazing at her as if she were already that woman, which was a worry. Annie shouldn't have a favorite, she knew that. But even when the other two girls had come along, she'd made certain to make special time for her firstborn. She'd been a perfect baby, a perfect child. They would set up a tent in the garden, under the vines, while the other two girls were napping. Elv never napped, not even as a young child. Sometimes the two of them went out and watched fireflies careen through the dusk. When it was pitch-dark, they took flashlights and made their own moons on the canvas tent. Annie would tell fairy tales then, the old Russian stories her mother had told her, stories in which a girl could triumph in a cruel and terrible world.

"YEAH, RIGHT," ELV grumbled as they headed toward the ballroom. She was silent for a while, considering. "Really?"

"Really," Annie assured her.

Their ama was waiting for them. Elv led the way as the girls ran to hug her. Natalia had made their dresses, stitching by hand, carefully choosing the yards of silk. They all wanted her to love them best and to take them to Paris for the rest of their lives. They vied for her attentions, though she vowed she loved them equally.

"My darling girls," she said as they gathered around. She held them close and ran a hand over Elv's hair.

The ballroom was white and gold, with huge windows overlooking the park. There was a five-piece band, and waiters were already serving hors d'oeuvres, salmon and crème fraîche, blini with sour cream, stuffed mushrooms, crab cakes, sturgeon on thin slices of pumpernickel bread. The girls were insulted to discover they'd been seated at the children's table along with a troupe of poorly behaved little boy cousins from New Jersey and California. At least Mary Fox was there. She was their favorite cousin, also fifteen, a month older than Elv. Mary was so studious that she made even logical Meg seem frivolous. She planned to be a doctor, like her mother, Elise, who was Annie's first cousin. Mary didn't notice the sisters' glamorous dresses; she didn't care about appearances. She had no idea that she was pretty with her milky skin and pale hair. For this festive occasion, she had on a plaid dress and her everyday shoes. Because she wore glasses she assumed she was ugly. Mary was honest to a fault and never bothered to be polite. Maybe that was why the Story sisters liked her.

Natalia and Martin's friends, including Natalia's dearest old friend, Madame Cohen, who had flown in from Paris, were seated at the best tables, chattering away. They sipped mimosas and kir royales while at the children's table root beer and Cokes were served. The boy cousins were slurping their sodas through straws.

"Can you believe these morons?" Mary said to Elv. Mary had neither a censor nor a fear of adults. She was particularly ticked off that they were sitting with a bunch of ill-behaved little boys who had no manners at all.

"They probably thought we'd have fun with all the cousins

sitting together," Meg said, reasonable as always. "There's no one else here our age."

"They're not our age," Mary said. "They're infants. In two-thirds of the world we'd already be married. Well, maybe not Claire, but the rest of us. We'd have our own children by now."

While the Story sisters thought that over, Elv asked the waiter to take the bread basket away. Mortals slipped slices of bread into their babies' blankets to keep the faeries away. In most fairy tales it was the mortal child who had been stolen, but it had been the other way around on Nightingale Lane.

The boy cousins were now situated under the table playing poker, betting with toothpicks.

"Ugh. They are so gross," Mary sighed. "And this party is such a waste of money." She couldn't tolerate the extravagance of the event. She'd spent her Christmas vacation working on a project in Costa Rica for Habitat for Humanity. "Your grandparents could have donated the money to the Red Cross or the American Cancer Society and saved lives, but instead everyone is dancing the cha-cha."

"I think it's romantic," Meg said. "Fifty years of marriage."

"I think it's revolting," Mary countered. "I'm never getting married."

The girls looked to Elv.

"Love is what matters," she said. "Real love. The kind that turns you inside out."

That didn't sound particularly appealing—it sounded painful, as if blood and bones and torture were involved—but no one had the courage to question Elv further, not even the cantankerous Mary Fox. They stared at Elv solemnly, each of them wishing they knew what it was like to be her, for a moment, or better still, for a day.

At the end of the meal, plates of iced petits fours were served in pastel colors, green and yellow and pink and a pale eggshell blue that was nearly the same shade as Claire's dress.

Mary turned up her nose. "Fat and carbohydrates," she said, opting for frozen yogurt instead.

Elv put her sweater on, even though the room was quite warm. The waiter had been skulking around, trying to get close to her, breathing on her hair, looking at her as if he knew her.

"Did you want something?" Mary Fox asked him.

"Don't talk to him," Elv said.

Claire was busily collecting cakes in a napkin. The grown-ups had started drinking and dancing in earnest. Even Madame Cohen, who was so refined and scared the Story sisters with her direct questions, danced with their grandpa Martin. The boy cousins had come out from under the table and were smashing the petits fours to smithereens, using their water tumblers as hammers. Each time one crumbled they called out "Hurray!" in the most annoying voices.

Elv didn't pay them the least bit of attention, not even when they stole the cakes off her plate. In the faerie world, the old Queen was dying; she was a thousand years old. She had summoned Elv to her side. *Which of the three is the bravest? She who has no fear of what is wicked is the only one who is worthy. She alone will follow me and be our Queen.*

The girls' mothers were enjoying martinis while discussing their divorces. Why not be brave, indeed. It was the perfect time to sneak out. The city was waiting, and the Story sisters had the chance to be on their own in Manhattan, a rare circumstance. They let Mary tag along. She was their cousin, after all, even though she was so serious and dour. Now she endeared herself to them by saying, "Let's split like pea soup." She was so corny and honest, they laughed and grabbed her and brought her along.

Once they got past the doorman, the girls made a mad dash for the park. They were all giggling, even Mary, who had apparently never jaywalked before. "We're going to get arrested!" she cried, but she galloped across the street without bothering to look both ways. They all loved New York. The pale afternoon light, the stone walls around the park, the radiant freedom. They threw their arms into the air and turned in circles until they were dizzy. They shouted "Hallelujah!" at the top of their lungs, even Mary, who'd been an atheist from the age of five.

When they settled down, the girls noticed that Elv had wandered off. She was walking toward the horses. Some of them had garlands of fake flowers around their heads. They wore blinders, and heavy woolen blankets were draped over their backs. They seemed dusty, as if they'd been housed in a garage at night rather than in a stable. The air smelled like horseflesh and gasoline. The other girls would have been happy to dart down the stairs and head for the zoo or the fountain, but Elv lingered, eyeing the horses. She had thoughts no one else had. She alone could see what they could not. When she narrowed her eyes, all that was wicked in the world appeared, exactly as the Queen had predicted. It was like a scrim of black ink spread across the earth and sky.

Elv saw past the luminous *now* into the murky center of the *what could be*. Would anyone else at the party have seen how tired and beaten down the horses were? Most people looked at what was right in front of them. A glass of champagne. A dance floor. A piece of cake. That was all they knew, the confines of the everyday world.

A couple got into the first carriage in line. They were on their honeymoon, arms draped over each other. The driver whistled, then clucked his tongue. He tugged on the reins. The horse, resigned, began to move. One of his legs seemed wobbly.

"This is animal cruelty," Elv said. Her voice sounded far away. She had the desire to cut off the hansom driver's hands and nail them to a tree. That was what happened in fairy tales. Evil men were punished. The good and the true were set free. But sometimes the hero was disguised or disfigured. He wore a mask, a cloak, a lion's face. You had to see inside, to his beating heart. You had to see what no one else could.

The next horse on line looked the worst, old and dilapidated. He kept lifting one hoof and then the other, as if the asphalt of the city street caused him pain. He wore a straw hat, and somehow that was the saddest thing of all.

"I don't see why you're so concerned about a bunch of fleabags," Mary Fox huffed. "There are human beings starving to death all over the world. There are homeless people who wish they had as much to eat as these horses."

Elv's beautiful face was indignant. She flushed. She spoke to her sisters in Arnish, something she rarely did in front of outsiders. "Ca bell na." *She knows nothing.*

"*Amicus verus est rara avis,*" Mary shot back. She was vaguely insulted that she hadn't been included in the invention of Arnish. "That's Latin," she added. "FYI."

The old horse on line was foaming at the mouth. There was a river of noise on Central Park South. The driver snapped his whip.

"Ca brava me seen arra?" Elv said softly. *Who among us has the courage to do the right thing?* "Alla reuna monte?" *How can we save him?*

Elv was the dancer, Meg was the student, but Claire was the one who knew how to ride. She had been attending classes at a stable not far from their house. Her instructor had said she was a natural. Elv and Claire exchanged a look. They could communicate without speaking. Exactly as they had in the horrible man's car. In

Arnelle, it was possible to read each other's thoughts, especially if the other person was your sister. Your own flesh and blood.

The owner of the hansom was busy talking to the driver behind him. They were both lighting up cigarettes. There was blue-black exhaust in the air as taxis and cars sped by.

Elv went up to the men.

"Excuse me," she said.

Both men turned and looked her up and down. She was gorgeous, a peach.

"Did you ever hear the story about a princess the enemy tried to capture?" Elv said. Her voice sounded funny—but she went on. "The princess got away, but they captured her horse instead." This was the way all the best stories started, in a country nearby, a world full of human treachery.

"Oh yeah?" The driver of the hansom drawn by the old horse with the straw hat signaled her over. "Why don't you come closer and tell me about it."

The men laughed. Elv took three steps nearer. Three was a safe number. There were three sisters, three beds in their room, three coats in their closet, three pairs of boots on the floor. The smell of horseflesh made her feel sick. Her throat was dry. The second driver had his lunch in front of him. A hero sandwich wrapped in brown paper. Elv's mother had been the one to tell her the story of the loyal horse in their garden one night. It was one of the old Russian stories that never shied away from cruelty. *Are you sure you want to hear it?* Annie had asked. *It's such a sad story.* There had been white moths fluttering around the tent they'd set up. The other little girls were upstairs, asleep in their beds. *Oh yes, please,* Elv had said.

"They burned him and stripped him of his flesh," Elv went on. "They cooked him in a cauldron. Then they nailed his skull to a wall."

"That's not a very nice story." The second driver clucked his tongue.

"Come on closer. I'll tell you a story," the driver of the bad hansom urged. "I've got a much better story for you."

Elv looked at them coolly, even though she felt a wave of dread. If they knew she was nervous, she'd be at their mercy. But if they thought she was ice, they'd be afraid to touch her. "Later, they tricked the princess and trapped her in a garden maze. But she made her escape because the skull spoke to her. Run away, it told her. Run as fast as you can."

No one noticed that Claire had gone up to the carriage horse. The horse snorted, surprised to have been approached by a stranger, skittish until Claire opened the napkin filled with petits fours she'd taken from the party. At the stable down the road in North Point Harbor, the horses crowded around for carrots, but Claire knew they preferred the oatmeal cookies she often had in her pockets. The old carriage horse seemed to appreciate the French pastries he was offered.

The driver's attention was still diverted, so Claire went around to the steps and climbed into the carriage. She didn't know what she was doing, but that didn't stop her. She was thinking about animal cruelty, and ribs showing under the skin, and the way those men were looking at her sister. She had never been brave in all her life. Now she had the definite sense that something was ending, and something was beginning. Maybe that's why her hands were shaking. Maybe that was why she felt she had already become a different person than she'd been that morning.

Claire had never even been in a hansom cab, although she'd ridden in a horse-drawn sleigh in Vermont. Last winter, their mother had taken them to an inn where there was a cider festival. It was supposed to be a fun getaway, but the local teenagers mocked them. The ringleader, a skinny boy who was nearly six feet tall, had called Meg an ugly bitch. He'd gone to grab her hat, but Elv had come up behind him. She kicked him so hard he'd squealed in pain and doubled over. "Now who's the bitch!" she had cried. They'd had to run back to the barn where their mother was waiting, wondering where they'd disappeared to. They'd been laughing and gasping, exhilarated and terrified by Elv's daring.

Claire thought it would be difficult, maybe even impossible, to figure out the particulars of the carriage, and she'd have to struggle to get it to work, but as soon as she picked up the reins, the horse started off. Maybe it was her light touch, or perhaps the old horse knew he was being rescued; either way he took the opportunity to flee, not slowly clip-clopping like the previous horse and carriage. He took off at a trot. Claire felt light-headed. Horns honked and the carriage jostled up and down precariously, wooden wheels clacking.

The driver turned from Elv to see his carriage disappearing down the road. He took off running, even though it was impossible to catch up. On the sidewalk, Elv leaped up and down, applauding. "Yes!" she cried out. She wanted the horse to run as fast as it could. She felt alive and free and powerful. They had made their plan in absolute silence, that was how deeply she and Claire knew each other.

Meg and Mary Fox watched, stunned. The horse was at a full gallop now. Runners and cyclists scattered. The carriage was shaking, as though it might spring apart into a pile of wood and nails.

It took all of Claire's strength to hold on to the reins. She remembered the number one rule her riding instructor had told her. Never let go, not under any circumstances. She could feel the leather straps cutting into her hands as she was tossed up and down on the seat. There was an upholstered pillow, but underneath there was only a plank of wood that hit against her tailbone. Maybe she should have been more frightened, but she had the impression the horse knew where he was going. He'd probably been along this same route a thousand times. Everything was a blur. There were sirens in the distance, blending together into a single stream of noise. Claire had never felt so calm. She had the sensation of floating, of following destiny in some way.

"Good boy," Claire called, although she doubted the horse could hear her. Everything was so noisy. He was running and the air was rushing by. The horse had kept to the asphalt path, but he suddenly veered onto the grass. There was a big bump as they went over the curb. Claire could barely breathe, but she held tight to the reins. It was quieter on the grass. Everything smelled fresh and green. Now Elv would be proud of her. Now she would be the one to make the sacrifice, save the day.

Se nom brava gig, Elv would say. *You are my brave sister.*

Slats from the carriage were falling off, leaving a trail in the grass. They had almost reached the reservoir. That's where the horse seemed to be heading. When they arrived, Claire hoped he would stop and drink. Everything would be fine then. She was certain of it. Maybe they could take him home, to the stables out on Long Island. She could bring him special treats every day, and he could be happy, and they could be too.

Mary Fox dashed back to the Plaza to look for her mother. She ran so fast that she began to have an asthma attack. She stopped when at last she reached the ballroom door. By then she was gasping. Tears were steaming down her face and she was shaking. Seeing Mary in such a state was shocking. Everyone knew her as logical Mary who read medical journals for fun. Now she seemed transformed. Her hair was straggly, her face ashen.

"Hurry!" she cried. Her voice sounded childlike, reedy. "It's life or death!"

The girls' grandfather, so recently ill, was taken home by Elise, who also had Mary in tow, her inhaler already in use. Madame Cohen was taken to her hotel by their uncle Nat so that she wouldn't get the wrong impression of Americans and their dramas. Still, Madame Cohen worried about the Story sisters, especially the eldest, who had the misfortune of being too beautiful and had a far-off look in her eyes. Madame Cohen had seen what could happen to girls like that; they were picked off like fruit on a tree, devoured by blackbirds. No one liked to hear bad news, but she would have to warn Natalia. She would have to tell her to look more carefully at her eldest granddaughter. She would tell her to look inside.

PEOPLE GATHERED IN ragged groups outside the Plaza, hailing cabs, wondering how the day had gone so wrong. Annie and the girls' grandmother raced to the line of carriage horses. When they explained to a policeman what had happened, he quickly called for a squad car. Everything seemed to be going at a different speed. Time was in fast-forward. At least the other girls were safe, running over to their mother and grandmother at the entrance into the park. Meg looked pale, but there was bright color in Elv's cheeks.

When the police cruiser pulled up, Meg got in alongside her grandmother. She felt irresponsible and scared. She should have watched over Claire. Something had gone terribly wrong and she hadn't done a thing to help.

Elv came to stand beside the squad car. There was green pollen in her hair. She looked shimmery and hot. Everything she touched smelled burned, like marshmallows held too long over a bonfire. "I hope that driver gets put in jail for a thousand years," she said. Her voice was powerful, as though she were reciting a curse.

Annie felt a chill. Elv was always at the center of things, gathering the other girls around her. "Whose idea was this? Yours?"

Elv narrowed her green eyes. "It was animal cruelty."

"Get in the car," Annie told her. "We don't have time to discuss it."

Elv climbed into the back of the police car, sitting in the middle beside her sister, so crammed in she was practically on Meg's lap. The cruiser took off through the park, siren blaring. All the windows were rolled down. The wind whipped through with such force that it stung. Elv wished they could go even faster. She liked the way her heart felt, thumping against her chest. As for Meg, she kept her fingers crossed and held her head down. She said a silent prayer. She couldn't bear for anything bad to happen to Claire, who always put others first, even an old horse she'd never seen before.

Midway through the park they spied the horse, galloping at full speed. He didn't look old, like skin and bones. He looked as if nothing could stop him. A patrol car was racing alongside of him, keeping pace. An officer who was a marksman took a shot from the window of the car. One shot and the horse stumbled. Another, and he fell with a crash. The carriage went up and nearly vaulted over him before it stopped, shuddering. For Claire, it was like a ride at an amusement park, one where your heart is in your throat, only this time it stayed there. She was afraid that if she opened her mouth her heart would fall onto the grass. She was still holding the reins. Both of her arms were broken. She didn't know that yet. She was in shock. She didn't see the horse anymore. Maybe he had gone on running. Perhaps he'd had made it to the reservoir and was drinking cool green water. But when Claire pulled herself up, she glimpsed the heap on the ground in front of her. She was fairly certain she could see his chest moving up and down. She thought he might still be alive, but she was mistaken.

The officers from three squad cars came racing over. Claire still wouldn't let go of the reins. An ambulance had pulled up and one of the EMT crew members came to talk to her. "Just let me unwrap them," he said. He would be careful, he promised, and it wouldn't hurt. But Claire shook her head. She knew it would hurt. She could still hear the clattering sound of the racing carriage through the quiet. She would hear it for a long time. A dappled light came through the trees and spread like lace along the ground. She smelled something hot and thick. Even though she'd never breathed in that scent before, she knew it was blood.

The girls' mother and grandmother were ushered from the police cruiser to the fallen carriage. The other Story sisters were told to stay where they were. They were too young to see what was before them. Death, broken bones, a trail of blood. But as soon as Annie and Natalia were across the lawn, Elv darted out.

"Come on," she urged Meg.

"We're supposed to stay here," Meg reminded her.

"It's Claire. She's hurt."

"They said not to." Meg's face was set. She had already decided. She was not going to listen to Elv anymore.

"Okay. Fine." Elv was disgusted. Those who could not be brave were condemned to the human world. "Stay."

Elv ran across the lawn. Her dress looked as though it had been made of blue jay feathers. Of course she would have the loveliest of them all. Meg had an odd feeling in her stomach as she watched her sister approach the horse. It was resentment, a pit she had swallowed that was already sending out tendrils, twisting through a tangle of her innermost self.

In the green bower of the park, Elv knelt down beside the horse. Snippets of grass clung to its black hide. There was blood seeping into the lawn, staining the hem of her dress. The blue fabric turned red, then black. Elv didn't care. She leaned close to whisper into the horse's ear. She had always believed that dead things could understand you if you spoke their language. Arnish was close enough to the lexicon of death. It was spoken underground, after all, by those who had known the cruelty of the human world. Surely, the horse would be able to hear her. Another girl might have shrunk from the bitter odor of blood and shit and straw, but not Elv. She wished the horse well on his journey to the other side. People in the park stopped to stare. They had never seen a more beautiful girl. Several passersby took photographs. Others got down on their knees right there in the grass as if they'd seen an angel. Looking out the back window of the squad car, Meg wasn't surprised by what she saw. Of course Elv's dress would be covered with blood and people would pity her, when she wasn't even the one who'd been hurt.

CLAIRE REFUSED TO speak to her mother. She wouldn't even look at her beloved ama. She closed her eyes so tightly she saw sunspots beneath the lids. If she let go, if she failed in any way, the horse's spirit might wander, miserable, panicked and in pain. It would all be her fault. Everything seemed to be her fault. She might have held on forever, but then she heard Elv's voice.

"Nom brava gig." *My brave sister.*

Claire felt comforted by the sound of Arnish. It made her think of birdsong and of their bedroom at home, things that were safe and comforting and lasting. Elv was never afraid of anything. She wouldn't compromise; she was stubborn and beautiful. There was no one Claire admired more.

The men from the ambulance continued to beg Claire to drop the reins.

"Go back to the car," Annie told Elv. Today the whole world had been turned upside down.

"Har lest levee," Elv said to her sister. *You can let go.*

Claire opened her eyes. It was a relief to finally drop the reins. Her mother unwound them and then the emergency technicians hurried to lift her and carry her to the ambulance. Claire realized there was excruciating pain in both her arms. The pain was terrible and growing worse. It felt hot, as though lit matches had been placed inside her bones. She didn't want her mother in the ambulance with her, she wanted Elv. She called for her sister, but the EMTs said no one under eighteen could accompany her. Claire started screaming, and when she did all the birds flew out of the trees, all the moths rose up from the grass in a curtain of white.

Elv's shoes were streaked with blood and grass stains. "I'm the one she wants," she told her mother. "I don't care what you say. I'm going."

Elv got into the ambulance while Annie begged the EMTs to make an exception this one time. Elv was already perched on the bench beside Claire. Meg and the girls' grandmother had come to wave, but you couldn't see a thing through the ambulance doors. Elv leaned in close.

"Se brina lorna," she whispered.

Claire couldn't make sense out of anything that was happening. She was dizzy and confused. Her mother was there now too, telling her she would be just fine. The siren they'd switched on was so loud it was impossible to hear anything more. But she'd understood what her sister said.

We rescued him.

Gone

The witch came to the village at noon. She moved into a cottage in the middle of town, got a fire burning, put up her pot.

The next morning a famine began. In the afternoon the roads were filled with frogs. By suppertime there was lightning. By early evening the birds all fell out of the trees.

They sent me to her because I was nothing, a cleaning girl.

I collected frogs in a jar as I went along. I took the charred wood from a tree hit by lightning and tied the twigs together in my shawl. I gathered the birds' bones and kept them in my pocket.

At the well, I stopped and looked down into the black water. Nothing was reflected back. Only the rising moon.

It was night and the streets were empty. Everyone had locked their doors.

What do you have for me? the witch asked.

I gave her the frogs, the charred wood, the bones.
She made a soup and offered me some. All over the
county people were starving. My poor sisters were
nothing but flesh and bone. I sat down to dinner.
When the witch packed up to leave, I was already at
the door.

HEALING TOOK TIME, EIGHT TO TEN WEEKS AT LEAST. CLAIRE
had to undergo an intricate surgery. A metal rod was inserted
into her left arm, and several pins were needed to repair her shattered elbow. She wore two heavy casts, from her wrists all the way
up to her shoulders. She never once complained. She'd done what
she had to, and now she bore the marks of her bravery. She didn't
say a word when she couldn't feed herself or turn the pages of
a book. She wasn't even able to take a shower without first being
wrapped in plastic. The most she could do was look out over Nightingale Lane from her window. She wanted to be as she imagined
Elv would have been had she been the one to be injured: a girl
who couldn't be broken, who refused to feel pain. But Claire's
arms still hurt and she couldn't get comfortable. Sometimes she
cried in her sleep.

Claire never told Elv that she still dreamed about Central
Park. It seemed so babyish and silly. Her dreams were nightmares of grass and blood. She urged the horse to leap, but he
stumbled and tilted over. Sometimes Claire startled in the middle
of the night, awakened by her own soft sobs. As the world came
into focus and her eyes adjusted to the dark, she could make out
Meg's sleeping form and the outlines of their room. There was

the pale wallpaper with its cream and lemon stripes, and the three white bureaus with their glass knobs, and the tall shelf filled with books. On some nights Elv was gone, her bed empty. Perhaps she could drift in and out of Arnelle, disappearing down the secret staircase at will, leaving her sisters behind.

When Claire heard the dusty leaves of the hawthorn hit against each other in the dark, she knew Elv was out there, perched in one of the highest branches. You had to look through the dark to see her, but she was there, breathing in the cool night air. That man wasn't a teacher at their school when they went back in the fall, but Elv whispered that you could never be too careful. She was looking out at the pavement, the asphalt, the trees with their swelling branches. It was so quiet Nightingale Lane seemed like the gateway to the otherworld.

Claire couldn't help but wonder what might have happened on the afternoon of their grandparents' anniversary party if Elv hadn't told her about the horses in the park. How would the day have ended if there'd been no mention of skin and bones and bravery? Perhaps the horse would still be alive. Claire got a shivery feeling thinking about it. She'd felt the same when she was eight and her parents got divorced. All the trees in the yard were covered with gypsy moth cocoons. The whole world seemed spun up in gray thread. People said they wanted to help you, then they did exactly the opposite. She felt safer with Elv out there in the tree.

In the afternoons, when she returned home from school, Elv always brought Claire a cup of soft vanilla ice cream. She fed her with a plastic spoon. She'd get into bed and tell stories about the three sisters of Arnelle. Each had a special task: one to find love, one to find peace, one to find herself. The sisters had a bond no one could break. That was something Claire understood. She and Elv spent more time together after the accident. Meg was busy with after-school activities—the school newspaper, painting lessons, the French club—but Elv came home early, skipping dance class. She murmured to their mother that she was quitting dance in order to help out with Claire, but there was another reason as well. She didn't like to look at herself in the mirror at the dance studio. She didn't think she was as graceful as the other girls. She was too tall, too clumsy. Her teacher, Mrs. Keen, insisted she had real talent. She'd come into the locker room while the other girls went in to warm up and told Elv it was time for her to be serious about her work. All Elv had to do was make the commitment. A dancer's life was one of both commitment and sacrifice. She was such a beautiful girl, she could have whatever she wanted. Elv had sat in the locker room afterward. Things echoed in there. The air was heavy and smelled of sweat. She could feel the beginnings of her black wings. She was from Arnelle, a stolen girl. Mrs. Keen hadn't seen who she was. She didn't know the first thing about her. That was when she'd begun skipping classes.

"Which sister am I?" Claire wanted to know when she was told that the old Queen was looking for someone to take her place. The next in line must be able to place her hand inside the mouth of a lion, her arm inside the jaws of a snake, her entire body into a nest of red fire ants. She must be able to tell the true from the false with her eyes closed. The scent of a lie was the stench of turpentine, dirty wash-water, green soap. She must be able to escape from ropes and metal boxes, to spy treachery from a distance.

"You're the best sister, Gigi." That was Elv's nickname for Claire, taken from *gig,* the Arnish word for sister. Elv's long black hair was pinned up. She stroked Claire's head, which was filled with knots from spending so much time in bed and from sleeping so fitfully.

"No," Claire said. "That's you."

Elv curled up closer. She spoke in a whisper. "Once upon a time I saw a demon on the road. I ran away, but then I realized I'd left you behind."

"You came back for me," Claire said.

Elv linked her arms around her sister. They both laughed when one of Claire's casts bonked against the side of the bed.

"Le kilka lastil," Elv said. *You could kill someone with that.*

"Je ne je hailil," Claire said. *I would if I had to.*

"No, you wouldn't." Elv smiled. "You're the good-hearted sister."

Meg came home, her backpack overflowing. She sat at the foot of the bed. She knew her sisters stopped their conversations whenever she was around. "Everyone's talking about you at school," she told Claire. "You're famous."

"No," Claire said. "I'm not."

"Oh, yes," Meg insisted. "Über famous. 'Page Six' famous."

Evidently there had been an article in the *New York Post* about the mistreatment of carriage horses. The reporter had mentioned the girl from North Point Harbor who'd done her best to control a runaway horse. There were animal rights activists who had built a shrine to her and the fallen horse in Central Park, on the Great Lawn. It was made out of horseshoes and stones. People brought flowers and left them strewn about the grass.

"Se breka dell minta," Elv said solemnly.

We should all bring you roses.

"Well, I brought homework instead." Meg brought forth the papers and books she'd picked up in Claire's homeroom. "I'll read the questions, then you answer and I'll write them down."

"Why don't you just do it for her?" Elv said. "It would be much easier."

"Because I don't know how she would answer." Meg had the habit of chewing on pencils, even though she was afraid it might give her lead poisoning. She had recently found she had a lot of nervous habits. More and more often, she wanted to be alone. She wished she could move into one of the smaller bedrooms downstairs, but she didn't want to hurt her sisters' feelings. She couldn't wait to go to college. She went to the school library to sift through college catalogs whenever she had a free period at school.

"Well, I do," Elv said. "I know her inside out."

Elv grabbed the homework assignment. It was a report on a European capital. Elv began to write about Paris. She wrote about the Louvre, where the girls had spent hours on their last visit. Later, when Elv read the report out loud, Claire told her not to change a thing. She had gotten it all right, even Claire's stop after the museum at her favorite ice cream shop, Berthillon. "Favorite flavor?" Elv had asked. All three sisters had shouted out "Vanilla" at the same time. Even Meg knew the answer to that. Claire never varied from her one and only choice. She refused to try a new flavor. For some reason, answering in unison made them feel happy, as if nothing would ever change, and they would always know one another completely, even if no one else did.

ANNIE HADN'T PUNISHED Claire after the incident with the horse. People said her girls would become sullen and spoiled if she weren't stricter. They said that adolescence was the time when girls flirted with destiny. But Annie was convinced there was no need for Claire to pay any further for her mistake. At the end of the month Claire understood why: spending spring vacation locked away was punishment enough. They were all supposed to go to Paris to visit their grandparents, but when school let out, only Meg and Elv went to France. The sisters had never been separated before. For the first time Claire was alone in their attic bedroom. At night when the leaves of the hawthorn tree rustled, she covered her head with her blanket. She didn't like being twelve. It was someplace between who she'd been and who she was about to be. It felt like no place at all. She had to count to a thousand in order to fall asleep. She missed having Elv out in the tree, keeping watch. She missed Meg's sleepy, even breathing.

In Paris, Meg curled up out on the couch in the red-lacquered parlor of her grandparents' home and wrote postcards to Claire. Meg was lonely and bored. Books didn't comfort her and even the ice cream at Berthillon wasn't as good this year. There should have been three of them, three was the right number. Paris wasn't the same, she complained. The weather was cold and rainy. A warm sweater and wool socks were necessary at all times. There was an old stone trough in the courtyard that had once been used to water horses but this year it had filled with ice, then cracked. The season had been so cold the buds on the chestnut tree never opened; the white buds were pasty and waterlogged around the edges, the glossy leaves more black than green. Plus, Meg and Elv weren't getting along. They got on each other's nerves and disagreed over everything.

"Let's not stay cooped up," Elv had said to Meg one evening. Recently it had crossed her mind that if she didn't know the human world, she couldn't defend herself against it. She had to experience everything. Go behind enemy lines. "We should go out after Ama and Grandpa are asleep."

When Meg had refused, unable or unwilling to break the rules, Elv had taken to sneaking out alone at night, tiptoeing down the back staircase, slipping through the cobbled courtyard. Each excursion was the work of a daring anthropologist: Where do lovers meet? Where can peril be found, and how is it best avoided? Where do squatters live? Can demons be avoided if you don't have the strength or the time to turn and run?

When she read Meg's cards, Claire couldn't help but wonder

if Elv was going off to Arnelle, if she'd found the gate under the chestnut tree, if she knocked three times, then whispered a faerie greeting. *When I walk, I walk with you. Where I go, you're with me always.*

That was what Elv had written on her postcard to Claire. She sat on a bench on the quay, overlooking the Seine while she wrote. She was barefoot, hunched over, scribbling furiously with a pen filled with pale green ink that she'd bought at a stationery store on the Rue de Rivoli. Paris had never been more beautiful, she told her sister, writing in Arnish. I feel free here. *Me sura di falin.* No one will hurt us now.

Elv had come to believe that if she did whatever she was most afraid of, its power over her would evaporate. She held on to metal railings. She went into *boulangeries* and looked at loaves of bread, and she didn't disappear the way most faeries would have. She tied her ankles together with rope, then slit the knots with a knife. If she had known these tricks, she might have been able to escape after she rescued Claire. She had come to believe that evil repelled evil, while good collected it. She could see it happening in the parks. The dark lacelike scrim, the goblins astride the billowy trees, the demons drawn to purity, unnoticed by women on the benches, children at play. A clever girl met evil on its own terms. She didn't get caught unawares. Elv bought a pair of black pointy boots at the flea market. She took up smoking, even though it made her choke. She kept at it until she stopped coughing. She could get used to anything. That's what she had decided. She perfected a look that said *Go away* in every language, most especially in Arnish. It was as though she now possessed her own arsenal of weapons. She didn't mind that men looked at her. Their attraction to her only added to her power.

All the while Meg lay in her bed reading novels, writing her whiny postcards, Elv was exploring the human world. She could feel herself growing stronger. She no longer panicked if the wind came up, if a stranger walked by. She wasn't the least bit spooked when the leaves on the trees rattled, always a sign of rain. The rain in Paris was beautiful, anyway, cold and clean and green. The Queen had told her that if she faced whatever she feared most, she would win the right to sit on the Arnish throne. *Water, sex, death.* Elv wrote the words in green ink on the back of a postcard. She folded the card into threes and kept it under her pillowcase.

One night Elv woke Meg from a deep sleep. It was late at night. Their ama's guest room with its two twin beds was bathed in blue light. Elv had brought home a kitten someone had tried to drown. She'd had to wade far into the water to save it. All the while she had a fluttery feeling in her chest. She imagined the water rising over her. She imagined she could no longer breathe. He had done that to her when she started screaming. She thought about her vow to the Queen of Arnelle. *Water, sex, death.* In an instant, her fear was gone. It was only green water, dirty and cold. She reached out and grabbed.

"It's tiny," Meg said of the kitten when Elv brought it out of the sopping burlap sack it had been tossed into. "Poor thing. It will probably die."

"It's not going to die," Elv said firmly. Why was it that Meg had to try and ruin everything?

The kitten was indeed starving and soon began yowling so loudly their ama came running into the guest bedroom, convinced one of the girls had been struck by appendicitis. Elv should have been in trouble for being out at night, but instead she talked Natalia into letting the cat stay. They named it Sadie and gave it a bowl of cream.

"We won't tell your grandpa," Natalia said. "One day he'll look down and he'll notice a cat and he'll think it has always been here. Anyway, she's a darling creature. Who would mind a little thing like her."

Elv looked elated, though her shoes were sloshy with river water and her clothes were soaked. "You have a good heart," Natalia said to her. Before she went out, she kissed Elv's forehead. Meg had felt herself burning.

Elv was singing to herself. She ripped off all of her clothes and left them in a dank pile in the corner. She was a woman and beautiful and fearless and the queen-to-be. She struck her fear of water off her list.

"You're going to get in trouble if you keep going out at night," Meg told her.

"I don't care," Elv shot back. "Anyway, trouble can find you anywhere. It's probably under your bed right now."

THE BEST PART of the trip was the art classes the girls took with Madame Cohen, at least in Meg's opinion. Elv only seemed interested in sleeping the days away so that she'd be refreshed when she sneaked out at night. The girls had been acquainted with their grandmother's dearest friend since they were little and had often visited her jewelry store. Her stupid grandsons were sometimes there as well, but the Story sisters ignored them; the boys couldn't even speak English. But they respected Madame Cohen. She had once been a watercolorist of some note. She had gone to art school in Paris and Vienna. She was a stern teacher who wore black even in the summer heat, still in mourning for her husband, who'd been gone nearly twenty years. The girls went to sit with her in the kitchenette behind the jewelry shop each day. Elv was sleepy from her wanderings. Sometimes she was so rude she actually put her head on the table and closed her eyes while they were supposed to be painting. Instead of punishing her, Madame Cohen gave her a cup of espresso. Elv didn't even try and her watercolors were beautiful. She only used shades of green. When asked why, she said, "I've been studying the river." Once she made a black painting and when Meg said, "I thought you were only painting the river," Elv laughed and said, "Can't you see what that is?"

Madame Cohen had peered over. "It's the Seine at night."

Elv had nodded, surprised.

"I think it looks like a shoe," Meg said.

"Sisters shouldn't argue. I was one of three sisters myself," Madame Cohen said ruefully. She knew there was evil in the world. She'd seen it with her own eyes. She never talked about the past and was surprised to find herself doing so now. She was older than the girls' grandmother by several years. You didn't see how old she was unless you looked very carefully. Her skin was patterned with very fine lines that made Elv think of the way leaves are veined, how beautiful they are when sunlight filters through.

"May I have more paper?" Meg asked.

"What happened to them?" Elv wanted to know.

Madame Cohen was well aware of the black scrim that stretched above parks and playgrounds. She saw it over her own roof sometimes. Just now, a black bug was trying to get in the window, bumping against the glass. You would think it was nothing, unless you knew better.

"They're gone." Madame Cohen clapped her hands together. That was enough of the past. "If you go out at night, I hope you're careful," she told Elv. Nearly everyone in the neighborhood had heard the stories of the girl who crept out of her grandparents' apartment house, then slipped off her boots so no one would hear the clatter of her heels on the cobblestones. It was the sort of neighborhood where everyone knew everyone else's business, or at least tried to.

Elv smiled and said she certainly would try her best, even though they both knew that being careful was only good for so much.

"I have a bad feeling," Madame Cohen told her dear friend Natalia that same week. It was late and no one knew where Elv had gone off to. She'd told her grandmother she was going to the bookshop, but Natalia had checked and she hadn't been there. Plus, Elv had worn a short black dress, black boots, and she'd lined her eyes with kohl she'd found in her grandmother's old makeup kit. That did not seem like bookstore attire.

"All girls need their secrets," Natalia said. "It's part of growing up. She's about to turn sixteen, after all. Not a child."

"They may need their secrets," her friend replied. "But do they want them?"

MEG SENT CLAIRE a watercolor of the chestnut tree in the courtyard, which Claire taped to the wall above her bed. She stared at it every night, but it was difficult to tell whether there were white flowers on the tree's branches, or dozens of doves, or if perhaps stars had fallen from the sky, only to be caught in a net of leaves. When Meg wrote about Elv's black painting, Claire found herself wanting that one instead. She thought she would be able to see the river, even if Meg could not.

Claire lay on her bed in her dark room, feeling sorry for herself. She loved Paris and ice cream and art. She loved her grandmother's parlor with its red-lacquered walls and the terrace where birds came to perch, begging for crumbs. She didn't know how Meg could be miserable at their ama's or how she could be lonely when Elv was right there or why she didn't dare go to see how many colors of green the river could be.

To cheer Claire, Annie spent huge amounts of time with her. She'd turn on the CD player and they'd sing along to Beatles songs and that was great fun. Or Annie would read from *Anne of Green Gables* or *Robin Hood,* or from old volumes of Nancy Drew that were hokey enough to make them both laugh. They watched movies for hours, all of Annie's favorites, *Charade* and *Alfie* and *Four Weddings and a Funeral.* They watched *Two for the Road* so many times they could both repeat the dialogue by heart.

Claire had never had her mother all to herself and it was lovely to be the center of attention. She even taught her a few words of Arnish. *Melina* was summer. *Henaj* meant dog. But afterward Claire felt she'd betrayed her sisters. It was their secret, after all. Secrets were only good if you kept them; otherwise they were worthless. That was why Claire didn't tell their mother when Meg wrote that there was a man who'd been hovering around Elv. He stood waiting for her out past the courtyard, besotted. He called out Elv's name while they were all seated at the dinner table. Their grandfather, Martin, asked if anyone heard anything and Elv smiled and said, no, she hadn't heard anything at all. Later, when Meg had asked who he was, Elv had merely shrugged. "Nacree," she'd said in Arnish. *Nobody.*

"There's a man following your granddaughter around town," Madame Cohen told Madame Rosen one day when they were playing cards out on the balcony. The weather had cleared. The girls were going home the following afternoon.

"She's beautiful. Lots of men will be showing up."

But Madame Cohen could see accidents before they happened. She saw one now. "Your granddaughter may not be looking for trouble, but trouble is looking for her."

"She's high-spirited," Natalia said. "Girls her age are meant to have adventures."

"He works in a bar, Natalia, dear." Madame Cohen sighed. "This is not some first love. He's thirty years old. I hear he's married."

"We'll take the girls to the airport first thing in the morning," Natalia decided.

"Good idea," her friend agreed, even though she knew that it was quite possible for trouble to find a girl anywhere.

Meg was in the parlor. She couldn't help but overhear. If her grandmother knew the half of it, she would have been shocked. When Elv sneaked in at night she was barefoot, holding her black boots in her hand, smelling like tobacco and perfume and something that Meg didn't recognize, the scent of something burning. Meg always pretended to be asleep, but Elv knew better. One night she had sat on the edge of her sister's bed. "He'll do anything I tell him to. He'd die for me, he said."

Meg had kept her eyes closed.

"I know you're listening." Elv had a rush of adrenaline when she broke rules. She wondered if that was what warriors experienced in the moments before battle. It was like jumping off a bridge. You had to do the thing you were afraid of; after a while you didn't feel anything. That was how it was whenever she was with Louis. He was the fool who felt something, not her. Maybe that's why she'd chosen him. He was a way for her to learn how to manage what life had brought her.

"I hope you never know the things I know," Elv told her sister. "I hope you read your books and think that's what life is."

Meg had thought Elv might be tearing up, but she didn't dare look. Elv slunk off to bed and then it was too late to ask why she went with that man if it only made her cry.

◆ ◆ ◆

WHEN THE STORY sisters went back to school, people said Elv had changed. She seemed far away, an indifferent, elusive girl who painted her nails black and walked through the halls barefoot until the teachers threatened her with detention if she didn't put her boots on. Not that the boots were any better; they were black, pointy-toed. They looked foreign and dangerous and they made the skirts she wore seem even shorter. Girls who used to sit at her lunch table were afraid of the stories she told, brutal, bloody tales in which hands and heads were cut off. People turned into frogs, ate poisonous bugs, were buried alive. No one wanted to hear stories like that anymore. The girls she'd grown up with wondered how she knew the things she knew. They kept their distance. After a while they didn't even bother to say hello.

The boys in town were the opposite. They followed Elv around, and even the brashest among them seemed bewildered. They didn't listen to her stories. They just stared. Elv seemed more beautiful than before, but in a hot, careless way. Boys she'd known since kindergarten begged for kisses. They telephoned late at night and threw pebbles at her bedroom window. She ignored them completely. For her sixteenth birthday Elv didn't want a party. Her sisters were friends enough. Alan showed up with his new girlfriend, who taught biology at the same high school. Annie noticed how young she was, how she was trying to make a difficult situation less strained.

"Alan talks about the girls all the time," the girlfriend said. Her name was Cheryl Henry and she yearned for children of her own. "They're his pride and joy."

"Really," Annie said. "How nice." She offered Cheryl a piece of cake. It was chocolate, with mocha frosting, Elv's favorite. Not that Elv had eaten a bite. They were in the kitchen and Alan had arrived too late for the actual birthday dinner. Elv had been waiting for him, but once he was there, she didn't even say hello.

Alan kissed her on the forehead and gave her a hundred dollars. That was her birthday present.

"Don't spend it all in one place," he'd said to her. Elv watched her father as he fixed himself a cup of coffee, then she disappeared while the others were having their cake. She got into bed and pulled up the covers. Sixteen was nothing. It was meaningless. Elv heard her mother come upstairs, open the door, see that she was in bed, then carefully close the door once more. Her mother was just as blind as her father. What had she thought that summer when Elv wept as the gardeners swept away the cocoons? "It's not a bad thing. It's necessary. Otherwise the moths will eat all the trees," Annie had assured her.

"I don't care," Elv had said. "I couldn't care less."

THE MORNING AFTER her birthday, Elv took the hundred dollars her father had given her and hitchhiked to Hempstead. The guy who picked her up kept looking at her, as though she was a mirage, a faerie who'd appeared in his passenger seat. "Do you have a problem?" she said coolly. She had a paring knife in her pocket, taken from the silverware drawer. "Maybe," the guy had answered. He looked at her as if he expected something to happen, so she got out at a red light and walked the rest of the way. She found the tattoo shop. Patrons were supposed to be eighteen, but Elv looked old enough, as if she knew what she wanted, so no one asked for ID. She had two black stars tattooed above each shoulder, in the place where her wings would be. She found the pain soothing in a strange way, a gateway out of her body, into Arnelle. There was an army gathering there: the Queen had posted them at the doorway.

Anyone residing in the human world was suspect, including Elv. *Prove yourself,* one of the guards said to her. She was wearing a black dress. Black ballet shoes. She could smell jasmine. The tattoo artist was a bit leery now that her shirt was off. He said, "This might hurt." As if she cared about that. He covered the tattoos with white bandages. "There might be some blood seeping through," he told her. As if that mattered.

She waited for the bus, then, once she was home, she walked along Main Street, her shoulder blades burning. She felt free in the dark. When she got to Nightingale Lane, she walked more slowly. She stationed herself across from her house and watched the family inside. Her mother and Meg and Claire and their cousin Mary Fox and Mary's mother, Elise, were all having dinner together. Elv wished she was inside with them, pouring the spaghetti into a colander, cutting up cucumbers, setting the table. She wished she was laughing at Mary's stories of how stupid her classmates were. But she was beside a hedge at the end of Nightingale Lane, and she could barely understand what they were saying, even though the windows were open and their laughter filtered outside.

She heard a rustling. She thought there might be a demon there. She put her hand on the knife in her pocket, but when she turned she spied a boy from school creeping out of the Weinsteins' yard. He was wearing a black sweatshirt and jeans. He saw Elv, hesitated, then came over. His name was Justin Levy and he was madly in love with her.

"Hey," he said, sitting down next to her beneath the hedge.

"Robbing the Weinsteins?" Elv asked.

Justin pulled two vials of pills from his pockets. "OxyContin. Mr. Weinstein has cancer."

He took one of the pills and offered Elv one. She swallowed it, then they lay back in the grass. Elv didn't feel a thing. She just felt quiet. She felt like she could stay under the hedge forever. Her tattoos didn't even sting.

"What kind of cancer?" she said.

"Pancreatic. My dad works with him. My dad said he doesn't have a chance. They're over at my house, having dinner, not that Mr. Weinstein can eat much."

"How'd you get in and out of the house? I thought they had a dog."

"I brought a hot dog with me," Justin Levy said.

Elv laughed. "I'll bet you did."

"He's a nice dog."

The Weinsteins had an old basset hound named Pretzel that woofed when anyone passed by. But if you bent down and patted his head, he instantly became your best friend. For some reason Elv felt like crying when she thought about the Weinsteins' dog. Justin Levy must have known she was upset. He took her hand. When she glared at him, he let go. "Just so you know, I'm not interested in you," Elv told him. "I'm never going to be your girlfriend."

"Okay." Justin Levy was stoned and taken aback. He'd never in his wildest dreams imagined that she would be. Every guy he knew was terrified of her and wanted to fuck her. He was happy just to lie beside her in the grass.

Elv sat up and took off her blouse. Justin Levy watched her, stunned. When she told him to remove the bandages on her shoulders, he did. There was hardly any blood, and underneath, the black stars.

"You know what it means?" Elv asked him.

"That you're beautiful?" Justin ventured.

Elv laughed. That was too funny. People saw with their eyes and nothing else. The day she met a man who knew her for who she was would be the day she would be rescued from this pathetic human world. "That I'm invisible," she said. *There,* she said to the Queen of Arnelle. *There's your proof.*

AT NIGHT, AFTER Meg was asleep, Claire got into bed with Elv to hear stories about Paris. She heard about the different shades of green the river could be, about the way the rain had fallen in sheets. Claire asked for the black painting, but Elv said she couldn't remember what she had done with it. It was ugly, anyhow. When Claire wanted to know about the man Meg had told her about, Elv said he was nothing to her.

"That Meg," she said. "What a bigmouth. She couldn't keep a secret if you paid her."

"Tell me something," Claire begged. "Tell me a secret."

"You have to swear you'll never tell."

"You know I won't."

Elv whispered to Claire that on the night she found the cat, stuffed and mewling in a burlap bag, thrown into the water like so much garbage, there had actually been two bags. She hadn't told Meg or their ama. Elv hadn't been able to reach the second kitten. That haunted her. She couldn't let it go.

"You saved one," Claire said.

"But not the other."

She showed Claire the black stars on her shoulders. Claire was hushed and impressed. "Mom will kill you," she said admiringly.

"She'll never know." Their mother was an optimist, which in Elv's opinion meant she was a fool. "She never knows anything."

They were whispering. They could hear the hawthorn tree and Meg's sleepy breathing and the wind outside. Claire had a lump in her throat. They had secrets they couldn't say aloud. "Where did he take you?" she asked. She had wanted to ask this question for four years. It had taken that long for the words to come out. Some words drew blood, they cut your tongue, they made you know things you couldn't unknow. Elv had been missing for an entire day. Claire had run back and waited at the stop sign. She'd stayed there until it grew dark, until the fireflies appeared in the woods. Until Elv came back. She wouldn't tell her then, and she wouldn't tell now.

"Go to sleep, Gigi," Elv said. "Close your eyes."

IN THE FIRST week of June, there was an unexpected heat wave, with temperatures reaching into the nineties. It was the kind of weather in which people did stupid things, such as throwing themselves off a dock into the cool water, only to break their necks on the rocks. Elderly residents were warned not to go outside. Birds died in their nests. On impulse, Claire decided to have her hair cut short. She usually was a follower and she thrilled herself with her own fierce determination to make a change. She was broiling in her casts, nearly fainting with the heat. Her scalp itched and there was no way for her to scratch it. Annie took her to the hair salon on Main Street, where a young woman named Denise fastened a smock around her shoulders.

"Are you sure? You have such beautiful hair. It seems a shame."

Claire was sure. Denise cut her mane of heavy black hair to just below her chin. They would donate what had been shorn to Locks of Love and a wig would be made for a cancer patient. Claire loved her hair short—it was so much cooler—but when her sisters saw her they were horrified. The older girls were at home watching an old black-and-white movie about a werewolf. They had been captivated by the poor werewolf's plight, enough so that they actually didn't argue the way they usually did. When they saw Claire's haircut, each let out a shriek. Elv said, "Who did that to you? I'll bet it was Mom's idea." Meg, near tears, cried, "Oh, Claire. Now we don't look alike."

Meg's own long black hair was braided and clipped atop her head. She didn't like anything to change. She favored long, involved books like *Great Expectations,* wherein the villains turned out to be heroes and there was always someone who would save the day just when it seemed all had been lost.

"Now we'll never look alike," Meg said sadly.

"There's only one way to do it," Elv advised, once their mother had left the room. "If that's what you want," she said to Meg. "But you're probably all talk."

Meg tilted her chin. She knew her sisters had secrets. She could hear them whispering in bed. "You think so?" she said. "I'll go first. Then we'll see if you have the nerve."

They went upstairs and sat on the floor. Elv lit a black candle she had brought home from Paris. She was wearing jeans and a white T-shirt she'd found at a shop on the Rue de Tournon. It had been hideously expensive, but she'd wanted it so. She slipped it into her purse when the shop owner wasn't looking. You could see right through the fabric but Elv didn't care. She went to get the scissors and a towel to drape around Meg's shoulders. Then she locked the bedroom door.

"Are you sure you want to do this?" she pressed. "A thousand percent sure? This isn't something you can change your mind about later."

Meg nodded. She was very calm. She hadn't had her hair cut since she was ten years old. She thought of it as her only good feature. She was just as beautiful as Elv, but she didn't realize it. Now she unplaited her hair. Perhaps she was even more beautiful than her sister when she wore her hair down.

Claire sat on the edge of Meg's bed. She felt guilty and responsible. "I only cut mine because I'm so hot in my casts and I can't braid my own hair. I can't even wash it. Maybe you shouldn't, Meg. You don't have to."

It was a surprise when Meg was suddenly decisive, as she was now. They had always looked alike and that was what she wanted. She firmly ignored Claire's protests.

"There's no other way. Cut it."

Elv unclasped Meg's braid and began to cut. It took a while because the scissors were old and hadn't been sharpened. She handed Meg the braid when she finally managed to saw through. She kept cutting after that, to even out the edges. Hair continued to fall on the towel and the wooden floorboards.

"You can donate it to Locks of Love," Claire suggested. "For a sick child."

"Or you can burn it and put a hex on someone," Elv recommended as she clipped some more. She was concentrating hard. She'd never cut someone's hair before. At last, Meg went to look in the mirror. Elv had cut her hair very short. Too short. The ends were raggedy from the dull scissors. She looked like a boy.

"It just has to grow out a little," Claire said. "Right?"

"I need a break," Elv said. Once things were changed you couldn't go back. She knew that. Now Meg would know it too. She went out through the window. The leaves outside their window were rattling. Claire could hear her climbing down the hawthorn tree. Meg was still looking at herself in the mirror. She seemed in shock. "She did this on purpose." Meg's face was blotchy, as though she might cry. She ran a hand through her hair. It stuck straight up. "She's not going to cut hers."

"Of course she will," Claire assured Meg. "We always look the same."

They waited, but Elv didn't return. She didn't come home until it was almost morning, climbing in through the window, exhausted. She'd spent the night in Justin Levy's bedroom. She'd made him sleep on the floor. He did whatever she told him, which was pathetic, really. They smoked weed, which didn't affect her in the least, and then she told him to get on the floor. She dreamed of black stars, black water, a black sun in the center of the sky. When the other girls woke up, Elv was finally asleep in her own bed, her long hair knotted, still in her clothes, as if she'd been out dancing in Arnelle all night long.

Annie took Meg to the salon. Denise did the best she could, but Meg's hair wound up being even shorter. She looked like an Olympic swimmer wearing a boy's haircut. When they got back home, she locked herself in the bathroom and refused to come out. Annie and Claire waited in the kitchen. They could hear her quietly sobbing.

"What made her do that to herself?" Annie wondered.

It was ninety-nine degrees, utterly sweltering, and the meteorologists were predicting triple digits and thunderstorms. True summer wasn't even here and it was already unbearable. Annie began phoning around to see if she could have central air-conditioning put in. There were fans set up all over the house. Some folks were paying double for air conditioners being sold out of the back of vans on Northern Boulevard.

Annie felt panic-stricken. Three teenaged girls took up a lot of space in a house. They grumbled and were moody; they kept secrets and cried for no apparent reason. They were moving further away from her. She could not remember the last time they'd all sat down for a meal together, had a discussion, watched a movie. Claire was trying to get Meg to come out of the bathroom, speaking that awful Arnish. The panic spread into Annie's chest. She called around for air conditioners, but there were no air conditioners to be had on all of Long Island. Everyone was hot and dissatisfied and out of sorts. If she wanted an air conditoner she'd have to buy it from one of the scam artists, who were over-charging like mad, and she wasn't about to do that.

"It's a good thing we cut our hair," Claire said when Meg finally emerged from the bathroom, her face splotchy, eyes red.

Claire was getting her casts off at the end of the week. Maybe she'd be happy then. Maybe everything would finally be set right, the way it used to be when she didn't always feel she had to choose between her sisters. "At least we'll be cool during the heat wave," she said to Meg. "And you-know-who won't be."

Their mother was still busy on the phone in her search for an air conditioner. Meg leaned in close. She didn't want Annie to overhear. She didn't even want it to be true, but it was, and it was her duty to let Claire know.

"Elv isn't who you think she is," Meg said in a strange, small voice. "Watch out for her."

ON THE DAY Claire had her casts taken off, the heat finally broke. It was wonderful and odd to suddenly have her arms back. She felt spidery and ill at ease. She was awkward doing the simplest tasks—pouring a glass of orange juice, brushing her teeth. She'd cut her hair, and now Meg and Elv weren't speaking. When they passed each other in the hall, they looked away, as if a shadow was passing by, one they needn't recognize. School would soon be over. Next year everything would be better. They would all go to Paris in the spring; it would be the three of them, the way it was supposed to be. In every fairy tale there were always three sisters: the eldest was brave, the middle one was trustworthy, and the youngest had the biggest heart of all. Elv had hung a map of Arnelle in their closet. Sometimes Claire sat in the closet with a flashlight and tried to memorize it. The rose gardens, the thornbushes, the huts made of stone and straw, the paths to the castle, the lake where the water was so deep no one could ever reach the bottom, the meadow where the horse that had been rescued wandered freely, without a saddle or reins.

AS THE SCHOOL term neared its end, Annie was called in to the principal's office. Elv was barely passing her classes. She fell asleep in Latin. She talked back to teachers. Annie could see her through the glass door, out in the waiting room. Just last week Elv had refused to take the SATs. She didn't want to go to college. She wanted something different. Maybe she'd live in Paris and work for Madame Cohen and sit in cafés in the evening and walk along the river.

The principal called Elv into his office when he and Annie were done with their meeting. "Did you have anything you wanted to say?"

"Ni hamplig, suit ne henaj." Elv looked at the floor. *You're a pig and a dog,* she had told him. A little smile played around her lips.

"I think you see what I'm talking about," the principal remarked to Annie.

"Can't you just go along with things and be polite?" Annie said as they walked out to the car.

"Is that what you want? For me to be polite?" Elv yanked the door open and folded herself into the passenger seat. She flipped down the visor so she could look into the mirror as she applied green eyeliner. In Arnelle, members of the royal family all had green eyes. She hadn't had the heart to tell Claire that she was not included in the top echelon, although she would have loved to let Meg know. Meg who was so perfect, who didn't know the first thing about real life.

"Are you upset about something?" Annie said. "You can talk to me. You used to talk to me."

Elv laughed. "A hundred years ago." In Arnelle, a hundred years went by in an instant. Time was transparent. You could see right through it. *Look through the glass,* the Queen had told her. *See how simple it is to walk back in time?*

Elv leaned forward to get a better look in the mirror. As she did, her sleeveless T-shirt pulled back. You could see her flesh through the fabric. Annie saw a flash of one of the black stars.

"What is that?" she asked. She had a tumbling feeling. She'd been shy as a girl and had felt a sort of desperation whenever she'd had to speak in public. She felt a wave of desperation now.

Elv gazed at her shoulder and pulled her shirt over her skin. "I've had it for a long time," she said coolly. "You just never noticed."

"Elv. Please. Talk to me."

"I'm not going to be polite, if that's what you want to talk about. You can forget about that. " Elv had a strange feeling in her throat. If she wasn't careful, she might say something. She turned to look out the window. Everything looked the same in North Point Harbor, everything was green. It was a relief to be invisible, to be marked by stars. She didn't have to listen to another word her mother said, even if she begged Elv to talk to her, even if she was crying.

"Can we just go?" Elv said.

Her mother started the car.

MEG WAS THE one who found the marijuana in the closet. It was in a shoebox, along with matches and some rolling papers. She pulled Claire inside and they sat there under the green map of Arnelle in the dark. Meg flipped on a flashlight. Claire had grown and was now as tall as her sisters. If only there hadn't been that stupid disaster with the haircuts, people would have thought they were triplets. They would have had great fun in school, tricking teachers and classmates alike.

"It probably belongs to Justin Levy," Claire said. "She spends a lot of time with him."

Meg grimaced. "I doubt that. Justin's not her friend. He's more like her slave. Everyone knows she's just using him."

Justin had his own car and would drive Elv anywhere she wanted to go. She didn't even walk to school with her sisters anymore.

Claire held the baggie up to her nose. "It smells like feet," she said.

"The question is—do we tell Mom?"

"No," Claire said. "Definitely not."

"We have to say something," Meg insisted.

"Why?"

"If you keep someone's secret, you're just as guilty as they are. You're an accomplice."

Claire felt hot in the closet. There really wasn't any air.

"Fine," she said. "We'll talk to Elv tonight."

ELV DIDN'T COME home for dinner. Annie and Claire and Meg had pizza and a salad. The sisters exchanged a glance when Annie asked if they knew where Elv was. They shrugged and said they had no idea.

"Is that Justin Levy her boyfriend?" Annie wanted to know.

"Hardly," Meg said. "He's just madly in love with her."

"Meg!" Claire said.

"Well, everyone knows he is. He spray-painted that thing on the wall."

"What wall?" Annie said.

He had spray-painted *I would tear out my heart for you* on the side of the old Whaling Museum in town. Everybody was talking about it.

"The salad's good," Claire said.

"I would tear out my heart for you," Meg said.

"That's about Elv?" Annie had noticed the shaky writing, the yellow spray-painted declaration of love.

"Yep," Meg said.

"We assume, but we don't know," Claire said. She gave Meg a look. "Justin Levy has emotional problems."

"Major ones," Meg agreed.

"For all we know, that graffiti could be about Mary Fox," Claire ventured.

They all laughed.

"I would tear out my cerebellum for you," Meg joked.

"I would conjugate Latin for you," Claire piped in.

"I would love you all the days of my life," Annie said to her daughters, glad that she wasn't Justin Levy's mother.

THEY WERE UPSTAIRS doing their homework when Elv finally came home. She smelled like burning leaves. "Hard at work?" she said. She picked up one of Meg's books—*The Scarlet Letter*—and thumbed through. "Who would name someone Hester?"

Meg reached under her bed and brought out the shoebox.

"Well, well," Elv said when she saw it. She put down the book. "Look what the little detective found."

"We don't want you to get in trouble," Claire told her.

"Trouble with a capital T?" Elv sat down on Claire's bed. She was sitting on Claire's feet, but Claire didn't complain. "I wish you wouldn't look through my personal belongings," she said to Meg. "Just because you're jealous."

"Jealous?" Meg laughed. She didn't sound very happy.

"It started in Paris and you know it. You couldn't stand that you didn't have the guts to do what I did."

"You mean sleep all day? Or be a whore?"

Elv reached over and slapped her sister. "You're a jealous bitch and you know it."

Meg clutched at her burning cheek.

"You wanted to blame me for cutting your hair, but that was your decision. It's not my fault you're ugly."

"Stop it!" Claire said.

"I told you," Meg said to Claire. "This is who she is."

Elv went to the open window and slipped outside. Claire got up, grabbed the shoebox, and replaced it in the closet. "Mom can't find this."

"Are you taking her side?" Meg said.

"No." Claire slipped on a pair of flip-flops. She wished Meg had never poked around in the closet. She wished she had left things alone.

"You are. You always do."

"That's not true."

"You're no better than Justin Levy. Another one of her slaves."

"You don't even know her," Claire said coldly. "You just think you do."

CLAIRE WENT DOWNSTAIRS, then out the back door to the garden. Behind her the house was quiet. There was the muffled sound of the TV as their mother watched the news. The evening was pale, the air unmoving. There was Elv, sitting beneath the arbor, smoking a cigarette. Her white T-shirt clung to her. She was barefoot, and the soles of her feet were dark with soil. Her black hair hung to her waist. She didn't look anything like them anymore. She looked like the queen of a country that was too far away to visit. There were moths in the garden, fluttering about blindly. The bedroom light was turned off now. Meg had probably slipped into bed, crying the way she did, quietly, so as not to disturb anyone.

"You shouldn't have been so mean to her," Claire told Elv.

"That wasn't mean. It was honest. She is a bitch."

"She said I was like Justin Levy."

"Yeah, right. Justin is pathetic and you're brave. If anything, you're opposites. Meg doesn't have a clue." Elv suddenly threw up her hands. "Don't come any closer," she warned.

Claire stopped where she was.

There was a tiny bird in her path. Both sisters knelt. "He fell out of his nest." Elv picked up the fledgling. "He's a robin."

Claire was startled by how fragile the baby bird was. She could see through its skin to its beating heart. There were only a few stray, luminous feathers.

The girls went in search of the nest, but they couldn't find it in the dark. There were spiderwebs that were frightening to walk through. Claire kept brushing them away, even when they were no longer there. The crickets were calling. Elv sat down in the wet grass. She looked so sad and beautiful. She was everything Claire wanted to be.

"It's too late anyway," Elv decided. "Even if we did find the nest, he's hardly alive. Do you want to hold him?" The Queen of Arnelle had decreed this was to be. *Water, sex, death.* This was number three. There was no way to save him.

Claire sat beside her and Elv slipped a hand atop hers. She let the bird settle into Claire's palm. Claire could feel it shudder. Its heart was beating so fast it reminded her of a moth's wings.

"Maybe we should say a prayer," she suggested.

"You do it, Gigi. You're good at that kind of thing."

Claire felt emboldened by Elv's praise. "Your life has been short," she began in a serious voice, "but it has been as important as any other life."

Claire heard something then. It was Elv, crying.

"Don't look at me," Elv said. She tried to think about the way time could go backward, far back, to the time when she was in the tent with her mother in the garden. There had been twelve princesses who had danced the night away in one of the stories her mother had told her. Twelve brothers had turned into swans.

"Okay." Claire lowered her eyes, stunned.

"Go ahead," Elv urged. "Finish."

"We hope you find peace." Claire was thrown by Elv's show of emotion. She ended the prayer as quickly as she could. She was probably doing it all wrong. She wasn't as good as Elv thought she was. "We hope you're blessed."

The sisters could hear one another breathing and the whir of the crickets. There was the tangled thrum of traffic from Main Street. Sound echoed for blocks on a clear night.

"Close your eyes," Elv said now.

"Why?"

The whole world seemed alive. The air was filled with gnats and mosquitoes and moths.

"Just for a minute," Elv said. "Trust me."

Claire closed her eyes. After a time the robin didn't move anymore.

"Okay. It's over," Elv said. "You can open them now."

The robin seemed even smaller, nothing but skin and bones. Elv went to the garage and got a shovel. She had faced the third fear on her list. Tonight she could tear up the postcard with the green ink. She came back and dug a hole beneath the privet hedge. Her face was streaked with tears. She shoveled dirt so fast she seemed more angry than upset. Claire was too much in awe to offer to help. When Elv was done, she tore off the bottom of her favorite T-shirt from Paris and carefully wrapped up the robin. Claire had never loved anyone more than she loved Elv at that moment. She felt something in the back of her throat that hurt. She felt lucky to have come outside, to have found her sister in the garden, to be with her in the dark.

After the burial they went back to the garden. They ducked under a net of vines and sat down cross-legged beside a row of cabbages. Nobody liked cabbages, not even their mother. They were a total waste of time. Elv lit a cigarette and blew out a stream of smoke. The night was so dark the smoke looked green. The rest of the world seemed far away. Without warning, Elv lurched forward. At first Claire thought she was about to be slapped, like Meg, but instead Elv threw her arms around her. She hugged her tightly, then backed way. When she lifted her T-shirt to wipe her tearstained face Claire saw she wasn't wearing anything underneath. She looked like a creature who belonged in the garden, who slept beneath leaves and spoke to earthworms and threaded white moths through her long black hair. She didn't seem quite human. Claire got a funny feeling then, the way Elv must have felt when she saw the bag with the other cat floating away. The one she hadn't been able to rescue.

In the summer of the gypsy moths when everything changed, when Elv was eleven and Claire was eight and Meg had stayed home sick, they had walked home from the stop sign in the dark.

Elv had been gone for ten hours. She was still wearing her bathing suit, but no shoes. They were gone. They held hands and went along the empty lane. Their mother scolded them when they got home. She told them to go upstairs and they would talk about their disappearance in the morning. Elv said it was her fault, and that Claire couldn't find her way home without her. Elv was going to be punished for coming home so late, but she didn't care. When she and Claire went upstairs, she got into bed, her knees drawn up. Meg was sprawled out on her own bed, reading *Great Expectations*.

"Have you ever read this?" she called to Elv.

Elv turned to the wall. Arnelle was like a black seed in the center of her chest.

Claire got into bed beside her. Elv smelled like ashes and garden soil. There were leaves in her beautiful long hair.

"It's about a boy who thinks he has no future, but then it turns out he does," Meg said. "It's a complicated mystery about fate and love."

Elv felt cold. Claire wrapped her arms around her. There was no way for her to ever thank her sister, no words that would ever do. Something bad had happened to Elv instead of to her. Elv's bathing suit was still damp but she hadn't bothered to take it off.

That was when Claire knew they would never tell.

IN THE GARDEN, on this night when the robin had died in their hands, June bugs flitted overhead. Elv shooed them away. The sisters were sitting beside the row of cabbages. No one knew where they were. They might have been a hundred miles away; they might have slipped down the steps that led underground. It would be August before they knew it. Elv bent forward to whisper. Her face was hot and tearstained. In the human world you had to choose your loyalties carefully. You had to see through to someone's heart. Elv's long hair grazed Claire's face. "You're nothing like her, you know." The garden was so dark they could only see each other's faces. That and nothing more. "You're much more like me."

Swan

My sister stayed in her room, hiding. She gazed at the sky and cried. You'd think she'd be happy to be human, but she kept talking about needing her freedom. I had lost sister after sister; was I supposed to lose her, too? She stood on the ledge outside the window. She had only one arm; if she started to fall she would dash to pieces on the rocks below.

I went out at midnight to gather the reeds, though there were wild dogs and men who thought of murder. I carried sharp needles and sticks. At night I wove the reeds together while my sister cried. When I was done, I threw the cape over her. She changed into a bird and flew away.

I watched until she looked like a cloud. Now she was free. Well, so was I. I walked to the city and got a job. I had a talent after all. When people asked if I had a family I didn't mention that once I'd had twelve

sisters. I said I took care of myself. I said I liked it that
way, and after a while I meant it.

AT THIS TIME OF YEAR THE STORY SISTERS HAD TOMATOES
at every meal. Fried tomatoes battered with bread crumbs, rich
tomato soup with celery and basil and cream, salads of yellow
tomatoes drizzled with balsamic vinegar. Once a pot of simmer-
ing preserves were left on the stove and forgotten; the girls
dubbed the remaining mixture Black Death Tomatoes, delicious
when spooned onto toast. They told tomato jokes: Why did the
tomato turn red? Because he saw the salad dressing! How do you
fix a broken tomato? Tomato paste! They tried crazy recipes that
took hours to complete: tomato mousse, tomato sherbet, green
tomato cake. But this summer Elv declared she was allergic to
tomatoes. She insisted they gave her hives. She wouldn't eat a single one. She pushed her plate away, no matter how much work or
effort their mother had put into the meal. Elv didn't care. She
would eat what she pleased. She would do as she wanted. She said
it quietly, but everyone heard.

The scent of the sultry vines in the garden in August always
reminded the Story sisters of their mother, who they sometimes
saw crying as she weeded between the rows. They wondered if
she was still in love with their father or if it was something else
that made her cry. Elv guessed she was feeling sorry for herself.
Claire thought it best not to pester her with questions. Meg went
out to ask if she needed anything, perhaps some help with the
weeding. Annie gave her middle daughter a hug. After that they
often worked together, late in the day, when the sun was low but
the mosquitoes weren't yet out. The quiet and the company were
a tonic to them both.

Meg was fifteen now, a studious, lovely girl. She wore glasses and spent a great deal of time on her own. Of all the Story sisters, she more than anyone reminded Annie of herself at that age: shy, serious, a fanatical reader. Meg had a job as a counselor-in-training at a summer camp. She was beloved by her campers. Every afternoon she had a book club, which quickly became the summer's favorite activity. The little girls tried to sit next to her so that they could have the honor of turning pages. They all began to wear velvet headbands, just like Meg, and several campers went home and asked their mothers if they could have their hair cut short.

Yet Meg remained a bit of a mystery to Annie. She was something of an outsider, even with her sisters. Well, all the girls were enigmatic, secretive. Elv and Claire still chattered in that language of theirs and laughed over private jokes. But they kept quiet when Meg entered the room. There was some bad blood between them that Annie didn't understand.

"I wish I knew what they were saying," Annie blurted to Meg one day as they worked in the garden, filling a barrel with the dusty weeds they had gathered.

"It's nothing worth hearing. They think they're better than everyone, that's all."

Arnelle no longer held any interest for Meg. Privately, she denounced not only the language but the world. There was a war going on there—faeries were set against demons and human beings. The stories Elv told were filled with brutal atrocities, some so awful they made Meg wince and cover her ears. Swans were murdered, their bloody feathers plucked out. Roses were hexed, turned into thorns that pierced hands and eyes and hearts. The more vivid and alarming the stories were, the more engaged Elv was in their telling. There was a man named Grimin she wanted to murder. Together she and Claire plotted the ways that would cause the most lingering pain: boiled in oil, pecked at by ravens, locked into an iron box with a swarm of bees.

Bees, Claire had decided. Thousands of them, the killer kind, from South America.

In the evenings, Annie and Meg sat out on the porch, reading novels in the fading August light. As for Elv, she'd found a job at the ice cream shop. It was a far cry from Berthillon, just a crummy stand that offered soft custard. Elv felt humiliated being in such a second-rate place. But she wanted her own money, her own timetable. When she came in at night she smelled of hot fudge and sulfur. She never told the truth about anything. Not to her mother, not to people in town, not to her customers, whom she often shortchanged, not even to herself. What people called the truth seemed worthless to her; what was it but a furtive, bruised story to convince yourself life was worth living.

ELV WENT OUT every night, the door slamming behind her. She was barefoot, sullen, in a rush. "See you," she would call over her shoulder to Claire, the only one she bothered to speak to, the only one who knew who she was.

"Later, alligator," Claire would call back, wishing she was old enough to go with her.

Annie always asked when Elv would be back, even though she knew what the answer would be.

"Whenever," Elv would say, aloof, impatient.

"Do you want me to follow her?" Meg asked one evening when the trees on Nightingale Lane were so green they appeared black, melancholy in the darkening sky. There were bands of clouds swarming across the horizon.

Annie had shaken her head. "If anyone should follow her, it should be me."

Annie slipped off her sandals. The soles of her feet were dusty. She marveled at the way Elv could ramble all over town without shoes. Nothing ever seemed to hurt her, not stones or glass or twigs. Their town was safer than most, with a nearly zero crime rate, but you never knew what could happen to a girl all alone. Down at the harbor there were said to be wild parties going on. The police regularly drove past on patrol, but the parties went on out on the sandbars. No one knew how the local kids managed to get so many kegs of beer, but they did. No one knew where the drugs came from, but they were there as well. Once, on her way home from the market in the evening, Annie spied a group of teenagers down by the bay, huddled near the flagpole in the park. They didn't look like bad kids. Annie stopped her car and got out to talk to them. Most of them scattered, but a few stayed, laughing and nervous to be approached by an adult. When Annie asked if Elv was around, they all looked away. One of the boys snickered. Annie heard some of the girls laughing as she walked back to the car.

Thinking of that group of kids and their reaction to Elv's name, Annie suddenly grabbed for her shoes. "I'm going."

"You can't stop her from doing anything. She wouldn't even get in the car with you."

"I could ground her. Take away TV privileges. I could make her stay in for the rest of the summer."

"Mom," Meg said sadly.

"I could lock her in the bedroom."

"She would climb out the window."

They could still see Elv, disappearing down the lane, stopping to pat the old basset hound on the Weinsteins' lawn before she disappeared into the gathering dark. She was like a shadow, something you imagined and couldn't quite grasp. When she wasn't at the ice cream shop, she was heading for the bridge. The group who banded together had bad reputations, but at least they knew how to have a good time. Yet even those girls stayed away from her, making sure to clutch their boyfriends when Elv was nearby. She seemed dangerous even to them, willing to try anything. Give her a pill and she'd take it, offer her a drink and she was always willing to accept. Her cool bravery was legendary. Justin Levy had seen her flustered, though. Once when they were down at the beach she saw a car in the parking lot and bolted. She was shivering by the time Justin caught up with her on Main Street.

"Is he still there?" she'd said to him. She was wearing her bathing suit, a damp towel wrapped around her. She didn't even think about calling the police. All she thought of was running.

Justin shrugged, confused. She'd made him jog back to check.

"No cars in the parking lot," he assured her when he returned, out of breath, her loyal messenger.

After that Elv continued to allow Justin to tag along until he foolishly proclaimed his love for her. He was getting tiresome. By the middle of August, she'd had enough.

"What's wrong with me?" Justin had asked mournfully when she told him to stop stalking her.

If Elv was someone else, she would have said *It's not you, it's me*—that's what everyone said to get out of someone's grasp. Instead, she was honest with Justin.

"You're not who I'm looking for," she replied. She was looking for someone who had no fear of iron or ropes. An escape artist, that's what she wanted. A man who could turn her inside out, make her feel something, because nothing else seemed to. She could sit in the bedroom closet and cut herself with a razor and still feel nothing at all. She could pass her hand above a candle and when it flamed up have no reaction. All she had to do was close her eyes.

Justin had actually cried when she dumped him, as if to prove her point.

"Oh my God, Justin. Find somebody nice. Someone better than me. I am the last person you should be with. You should thank me for giving you this advice."

After that, whenever Justin saw her he didn't say hello. He took to wearing a black coat even though it was August. He wore sunglasses at night. People started laughing at him.

"You look like an idiot," Elv said when she next ran into him. It was at the tea shop and she was there with Brian Preston, who was known for his drug use and also for burning down his family's summer house in the Berkshires. Brian was stupid and good-looking and entertaining. "At least take off your sunglasses," Elv told Justin.

When he did, she could tell he'd been crying again. Didn't anybody see what the real world was like? She felt repulsed by his weakness. Mr. Weinstein down the street had died and now his bassett hound was on the lawn all the time. Mrs. Weinstein didn't allow the dog in the house and whenever she passed him Elv felt like crying herself. She had to stop that. It was useless. It was like trying to win her place in the court of Arnelle, or trying to get rid of the black seed inside her, the taste of iron and of lye. She'd cried that day when the man in the car took her to his house and locked her in a room, until she realized it wouldn't do any good. She had done everything the Queen had asked and had received nothing in return. Arnelle was pointless.

She had decided to change the story.

She was going over to the other side.

THE TOWN WAS thick with Virginia creeper, wisteria, weeds that suddenly grew three feet tall. It had been that kind of summer. There were thunderstorms and hail. The news reported a strange rain of live frogs one wet, humid night. Children ran out with mayonnaise jars to try to capture them the way they used to catch fireflies. The air felt electric, sultry; it pressed down on you and made you want to sleep, turn away from your troubles, tell yourself lies. Even smart people are easily tricked, especially by their own children. When everything smells like smoke, how do you know what's burning? Things that should have added up for Annie seemed like mere coincidence: cigarettes found in the garden, doors slamming, boys throwing pebbles at the window, finding that neighborhood boy Justin Levy sitting in the hedges one evening in his black overcoat, crying. If she set the pieces side by side, she might have been able to interpret them.

When Annie visited her mother, she asked for her advice. She was worried about the Story sisters. One was quiet, one was stand-offish, one seemed to be disappearing before her eyes, becoming someone else entirely. Perhaps they'd been more affected by the divorce and Alan's defection than it had first appeared. Or maybe it was Annie's fault—she'd been depressed, wrapped up in her souring marriage. She went to the garden for solace rather than to her girls. She'd cut herself off, didn't date, rarely saw friends— a poor example of how to live in the world.

"Young girls are moody," Natalia told her. The task of raising children was a difficult one.

"Was I like that?"

"Well, you were well behaved. I never had to punish you. But you used to cry for no reason. It's an emotional time of life. You try things on, you put them away."

"Was I like Elv?" Annie wanted to know.

"No." Natalia shook her head. That man in Paris had skulked around long after the girls had gone home in the spring. Natalia had found a knife and a length of rope beneath the bed in the guest room later in the month when she was cleaning up. She'd brought the little rescued cat, Sadie, with her from Paris to New York. It sat in her lap in the afternoons while Martin took his nap. Natalia often thought back to that night when her granddaughter had sneaked back into the apartment, dripping with river water, managing to be both fierce and tenderhearted. "Not like Elv."

The last time the Story sisters had visited her apartment, Natalia had found Elv in her closet, asleep on the floor, curled up like a little girl. The jewelry box had been open and a gold chain was missing. Natalia was sure Elv would wear it, then return it to its rightful place. But she never saw the necklace again.

Sometimes when she looked at her granddaughter—her black-painted fingernails, the expression on her face when she thought no one was looking, the marks on her skin that were so even it appeared as if she cut herself—Natalia felt afraid for the child. Her friend Leah Cohen had told her that demons preyed upon young girls. They came through windows and found ways to open doors. Natalia had always listened to these stories with half an ear; now she was hesitant to dismiss them. She found herself locking the doors whenever Elv came to visit so that no one could get out or in. She had grown convinced that you could lose someone, even if she was in the very next room. She remembered her friend's warnings more clearly. Although Natalia didn't believe in butting into her daughter's business, she took Annie by the arm before she left for home.

"Look closely at Elv," she advised. "Look inside."

SHE STARTED BY searching the attic. It was one of the reasons they'd bought the house in the first place, the sloping eaves, the large space, the old hawthorn tree that cast shadows through the window. The perfect place to raise three girls. They had painted the woodwork antique white and papered the walls. Annie found the shoebox where the marijuana was hidden first, then a vial of pills—Demerol stolen from the grandparents' medicine cabinet. Taped to the closet wall there was a series of photographs of Elv kissing various boys. There was a mysterious map as well. Inky green paths led through a garden of thorns. Demons were wound in a frantic, scandalous embrace.

A journal had been left in Elv's night table. Annie took it down to the garden. Her hands were shaking. She felt like a witch in a fairy tale, raiding the castle, sifting through bones. There had been rain that morning, and the heat had broken. Birds were searching for worms and the tomatoes were covered with glistening drops. Most of the writing in the journal was in Arnish, with captions beneath green and black watercolor paintings. A girl with wings was held captive, abducted from her true parents. Roses died, iron bars were set around a beating heart torn whole from a now lifeless body, a man named Grimin tied up faeries and fucked them till they bled, goblins drifted through the trees ready for rape and destruction.

Annie hadn't imagined Elv knew about such things, let alone that she was filling a journal with erotic and dangerous drawings. She threw out the drugs, then went back upstairs. The house was quiet. It felt big when there was only one person in it. She thought about the year before she and Alan were divorced, how the fights they'd had must have reverberated up in the attic. Did the Story sisters place their hands over their ears? Did they all get under a blanket and wish they lived somewhere else? Annie replaced the journal, closed the bedroom door, then called her ex-husband. She was crying, so it was difficult for him to understand, but once he did, he insisted everything Elv had done was within the realm of normal teenage behavior. He was a school principal, after all.

Minor drug use and a fantasy world. He'd seen far worse, and many of those students had gone on to graduate, been accepted to college, lived their lives. Annie was overreacting, as usual. But did he know Elv was going out at all hours? Elise had reported that Mary had seen Elv swimming naked in the bay with some high school boys. What about her refusal to follow the house rules, sneaking out at night? He said to wait, things would turn around.

The next morning a police officer came by to inform Annie that her daughter had stolen a tray of cupcakes from the bakery. She'd been seen giving them out to children in the playground before the tots' agitated mothers swooped in to throw away the suspicious treats.

"They were only cupcakes," Annie said, quick to defend her daughter.

"They were stolen property," the officer said stiffly.

When he left, persuaded to let the incident go unreported, Annie went upstairs and knocked on the bedroom door. It was locked whenever Elv was at home. The locks clicked open and there she was, annoyed, half dressed, her hair in knots.

"The police were here," Annie said.

No response.

"The cupcakes?"

Elv's eyes had a yellow cast. She couldn't even do something nice without people getting on her case. If Meg had given out the cupcakes, she probably would have gotten a medal. She'd be on the town honor roll. "I refuse to be who you people want me to be," Elv said.

"What people?" Annie was confused. It crossed her mind that Elv might be high.

"The human race," Elv said disdainfully.

That night Elv burned all her clothes in a trash can. It was one more leap away from the brutality of the human world. She scooped out armfuls from her closet, collecting bathing suits, shoes, purses, socks. She saved two black skirts, a pair of black jeans, a few T-shirts, and the pointy boots from Paris. At the last minute she grabbed the blue dress her grandmother had made for her. Everything else went up in flames, even her winter coat. She poured on lighter fluid and lit an entire pack of matches. The whole neighborhood smelled like burning wool. The fire department was called in by Mrs. Weinstein, worried when she saw flames beyond her crab apple tree. Her husband's old dog set to howling.

Elv couldn't have cared less if Nightingale Lane was rife with ashes. She was barefoot and defiant when the firemen arrived. They made sure the bonfire wasn't out of control, then went away, sirens blaring. For hours afterward, Annie and Meg watered the garden, making certain the embers that had fallen weren't still burning. That night there was still the stink of scorched weeds and the sharp scent of singed tomato vines; the last of the peas on the vine made popping noises as they burst open, like firecrackers set off one at a time.

Elise told Annie she should contact the police the next time Elv didn't come home at her curfew. But Annie was afraid such a move would make Elv run away; she could easily become one of those mistreated, sullen girls you heard about on TV, the ones who disappeared and wound up murdered. Instead, when Elv didn't come home, Annie pulled up a chair and waited at the back door. By the time Elv finally straggled in it was early morning. The lawn had been wet and her footprints flecked the kitchen floor. She was neither surprised nor nervous when she found her mother in the kitchen. She plopped herself down on one of the stools at the counter and asked for pancakes. "I'm starving," she said. When her heart beat faster, she felt alive. When she was hungry, she was starving.

"You can't run around like this. It's dangerous to be out all night. Something terrible can happen to you."

"It already has." *Ask me. See who I am.*

"Elise thinks I should call the police. For your own safety."

Elv gazed at her mother, chin raised. "I take it you're not making pancakes."

"No," Annie said. "I'm not." This wasn't the child she'd told stories to in the garden, her darling, trustworthy girl. "If I find drugs again, Elv, I'm sending you to rehab. I mean it." That was Elise's other recommendation. Don't play around. Take charge.

Elv wondered how she'd misplaced the shoebox. Now she understood. Her mother had been there. "You went through my private belongings?" she said.

"It's my house," Annie said. "My rules."

"Okay," Elv said coolly. She took the confrontation as a challenge that would spur her on to battle. "Look as much as you want. You won't find anything."

Claire helped to toss away any incriminating evidence. They got rid of the needles and ink Elv kept for her homemade tattoos, the hash pipe, the rolling papers, the empty packets of birth control pills, the razor blades she used to cut herself. She said her blood was green, but it looked red to Claire when she watched the razor go into Elv's flesh. Several times Claire had found her sister in their bedroom standing naked in front of the mirror, gazing at herself. They both stared at her body, which seemed perfect to Claire. But Elv seemed disappointed in herself. She turned to gaze at her back, searching for the beginnings of black wings. There was nothing there but skin and bones.

One morning, Claire awoke in the middle of the night to see a boy in a black coat sitting on Elv's bed. He seemed like a dream. Claire closed her eyes and wished him away. In a little while he was gone, out the window, across the garden. It was Justin. Claire had seen him hanging around Nightingale Lane before. Once she thought she saw him in the woods nearby, crying.

AT THE END of the summer Justin Levy hanged himself in his bedroom. Elv didn't go to the funeral, which was held in a chapel in Huntington. That night, Claire looked out the window to see her sister digging up the robin's skeleton. Elv carefully placed the bones in a clean dish, then brought them inside. Claire crept down the stairs and joined her sister at the kitchen table. Elv had their mother's sewing kit. There was a spool of black thread and a long needle. She was making a necklace out of the bones that had been buried under the hedge. It would be an amulet in memory of the dead.

Elv's fingers were bleeding from her work. She had drilled little holes in the bones with a safety pin.

"Doesn't that hurt?" Claire asked.

Elv laughed. Something caught in her throat. That happened when she thought about Justin. He was so susceptible to pain. She should have taught him how to walk through this world. She should have showed him how to lock it all away. "I can hurt myself more than anyone else can," she told her sister. "I can do it with my eyes closed."

People in town said Elv was a witch after she took to wearing the bone necklace. But Claire thought the necklace was sad and beautiful. Elv let her try it on once. They stood together in front of the big mirror in their bedroom. Even with her short hair, Claire was pleased to see how much alike they looked.

As for Meg, she thought the necklace was a travesty. "She can't even let the dead rest in peace," she murmured to Claire once after Elv had left the room. Their older sister released so much energy and turmoil, it was as if a storm had been trapped in a jar, then set free on the third floor every time she was around. When Elv drifted back into their bedroom, Meg fell silent.

"What's wrong with you?" Elv asked her sister. In Arnelle, everyone understood that it was possible to cry without tears, to be brave even when riddled with fear. But Meg didn't understand anything. "Cat got your tongue?"

In Arnish, cat was *pillar*. Said aloud it sounded vicious.

"Nothing's wrong with me," Meg said.

Elv knew what she meant. *It's you. Always you.*

THE WEATHER WAS changing. It was September and school had begun. In the evenings, Elv began to smoke a white powder. She used a glass pipe that looked as if it would catch on fire when she inhaled. Claire sat out in the hall on the third floor, guarding the bedroom door. "Thanks, Gigi," Elv would say when Claire came back into the room. "Now I can breathe."

When Claire asked what was in the pipe, Elv said, "The antidote to humanity" and laughed. "Seriously, it's nothing. It's chalk dust."

Even though school was in session, Elv often didn't come home until dawn. She didn't mind getting wet as she ran across the damp lawn; she was burning up under her skin despite the change in the weather. At the hour when her sisters got ready for school, she would creep into bed, naked and wet. If you shook her, she didn't budge. If you talked to her, she didn't answer. She was exhausted most of the time, but agitated. When she managed to go grab some sleep, she talked through her dreams, always in Arnish.

Claire would perch at the foot of her sister's bed on these school-day mornings, worried. She had begun to dread the future. Elv was being swallowed up. Claire wondered if the door to Arnelle could close when a person least expected it to, shutting her into that underground world. She whispered Elv's name, but there wasn't an answer. She traced a finger over the scars Elv had left on her own skin. Would she know how to rescue Elv if the time ever came? Would she stand there mutely and watch her sister be carried away or would she dare to be brave?

MEG BEGAN TO hide everything she cared about. She kept it all in the guest room closet, which she secured with a lock she bought at the hardware store, keeping the small key in her backpack. Things had been disappearing: headbands, jewelry, clothes. Elv had burned her own belongings, and now she was taking whatever she wanted. Elise phoned Annie to say that Mary had come home to find Elv going through her closet. Elv had pried open a window and managed to climb into Mary's bedroom. When Mary walked in to find her cousin loaded down with her belongings, Elv threatened to burn down the house if she told. Mary had had such a bad asthma attack afterward that Elise had rushed her to the hospital.

After that, Annie stopped seeing her cousin, just as she avoided most people in town. She didn't want to hear about anyone else's children, their high SAT scores, their good grades, their bright futures. She didn't want to see the looks of pity when they asked after Elv. People in town talked about Elv endlessly. Her antics provided for a steady stream of conversation. She was seen sitting in the graveyard, barefoot, smoking, haunting the plot where Jason Levy was buried. She'd talked back to the history teacher all the other students feared, and now Mrs. Hill was out on medical leave. She stole handfuls of prize roses from Mrs. Weinstein's yard and hung them over her bed on a string, a charm of mintas for protection, she said. "So the goblins don't eat us alive," she explained when Mrs. Weinstein came knocking on the door. "Or would you like that to happen to us? Would you like us to die the way Pretzel did?" Pretzel the basset hound had been hit by a speeding car earlier in the month. He was too old and blind to stay outside, but Mrs. Weinstein had kept him out of the house anyway. Elv had egged Mrs. Weinstein's Honda, a crime Mrs. Weinstein hadn't unraveled. When people on the street turned to look at Elv's black outfits, her pointy boots, she shouted out, "What the hell are you staring at?"

"People in this town are so stupid," she confided to Claire, who was beginning to wonder if there was such a thing as being too fearless. She had begun to have nightmares, about the horse in Central Park, the boy on Elv's bed, the dog down the street. "Trust me, you have to watch out for yourself," Elv assured her little sister. "Otherwise you'll just get dragged down by all their asinine rules."

A girl Meg knew named Heidi Preston said her brother boasted that he could have sex with Elv whenever he wanted in exchange for drugs. He had access to methamphetamine and OxyContin and Ritalin. Heidi didn't seem judgmental about this; she told Meg as if she were a newscaster, merely reporting the facts. For a couple of weeks Meg let Heidi be her best friend. She found Heidi's knowledge about drugs and sex to be fascinating and quite unexpected. Then Elv spied them together. Outraged, she pulled Meg aside that afternoon when she got home from school. "Stay out of my life," she snapped. "And keep the hell away from Brian's sister."

They were up in the bedroom, the door locked. Elv had flown at Meg, pushing her against the wall, pinching her. To Claire, the third floor felt as if it was part of the otherworld, not quite connected to the rest of the human realm. Elv had written on the walls with green ink. The floor around her bed was littered with crumpled paper and used cups and glasses.

"I'm serious," Elv said. "Don't ever talk to that girl again."

"Stop it!" Meg said. She tried to pull away but couldn't. She was crying, and trying not to let her sisters see. Red welts were rising on her skin where Elv had pinched her.

"You're like a stupid cow, butting into everyone's business. That's why Claire and I hate you. You're such a nothing, Meg."

Meg looked down at the floor and made a sobbing sound.

Claire felt her blood rise. "Don't talk to her like that!"

Elv turned to stare at her, stunned.

"Meg can do as she pleases," Claire told Elv, surprising even herself. She and Elv had been each other's so completely. But since Elv had started smoking that white powder she was different. You have to be mean sometimes, she'd whispered to Claire. You have to protect yourself at all costs. "Meg can be friends with whoever she wants," Claire said.

Meg got into bed. She pulled up the covers. She did that whenever she cried, thinking no one would know.

"Fine." Elv's face was flushed. "I don't care about Meg."

"I do," Claire said hotly.

"Really?" Elv said. "Would she have rescued you?"

That was the end of Meg's friendship with Heidi. She and Claire walked home from school together. The September light was incandescent: the lawns were brown. People in the neighborhood looked out their windows and thought the two Story sisters looked like twins. In the evenings they did their homework in the kitchen while Elv prowled around town. It didn't matter to Meg if she ever talked to Heidi again. She wasn't really interested in friends anymore. She had Claire now. That was enough.

THE WEATHER BECAME chilly at night. You had to wear a sweater or a light jacket. The edges of the leaves were already turning. Autumn was early this year, especially welcome after the hot, humid summer. Annie had dug up most of her garden, tossing away the spent lettuce and the squash vines with their yellow-white blossoms and the singed pea pods. Meg helped, and soon Claire decided to lend a hand as well. They worked well together, in a steady rhythm, pulling weeds, turning the soil, gathering the last of the vegetables. They stepped on the fallen tomatoes and heard them squish and laughed till they nearly fell down.

"Do you think your past stays with you forever?" Claire asked Meg one day. They were removing the wooden stakes used to tie up the heaviest of the vines. "Do you think you can ever escape it?"

There was a slight drizzle, and the two Story sisters were wearing raincoats. Their mother was collecting the cabbages that no one liked. She would take them to the town hall, where there was a food pantry for the needy.

Meg shrugged. "I think you are who you are."

"But what if you're attacked by sharks or kidnapped? Those things change you, you know. You can't be the same after that."

"There are no sharks in North Point Harbor," Meg said.

"There was one once." Annie had overheard and now came over to join in. She loved spending time with the two girls. "It came around the tip of Montauk."

"No, it didn't!" Meg and Claire laughed.

"It was ten feet long," Annie vowed, a grin on her face. She felt the way she used to, when her daughters were young and she was young, too. Even before the divorce, Alan was never around. It was just the four of them, all in it together.

"It had a thousand teeth," Meg added to the story. "It could swallow an entire horse. A whole cow."

"It could eat an entire town," Annie said. "Houses, stores. And then one day it went away. It went to sea where it belonged, and never thought about the town called North Point Harbor."

"It was lost and never found," Claire said. She could see their bedroom window. The leaves on the hawthorn tree looked like black wings. She closed her eyes and wished that nothing bad would ever happen to Elv. She wished they could go back to who they had been before they'd become who they were now.

THE FIRST SEMESTER of school was over. Elv had failed every one of her classes. She had been picked up by the police for shoplifting, but the charges were dropped in exchange for a promise that she would no longer frequent the local pharmacy. It was only nail polish and mints, she complained. Hardly a federal offense. At least Alan had gotten a decent lawyer and paid the bill, which was substantial. The tension in the house grew worse. Elv seemed to have a different boyfriend every week. They followed her like dogs, then disappeared, replaced by someone new. It had happened slowly, but she had become a stranger in their house. She barely spoke; she drifted in and out like a shadow. Ever since the fight over Heidi Preston she'd been standoffish even to her beloved Claire. She needed room to breathe, that's what she told Claire when Claire got into bed beside her. She told her to go away, even though she was crying and her skin felt cold and she was so alone.

Meg did the research about methamphetamine. She and Claire sat in the library and read about the effects: rashes, paranoia, violent outbursts, inability to sleep. It all seemed familiar. Meg ran into Heidi Preston, who said her brother, Brian, had been sent to school in Maine because of Elv. Heidi's parents had found them getting high in the basement. Now Brian had run away from boarding school and they didn't even know where he was. Meg and Claire went upstairs and searched through the shoebox. They studied the map on the wall of the closet. Claire had never before noticed that all of the roads in Arnelle were circles. Each one led to the same place.

ONE NIGHT IN early October there was a sudden frost. Annie wanted to protect the last of her crop. She often continued to have fresh tomatoes at this time of year, which she used for spaghetti sauces long into the winter. She went out to lay plastic over the few tremulous vines that remained. When she looked up, she saw Elv climbing out of her window. She shinnied down the tree. Annie stayed perfectly still, hidden by leaves. She could hear the wind and the fluttering sound of the last few moths in the garden, luminous against the dark.

Elv was wearing a thin black blouse that clung to her breasts. She had on her black jeans. Despite the frost, she was barefoot. She began to run as soon as she touched the ground. For some reason Annie ran after her. She didn't think, she merely acted. It was as though someone had pressed a button that had activated a spring and Annie had no choice but to go. Elv's footsteps were muffled and she was surprisingly fast. Annie was out of breath in no time, but she went on, following her daughter. It seemed as if everyone in the world was sleeping, unaware that time was hurtling forward. Dogs barked in backyards. Though the leaves had begun to turn color, in the dark everything looked black.

Elv was headed to the parking lot of the convenience store. An old car was parked near a few locust trees that had grown up through the asphalt. The car engine was running and exhaust filtered into the dark. Annie stopped in a thicket of thorny briars. Her breath echoed inside her head. She was sweating even though the air was cold. She saw the car door open. A burst of loud music escaped. Once Elv climbed inside, the car pealed out, tires squealing. Annie stood in the brambles, breathing hard. She walked home slowly, a stitch in her side. There were boys inside the car. No one local. No one Annie recognized. She thought she'd heard Elv laugh.

When she got home, the kitchen light was turned on. Annie had a surge of hope—maybe Elv had been dropped off and was already back—but when she went inside only Meg and Claire were waiting. They had made a pot of tea.

"Did you find her?" Meg asked.

Annie shook her head. She went to sit with the girls. Claire got her mother a wet paper towel. The brambles had left scratches. Her forehead and arms were bleeding.

"Thank you," Annie said.

"She's using ice," Meg told their mother.

"What?" Annie looked at her daughters. They had school in the morning. They shouldn't be up in the middle of the night. Claire was only thirteen and Meg was fifteen.

"It's methamphetamine," Meg explained. "Brian Preston's sister Heidi told us. He used to go to our school till he got kicked out."

Meg and Claire sat close together, knees touching. They had united and were turning Elv in even though they knew they would surely pay for their disloyalty. Elv wasn't the forgiving type. "Je ne sprech suit ne rellal har," Claire had overheard Elv say when Meg found the glass pipe and the packet of chalky powder. *Say one word and I'll make you regret it.*

She had made them both promise, but they'd kept their fingers crossed behind their backs. They'd always learned their lessons from Elv, and that was how they'd learned to lie. Meg brought Elv's backpack to their mother. If they didn't stop her, she wouldn't stop herself.

Meg had convinced Claire it was the right thing to do, but even now Claire wasn't certain. She'd had trouble sleeping of late. She was afraid that Justin Levy's ghost would appear at their window, still searching for Elv. She thought about demons and women with black wings. On the terrible day, she had waited at the corner by the stop sign for hours. She had been covered with blackfly bites. She would have waited a thousand years before she went home without her sister.

If we don't help her, no one will, Meg had whispered tonight. *It's now or never.*

Claire imagined that Elv was calling for her, unable to speak or form words, but summoning her in silence, using the spell meant for the most desperate of times. *Reuna malin. Rescue me.* There was no other choice. That's why they were waiting when their mother came home. They had come to tell her the truth about Elv, even though they knew that once they did, nothing would ever be the same.

Iron

We only wanted to look at him. We set the trap in the meadow. It had metal bars and a gate that slammed shut whenever footsteps crossed the threshold. People barely believed in him anymore, but we did. We'd seen his shadow.

We caught him the first time out.

We thought it was luck. We thought it was fate. We were proud of ourselves.

There he was, hiding from the sunlight. Crows circled overhead.

He didn't move, so we poked him with sticks. We were afraid that if we opened the gate he would run, so we watched him all through the day.

Tell us your name, we said. We knew if he did he'd be ours forever.

He said nothing. Perhaps he couldn't speak.

He was growing paler. He looked like moonlight.

He was so beautiful we couldn't stop looking at him.
We watched him all day long.

Tell us, we asked, again and again.

He said nothing until he disappeared, curled up
like a leaf, gone. We heard clearly that his name was
sorrow, and now it was ours forevermore.

THEY WENT ON A SUNDAY. IT WAS THE HEIGHT OF THE FALL
foliage season, and they were driving to New Hampshire. Everything was red and yellow. The whole world was shimmering. The
other girls were brought along so that nothing would seem amiss.
Family time. Nothing more. An adventure into the countryside.
It was rare for Alan to spend even an hour with his ex and the
girls, let alone an entire day. It was a stab at a new, more civilized
approach to the divorce, that's what Elv was told. In truth, Annie
had to force Alan's involvement—she'd fought and begged until at
last he'd given in. Still, they must have been convincing, because
there Elv was, in the backseat, sleeping. Every once in a while
Annie could hear Claire and Meg whisper to each other in Arnish.
They were worried, two anxious doves. Se sure gave ne? *How*
much longer till we get there? Sela se befora. *What if we're wrong?*
Quell me mora. *Don't ask questions.*

Annie was quick when it came to languages. She'd learned
French by eavesdropping on her parents, and now, because of the
bits Claire had taught during her recovery, she understood a little
Arnish. Recently she had gone to see a therapist, who had informed her that she should have never allowed a separate reality
to be constructed, especially one that excluded parents. The Story
sisters had isolated themselves from the rest of the world, as

though they were mere travelers in the here and now, meant for some other time and place. Such activities caused nonattachment, delusions, disloyalty. The world they lived in should have been enough.

Elv was stretched out, wearing the clothes in which she'd slept. They'd woken her early. She had grumbled and complained, but when she saw that her father was visiting, she'd pulled on her boots, grabbed a sweatshirt, and thrown herself into the car, where she quickly fell back asleep. She was dreaming while Meg looked out the window and Claire bit her nails and her father navigated and her mother sat in the front seat wearing sunglasses even though there was no sun that day. Annie had brought along a cooler of drinks and sandwiches, not that anyone was interested in eating. The trees were so red by the time they reached New Hampshire that the leaves looked like flames. Elv yawned and sprawled across Claire's legs.

"Halav semma burra." She was half in a dream. *This is so uncomfortable.*

Elv still wore the robin's bones. They were turning yellow, black lines striating the marrow, but she didn't mind their decay. Every girl needed protection against evil.

Elv was heavy, but Claire didn't complain. She ran her fingers through her sister's knotted hair. Elv didn't brush it or take care of it and it was still beautiful. For an instant Claire thought she should wake her. If they escaped, they could live in the woods. They could eat wild berries, commune with bears, never be found.

"Let her sleep," Meg whispered.

Ever since Meg's hair had been cut, it had turned coarse. It wasn't straight anymore and on humid days it grew curly. She had turned sixteen and for a little while was the same age as Elv. In fact, she felt like the older sister, the one who had to get up and do all the chores, weed the garden, complete the schoolwork, keep quiet when she wanted to scream. Earlier that morning, as they went out to the driveway, Meg had leaned in close to whisper to Claire. *Do what I tell you when we get to New Hampshire.*

Their mother had confided in Meg. She'd told her the intervention was for Elv's own good. They wanted to save her. When Meg had revealed some of this to Claire, Claire couldn't help but wonder if Elv wanted to be saved.

As they drove on, Meg remembered reading somewhere that tigers could smell fear. The best thing to do if one ever attacked you was to think of chocolate or cinnamon, scents that would mask your terror. She forced herself to think of chocolate sauce and hot apple pie and the marshmallow s'mores they used to make on the grill in the summertime. She thought so hard she could taste the chocolate, but it had a harsh flavor and she wished she could reach the cooler her mother had brought along, in which there were bottles of spring water.

When Elv woke, she lay there prone, tired, and out of sorts. She could see fleeting images out the window: red leaves, the black bark of the trees, the shadows of other cars. She knew they'd been driving a long time. "Harra leviv jolee," she murmured. *Our parents are crazy.* "Je below New Hampshire." *I hate New Hampshire.*

In spite of their nerves, Meg and Claire both laughed. They hated New Hampshire too. The day was already too long. Their legs were falling asleep under their sister's weight. Elv had little red marks all over the backs of her hands where she'd burned herself when she was bored. The burns had scabbed up and it looked as though she was recovering from the chicken pox. She had fifteen black stars on her body, most in places her mother couldn't see, homemade tattoos she'd made by plunging an inky needle into her skin. There were dozens of broken-down Bic pens on the floor of their closet. Since their mother didn't see anything, Elv had gotten away with it. She had perfected household deception. A secret, after all, was only a secret if no one heard it.

Annie switched on the radio to a song about falling in love. She looked straight ahead at the road. Being in the car with Alan was even more uncomfortable than she had imagined. But he was the girls' father, despite the fact that he'd moved in with his girl-friend, that nice woman who'd been there for Elv's birthday cake. Well, what difference did it make who he was with? If Annie had ever loved him, she didn't now. As they drove along, she wondered if she would ever feel anything again. Maybe she was heart-less. What sort of person tricked her own daughter? She had become the witch in the woods, just as Elv's diary had predicted, leading the way with a trail of sandwiches and good cheer. She was the old woman who stole children and coaxed them into the forest. Where they were going, no one escaped. That's what the brochure had said. Not a single student had ever successfully run away.

The rain had begun, and there was the rhythmic sound of the windshield wipers. The windows were foggy and streaked. Red leaves fell in clouds. They drove through a little town where everything but the gas station seemed to have closed for the day or gone out of business. Annie had done nothing but research for the past few weeks. She had hired a consultant and seen a therapist. She had been on the Internet and talked with other distraught parents halfway across the country. The consensus was always the same. The Westfield School was the best. It was ridiculously expen-sive, but was said to have the most success with kids like Elv. Annie had borrowed the money from her parents. Her father had writ-ten out the check without even asking what it was for. He was ail-ing, struck with congestive heart failure, and she hated to ask him for anything. But he'd been in Paris with the girls in the spring. He'd seen what was happening to Elv. When they'd gone back to

Paris after spending the summer in New York, that man she'd gotten herself involved with was still skulking around. Once they had returned home from the opera to find him weeping beneath the chestnut tree. Martin had had to chase him off with a broom.

After the Storys had driven through the sleepy little town, they turned onto an old logging road that snaked through the mountains. Along the roadside were stone walls marking the boundaries of abandoned apple orchards. The fields were still dotted with twisted black trees. The school was located on a run-down estate. A fence rimmed the property. It was hidden in the pines, but when you looked carefully you could see it, a crisscross of barbed wire. Claire spied it right away; it made her think of a sharp spiderweb. She imagined thousands of spiders, and her skin crawled. She was having a panic attack. She didn't understand why it hurt every time she took a breath. They drove through an automatic gate that clicked closed behind them. It was still raining, a cold rain for October. They had to navigate through pools of mud. No wonder they all hated New Hampshire.

Elv had been very stoned the night before. She was hungover, exhausted, more compliant than usual, quite surprised by the notion that their father, usually so disinterested, would be with them. She had no idea that the counselors were ready for her, two large men who didn't look the way Annie had assumed school counselors would look. They seemed like prizefighters or bouncers in a nightclub. They wore black rain jackets and work boots. They were standing in the rain, waiting. If Annie could have felt anything, she might have been flooded with second thoughts. She might have made Alan turn the car around. But she was paralyzed. They all were. Meg and Claire gazed out the window. The place looked like a prison. The car stopped, and Alan opened the door and got out. Annie turned to her younger daughters. Meg thought she could smell her mother's fear. No one had told her to think of chocolate.

"Stay in the car," she told them.

When Annie got out, she was immediately drenched. The rain was coming down so hard it was deafening. While Alan went to talk to the counselors, Annie opened the back door and leaned in.

"Elv." She sounded like a betrayer, even to herself. "Get up."

Elv yawned and stretched. Rain was splattering on her legs. "Al je meara," Elv said. *Leave me alone.*

Annie reached in and shook her by the shoulder. "We're here."

No destination had been mentioned before. It was a ride in the country. Just an autumn picnic. The chance to spend some time with their dad. She'd agreed to go. She'd let down her guard. Suddenly there was a *here*. Elv didn't like the sound of that. She rose from the backseat and looked out, eyeing her father and the two men talking to him. The building behind them seemed like a prison to her, too. She didn't need to see any more. She could tell it was a trap. She pushed past her mother. Annie was no match for her; she toppled backward as Elv leaped out of the car.

Elv wasn't as stupid as they thought. She didn't give a damn about the mud all around, splashing up as she ran. Her hair was like a waterfall as she raced through the rain. She focused on the woods in front of her. The red leaves, the black bark. She thought she was far out in front, flying, but then she heard their heavy breathing. They sounded like horses, close behind her. They took her down so hard three of her ribs were fractured. She could hear the bones crack. The breath was knocked out of her in a searing flash. In the mud, she tried to wrestle out of their hold. The robin's-bones necklace fell to pieces. It shone like opals as it scattered. She reached for the broken pieces but they slipped out of her grasp. The ground was cold and slimy. The mud could choke you if you were screaming and struggling and they had you face-down on the ground. They were hurting her, but she didn't stop trying to get away. She had practiced escaping from ropes so no one could ever do this to her again. She had cut herself to strengthen herself and inure herself to pain. She wished she could find the door that led to the otherworld, but she was too far away. She felt herself being overtaken, so she bit the hand of the man who'd grabbed hold of her. He shook her and spat out some curses, then held on more tightly. Elv saw stars, but she didn't care. She'd drawn blood. She would never again let herself be tied in knots, shackled in iron handcuffs, gagged.

The director's assistant had come to usher Alan and Annie inside, holding a black umbrella above their heads. There were some things no parents should see. After a quick half-hour orientation, they would be asked to leave. No phone calls or visits were allowed during the first three months, no packages from home. Students needed to be out of their element, away from the triggers that had driven them to drugs and out-of-control behavior. Annie was shivering. Alan was drenched. Pools collected on the tile floor under their feet. The school smelled like Lysol and that morning's breakfast, bacon and overdone toast. They sat at a conference table and signed the papers registering their daughter while the counselors dragged Elv to the door of the residence hall. It was a concrete building, painted pale green. Claire and Meg watched through the car window. Claire's throat was closing up.

"Nom gig!" Elv screamed. "Reuna malin." *Rescue me.*

One of the big men picked her up; he had his hands all over her. He touched her in places he shouldn't have just because he could. He hoisted her off the ground as though she were nothing more than a sack of skin and bones.

Claire and Meg couldn't move.

"Come and help me!" Elv screamed to them.

One of the men opened the door into the dormitory. The other one had Elv. Claire lowered the window to see more clearly. They were hurting her. The rain came inside. It was cold.

"Don't listen," Meg told Claire. She closed the window. They couldn't take back what they'd done. The rain was coming down harder all the time. There were so many leaves on the windshield the girls couldn't see through the glass anymore. They crouched on the floor of the car, arms around each other. Claire was thinking of the blackflies circling on the corner with the stop sign and of the sinking feeling she'd had and how paralyzed she'd been on the bad day.

Meg couldn't get the image of tigers out of her mind. It was said they never forgot an act of cruelty or an act of kindness. They were known for being vengeful; they returned to villages where traps had been set and wiped out everyone in their path. They dreamed of skin and bones. Everything they ate tasted like revenge.

"They're not going to hurt her." Meg crossed her fingers behind her back, hoping that what she vowed wouldn't be held against her if it turned out to be wrong. "And when she comes home, she'll be the way she used to be."

Claire didn't say anything, but she knew it wasn't true. She wished she could go out and gather up the robin's bones. She wished she could make this day disappear. The spell had been said aloud and she hadn't responded.

She kept listening to the rain. She understood what was happening. The world they'd known was slipping away from them.

AT LAST THEIR parents came back. They got inside, bringing the damp and cold with them, not speaking. They slammed the car doors shut. Alan turned the key in the ignition. There was nothing to say anymore. It was the last time they would all be together. Alan saw his daughters less and less frequently after that, and they never reached out to him. When they did see him, they would always be reminded of this day when he cried as he started up the car, sorry not for them, or for Elv, but for himself.

"If you'd been stricter with her, none of this would have happened," he said to their mother.

Annie didn't answer, and the girls didn't blame her. She still had bramble scratches on her face from chasing through the woods after Elv. She had lost ten pounds without trying. Claire and Meg stayed where they were, on the floor of the car, as they drove away. They were too old to be acting so childishly, sixteen and fourteen, as tall as grown women. Ordinarily their mother would have insisted that they wear their seat belts, but she didn't say anything. She didn't even seem to notice they weren't in their seats.

It was bumpy going on the rutted driveway, but as soon as they turned onto the paved town road the ride was smoother. The car twisted through the mountains, went past the town, then reached the highway. Claire leaned her head against the seat; she nearly fell asleep. It rained and rained, and then it stopped. They had been driving for a long time. All day. Alan pulled into the parking lot of a diner. The sandwiches Annie had made were ruined, soggy after so many hours in the cooler. Nobody wanted them. By then the light was fading and even the red leaves looked dark. All four got out of the car. Anyone would have thought they were a family. The wind was blowing and Annie was still shivering.

"Let's have hot chocolate," Alan suggested.

They were exhausted and cold. They couldn't wait to get out of New Hampshire. None of them had eaten, not even breakfast, and their stomachs growled. Their father didn't know that Claire and Meg didn't like hot chocolate anymore. He didn't know the first thing about them. They had started drinking coffee. They were old enough for that now. They smoothed down their hair, their coats.

"What happens next?" Claire asked her sister. She could still feel her throat closing up. Her loneliness was like a black stone she couldn't swallow.

They were walking behind their parents. They had no idea where they were, if it was a town or just a spot on the map no one had ever heard of. The diner had a blue neon sign that looked like rain on a black road.

"Don't ask," Meg said.

WHEN ELV WOULDN'T calm down, they put her in a straitjacket for thirteen hours. She should have been released after seven, but the shifts changed and she was forgotten in the behavior room. The nurse on duty who found her apologized. She said it would never happen again. Surely it wouldn't if Elv had anything to do about it. She knew how to mind her manners until she could get free. After that initial incident, she was so quiet anyone would have guessed she was calm, quite well behaved. She had good reason to appear so: The buckles from the jacket had left marks in her skin. She understood iron. She knew what sort of marks rope could leave. When she refused to eat, they threatened to force-feed her. She quickly accepted their bread. She was a quick learner. What happened once would never happen again. She grew quieter and quieter still, crouched in Arnelle, biding her time.

The doctor who examined her gave her Tylenol for her ribs. He said that if she wanted to behave so poorly, there would be consequences. She went to the room she was assigned and didn't

complain, not about her ribs and not about the cold linoleum
floor or the little black bugs that skittered away when she turned
on her bathroom light. She approached everyone and everything
with caution. She felt anxious, panic-stricken, and often woke
from her dreams gasping. She'd been betrayed and tricked, but
she wouldn't let them destroy her. The same thing had happened
to the new Queen of Arnelle. The old dying Queen had warned
her to trust no one. To never once shut her eyes. Betrayal was
quick, sharp, unexpected. One of her sisters was jealous and petty,
the other was kindhearted but weak. They had joined forces with
the human world. Elv had come to despise faeries, those simper-
ing backstabbing creatures. The story had changed, and so had
her allegiance. She realized now that there was a grave distinction
between a demon, who was a pure dark spirit not unlike herself,
and a goblin, a human with an evil heart. As the new Queen she
chose to recruit demons. They alone were powerful enough to
come to her aid, unwinding the black vines used to tie her
beneath the stump of a chestnut tree.

She made certain to adhere to the Westfield rules. She didn't
mouth off to the guards or the counselors or whatever they were
supposed to be. She sat through group therapy and pretended to
listen. Sometimes she even spoke, tentatively, not giving too much
away. All the while she let herself wander more deeply into Arnelle. What was a demon but a lost soul, one that had been forced
to use his skills to survive? She found sanctuary among them,
escaped from the vines that tied her, ran far into the woods. She
found a garden of black roses there, the perfect place to hide from
faeries and goblins and humans alike.

Before long Elv was able to be in both places at once. It was a
great triumph and an even greater relief. She was able to speak to
a teacher and at the very same time be in the black garden. She
made an Arnish promise, one she planned to keep. She would get

through this, then she would make them pay for what they'd done to her. She and the demons would take back Arnelle from the rebels who were after her still. The faeries and their human coconspirators were scooping up demons in butterfly nets, then releasing them into the waking world, in New York City, in Paris, right there in the New Hampshire woods. Each of these demons had been betrayed just as she had, cast out and reviled. Each one was utterly alone.

The brochure said Westfield was a therapeutic school, but as far as Elv could tell, it was simply a holding tank for spoiled, drug-addicted brats with personality disorders. Most of the students came from middle-class families. Those who did not were there via court orders that ensured that the state or county or town where they'd lived would pay the academic fees. By the end of the first month Elv had come to understand the school's philosophy. They swiftly broke you down until you were nothing. They destroyed you, then built you back up again. Only they did it their way, the Westfield way. What they wanted were clones, people without minds of their own who had the Westfield agenda imprinted on their souls. They hammered at people, tearing them apart in therapy groups. During the first month, Elv had a piece of cardboard strung around her neck that proclaimed I AM A LIAR. She had told a teacher she had missed class because she felt feverish, but when her temperature was taken it had been normal. Well, she'd hated that class. And if she was a liar, at least she was good at it. They'd have to do a whole lot more than dangle a sign around her neck if they wanted to humiliate her. Thankfully, she wasn't in the group with the therapist who insisted his patients strip naked and stand in a circle so they couldn't hide their inner selves. They would have had to tear her clothes off, and even then she wasn't about to reveal anything.

◆ ◆ ◆

ELV HAD HEARD about the worst Westfield technique from her one and only ally, Michael. Michael came from Astoria, Queens; he'd dodged jail time for car theft in exchange for a year at the school. For those students who didn't improve and continually refused to cooperate he told Elv they did something called blanketing. They wrapped you up and wouldn't let you move for hours, no matter how you might struggle, until at last you were reborn with a fresh, compliant ego. It was meant to be a rebirthing, but it was total control. Sometimes they held you immobilized for hours. If Elv had thought the straitjacket was bad, Michael said, this was a thousand times worse. When you could barely breathe, when you were choking on your own fury and bile, you had no choice but to give in. That was the way in which you were converted to their world.

Demons were said to be cruel, but a demon would never have been so brutal as this. A demon merely called you by name, threw his arms around you, whispered his plight, understood yours, then took you for his own. The extent of human cruelty continued to amaze Elv. If you wanted to survive in this place, you had to let them think you had given in. The harder you fought, the harder they broke you. You had to hide yourself away. She understood that. She had once talked a goblin into setting her free. She had spoken so sweetly he had untied the ropes, turned his back on her, left her alone to fetch her a cup of water. The window was open. Even at the age of eleven she had known that there were no second chances.

FOR THE FIRST three months Elv had level-one privileges—no phone calls or visits. She was given latrine duty, meant to break her down. It was filthy, disgusting work. She didn't complain.

She wasn't going back to solitary under any circumstances. Every day she took a mop and a pail of soapy water and did her job. There were beetles in the bathrooms. Elv was supposed to kill them with bug spray, but she let them live. She wished she could slip them into envelopes and mail them to Meg. *Thank you for betraying me,* she would write on her note. She was a fairy-tale girl, scrubbing away at the first break of light, but she had fur and teeth and wings. She didn't mind getting up at five thirty. She loved the dark blue color of the sky at that hour. She treasured the feeling of being alone in the world. *You'll be repaid for what you've done to me.*

The girls at Westfield didn't like Elv. She wasn't surprised. People were jealous and petty and mean. She didn't care what they thought. She was already alone. When a volatile girl named Katy came after her, calling her names, shoving her, it was hard for Elv not to fight back, but she stuck to her plan. Play them all and you had a better chance of getting what you wanted. Let the person in power think you were on their side.

"Did anyone ever tell you you were a bitch?" Katy said. She'd had it in for Elv ever since Elv had suggested she had an anger management issue during group therapy.

Elv had already decided that the more trouble Katy made, the better off she herself would be. When Elv turned to walk away, Katy grabbed a glass vase on the reception table and slammed it into Elv's head. There would only be plastic vases allowed after that. The glass shattered into hundreds of jagged pieces. For weeks afterward tiny star-shaped bits of glass were swept up.

When the counselors ran into the room to separate the girls, anyone could clearly see Elv was the victim. Shards from the vase were threaded through her hair, where they shimmered like beads of ice in a thin trail of blood. Her face was pale. Her eyes closed. She was in the garden in Arnelle as they carried her to the nurse's office. *Reveal nothing, say nothing, and you'll get what you want in the end.*

Katy was immediately transferred to solitary. Elv, on the other hand, was released from latrine duty. She wanted to jump up and cheer. Instead she said "Thank you" in a solemn, soft voice. "I'm grateful for your trust and support." She had the language of self-help down pat. In group therapy, she told sorrowful stories that shocked everyone. It felt as if she was lying even if it was the truth, how she'd been fed bread and water, how he'd tied her down. When she cried, her tears were made of glass. They broke in half when they fell to the floor. No one noticed; they thought they were real. As if she would ever cry over what had happened.

The staff began to like her, she could tell. They pitied her. They thought she'd been treated unfairly at home, that she'd came from a dysfunctional family of divorce and shared secrets and was trying to reclaim her life. She was a model student and had soon won over her teachers. She attended all of her classes, even though they were a waste of time. All you had to do was show up and you'd pass. Westfield wanted to boast that 100 percent of enrolled students earned a high school diploma, even if no one learned anything. It was all a big show for the parents.

Soon Elv was granted permission to walk around the grounds. She searched for the robin's bones, those glinting opalescent shards, but too many leaves had fallen. She couldn't find a single one. She lay down in the leaves and listened to her name being called by those below. She hated herself for crying, even if they had been false tears. Right here, right now, she intended to give up all of her human traits. They had gotten her nothing. They'd gotten her here. In Arnelle, she was the one who freed demons from the nets that trapped them. She was known as their savior. In their world, she mattered. In their world, she was a queen.

ELV'S MOTHER SENT a present at Thanksgiving—a black cashmere sweater. *Now that the weather is getting cold,* Annie had written. Was she kidding? She never wanted to know the truth about anything. She wanted to believe everything was just fine—no skin and bones, no goblins, no rules. Students weren't allowed to wear their own clothes at Westfield. Elv gave the sweater to Julie Hagen, the counselor in charge of job assignments. Elv couldn't have anything but the ugly jeans and green T-shirt everyone was forced to wear. What did it matter? She might have been trapped in Westfield, but she was hiding out in Arnelle. She picked up the fragrance of hypnotic black roses as she walked down the corridor to the cafeteria. She could feel her wings emerging through her skin, feather by feather, bone by bone. She hadn't expected it to hurt so much.

IN DEEP WINTER, when the snow was three feet high and the white birch trees faded into the landscape, Elv earned the right to take care of the horses. She'd worked hard to get the job that would give her the most freedom. She swore that sugar made her hyper and brought her desserts to Julie Hagen, the counselor she'd presented with the black cashmere sweater. Miss Hagen was a soft touch, so Elv hung around her office on the pretext of being lonely. She began running errands and quickly became Miss Hagen's pet and her success story. In the end, it paid off. When the snow covered everything and the days ended in darkness at four, Elv got the plum job that she coveted.

Some of the other students might have been afraid of horses. They might have refused to shovel manure or resisted getting up so early, forced to tumble into the snowy field hours before breakfast. Elv was thrilled with her new position. She relished the time alone. She went to the stables early and stayed there most of the day, except for the few hours she had to spend in class. The glinting first light of morning was the perfect time to glimpse owls settling in the tall trees after a night of flight. Once there was a fox in the snow. Elv had stood there, quiet, breathing in the cold air, watching the scarlet color of the fox's coat. She felt bewitched and lucky. She could have been anywhere, a heath, a moor, a garden.

Annie phoned every week, but Elv never took her calls. When she had the flu, it was Miss Hagen who brought tea and a cold washcloth for her forehead. When the holidays came, the only one who sent a card was Claire. Elv sat on her bed to read it. It was in the shape of a bassett hound, resembling Pretzel, who'd lived down the street. The card read *Doggone, I miss you.*

Come back, Claire had written. *Nom brava gig.*

Claire wrote weekly letters, and although she read them hungrily, Elv didn't answer them. If Elv had been the one in the car, she would have never sat there, paralyzed with fear, while they'd carried her sister into the school. She would have done anything to stop them. But Claire didn't know what Elv knew, and Elv was grateful for that. She didn't know how to be vicious, how to bite back, how to fight for your life.

Elv didn't write to her, but she slipped the card under her pillow. It was the only thing she kept from home.

WHEN ANNIE CAME to visit, it was unannounced and unexpected. It was also unwanted. She thought it might be the only way she could get through to Elv. That if they sat down and talked they could work out what had gone wrong. All that week she had been dreaming of her daughter. Lately, she'd been afraid to fall asleep. Their lives had gone on as though everything was normal, or so it might appear. Annie and the girls had breakfast together, then Meg and Claire went off to school. Annie had stopped working. She had decided to focus on her family. She had savings and they would make do. She yearned to devote herself to something, even if that something was being a chauffeur. She cooked intricate dinners, learned how to make sushi, began to knit. She helped the girls to paint their bedroom a fresh eggy yellow in the hopes of brightening the third floor.

In the night, however, nothing seemed normal. The house echoed. Branches hit against the roof in a strange melody. Sometimes she dreamed about taking Elv to Westfield, the same turns on the highway, the same falling leaves, that dreadful moment when Elv glanced out the window and realized where they were. Everyone said to wait. Elv would contact her when she was ready. They said her oldest daughter would turn around and come back to her. But she had waited long enough.

One day, after Claire and Meg had left for school, Annie got in the car and started for New Hampshire. She'd felt such urgency she hadn't bothered to listen to the weather report. By the time she'd made it to the New Hampshire state line, it was snowing so hard the road didn't look the same. She stopped at a market and put together a care package of food, then headed on. She grew confused and had to stop several times to ask directions. The area around Westfield was a mystery. The roads were badly marked and turns came up suddenly. Everything was white and the woods were endless. Fir and oak and crumbling stone walls zigzagged through places where there were once farmers' fields. Annie pulled over to the side of the road, completely lost. The terrain was wild and hilly and she had mistakenly run over some felled logs. Somehow, she'd missed the turnoff to the Westfield School.

A police car came up behind her. Annie knew she was about to cry. She slipped on her sunglasses. The officer came around and tapped on the glass.

"Everything okay?" he asked when Annie buzzed down the window. He looked at her curiously.

"I missed the Westfield School. I didn't see it. My daughter's there."

"You can make a U-turn," the officer allowed. "I'll make sure the road stays clear."

He pitied her. She could tell. She saw that same look from neighbors and friends.

"It's about a quarter of a mile on the left. Why don't you stay here until you're ready to drive," the officer suggested. "I'll wait. No rush."

Annie sat there parked for a while, then turned and headed back down the blacktop. The officer waved to her. She felt as though he was the only person on earth who knew she was alive. The snow was coming down harder. As she edged along, Annie still couldn't see a thing. She drove slowly. When she squinted through the large fluffy flakes, the Westfield gates appeared inside a white fog. This time she didn't miss the turnoff.

The care package was perched on the backseat. Fruit and cookies and a plant. Annie parked and retrieved her offering. She kept on her sunglasses and tied a scarf around her head. The school looked different in the falling snow, as though it had been caught in a snow globe. The campus seemed so far away it might as well have been in the Russian steppes. Annie's mother always said that her childhood in Moscow was a childhood spent in winter. The first thing Natalia's parents had done when they'd reached

Paris was to buy fruit, something they'd rarely had beyond a few brown apples at most. It was Natalia who had started Elv on her love of apricots. *Fruit is always a gift,* Natalia always said to the girls. *No one knows that better than those who've never tasted it.*

Annie could hear the crunch of her boots and the sound of her own breathing as she walked the icy path to the administration building. She thought she saw something in the tall, plumy weeds, an opossum or a raccoon. Whatever it was, it was watching her as she tried her best not to slip on the ice. Inside, two guards were at the front desk, chatting. They stopped talking when Annie approached.

"I'm here to see my daughter," she told them.

When neither responded, Annie had a wash of panic. Didn't they know their own students?

"My daughter," she insisted. "Elisabeth Story. Elv. She's a student here."

"Did you have an appointment?" one of the guards asked.

"Do I need an appointment to see my own child?"

Apparently she did. The guard called down to the administration office. All Annie could do was wait as the care package was examined. Only the fruit was acceptable. The plant would have to be confiscated. They handed her a list of dos and don'ts for the future. Annie thought about the cashmere sweater she'd sent at Thanksgiving. She'd taken hours choosing the right one, nothing too fancy or frilly.

Elv was coming back from lunch in the cafeteria when she spied her mother in the lobby. She ran to her room and shut the door. Her heart was beating fast. Her mother looked like a stranger in her black winter coat. She'd been wearing sunglasses even though it was snowing outside. Elv felt a wave of sadness. She thought about being in the garden with her mother when the other girls were little, asleep in their cribs. Only Elv helped to gather tomatoes and peas. Her mother lifted her up so she could reach the highest of the climbing tendrils and pull down the sea green pods. There was pollen in the air, and the hawthorn tree sent the light through the slats of the trellis, and her mother laughed at how many pea pods Elv managed to gather at one time, dozens in a single handful.

Elv went into the bathroom and forced her fingers down her throat so she could make herself sick. When Julie Hagen came to get her, having made a special allowance for a family meeting, Elv was on the bathroom floor vomiting. Miss Hagen went back to the lobby to tell Annie the visit would have to be postponed; her daughter was sick, not the optimum time for a first encounter. Nothing to worry about, probably a stomach virus. Nothing for Annie to do but leave despite her protests.

Elv went to her window to watch her mother's car cross the parking lot. It drove away slowly, as though caught in dreamtime. It stopped at the end of the long driveway, and Elv felt something flutter inside her chest. Then the car started off again. It went through the gates and was gone. There was no point in feeling anything. Elv was weirdly protected, as if she lived in an Arnish castle made of stones and sticks. As if the wire fence was there to protect her from evil. When they brought her the care package her mother had left, Elv let it sit on her dresser until the fruit rotted. There were yellow apples and blood oranges and tangerines, but soon enough they all turned black and poisonous. In the end, Elv threw the fruit out her window for the birds to peck.

She curled up on her bed and thought about the otherworld. One of the demons tugged on her sleeve. A tiny lost creature with wings the color of blood. Human beings had been just as cruel to the demons as they had been to her. She pitied them and she pitied herself. If only she hadn't been stolen from her true life, she could have been happy. She let the demon lie down beside her, the poor, sweet thing. She let it crawl under her skin.

ELV HAD BEEN doing Michael's schoolwork in exchange for cigarettes. Though at first she planned to skim the books, she'd actually begun to read the novels assigned. Recently she'd been making her way through *The Scarlet Letter*. It was surprisingly good. She remembered when Meg had been reading it, she'd thought her sister was wasting her time, but she liked the way Hawthorne seemed to take Hester Prynne's side. She knew what it was like to be marked. When she gazed at her tattoos in the mirror, she felt set apart in the very same way as Hester did, revealed and ruined, exposed for all to see.

The only time when Elv didn't slip into the otherworld was when she was taking care of the horses. She loved the job. That was why she didn't dare tell anyone, not even Miss Hagen, who was usually on her side. She was afraid that if anyone knew she was happy, it would all be taken away. The horses were called Daisy and Cookie and Sammy and Jack. They'd been left behind when the person who owned the estate went bankrupt and sold his land to the school. He'd abandoned the horses along with the real estate and the furniture, as if they were nothing more than goldfish in a pond. Daisy and Cookie were young, high-spirited. But Sammy and Jack were her favorites. Sammy was a little palomino, skittish with anyone he didn't know. Jack was old and huge and dignified with enormous hooves. The horses all knew her and were waiting for her no matter how early she arrived.

Christmas had come and gone. There was a turkey dinner, and then Elv escaped out to the stables. Winter went on, darker, the days so short they passed by quickly. North Point Harbor was so far away it might as well have been on the other side of the world. Elv lost weight, but she got stronger working with the horses, hauling around bales of hay, mucking out the stalls. All through January and February the weather was so cold the horses had to wear wool blankets. When they breathed out, they looked like steam engines. Elv loved being with them; she loved the smell of hay. She thought about Central Park and the horse that had run away with her sister. Better to die than be a slave of men, tied up, an iron bit in your mouth.

Jack banged his body against his stall and whinnied like crazy when Elv got there in the morning. When she whistled, he came right over, like an enormous, well-trained dog. Sometimes she sat in the straw in his stall and just talked to him. He looked at her with his big dark eyes and she felt tears rising. Not crocodile tears, but real ones. Maybe when she left she would steal him. Or she would leave his stall door open and he could run away and be free. The horses didn't judge Elv by the way she looked or discern that she was marked and ruined. They didn't care that something bad had happened to her and that no one saw who she was. They didn't care that she wore ugly clothes, or that she burned herself with cigarettes, or that she sat in the hay and wept when she thought about how long Claire had waited for her at the corner, all day, until darkness fell and the mosquitoes filled the air. Claire was the one who had been crying for hours, her face streaky and hot. It was Elv who'd had to comfort her.

Sometimes Elv and Michael would hide out behind the stables and smoke the cigarettes his brother smuggled to him on visiting days. Elv was now doing all of Michael's schoolwork, even the math. Lately, she skipped evening activities in order to get back to *The Scarlet Letter*. Sometimes she chose it over drifting into Arnelle. She hated Dimsdale and wanted to see him get his comeuppance. It wasn't real life, so perhaps a horrible human being really would get what he deserved and the girl who'd been ruined would turn and walk away.

SHE WAS HEADED back from the stables one windy day as Michael was leaving the administration building. He was an honor student, due to Elv's hard work, and as such he was allowed unsupervised visits with relatives. He had only one visitor, his brother from New York City. Elv was standing in the tall grass, which had turned a pale green. It was early spring and the ground was muddy. The air was chilly and fresh. She had been away for six months. The outside world didn't even exist anymore. She could barely picture her mother's face. She didn't bother opening her letters. Everything that came before her time at Westfield was a blur. Elv was ready for the next thing to happen. She was waiting for a new life.

On the first day that it seemed as if winter might actually be over, she left her jacket behind, even though the air was still cool. In New Hampshire, people were desperate for spring, and she was among them. She wore oversized jeans and a sweatshirt over her green T-shirt—hideous clothes she knew were supposed to make her feel less like an individual. Everyone was equal at Westfield, even if that meant feeling ugly. Elv had on tall rubber boots that were splattered with mud. Her long black hair was all she had of the person she used to be. Still, she felt hopeful when she stood out in the grass. Another world must surely exist somewhere, one where she would be known in some deep way that was far beyond words.

Michael was telling his brother about some guy from their old neighborhood who had just been busted, but Lorry wasn't listening. He was twenty-five, his own man. There was a gap of eight years between the brothers and they were different people entirely. Whereas Michael was a braggart, Lorry was more of a storyteller. Whereas Michael was a car thief, grabbing for what he wanted greedily, always getting caught, Lorry liked people to hand over what was precious to them, convinced that they had made their own decision to do so. He was tall and thin, handsome, dark, with hooded eyes and an uncanny ability to read people. Women said he had a lethal smile and that he was difficult to resist. Everyone agreed—he could talk himself out of just about any kind of trouble. In the city he was known for his tattoos. On one hand there was a crown of thorns, on the other a crown of roses. Above each was a black star. The back of the hand was one of the most painful places to be tattooed—the skin was paper thin—but Lorry hadn't minded. He told himself there was a price to pay for any story worth telling, and that his tattoos would tell the story for him when he didn't have the time, or the energy, or the heart to tell it himself.

He saw the girl who had come out of the stables standing in the grass, her hair flying out behind her. There was pollen in the air; everything looked hazy and green.

"Who's that?" he asked his brother.

"Her? She's a little suburban bitch whose parents thought she was uncontrollable. I've got her doing all my schoolwork." Michael always had to show off for his brother. "She does whatever I tell her."

Lorry laughed. Unlike his little brother, he didn't have to brag. He simply knew what he wanted. "Not anymore."

Elv saw Michael and his visitor, but assumed they hadn't spied her. She thought she was invisible. She was in Arnelle, far from the muddy green-edged spring. She was in a field where the violets were as big as cabbages, where the tomatoes were black and poisonous, love apples that dared you to take a bite. She went there whenever she left the stables. In New Hampshire, she was nothing, a speck in the grass, but her demon court had taken over the otherworld. They'd chased out the turncoat faeries who'd turned out to be cowards, willing to make bargains with human beings. They'd built houses of straw and mud, ringed with the black stones of vengeance, a curse to anyone who tried to harm them.

Elv assumed the handsome man approaching was on his way to the parking lot beyond the field. She'd never seen Michael's brother before, but she'd heard about his exploits. He was like a magician, Michael had said. He could make things appear when you least expected it—money, drugs, a free apartment, a car with a full tank of gas. Elv suddenly realized he was headed straight for her. She felt light-headed, forced to step out of Arnelle. It was as if she was being torn out of something. She heard a crack, as though the atmosphere was breaking apart. She moved into this world. She could feel her heart beating hard.

"Nobody as beautiful as you should be here," Lorry told her.

The first words he ever said to her went right through her. She was there in New Hampshire, standing in the grass in her terrible clothes, pushing the hair out of her eyes so she could see him more clearly.

"They should have never put you here," he went on, as though they were in the middle of a conversation, as if he knew her better than anyone.

He was almost too good-looking, like a movie star who'd wandered into the New Hampshire meadow by accident. He wore a black coat, jeans, boots, black leather gloves. He was so tall, Elv had to look up to see his face. No man had ever spoken to her that directly. Usually, Elv would have flirted or, if she was in a foul mood, walked away. But in his presence, she felt overwhelmed. She lifted her chin like a child setting out a dare, trying to undo whatever spell had befallen her.

"I'll bet you don't even know my name."

He squinted through the green pollen in the air. "It's Elv."

Her own name sounded beautiful to her for the first time. The spell intensified twofold.

"Let's get out of here." Lorry had a fluid energy that took control. He grabbed her hand and they went past the stables, into the woods. The air was chilly, but the grass was green. Little bits of it were sticking to her clothes. The woods were thick, filled with birch and pine. The fiddlehead ferns were unfolding, and masses of swamp cabbage were greening, with huge, musty leaves. Lunch in the cafeteria had already been served, but no one would miss her. She often stayed with the horses until she had to be in class; sometimes she didn't appear until the dinner hour. Julie Hagen gave her an absence note if she needed one. She was Miss Hagen's pet, after all, the girl who had been controlled and transformed, who knew how to behave, until she found a way to escape.

As they walked along, Lorry began to tell the story of his life. He had grown up in Queens, but his parents had abandoned him and his brother. He'd been on his own from the time he was ten. He'd learned how to survive when everyone else turned away. He stopped suddenly, in midsentence, so that she crashed into him. Lorry grinned. He put a hand on her waist to steady her. His touch was hot; it spread along her body. "Unless you don't want to hear it," Lorry said.

"No. Tell me." Elv was overcome with emotion. Most people were so boring, she tuned them right out, but not him. She was ready to listen. "Once you start a story you have to finish it."

"It's not the kind your mother told you at bedtime," Lorry warned. "It's scary," he said in a fevered tone that warned her to think twice. Some stories stayed with you even when you wanted to forget them.

Still, Elv remained stubborn. "Those are the best kind of stories."

Lorry laughed, charmed. She was such a gorgeous girl, delicious in her stubbornness and her beauty. He had good reason to charm her right back. He put everything on the slow burner; he'd let her burn and come to him. "Once upon a time," he said and again they both laughed. There were crows calling from the trees. He waited for quiet and soon enough the noisy crows in the pines took flight. He told her he'd been on his own since they tried to beat him to death at his last foster home. It had been bad before that—at one place they'd made him stand out in the pouring rain and he'd come down with pneumonia. In another, they fed him only bread and water. In a third, they'd put pennies on his eyelids, the way they did for the dead, and he'd had to sleep without moving all night long so that the pennies didn't shift. But the last house was the worst. They'd kept him locked in a tiny room they called his bedroom whenever he wasn't in school. It was an airless closet. It was where they kept their trash and old shoes. When he'd had enough, he slipped a knife into his pocket in the school cafeteria. That night he cut through the ropes.

"They tied you up?" Elv was mesmerized. She put her hand up to her chest to try to stop her heart from pounding. Her secret incantation had somehow been revealed. *Rope, Iron, Water, Bread.*

"People who are weak do that. It's the only way they can get power. They don't have anything within themselves, so they try to tie you up, hold you captive. That wasn't going to happen to me."

He climbed out the window and never looked back. One cold night when he thought he'd freeze to death, he found a hidden staircase on Thirty-third Street behind an iron gate. It was the way all treasures were found, when you weren't even looking for them. Like today, for instance, seeing her across the field.

Elv thought about the word *treasure* and told him to keep going. He pulled her down and they sat close together. The sun came through the trees with pinpricks of light.

He opened the iron gate, then went down so many steps that before long the subway ran above him. He could not believe what he'd found.

There were gnats circling in the air, but Elv barely noticed. Her breath came fast.

"You lived underground?"

"I'll tell you about it sometime." Lorry shrugged. "It's a long story."

"No." Elv's tone was urgent. "Tell me now."

He had her and he knew it. He said it would have to wait until next time. The dinner bell had been ringing, Elv just hadn't heard it. She'd miss dinner if she didn't hurry. Then there would be one of the Westfield punishments, either isolation or humiliation. They had been in the woods for hours. It was the time when the field mice ventured out, after the hawks had settled in the trees but before the owls came to hunt. The sky was now the color Elv liked best—a tender dark blue, falling to earth like ashes.

"I don't want you to find yourself in trouble," Lorry said. He walked her back, stopping to light a cigarette. He had bad habits, but he could control his excesses, unlike most of the fools he knew. "I can quit anytime I want," he told Elv. "I'm not a slave to anything or anyone."

He'd taken off his gloves to strike the match, revealing the black stars, the roses and the thorns. Something dropped in the pit of Elv's stomach. These were the images from her own stories, skin and bones, flesh and blood. She thought, *Is this how it happens?* When she looked at him, a shiver went through her. She had talked about being turned inside out by love. Now for the first time she had an idea of what that meant. She had the same feeling she'd always had before she jumped off a dock into deep, cold water. Half wanting it, half terrified.

Lorry came close. She thought he was going to kiss her, but instead he wrapped his arms around her. Sheltered by his embrace, she could scarcely breathe. Before she could contain herself, she started to cry. She knew she was about to surrender to him. She didn't even try to stop herself.

She didn't care about time. Lorry walked her back in the fading light. When he left, Elv went to the window of the dining hall and gazed out. She had become a sky expert. She could tell the hour by the position of the sun and the stars. She made a wish, the way she used to, when her mother took her into the garden to tell stories, to watch the white moths, to see the moon rise above North Point Harbor.

"Where the hell have you been?" Michael asked when she had grabbed a dinner tray—meat loaf, soggy green beans, and a sad-looking ice cream sundae.

Elv sat down at the long metal table, across from him. She wasn't sure herself, so she merely shrugged and asked if he wanted her dessert. Greedy as always, he grabbed it. Not that she wasn't greedy as well. When Lorry's next visit came around, she was waiting by the gate.

HE VISITED WESTFIELD every other week. It was some time before he even kissed her, but when he did, she felt her world fall away. She fell in love feetfirst, as though dropped from a bridge. Headfirst was too rational for what happened to her. By then she knew more of the story. He had lived underground for seven years after fleeing his last foster home. He set up camp on a platform eight stories below Penn Station. You wouldn't think the world was that deep, but it was. He had a tent, a lantern, a canteen. It was homey, if you didn't notice the trains screaming past at all hours. He was a Boy Scout, only in reverse, not in it for fun and games, merely trying to survive. The others there called themselves the People, but they were nothing like the human beings aboveground. They were kinder, braver, stronger. Some were so dangerous they were combustible—one wrong word could be the match that set them aflame. Some were lost. There was a giant who was so difficult to find you had to write his name on a piece of wood and leave it beside the train tracks and a week later he might show up to sell you weed or mushrooms. The best of the People took pity on Lorry. They taught him to get fresh water from the restrooms in subway stations built decades ago by the city, but never used. They showed him how to pick pockets, how to bind a wound with a spiderweb to keep away infection, how to chase away rats, how to wait outside bakeries above-ground till closing time when what was day-old to them was a treasure to him.

He was ten, but hardly easy prey. He had a knife, the ability to sleep with his eyes open, and a talent for hiding. He had enemies underground, but he had friends as well, people who saw him through such tough times anyone else would have died.

The giant took a liking to him and so did the giant's wife, who worked at a restaurant aboveground and often left Lorry a cooked dinner. "You don't belong here," she told him. "I want to see the day when you leave here and go back up to the world."

But there was nothing for him in that world. He soon realized that the realm he'd chosen to replace it was just as dangerous as the world aboveground. Luckily, only a few weeks after he arrived underground he adopted a dog he named Mother, half husky, half German shepherd, abused by an unbalanced homeless owner, turned vicious, then abandoned. Mother had saved his life more than once. Hence the name. The mother he never had, one with teeth and claws. A beast whose very presence scared the evil residents away, but who would eat from his hand and never once bite. That's how he came to understand what loyalty was. It was the first worthwhile human trait he ever learned.

THEY WERE IN the grass in the place where the robin's bones had been scattered, where they'd broken her ribs. His arms were around her, under her clothes. He was so hot she felt he was the match that had been set to her skin, like those combustible men belowground, just waiting to be ignited. "Should I let go of you?" he asked.

Being close to him was like being in another world. Elv felt safe in a way she didn't understand. She closed her eyes. She thought about the wild dog and the subway platform lit by torchlight. Most men would have rushed her, but Lorry had waited until she was ready. She told him not to let go. Nothing else seemed to matter anymore, not even Arnelle. Everything that had happened to her before was part of a ghost life. This alone was real and beautiful.

"You can trust me," he said. "People tell you that all the time, and you know you can't believe them. But this is me, Elv. Just me."

She could not remember the last time she trusted anyone. He slipped her clothes off, ran his hands over her, took his time. She gave herself to him completely. It was pointless to fight what was happening; it seemed preordained. She wanted someone to protect her, to know her. She felt herself swoon like some foolish girl who believed in love and fate. He talked to her the whole time, and the more he spoke, the more entwined they were. She gasped when he moved to enter her, shocked by how much she wanted him. With all those boys back home, she'd stood outside herself, watching. Now she was on the inside looking out. What she saw was a man who couldn't take his eyes off her. It was exactly what she wanted.

He didn't kiss her until the very end. By then she belonged to him. He told her that he'd made a vow to never kiss a woman he didn't love, that it went against his nature, because it was the way you entered into another person's soul. He waited while she pulled on her T-shirt, buttoned her jeans. When he drew her to him once again, Elv realized that he'd never taken off his coat. He'd spent his life on the run, he told her. But he wasn't running now.

They were hidden in the woods. Elv could see the angles of the school through the trees. She didn't want to go back. She curled up, covered her face, distraught. Once you started to feel things, this is what happened, it went on and on, taking you over.

"Come on," Lorry said. "I'll do anything to make you happy. I'll get you whatever you want. Seriously. Just tell me."

"I want Jack," she said.

He backed off, frowning. "Jack?"

Elv felt a little rise of pleasure. He was jealous. She nodded to the stable. "The old horse. He's the best one."

Lorry laughed, relieved. Any air of menace dissipated. "I can't manage that right now. But I have something else that will make going back easier." He took a small envelope from his pocket and snapped his fingers against the waxed paper. He called it the witch. "My fatal flaw." He laughed.

Elv shook her head. She could see it wasn't true. He was flawless, exactly what she'd been waiting for. How had this happened? How had she been so lucky? He had walked across the meadow and it had all begun, her real life, her life on earth. He laid out the lines of heroin. It made her think of the way the grass froze into a white patchwork of dew.

One breath of the powder and she was blown away. Nothing she'd tried before compared to this. She leaned up against him.

She was miles away from the mud in the fields and the bitter green scent of swamp cabbage. Neither of them cared that it was getting cold now that the light was fading. She hadn't seen how beautiful it could be in New Hampshire. The grass looked black. The peepers out in the marshlands began to call. Elv really didn't care about anything except for him. She kissed him for as long as she dared.

SHE WAS LATE, missing dinner by nearly an hour. Anyone else would have been put in solitary, but Miss Hagen, so earnest and well-meaning, came to her defense. As punishment Elv was assigned to a second job. "It was the best I could do," Miss Hagen said apologetically.

"It's fine," Elv assured her. "I just got lost."

She laughed because it was true. She was lost and he had found her and she didn't really care about punishment. She worked in the stables in the mornings and had latrine duty at night, after supper. It didn't matter. She was just biding her time. Counting off the hours. Michael came around to watch her mopping out the rec room bathrooms. He was resentful, sullen, someone with a jealous soul. He rarely saw his brother now that Lorry was so taken with Elv. He just checked Lorry in at the administration building, then slunk away while Lorry went to meet Elv at their pre-arranged spot in the woods.

Now Michael tried to unwind their bond. He perched on a chair to tell Elv she was an idiot if she thought she could keep Lorry's attentions. Every woman who saw him fell for him. Did she think she was the first? They'd hand over their hearts and their savings and when he was done he'd walk away, on to the next. In case she hadn't noticed, that fatal flaw Lorry joked about wasn't a joke. He'd been hooked on heroin for years. This wasn't a baby habit, it was King Kong—his everything. Lorry was a liar, one of the best. He was dangerous territory for a girl like Elv, too stupid to see him for what he was. Michael was his brother, of course, but he was a wolf as well. Maybe it would be better if Lorry was taken off the visitors' list. Michael grinned when he suggested it. Elv glanced up, eyes narrowed. Just as Lorry had said: those who are most powerless are the ones who do their best to hurt you.

Elv told Michael that if he didn't shut up, she wouldn't do his schoolwork anymore. Her ex-friend was clearly an idiot. Their relationship dissolved then and there. He was nothing like his brother. He couldn't even pass simple geometry without her help. And her help was something he had only as long as Lorry was kept on his visitors' list.

A FEW WEEKS later, Elv thought she might be pregnant. She was panicky, scared to tell Lorry, but when at last she did, he surprised her. He said they would deal with whatever happened. They'd raise the baby just fine, the two of them. They'd do a hell of a lot better than their parents had.

"We're together," he said. "I told you that. I won't walk away."

When Elv got her period a few days later, she was overwhelmed by sadness. She locked herself in the stable and cried while the horses watched her. She wished she was a normal girl who lived in a house and could call the man she loved and talk to him, listening to his voice all night long. She was besotted. She wrote his name on pieces of paper the way she had once mapped out the lanes and alleyways of Arnelle. She didn't think beyond the next visiting day. And then the worst thing happened, something so terrible she hadn't even imagined it. Michael was being released. He had turned eighteen and had finished out the school term with A's and B's thanks to Elv. He was actually graduating.

She went to the graduation—ten lackluster students and a few family members who didn't know whether to be worried or relieved. She sat in the last row. Lorry came in and took the seat beside her. They held hands under the chairs so no one would see. Elv cried all the way through the ceremony. Lorry leaned close. "This is temporary," he told her. "It has nothing to do with our real lives."

They quickly planned a meeting at the end of the week. After the ceremony, once Michael had packed up and left, Elv stood out in the empty parking lot. Miss Hagen came to comfort her, just as Elv had hoped. Miss Hagen knew Elv and Michael had been close. It was difficult when friends moved on, but Elv had made such progress. If she stuck with it, it would be her own graduation before long.

There were June bugs floating through the heavy air. Elv didn't have to fake blinking back tears. She thanked Miss Hagen for all she had done. For changing her life. But today had been so sad, perhaps if she could have an afternoon off. If she could walk through town, sit in a restaurant, make a phone call, she might be strong enough to carry on.

The pass came through the very next day.

ELV HAD NO interest in the small New Hampshire village, where there was only a pizza place, a Laundromat, and a grocery that was closed half the time. That wasn't why she hadn't slept all night. She went to feed the horses earlier than usual, when the sky was pitch-black, then came back to sit on the edge of her bed. She waited, dressed up in a skirt and a blouse that the school had approved for an "out" day. She was allowed to leave the grounds at ten and had to be back at three. She wasn't thinking about coming back. She was only thinking about how long it would be before she was with him.

It usually took half an hour to walk along the road to town, but Elv ran. Lorry was waiting in the parking lot behind the Laundromat, just the way they'd planned. They drove off and found an old logging road that led into the woods. They could be as reckless as they wanted. They could do as they pleased. They made love in the car, quickly, desperate for each other. Lorry pulled Elv into his lap and told her that this was their real life. This was what they'd been waiting for. When they got out of the car, they went exploring. They found a pond and took off their clothes and dove in heedlessly. Frogs plashed out of their way. The cold water shocked them and made them cling to each other. The sunlight was thin and pale, but when they came out into the chilly air, Elv stayed undressed. She unfolded herself onto an old blanket Lorry had put down for her. There were black-eyed Susans and thistle and dozens of small butterflies skittering over the blooms. Elv braided her hair and pinned it up. If Arnelle really had existed, it would have had this same tawny landscape of pine and oak and birch, the same banks of ferns speckled with sunlight.

Lorry pulled on his clothes and went to retrieve something from the car. He was singing to himself. Elv thought, *This is what happiness is.* He'd brought along ink and needles to mark this day. He'd brought the witch as well. "My fatal flaw," he remarked as he knelt down beside her. When Elv wanted to shoot it, Lorry was reluctant, but she teased and coaxed and at last he agreed. He did it for her, tying his belt around her arm, telling her to close her eyes, mixing it up over his lighter until it was melted and liquid. She drifted into this delicious thing she now understood to be happiness. She wanted a tattoo, so he told her to lie down and turn over. She pried herself out of her dreams and did as he said. She didn't even feel the needle. She was floating and it was perfect and when Lorry leaned in to ask if he was hurting her, she answered no, not at all. How green the light was. How quickly the dragonflies darted along the surface of the pond. When Lorry was done with the tattoo, Elv went to the car and glanced in the sideview mirror. There was a small black rose at the base of her neck.

She didn't want to go back. She gave him every reason she could think of to take her with him, but in the end she understood why he said he couldn't. She wasn't eighteen. If caught, she'd be sent back to Westfield, but Lorry would go to jail. She got dressed and unplaited her hair. It was late. That meant trouble.

"They're going to do something terrible to me," Elv worried.

"Even if they do," Lorry said, "they can't touch you."

He drove her halfway back to school, then pulled onto the side of the road. She scrambled back into his lap, her arms and legs around him. She didn't want to let go of him. This world, so bright with him in it, was meaningless without him.

"What if I never see you again?" she asked.

Lorry vowed that when she got out of Westfield, he would be there for her. He would find her no matter where she was.

"What happened to the dog?" she asked. "Mother? At least tell me that."

After a while, some of the worst of the People had put a price on his dog's head. Lorry had been invincible with Mother by his side, from the time he was ten until his seventeenth birthday. Some people didn't like that; it threatened the hierarchy that existed in the world below, where evil was sometimes its own reward and the good and kind often suffered. It had happened in midsummer, when the tunnels were hot, and tempers were twitchy. His heart sank when he woke to find his dog gone. Mother would have never left Lorry of his own will.

"Then what happened?" Elv wrapped her arms more tightly around him.

There wasn't time for the rest of the story. The sky was already that deep summery blue of early evening. There was no time left at all. After he drove off, Elv had a sharp instant of panic. She felt like running after the car along that stark stretch of road. But she didn't dare wreck their future with some hasty, love-crazed act.

She went back the way she'd come, ignoring the truckers who honked their horns, following the road to Westfield. It was long past curfew. They were waiting for her. Five more minutes and they would have handed her disappearance over to the state police. Even Miss Hagen couldn't get her out of this one.

They chopped off her hair, then used an electric razor. She remembered the way he'd held his arms around her, the promises they'd made. She thought of the green water, the frogs, the swamp cabbage unfolding, leaf by leaf. She thought of his first kiss and all it had revealed. Elv had always believed her long hair was the only worthwhile part of her, her single bit of beauty. Frankly, she'd been shocked by how brave Meg had been on the day she'd cut it all off. Now it was her turn, but she wouldn't resent the loss the way Meg had or let it define her. She refused to hide herself away. The rest of the world didn't matter. She was one thing only, and that was his alone. When the counselors held up a mirror, Elv wasn't like the other girls, who cried and covered their heads. She wasn't like her sister, willing to betray her own flesh and blood. She didn't flinch when she saw her reflection. Now that her hair had been shorn, the black rose at the base of her neck was visible, as if in bloom. So much the better.

This was who she was inside.

✦ ✦ ✦

THEIR GRANDFATHER HAD died of heart failure at the end of the winter. The funeral was in New York. It was a somber occasion, attended by a small circle. No one spoke about the fact that Elv wasn't there, though everyone knew what had happened. She'd been sent off because of her erratic behavior; there'd been drugs involved and a series of boys. She'd been a charming child one minute, an out-of-control teenager the next. Of course the family was crushed. Annie looked ten years older, and the younger daughters were exceedingly quiet, their complexions pale. Not a single one of the relatives mentioned that only two of the Story sisters were in attendance, dressed in black coats, standing at the grave site beside their mother and their beloved ama. Mary Fox, always so serious and clever, cried her eyes out and needed to be comforted by her mother. She then went to try to compose herself beneath the hanging branches of the pine trees, turning her back so the others wouldn't see her sobbing. Meg and Claire, however, had remained stoic, their faces expressionless, arms linked. Afterward, their grandmother went back to Paris. Once school had adjourned for spring vacation, Claire and Meg went to join her. They were still in love with the city. The sunlight was a thousand different colors in Paris. Every day it changed. But it was a time when everyone was lonely, even when they were together, even when they were in their favorite place in the world, their ama's apartment in the Marais.

The chestnut tree was in flower, and the leaves were especially lustrous this year. Every morning the girls and their grandmother had soft-boiled eggs for breakfast. They drank bowls of hot milk laced with coffee. They did not talk about Elv. They tried not to think about her. But of course the cat that Elv had rescued was always underfoot. Natalia was terribly attached to her and brought her back and forth across the Atlantic in a carry-on case. Sadie had grown to be a large, disagreeable tabby with green eyes. For some reason the cat took a dislike to Meg; as soon as she heard Meg's voice, she skittered into the closet to nest among boots and umbrellas. Meg didn't seem to mind. She said she was allergic to cats and avoided Sadie completely. But Claire often lay on the floor to play with the cat's favorite toy—a crocheted mouse on a string—until Sadie came to halfheartedly bat at the mouse with a paw.

Claire and Meg seemed older than their ages. They were wary and never spoke to strangers. Sometimes Elv's name tumbled out in conversation as they remembered other years in Paris, recalling how they would hide behind the old stone trough when their mother came looking to call them to dinner; they remembered the memory game they'd played on the day they'd taken the train to Versailles. They bit their lips then and looked at the ground. Meg thought about the way her sister had pinched her when she was angry. But Claire thought about the time that Elv had told her the story of Grimin, the most evil human in the world. *He thought I would drown, but I didn't. He thought I would bleed to death, but I'm still here.* There wasn't a day that went by when Claire didn't regret not opening the car door at Westfield. She should have gotten out and rescued her sister. If they had run far enough, New Hampshire would have disappeared behind them. All the stories they'd ever known would have disappeared as well, the words falling down around them, letter by letter, down to the bottom of the deepest well.

When Madame Cohen came to dinner and asked how Elv was, the Story sisters fell silent. Claire had written letters and cards but hadn't heard back. Meg was actually dreading the time when her sister returned. Natalia had fixed a sun-dried tomato rice pilaf to accompany the roast chicken she served. Madame Cohen offered the bowl to the girls but they said they weren't hungry. "Here in this country, herbalists thought tomatoes were bad for you well into the nineteenth century," she told them. "It was considered an act of bravery simply to eat one."

Meg excused herself to help their ama carry out the drinks, homemade lemonade and a bottle of local white wine.

"You can't always believe what everyone tells you," Madame Cohen told Claire, whom she found to be the most sensitive and emotional of the Story sisters. She pointed to their dinner. "We'd think this was as deadly as mandrake if we did." She ate a forkful of the pilaf. "I had two sisters," she said. "I was the youngest. Much like you."

Claire had always been a little afraid of her grandmother's friend, wary of her black clothes and stern appearance. Madame Cohen wore her white hair up, neatly held in place with tortoise-shell combs. She always had sensible shoes and often carried an umbrella, even on sunny days. Claire didn't know if her French was good enough to speak to Madame Cohen. "What happened to them?" she asked.

"Exactly what your sister Elv wanted to know," Madame Cohen told her. "They've been gone for a very long time. For other people, that is. Not for me."

"What do you think happened to Madame Cohen's sisters?" Claire asked Meg as they were getting ready for bed. Meg had recently made a vow to read all of Dickens. She had just begun *Oliver Twist*.

"Madame Cohen had sisters?" Meg got into bed and reached for her book. Claire got in beside her. She didn't mind if Meg stayed up reading. She liked sleeping with the light on. But even with the lamp's yellow glow, even though she heard the rustling of pages and the familiar sound of traffic on the streets nearby, even though she knew Meg was right there beside her, she still felt alone.

◆ ◆ ◆

THAT SPRING THE girls' grandmother gave them much more freedom than their mother ever would have, considering what had happened with Elv. Natalia believed freedom was never a problem, only those who didn't know how to handle the responsibilities that went along with it. In the afternoons, while she took her nap, the girls walked toward the Île Saint-Louis, stopping at Berthillon. Meg liked to try something new each time, blood orange, for instance, or caramel-ginger, but Claire stuck with vanilla. She was loyal to her favorite things. The Story sisters would then go to gaze into the green water of the Seine as they ate their ice cream. Sometimes they sat in front of Notre Dame and watched tourists. They liked to guess which families were happy and which ones were only pretending. They figured they were right 99 percent of the time.

Many people thought the girls were twins. Their hair was styled exactly the same, falling straight to the jawbone, angled in front. They explored the Left Bank, spending hours at Shakespeare and Co. searching through old volumes, reading the dedications scrawled on the frontispieces, wondering who had truly been in love and who was just offering up an insincere gift. They could speak enough French to order well in cafés. They loved the ones on Saint-Germain where they ordered espressos or cafés au lait and sometimes had the nerve to ask for glasses of kir, which the waiters always brought without question. They flirted with boys, but never divulged their real names or where they lived. They didn't trust anyone except each other.

They no longer believed in Arnelle. They were far too old for stories about faeries. They never spoke Arnish. It made them think of things they didn't want to remember. Red leaves, rain, New Hampshire. They were already forgetting the words Elv had taught them and they could no longer recall if *henaj* meant *wolf* or *dog,* if *nejimi* meant *hero* or *coward.* In dire circumstances, however, their private vocabulary sometimes surfaced in a rush, surprising them. They had fleetingly whispered to each other in Arnish when they'd become lost at the airport upon arrival. And then again when Claire had stomach pains and thought she might be dying of appendicitis. They'd had a tearful panicked conversation in Arnish then, though what had befallen her turned out to be severe indigestion, nothing more.

Although there were two beds in their grandmother's spare bedroom, the sisters slept together. They were too old for this, but they didn't care. They didn't talk about the reason they shared a bed nor did they discuss their dreams. Each had her reasons. The tiger at the door. The boy on the edge of the bed. The shower of red leaves. The man saying, *You know me; get in the car.*

In the last days of their vacation, their mother came to Paris to retrieve them and also to check in on her mother. Perhaps someone should have been checking on Annie. She didn't look like herself anymore. She had lost more weight and wore her dark glasses most of the time to hide the circles under her eyes. While the girls were away, she'd suffered terrible bouts of insomnia, sitting up until morning, gazing into the backyard and wondering when it had gone wrong. She thought it was that day at the Plaza. The way Elv had looked at her when she'd been accused of masterminding the theft of the carriage horse.

After Annie arrived in Paris, she was so tired she crawled into the second bed in the girls' room and slept for seventeen hours. She curled up beneath a snowy linen coverlet, the same she'd used during summers here in Paris when she was a girl. There had been some talk about staying on in France when she was twelve or thirteen, but her father's business was in New York and so they'd returned to Manhattan. Lately, Annie had become obsessed with the different life she might have had if they'd remained in Paris.

The man she might have loved, the apartment where she might have lived, the daughters whose only language would have been French.

The sisters sat by their mother's bedside. Today, the light through the window was pink and clear. They were glad she was there. Ever since Elv went away, she had been too quiet. She forgot to go shopping or make dinner. The milk in the refrigerator was often sour, and Meg had taken to cleaning the house once a week. Sometimes Annie didn't seem like their mother anymore. Now, for instance, she seemed like a little girl sleeping in the guest room bed. She was disappearing before their eyes. Meg made sure she was breathing; she held a mirror close to their mother's mouth—she'd seen this done in an old movie. When the glass fogged up, the girls knew she was still alive.

Natalia finally woke Annie from her long sleep, shaking her, calling her name, bringing her a cup of hot tea. She insisted they all go out for the day. They went to the Musée d'Orsay, where they thought they were enjoying themselves until they noticed Annie standing in front of Van Gogh's self-portrait, crying. Annie excused herself and went off to the restroom. Claire was reminded of the black river Elv had once painted. She wished she had begged for it. She wished she had it right now.

The rest of the weekend was better. The Story sisters took their mother to all the places they loved most: the ice cream stand, the bookstore, the Jardin du Luxembourg, the bench in front of Notre Dame, where they all sat together holding hands, and anyone who passed by would have thought they were happy. Annie slept through the night for the first time in ages under the white coverlet. She ate soft-boiled eggs. She painted her nails red, then polished the girls' nails as well. On their last day in Paris, the sisters were in the kitchen cutting up pears for a tart. Their mother and grandmother were on the terrace having their morning coffee. Below, in the courtyard, two elderly tenants were arguing over whether or not a third could tie his bicycle to the now broken stone trough. Their mother laughed when one tenant called the other a stupid boot. Meg and Claire looked at each other. They could hear the clock over the stove, ticking. They could hear doves in the courtyard. They wanted this moment to last forever. The sunlight was orange. They had to remember that. Meg would make certain they did. She fetched a piece of paper and wrote down the word *orange,* then folded the paper in half. They could cut up pears and write down all of the colors of the light and listen to people laugh and smell the blooms on the chestnut tree and forget about the rest of the world. They wanted to stay in their grandmother's apartment always, but instead they would have this memory of sitting in the kitchen, being happy.

They flew home on Air France. They spoke French to the stewards, and their mother was proud of them and let them each have a glass of champagne. Claire felt dizzy and sick right before landing at JFK. She had to go to the restroom even though the seat belt signs were already switched on. Once there, she vomited into the horrible, messy toilet. She clung to the sink, stricken that she had imagined she was happy, or that she might even have a right to be. She must have been gone for a long time, because her mother came looking for her, worried.

Annie tapped on the door. "Claire? Are you all right?"

Claire opened the door.

Annie touched her forehead. Burning hot. "Claire," she said. "Darling."

"I'm fine," Claire insisted. "Really. I am." And then, before she could stop herself, she said, "Maybe I just miss her."

Claire would certainly miss her beloved grandmother, but that wasn't who she was talking about and they both knew it.

"I miss her too," Annie said.

They went back to their seats. They were closer to home than they'd thought, all the way across the Atlantic. They put their seat belts on, and after that they didn't think about Paris anymore.

ELV WAS FINALLY ready to see them. They didn't have to coax or beg. She herself asked for the meeting. She wanted it right away. Sometimes Annie felt as though she had invented Elv, and all those years they'd spent together had been a fevered dream. It was decided that Alan and Annie would drive up separately. Neither wanted to be in the car with the other for five hours. Annie wore black slacks and a black sweater. She looked as though she were going to a funeral, so at the last moment she added a pink silk scarf, one the girls had convinced her to get at a tiny shop on the Rue de Tournon. Watching her get ready to go, Meg took out the piece of paper on which she'd written the word *orange* to remind herself of the day when the light had been so beautiful in their grandmother's kitchen. She told her mother not to worry; she would make dinner for herself and Claire. She reminded Annie to be careful on the road, as though she were the mother. Then Meg sat down in the kitchen, worrying about what would happen next.

As Annie drove along the highway, she thought of her three little girls helping her in the garden when they were small on a day when Natalia and her friend Madame Cohen were visiting. The older women had been perched on garden chairs, applauding every ripe tomato the girls picked. The girls had then gathered around Madame Cohen cross-legged in the grass and she told them that tomatoes were in the same family as belladonna, henbane—all poisonous, all associated with witches. "The fruit is so delicious," she'd said as she held up a ripe Indian Orange tomato. "But the leaves can be lethal."

◆ ◆ ◆

THEY MET WITH Elv in a carpeted therapy room. Alan and Annie were anxious, as though they were meeting someone for the very first time. Alan's girlfriend, Cheryl, was waiting in the car for him. Alan had bought himself a Miata convertible, with room enough for two. He and Cheryl lived in a house on the west side of North Point Harbor, which they were now considering putting on the market. They were thinking of applying for positions out in the Hamptons. They had recently taken up sailing.

"Frankly, I don't see what good we can do here," Alan said. Annie took that to mean he was done with the children and their problems and that he wanted to get back to Cheryl. She really didn't blame him for being defensive. She wasn't even angry anymore. She had already decided that no matter what Alan thought, she was going to remain hopeful.

"Elv wanted this meeting," she said. "Let's look toward the future."

The counselor was dressed casually in jeans and a black sweater. Miss Hagen told them she herself was a recovering substance abuser and that it was important to let go of the past and not be overly judgmental. Elv had made mistakes, she'd been an easy target for drug use—the sensitive child of divorce—but she was a lovely, intelligent girl, ready to start anew. Of course there were still issues. It would take time to build trust.

When at last Elv came into the room, Annie had to will herself not to cry. Elv stared straight ahead as she sank into a chair. She had done something awful to her hair. It was shorn so that bits of her scalp showed through. She wore shapeless blue jeans and a sweatshirt. There was a new tattoo she'd tried to hide by bunching up her sweatshirt.

"Hey," Elv said to no one in particular, eyes downcast.

"Let's just sit in silence for a while," Julie suggested. "That way we can get used to sharing the same space without hostility or aggression."

Alan and Annie shifted in their chairs. There was some sort of ruckus out in the hallway. Two students argued, calling each other *asshole*. Annie looked up at the same moment Elv did; for some reason they both laughed. It was probably nervous laughter, but it was laughter all the same. That was good.

It was cold in the therapy room. Elv's fingernails were bitten to the quick. She had picked up the habit of tapping her foot. She'd been begging for this meeting for the past two weeks, ever since she'd last seen Lorry, but her father was always too busy.

"You cut your hair," Annie said, genuinely shocked.

"I look great, right?" Elv said. "Just kidding," she added. She didn't seem as angry as she had before. Her clothes were so baggy, they didn't seem to belong to her.

"Actually, it was part of the life skills management program. The staff made the decision to cut it."

"You mean as a punishment?" Annie was outraged.

"It's behavior management," Alan said, correcting her.

Elv's eyes flitted over to her father. Annie remembered what they'd been told, not to expect too much.

"People start to think about going home when they finish a year of school," Julie said. "So it's entirely appropriate for Elv to start coming to terms with that idea. This might be a perfect time for her to reconnect with her family. A move home could be very beneficial."

Alan interrupted. "Isn't it a little early to think about that? This is our first meeting."

Elv was biting her nails. She tried to think about the woods, the pond, the way Lorry had held her, what the next part of the story might be. Did he find his dog alive or dead? Did he seek retribution or flee?

"Well, I think we need to consider how well she's been doing. Elv has been one of our best students," Julie Hagen said proudly. "She excelled in her English class."

It was a bullshit class, but there was a wash of pride across Elv's face. No one else had bothered to read anything even though they could choose whatever they wanted, even a comic book; they all sat silently. The other students looked at her, stunned, when she'd stood up and talked about the way Dimsdale represented all of the repressive factors in society, the people who judged you for all the things that had happened to you that you didn't have any power over anyway, things like love and faith and tragedy. She actually sounded moved, as though she might cry.

"Good. Then maybe she's where she belongs," Alan suggested. "This place has a great deal to offer a student."

"You shouldn't have come," Elv said to her father. "You don't care what happens to me. You never did. I don't even know why you bothered."

"Because you're my daughter," Alan said.

"Am I? Where was I all summer when you were getting your stupid divorce?"

"I don't know why she's bringing this up," Alan said to the counselor. "It was over five years ago."

Miss Hagen said she could see they had a long way to go before they were communicating effectively. Everyone had the best intentions, but maybe this was enough time for their initial meeting. They could meet again next month.

"I can't wait till then," Elv said, panic-stricken. Miss Hagen was trying to usher them out, but Elv urged her to continue the meeting. "I want to leave now," she pleaded.

When Miss Hagen opened the door, it was clear that the commotion in the hall had escalated and grown violent. Two heavyset male counselors were holding down a tall, skinny boy. They had a blanket wrapped around him so he couldn't struggle. The boy was screaming, but his cries were muffled. One of the counselors moved to sit on the boy's back; he looked big enough to crush him.

Miss Hagen quickly led the Storys back into the therapy room. Annie felt dizzy, stunned by what she'd seen. Is this how the staff treated a disturbance at Westfield? Alan was beside the counselor, asking to see Elv's grades. As they went back inside the therapy room, Elv came up close to her mother, so close Annie could smell the industrial brown soap students used in the showers.

"Please," Elv whispered. She was so close Annie could feel the heat of her body. Her voice was small and reedy. She didn't even sound like herself anymore. "Get me out of here. I'm begging you."

In the parking lot, Alan insisted they had to stick with the program; they had to commit to the Westfield philosophy in order for it to work. Annie watched him drive away with Cheryl, then she got in her car. She drove to the spot where the policeman had let her turn around, where she'd pulled over when there were snowdrifts and the woods were muffled and white. Now she could see blackflies drifting through the air. The leaves were pale green. Pools of shadows fell across the road. She thought of the boy in the hall, and of her daughter who didn't sound like herself. She remembered standing in the yard with Elv, pointing out Orion and telling her a story in which a girl had finally woken after a hundred years' sleep.

Annie made a U-turn and went back. She headed directly for the administration office and signed the release papers. She did not wish to speak to any of the counselors or to the dean. Her mind was made up. It was that boy in the hallway and her daughter's desperate plea. It was the way everything was spiraling forward in time, winter becoming spring in seconds, it seemed. Elv was in the front hall ten minutes after Julie informed her she was being released from Westfield. She was clearly delighted. To Annie's surprise, Elv actually threw her arms around her, which was totally unexpected, then just as quickly Elv backed away. She had only one small backpack. She left everything else behind. Elv shifted the backpack over her shoulder. With her clipped hair she looked younger than her age. She glanced around the hallway.

"No Dad?"

"Nope," Annie told her. "It's just you and me."

That was fine with Elv. She didn't care about the particulars. She just had to get out of Westfield. She didn't say good-bye to anyone, although she left behind her copy of *The Scarlet Letter* for Miss Hagen. If she thought about the horses, it would be too sad, so she wasn't going to think about them. She was wary as they walked out to the parking lot, yet joyful. She wanted to remember the moment of her release. She hoped the horses wouldn't be waiting for her in the morning, banging against their stalls, looking out the rough doorway into the field.

Elv was surprisingly polite in the car. At Westfield she'd learned it was best to speak only when spoken to. She'd learned a great deal there, as a matter of fact. She wouldn't miss it, but it held certain memories that in their aftermath had changed everything, including who she was.

"We'll work everything out," her mother was saying. Elv didn't disagree. She gazed out the window; she couldn't believe it was almost summer. She tried not to let on how excited she was. She was seventeen and ready for the world, whether or not it was ready for her. She could actually feel things after all. That's what Lorry had taught her.

They stopped at a rest area for coffee and doughnuts. Elv excused herself, saying she had to go to the restroom; she'd be right back. She asked her mother for money to buy some Tampax—how could she say no to that request?—then went down the hall to call Lorry from a pay phone. Just hearing his voice made her swoon. She felt so much realer when she talked to him. "Baby," he said. "Where are you?" Just those few words and she was undone. She, who had prided herself on her distance from all things human, was consumed by emotion. She'd been worried that he wouldn't want her in the real world where there where so many distractions, so many other girls.

She told him she was finally free. She whispered, "I'll die if I don't see you."

Lorry laughed. "I wouldn't let that happen," he told her. He sounded so sure of himself, so sure of them. When she hung up, Elv danced around even though people were looking at her. "Boo," she said to a little boy who was watching her, brow furrowed. He laughed and said "Boo" right back. They grinned at each other until his mother grabbed his hand and led him away. Elv had nothing to worry about. Michael had said that among his friends Lorry was famous for getting bored with his girlfriends and turning them out. That wasn't the case now. He still wanted her.

When she went back to the coffee shop, Elv saw that her mother looked nervous. Annie hadn't thought anything through; she'd acted on impulse and now here she was, drinking a tepid cup of decaf, waiting for her daughter. From a distance, as Elv approached down the hall, she appeared to be a complete stranger, with her clipped hair and her oversized sweatshirt, and the black rose tattoo there like a fresh wound. She had a new way of walking, light on her feet, looking to either side cautiously. She wore the sneakers everyone at Westfield was forced to wear. Slip-ons, no laces. They were the first things she planned to burn.

"I told you I'd be right back," Elv said.

They were about three hours outside of New York. They hadn't spoken more than a handful of words for nearly a year. All at once, Annie felt she had made a terrible mistake. She had no idea how Westfield might have affected Elv, for better or for worse. She had an almost uncontrollable desire to run, just leave the car for Elv and take off into the countryside. She could live among the deer, in the deep, dark woods. She could drink from a cold spring, clear New Hampshire water. At night there would be an endless sky filled with stars.

Elv tossed her empty coffee cup in the trash. She couldn't wait to see what happened next.

"Ready?" she said.

Rose

Everything was red, the air, the sun, whatever I looked at. Except for him. I fell in love with someone who was human. I watched him walk through the hills and come back in the evening when his work was through. I saw things no woman would see: that he knew how to cry, that he was alone.

I cast myself at him, like a fool, but he didn't see me. And then one day he noticed I was beautiful and he wanted me. He broke me off and took me with him, in his hands, and I didn't care that I was dying until I actually was.

MEG LOCKED THE BEDROOM EVERY NIGHT. ELV HAD HER OWN room now, one of the bedrooms on the first floor. She said she needed privacy and that at seventeen she was too old to share a room with the younger girls. But Meg knew the truth. Elv didn't want to be up in the attic with them. In her little bedroom she could talk on the phone all night. She could sneak out the window and no one would be the wiser. She could cook up a potion of drugs, dreaming her way through her entrapment at home until at last she turned eighteen and could be free. Their mother had given her everything any girl could have wanted—her own TV, her own telephone. Still she wasn't happy. She pouted and ran off to the city every chance she got. She told their mother she was seeing friends, spending nights with them. But anyone with half a brain could tell that was a lie. Elv had never had a friend in her life.

Sometimes Meg thought she was the only one who saw her sister for who she really was. She certainly wasn't someone you wanted wandering around your house. Meg was reluctant to be in the same room as her sister. You could never trust a tiger, someone out for blood, convinced you had betrayed them. Meg waited until Claire fell asleep, then eased out of bed and tiptoed over to turn the key and lock their door. Sometimes she took out the worn piece of paper on which she'd written *orange* that she kept in her wallet, along with her school ID. Once or twice she'd fallen asleep holding it. She was glad she'd thought to write it down when they were in Paris.

Their mother had gone for a visit to New Hampshire and returned with their older sister, won over by her lies and pleas.

"Are you happy now?" Elv had remarked to Meg soon after she came home. That was when Meg knew nothing had changed for the better. "My hair's shorter than yours. Does it make your day?"

Meg felt wounded that her sister would think her so vindictive. But in fact she had noticed that her hair was now much longer. Elv wasn't as luminous or as obviously pretty as she used

to be. She had a darker beauty now; she was thinner, edgier—
even her eyes seemed a deeper green. The first week after she'd
come home, Meg had spied her with some man in a parked car in
the lot by the beach. Elv was sitting in his lap, kissing him—the
kind of kisses Meg was embarrassed to see. It was daylight and
many of the children Meg knew from the camp where she was
once again a counselor were running around the playground. She
hurried past, shamed, head down, but Elv had glanced up and
spied her. That evening Elv had come up to Meg in the kitchen
while their mother was out in the garden and Claire was in the
living room, threading a strand of beads as a gift for their ama.

"Don't tell Mom." Elv grabbed Meg, the way she used to. She
seemed stronger now.

"I told you, I don't care what you do." Meg's heart was pounding hard. She pried herself out of Elv's grasp.

"Seriously. If you open your mouth, I will make your life miserable." Elv's voice was matter-of-fact. Meg had no reason to
believe that she wouldn't do exactly as she threatened. She was
already making things miserable without even trying.

"I'm not stopping you." Meg shrugged. "You can take off all
your clothes right in public if that's what you want."

Elv laughed. "You're jealous. You always want what I have.
Don't think I don't know it. And don't think I don't know you
were the one who had me put away. Pretend all you want," Elv
told her. "I know it was you."

Sometimes Meg couldn't believe how much she hated her
own sister.

Recently, she had run into Heidi Preston, who reported that
her sources had told her Elv was using heroin.

"I doubt that," Meg said, still defending her sister. But she
thought about how Elv stumbled out in the mornings and late at

night, about how thin she'd become. She thought about the bruised marks on her skin.

"Okay. Fine." Heidi shrugged. "Some people are saying her boyfriend is a movie star."

"Equally questionable."

Meg didn't want to think about the handsome man in the car or the kiss she'd seen. There was something illicit in it, something that suggested how little she knew about men and women. She asked Heidi about her brother, Brian. Heidi said she thought he was somewhere out west because he had once told her that a man could always make a living on a ranch. Meg wished the same thing would happen to them. Maybe once Elv turned eighteen she would take off the way Brian Preston had. She'd send them postcards from mysterious locations in California and Oregon. She'd promise she was never coming back.

Until that time came, Meg tried her best to avoid her. She was glad there were only two of them up in the attic now. Elv did as she pleased and took what she wanted. That was why Meg had recently taken a hammer and nails and permanently shut their bedroom window as a precaution. No one could get in now.

Sometimes Annie worked in the garden at night, waiting for Elv to come home, worried that Alan had been right. Annie dodged the truth, trying to maintain her optimism. But who did she think was calling late at night? Who was parked at the end of the street, waiting for Elv to sneak out her window and run down Nightingale Lane? Perhaps she had brought Elv home too soon. Perhaps as a mother she simply wasn't up to the task. There had been a drought, and the soil was dusty in the garden. The leaves on the hawthorn tree curled and rattled in the wind. No tomatoes appeared on the vines. The star-shaped blossoms had fallen off before they could bear fruit. Annie had planted seven varieties, two more than usual, adding Arkansas Travelers and a new variety of Cherokee, but she'd wound up with nothing. She discovered hornworms, so pretty when they were moths, so deadly to tomato plants in their larva form. As soon as the harvest season was upon them, she pulled on her gardening gloves and tore out the tomato plants. There were red and brown leaves everywhere. She hadn't the budget to hire a gardener anymore. All over town there were bonfires of burning leaves. Black ash drifted through the air. Annie looked up and glimpsed Meg behind the locked attic window. There was still the pungent scent of tomato vines. The metal trash can was full of tendrils and leaves, all turning yellow in the dark. This was the way her garden grew now.

WHEN THE SCHOOL term began, people avoided Claire and Meg. Everyone was talking about the Story girls and their crazy sister. There were all sorts of rumors, some true, some too far-fetched for reasonable people to believe. Some of the girls' classmates swore that Elv had been gone all that time because she'd had a baby. Others whispered that she'd robbed a bank, been to jail, that she now met her lover in the church in the town square, willing to defile the altar with black masses, sexual encounters, drug use. Many in town had spied Elv hitching to the train station. That was a fact. They'd glimpsed a car dropping her off in the center of town late at night. When she saw them gawking, she'd laugh and shout, "What the hell are you looking at!" Whoever was standing there staring would slink away, even if it was a well-respected neighbor, someone's father or mother.

Elv had lasted only two days before she announced she was dropping out of school. She vowed to attend night classes and earn a high school equivalency diploma. After Westfield and all she'd been through, she couldn't be expected to sit in a classroom with a bunch of suburban kids who thought going to the mall was the high point of civilization. "They're all talking about me," she said. "You expect me to sit there and take that?" She begged and pleaded, promising her mother that she would study hard. She'd already read *The Scarlet Letter,* the book on the list for the GED English class, and had gotten an A on the paper she'd written. She crossed her heart and took a vow to be the best student she could be, but her fingers were also crossed behind her back to negate the lie she told. She hadn't picked up a book since she'd returned home. There was only one story she was interested in, and only one storyteller.

Meg had read *The Scarlet Letter* when she was a freshman. This year she was in an advanced English seminar for juniors, assigned Virginia Woolf's novels. She enjoyed reading *To the Lighthouse.* It took her mind off Elv and stopped her from obsessing about getting good enough grades to get into Wesleyan. She wanted to be accepted there more than anything. She was desperately afraid of failure, not that she made her fears public. She wished she was as smart as Mary Fox, who had already been accepted early decision to Yale. Everything came so easily to Mary, while Meg had to work for her grades.

The one bright spot was that she was now rid of Elv at school. Those two days when she'd been enrolled had been rough enough—Elv had worn a short black skirt, a shirt that was all but see-through, and her black pointy boots from Paris. Recently, someone had spray-painted a pentagram on Meg's locker, as if the rumors were about her rather than her sister. Two janitors came down and repainted the locker. Sooner or later people would forget all about Elv. She'd disappear out of their consciousnesses as soon as she disappeared from town, which could not be soon enough, if you asked Meg. Now Meg had lunch with Claire every day in the cafeteria. Just the two of them. They usually had egg salad or peanut butter sandwiches. They had plenty of space. No one sat at their table.

MISS HAGEN SUGGESTED they try family therapy when Annie called to discuss how troubled Elv appeared. They went, but everyone was reticent and uncomfortable. Meg especially was too nervous to say anything. She worried about retaliation. She had to go home with the unfathomable person who glared at her from across the room. Even when asked a direct question, the most Meg would say was "I don't know." She didn't even seem very sure about that. Meg and Claire looked at each other for assurance and sat close together on a couch. Sometimes they held hands without thinking. Then Claire would notice Elv staring. She'd quickly drop Meg's hand.

The therapist suggested a game of trust in which you closed your eyes and fell back, letting another person catch you. They all refused to play. Only Claire thought it was a good idea.

"Let's just try it," Claire urged, but the others shook their heads. Elv rolled her eyes.

"If you're not going to be involved, I don't see what I can do for you," the therapist said to Annie and the girls. Meg agreed. She didn't believe therapy would do any good. It would never help them to reach a consensus on what their lives had become. She had taken up the premise of individual vision in *To the Lighthouse*. Everything depended upon a person's point of view. Even the tiniest detail was subject to interpretation. The old hawthorn tree outside the bedroom window, for instance, was covered with ice early that fall, but sometimes Meg could look at it and imagine it was the chestnut tree in the courtyard of her grandmother's apartment building. When she saw Claire sitting with Elv on the couch, chattering away as they made necklaces together, she wondered who it was Claire saw and who she imagined.

THAT FALL, EVERY encounter with Elv was difficult for Meg. She realized she was clenching her teeth, that she had several nervous habits. She bit her nails, and she often found she was silently counting to a thousand in order to clear her mind of bad thoughts. She wanted Elv to disappear, be eaten by tigers, live on a ranch where there was no telephone service.

"You know, you really don't have to study so hard," Elv told Meg one morning when they happened to meet up in the kitchen. Meg looked up from the table. When she saw Elv, her heart sank. Meg had been eating an English muffin and studying for a Latin test. She'd almost convinced herself that Elv no longer existed. Now, face-to-face, she had no choice but to accept the fact that she was back. Elv was a lot skinnier than she used to be. In the murky light of this overcast morning, she somehow looked more beautiful than ever. She ran off to the city at every opportunity, but she'd also settled in, made the house her own. That still didn't mean she was trustworthy.

"I don't mind studying," Meg said. "I like Latin."

"How nice for you. In case you didn't know, Latin is a dead language. Who do you think you are? Mary Fox? Don't bother. I doubt you'll get into Yale."

"I'm not applying there."

Claire had come into the room. She got a banana and some peanut butter. It was her favorite sandwich combination. Their mother was usually up late waiting up for Elv to come home, so Claire and Meg had made a vow to let her sleep in in the mornings.

"And here's your shadow," Elv announced as Claire got out

the loaf of bread. Lately, she felt jealous of Meg. Elv sat down next to her. She made sure she was a little too close. Suddenly, she was famished. "Are there any more English muffins?" she asked Meg.

Claire laughed as she prepared two sandwiches.

Elv turned to her "What?"

"You're mean to her, but you want her to make you breakfast."

"You've just turned against me because you used to be my slave and now you're hers," Elv said smartly to Claire.

Claire stuck out her tongue and Elv laughed, amused. "Am I supposed to be insulted?"

"Claire is not a slave." Meg said quietly. She packed up her books and got her coat.

"I guess you're not eating that." Elv grabbed what was left of Meg's English muffin and stuffed it into her mouth. "Bye, slave," she said to Claire, who was following Meg out of the room, carrying the two sandwiches in a lunch bag for later. "Bye, Curly Sue," she chirped to Meg, who cringed, ever conscious of her hair.

"Bye, bitch," Claire shot back.

Elv laughed out loud. Claire had spunk. "Ouch." Elv clutched at her heart, grinning all the while. "That hurt."

"I was kidding!" Claire protested.

"Come on," Meg said, pulling on Claire's arm. "I told you. Don't talk to her."

Claire thought about Elv all that day. She thought about her while she should have been paying attention in her classes, and again during soccer practice, which was held in the gym where Elv used to work on routines with the gymnastics team and the dance club, and then again at her piano lesson. Ever since the bad thing had happened, Elv had hid her true self away. People thought they knew her, but they didn't know the first thing about her.

✦ ✦ ✦

IT STARTED SNOWING late in the afternoon, big wet flakes, the first snow of the year. Everything smelled fresh, like clean laundry. Claire walked home because the bus had already left while she was at piano lessons in the music room. She was wearing sneakers and her feet were freezing. In some ways it was liberating not to have any friends. Ninth grade was rife with petty jealousies and cliques. Claire had nothing to do with any of it. The Story sisters were on the outside.

As she headed through town, Claire saw her father's white Miata parked behind the grocery store, in the far lot that nobody used. He took such good care of that car, Claire was surprised he would drive it in the snow. He had a Jeep that was his everyday car. The Miata, their mother had said, was his midlife crisis car. Claire had seen Alan and Cheryl driving through town in the summer, the top down, looking like the couple in *Two for the Road,* her mother's favorite movie. Maybe their relationship would fall apart for them the way it had in the film. Maybe they'd get what they deserved.

Claire walked around the market in the falling snow, past the trash barrels. It was already getting dark and the sky was inky. The snowflakes had taken on a blue cast. Claire went up to the car and knocked on the window. The glass was foggy and she couldn't see inside. "Dad?"

The window rolled down and there was Elv. "I can't get this fucking thing in gear."

"Are you crazy?" Claire took a step back. She felt a wave of excitement. "What'd you do? Break into his house?"

"Get in," Elv said. "I need you to help me."

Claire stared at her sister. Elv wasn't wearing a coat. Her hair was pushed back with a black velvet headband that Claire recognized as Meg's.

"Get in! I just wanted to have some fun, so I borrowed it for a little while. But I can't shift and drive at the same time. Hurry up."

Claire went around and got into the car. It smelled like smoke. She and Elv looked at each other and laughed. They had missed each other.

"You are crazy," Claire said.

"Crazy like a fox." Elv grinned.

"Crazy like a loon," Claire added.

"Crazy about you." Elv got down to business. It would be so much easier getting back and forth to see Lorry if she could drive into the city. She needed to practice. "You see the picture on the gearshift? Follow that. Do what I tell you and we'll be just fine. Okay?"

"Okay," Claire agreed. She took her sister's hand. "I shouldn't have let them do it," she said. She'd been wanting to say this ever since that day when they went to New Hampshire. "We thought they would find a place that would help you."

Elv withdrew her hand and looked away. "I can help myself."

"I was afraid you would die from using drugs." Claire blinked back tears.

Elv handed her a Kleenex from a box in the back of the car. "I don't blame you. I know it wasn't your idea."

Claire began to cry in earnest.

"It's okay." Elv wrapped her arms around her little sister. "I know you'd never do anything to hurt me." That's when Claire knew they didn't have to talk about it anymore. She felt lucky and free and utterly grateful to be with her sister, who was more beautiful than anyone else in the entire stupid town.

It took a while to get the car going. The car made a wrenching noise when Claire pulled the shift into first gear, which made them laugh all over again. Finally they figured out a system in which Claire shifted and Elv steered as she worked the gas and the clutch. They stalled out at the stop sign on Spring Street, got the giggles, then managed to get going again. They drove to the house where their father and Cheryl lived. They had both transferred to another school, out in the Hamptons. There was a For Sale sign out in front. Claire and Meg had never even been invited over for dinner. Not even while Elv had been gone. Thankfully, no one was home when they pulled the Miata into the garage.

"Good work, kiddo," Elv said appreciatively.

"Leave the windows open." Claire couldn't help being practical. It was in her nature. "That will air out the smoke."

"Very smart." Elv rolled down the windows of the Miata. "But of course you would be. You're my sister."

Claire felt a flush of pride. She wondered what it was like to be so fearless.

Elv returned the car keys to a peg on the garage wall. "He'll never know. Self-involved people never look any farther than their own asses. And he definitely is an ass."

"Maybe he'll think Cheryl took it for a spin," Claire said. "Maybe they'll fight and break up and he'll come back to Mom."

"I don't think so," Elv replied. "I wouldn't wait around hoping for that."

They snuck out of the garage and walked through town.

"You're a pretty great accomplice," Elv said. "A plus."

Claire felt a shiver of pleasure. They shouldn't have taken their father's car. Still, it was a compliment.

Elv was a fast walker, and Claire had to hurry to keep up with her. She found her sister fascinating. When they got to their block, she thought she saw Mrs. Weinstein looking out of the bay window of her living room. Maybe she was thinking of that time Elv had torn up the roses from her yard for a protection charm to hang above her bed or the time Elv yelled at her for mistreating Pretzel, keeping him tied up on the lawn.

"You're a pretty good driver," Elv told Claire. She missed having Claire as her ally. Meg had done her best to steal her away, but that was over with now. "Let's celebrate by eating." They used to do that all the time. Sneak food up to their room and snack all night.

When they arrived home, Claire and Elv went to the fridge and took out everything chocolate: ice cream, fudge sauce, brownies. They were laughing about how many calories they could fit into one bowl when Meg came downstairs. She stood in the doorway, watching.

"Hey," Claire said when she noticed Meg. "You'll never believe what we did." Claire had poured a ton of chocolate sauce into her bowl. Now she was adding chocolate chips. "Oh my God," she said to Elv. "This is probably a million calories."

"More like a zillion." Elv grinned. "Add more chips. Oh, and candy bars!"

"Don't you have homework to do?" Meg reminded Claire.

"What are you? Her mother?" Elv was at the snack drawer getting out a Kit Kat bar, which she broke into pieces to add to the sundaes. "Let's utterly pig out," she said to Claire.

"Yum," Claire said. "These look amazing."

"You have a paper for American lit," Meg said to her. "You told me you did. I said I would help you."

"You're such a baby," Elv told Meg. "Miss Goody Two-shoes. Why don't I just hand you a knife and you can stab me in the back?"

"Come on," Meg said to Claire.

Claire left her sundae on the counter. She put her spoon in the sink. She could smell the smoke in her own hair. "I guess I'm not that hungry," she said.

She grabbed her book bag and followed Meg upstairs.

"Go ahead," Elv called after them. "You're both babies!"

The girls went to their room. They set to work on the term paper in bed. The lock on the door was clicked shut. Claire glanced at the space where Elv's bed used to be. She missed there being three of them. She missed the way things used to be.

"She's really okay," Claire told Meg. "She's not exactly the same, but she's Elvish."

"If you say so."

Meg had begun to see the school counselor. She hadn't told anyone, not even Claire. She stopped by Mrs. Morrison's office every Tuesday and Thursday at ten o'clock. Sometimes she talked and sometimes she didn't. Sometimes she sat there and cried. She didn't exactly know why she wanted to see Mrs. Morrison. Maybe it was because she felt alone even when she was in a room full of people, even when she was in her very own bed talking to Claire. The one thing she knew for certain was that it would never be the three of them again.

"She's still Elv," Claire ventured.

"Take my advice," Meg said. "Don't trust her."

IT WAS THE middle of the night when it happened, a blue-black rainy night. The rain began at midnight, tapping on the windows before coming down in sheets. Claire suddenly woke with a fever. There had been midterms at school, and she'd been coughing and had a painful sore throat; now her illness suddenly took a turn, her fever spiking to 103. She got out of bed in her nightgown, drenched. Everything looked funny: her room, the light through the window. Meg was sound asleep. Claire wished Elv was in the next bed and she could get under the blanket with her and Elv could tell her she would feel better soon the way she did when Claire was little.

Claire went downstairs for a glass of water. Her head was throbbing. She should have gone to her mother, but it was Elv she wanted. As she went down the hall she heard people talking, a murmur, as if a radio had been left on. A muffled laugh pealed, then dissolved. Things looked different in the dark. The hallway seemed longer. A pale glow was cast by the moonlight coming in through the windows in the living room. It pooled on the hallway carpet like puddles of milk. Elv always locked her door, but she'd shown Claire how to get in. Only for emergencies, Elv had said. *Reuna malin,* she whispered. *Reuna malin,* Claire echoed.

She should have rescued Elv from Westfield. Elv had officially forgiven her, but Claire often couldn't sleep, kept awake by her shame. She rewound that day in New Hampshire inside her head. The way those men had grabbed Elv, the red leaves fluttering down like birds. She kept thinking about how Elv had opened the car door and run and kept running without looking back. Claire would never get back to sleep tonight. She was burning up, the way she had been when there'd been the heat wave and her arms were in casts and she had to sleep all alone in the attic while her sisters went to France. She still wanted that black painting of the river. She wondered if Elv had it, or if she'd thrown it away.

Elv kept a key under the hallway carpet. Claire bent to retrieve it. She thought she might faint. It was definitely an emergency.

Long before the rain began, Lorry had climbed through the window. He'd been to their house a dozen times or more with no one the wiser. That's what he did, after all. He was a thief, and he was good at it. All fall, Elv had been going to meet him in Astoria, at a basement apartment Michael had rented before he'd been picked up again for auto theft. He'd been sent to Rikers this time.

Now that he was eighteen he had been tried as an adult. The apartment had been empty for several months, but now Lorry had to relocate. In the meantime, North Point Harbor would have to do. He'd gotten to know the town. It was easy to pull off a robbery. People rarely locked their doors; they left cash and jewelry scattered around. Even the dogs, mostly cheerful golden retrievers and Labradors, seemed happy to greet him.

On this evening he'd arrived at dusk, hastening through the garden, where Elv's mother used to tell her stories, hands in his pockets. It was drizzling and the green trees loomed. He always wore the same black boots, though they now had holes in the soles, and his black coat. Her family had no idea what went on. Sometimes he was there waiting in her room all through their dinner, his car parked around the curve, past the Weinsteins' house. It felt illicit and crazy when they had sex in her bed. They wanted to laugh, but were afraid to make noise. He covered her mouth with his when she did laugh. *Shh,* he told her. *Don't say a word,* and she didn't. Only a few more months, and she'd be his. Then she could shout out loud. They wouldn't have to slink around or play by anyone else's rules. He knew he hadn't lived a perfect, blameless life, but this was different. He was careful not to let her get high too often. There were limits, and he'd been around long enough to know what they were. One of them with a fatal flaw was enough. Not that he didn't have other flaws as well. Elv being one of them. He couldn't stay away even though he knew he was risking too much, being with her in her mother's house when she was underage. He was in love, and people in that condition did stupid, unfathomable things. They were all flawed, every single one.

"Tell me a story," she whispered in bed. "Tell me about the dog."

He spoke softly, arms around her. A posse had been formed.

They had lanterns, torches, and knives. It didn't take long for them to find the gang who had killed Mother, his grand watchdog, the mother of all vicious, loyal beasts. The gang responsible was made up of a hodgepodge of thugs who terrorized women and children living underground, demanding protection money from the sick and the weak.

They went after a little girl named Emma, having been contacted by a couple aboveground who would pay two thousand dollars in exchange for a child. Emma was perfect. Her mother brought her to a public school kindergarten every day, waiting on a bench outside until the school day was done. That's where the unscrupulous couple had first spied her, deciding they wanted her for their own.

On the day of the planned abduction, Lorry and Mother had been passing by the tent where the child and her mother lived. Mother knew evil so well he could smell it. He stopped and bared his teeth. The fur along his back rose up in a ridge. The gang scattered now that Lorry and his dog were on the scene. Still, their intentions were clear; someone had cut through the tent where Emma and her mother lived. Someone was just about to grab her.

As a reward, Lorry and his dog were offered bowls of stew. It was all the woman had to show her gratitude, and on that night it seemed a great gift. Lorry and Mother were both starving.

The death of his dog was payback for thwarting the plan to take the little girl. Well, payback it would be. There were pools of blood when Lorry and his friends were done with the gang, and then a scattering. Two bodies on the track, the worst of the worst. Some things were meant to never be mentioned again, not then and not ever. When those who'd been there on that evening passed each other in the future, they nodded and rarely said more than a few words in greeting, yet they were brothers in some unspoken way. Lorry wrapped up the dog's body in the only blanket he owned, then carried him outside. He buried the dog in Central Park, not far from the zoo. He wanted his dog to be where snow would rim the ground, where the grass grew. There was a freedom in that, even for the fallen.

Elv was naked, she seemed like snow herself, her skin was so pale. She was crying over Mother as Lorry kissed her. She felt unwound in his arms. They were completely entwined when they heard the door open. Claire was there, whimpering, apologizing. Elv leaped out of bed and went to the door.

"God, Claire! What the hell are you doing?" She touched her sister's forehead. "You're burning up."

Claire peered around her sister. "Was that Justin Levy's ghost?"

Elv turned to look. Lorry had gone through the window, into the rain.

"Justin doesn't have a ghost," she assured Claire.

She brought Claire into her room, closed the door, then took her sister into bed.

"You don't know that," Claire insisted. She felt panic-stricken and faint. "He used to come into our room. I think he's still doing that."

"It was Lorry, silly. I told you about him."

"The one you're in love with."

"The one who turns me inside out."

"Doesn't it hurt?" Claire said in a hushed voice.

"Yes." Elv looked out at the rain. "It does."

She shoved the drug paraphernalia he'd left behind into the night table drawer. Lorry hadn't had time to collect it all. She could still feel him all over her. She pulled on a nightgown and got into bed with Claire. She had Lorry's works and enough for her to get high later by herself. She loved the dreamy way she felt. There was the sound of the rain, comforting against the windowpane. He'd be drenched as he ran to his car. He'd be thinking of her all night long.

"He comes from the world underground." Elv gave her sister a sip of water from the tumbler on her night table, along with two aspirin.

"No, he doesn't." Claire almost laughed, but she felt too weak.

"You can find the gate if you walk along Thirty-third Street right behind Penn Station. You have to go down eight stories, under the trains, under the subway. There are ten thousand steps with wild creatures all around. There are black roses growing beside the tracks."

"He comes from Arnelle?" Claire was confused.

"Go to sleep," Elv told her. "You'll be better in the morning. You won't even remember this."

"Yes, I will." Claire was so glad that her sister was back. "I always will."

MRS. WEINSTEIN WAS the one who phoned to report seeing a man slinking through their window. She had nothing to do but gossip and butt her nose in where it wasn't wanted. Elv came out of her room to find her mother calling the police. She grabbed the receiver away.

"It wasn't a criminal. Don't report him," she pleaded.

"Elv," Annie said. "How could you?"

"How could I what? Find true love? Get what you never had?"

Claire was still in bed; she stayed under the covers, listening to them fight. She'd found a photograph of Lorry under the pillow. She gazed at him, then hurriedly returned the picture when Elv slammed back into the room. She was being sent away to their grandmother's, and that suited her perfectly.

"Help me pack, Gigi," she said to Claire.

Claire got out of bed and went to the bureau. Elv had burned most of her clothes. They tossed everything she had into a single suitcase. Right before she left she retrieved the photo from under her pillow. She kissed Claire on either check and told her not to forget her, as if that would ever happen.

AFTER HER GRANDDAUGHTER moved into her New York apartment, Natalia had the same feeling of dread she'd had in Paris when Madame Cohen warned her to keep an eye on Elv. Some girls were in danger of vanishing just as children in fairy tales disappeared, out the door, under the hedge, never to be found again. But in fact, Elv was well behaved. She helped with the dishes. She played cards with her ama. She slept on the clean, white sheets and took baths in verbena bath oil in the big marble tub in her grandmother's bathroom. She tried on all of her ama's old clothes— black satin suits, white lace blouses, high heels, blue cashmere sweaters with crystal buttons, Chanel jackets that fitted her perfectly—then paraded around for her grandmother's approval.

But she often disappeared for hours, even days, and when she returned she was too exhausted to talk; she simply crawled between the white sheets and fell so deeply asleep that Natalia couldn't wake her for dinner. It snowed nearly every day, and Elv usually woke in the late afternoon to go meet Lorry. They had their rendezvous spot in Manhattan, as they'd had their meeting place in New Hampshire. It was just beyond the meadow where the dog, Mother, had been buried. Lorry had taken Elv there, and they'd left a handful of roses stolen from the market on the corner. The weather had turned and Lorry was still looking for an apartment, so they met in an underpass near the zoo. It was easy to forget you were in Manhattan in their corner of the park. Everything was muffled and quiet. It made Elv think of New Hampshire. She still missed the horses. She wondered who was taking care of them and if they would remember her if she ever went back.

Elv hadn't thought she needed to get high, but sometimes there was something needy snaking through her, rising to the surface. It was hot, dangerous. It felt like the way she needed him. At last she heard footsteps on the path. Lorry appeared, wearing his black coat and a black woolen hat. He looked beautiful in the snow. Snow didn't bother him. Nothing did. He reminded her of a man in a fairy tale who could always find his way, even without a map.

Everything was white. There were snowflakes on Elv's eyelashes. Inside the tunnel there was the smell of piss and hay, not that it mattered. Elv heard a wolf in the zoo. She thought of all the animals out in the snow in New York City; she thought of the time Claire stole a horse just to please her. She loved her sister and Claire loved her back and they didn't even have to speak to understand each other. She wondered if the carousel horses were still in the park or if they'd run away too. Elv shrugged off the cashmere coat she'd borrowed from her grandmother's closet. She told Lorry she couldn't sneak him into her grandmother's apartment the way he'd come to the house in North Point Harbor. Her grandmother would have a heart attack or something, and the apartment wasn't that big. For the past few days, Lorry had been living hand to mouth, staying with friends, waiting for a big break-in to go down someplace in Great Neck. Elv hated lying to him, but she claimed the apartment was haunted by her grandfather's ghost. Lorry had a fear of ghosts. He said that was the only thing he'd worried about when he'd lived underground.

There were so many ghosts down below you could hear them moaning in the night.

Elv knelt with her back against the tunnel and offered him her arm. She laughed when he said he hoped it wasn't becoming her fatal flaw. "That's you, baby," she said, leaning to kiss his cheek. She didn't like to put the needle in—the metal scared her. It made her think of handcuffs, pricked fingers, blood seeping down, a sleep that lasted a hundred years. She gazed at the graffiti on the wall. It all looked like Arnish to her, only she couldn't understand that language anymore. Lorry took something out of his pocket, a small velvet box. He tossed it to her. Inside was an emerald ring with a red-gold band. It was exquisite.

"Just so you know I'm not playing," he said.

She leaned to kiss him. She belonged where she was, with him. Everything was beautiful, especially the snow. After Lorry got high, he put his head in her lap and closed his eyes. He sang "Blackbird," such a beautiful, sad song. He told her he sang that song when he buried his dog in the park, when he stood there alone in the greening light, having lost his best friend, his only protector. Elv studied his face. He was perfect. He was always there for her. She gazed at the falling snow. She could still hear the wolves in the zoo. They listened together.

She took him to her grandmother's the next time her ama went out for the evening.

NATALIA WENT TO dinner on Long Island with Elise and Mary Fox. She was caught by a snowstorm and had to spend the weekend. "Don't worry," Elv said. "I have tons of canned soup and frozen pizza. I don't even have to go out." When Elise and Mary brought Natalia home, they were shocked by what they found. Mary went to the spare bedroom. There was Elv, passed out on the bed, naked. Mary noticed the glint of needles in an ashtray before she went back to the hall. The door to the bathroom was open. Lorry had a towel wrapped around him. His dark hair was slicked back.

They didn't know his name or anything about him, only that he threw on his clothes and skulked past them, put out, as if they were the intruders. "Tell her I'll be back," he said. He was a whirlwind, handsome, sure of himself. Natalia could see how he could enthrall a young girl, to whom he would seem forbidden, beautiful. She might not notice that wherever he went, destruction followed.

Annie drove in the next morning and waited for Elv to explain herself. Elv had been crying and she was exhausted. Natalia seemed so disappointed; she looked her age, a woman who didn't know how to handle her favorite granddaughter. Elv was fidgety and apprehensive. She wore the emerald on her left hand.

"Where did you get that?" Annie demanded. "Have you seen it before?" she asked Natalia.

"It's mine," Elv declared. She hid her hand. "I didn't steal it from Ama if that's what you're getting at."

"Did you get it from that man?"

"*That man* cares about me. Unlike you."

"She can stay here," Natalia said. "We'll talk things over. We'll figure out how to make it work."

"It's unworkable," Annie said. "I'm not having her do this to you."

"Do what to her? I would never hurt you," Elv told her ama.

They left and went down to the car, parked around the block. Elv got in and slumped down. She was tapping her foot. She looked ready to explode.

"Elv. You know I care."

Elv stared out the window. She wasn't listening to her

mother. She was biting her nails. "You're going to look back on this and see what a terrible mother you were."

"That man is not to come to our house."

"Do you think you can make me listen to you?"

Annie reached across Elv and opened the car door. "Then don't come home. Go to a residential school."

Elv glared at her mother, then pulled the door shut. It was freezing out there. It was so cold your fingertips could turn blue in seconds flat. She'd known all that talk about caring was a big fat lie. "Fine," she said bitterly.

"Fine," Annie agreed. It should have felt like a victory, but it felt like a loss. It took them a long time to get home because of the road conditions. Even so, they didn't speak a word.

THE WINTER LASTED forever, with record snowfalls reported. It was March and still snowing. And then, one morning, Claire awoke to find it was spring. It was a Sunday and the bluebells on the lawn had suddenly appeared. When she went downstairs, her mother was already dressed. Annie was going into the city to have lunch with Natalia. Their relationship had been strained since the incident with Lorry. They usually agreed on the important things, but not anymore. Natalia felt Elv should move in with her again, but Annie seemed to have given up hope.

"There has to be a way to bring her back to us," Natalia continued to say.

"If I knew what that was, I would do it," Annie told her.

"Maybe we should get to know that fellow of hers," Natalia said.

"Absolutely not," Annie had told her mother. "Not him."

"Give Ama a big hug from me," Claire said when her mother was about to set off for the city.

"Can you keep an eye on your sister?"

"Absolutely," Claire said, even though she knew Elv had been in a wretched mood since her return.

When her mother left, Claire gazed out the window. A robin was hopping about on the lawn. It made her think of the baby bird they'd found and the necklace of bones Elv had made. She wondered if she was the only one in the world who thought the things Elv did were beautiful: the robin necklace and the tattoo of roses, the language made up of words that sounded like birdsong.

After a while Meg came down and they sat there together in their nightgowns—presents from their grandmother, the smocking stitched by hand—and had a quick breakfast. They went back upstairs and got dressed. Claire pulled on jeans and boots and a sweatshirt. She'd packed her gym bag with her equestrian equipment, her helmet and gloves. She had taken up riding again and it was a perfect day for going to the stables. Claire had completely recovered from her broken bones, although she still had twinges on humid days. She could always tell when it was about to rain. It had taken a while for her to get over her fear of falling, but she'd done so with practice. Now she was horse crazy. That was the best thing about spring finally arriving. She would be able to ride every weekend.

Meg was heading out with Claire. She'd study for the SATs in the tack room at the stables, where she could curl up on an old leather couch. She was also bringing along her copy of *To the Lighthouse* to reread as a treat if she happened to finish studying. The truth was, she didn't like to stay alone in the house with Elv. Not that Meg would ever consider riding. She wouldn't even try it when Claire begged, insisting they'd have great fun. Meg was afraid of horses. She'd seen how hard and how fast the carriage horse in the park had gone down. She'd felt the thud right up through the tires of the police car.

They were just about to leave when Elv came into the

kitchen. She'd slept for seventeen hours and was groggy. She got herself a cup of coffee, then sat down at the table and pinched one of Claire's half-eaten waffles. Her skin was pale and she was wearing a velvet headband, the one she'd stolen from Meg. "I miss Lorry," she said plaintively. She sounded almost human.

"Who's Lorry?" Meg asked Claire when Elv went to get herself some juice.

"He's her boyfriend. He gave her the ring she wears."

"He must have been the one who was in Ama's apartment." Meg went to rinse the dishes and load them in the dishwasher. Then she got her jacket and Claire's. "Let's go."

Elv was drinking right out of the container of orange juice. She had to fill up the next few weeks until she at last turned eighteen and no one could tell her whom to love and how to live her life. "Where're you going?" she asked when her sisters headed for the door. "Where's Mom?"

"She went to see Ama." It was so beautiful outside Claire didn't think she needed a jacket, but when Meg handed her one, she put it on anyway. "She'll be back at dinnertime. We're going to the stables."

"Wait a minute," Elv said. She didn't want to be alone.

"We're already late," Meg said. "Come on." She guided Claire toward the back door. "We have to go."

"I know more about horses than the two of you put together," Elv said. "I ran the stables at Westfield. I wasn't some spoiled brat who has a hired hand to pick up the shit and clean out hooves. I did it all."

"Let's go," Meg said to Claire. She had the curdled feeling she had whenever Elv was around.

Elv put the OJ container on the counter. She wanted to have fun, the way they used to. "I can give you a ride," she said. "You'll get there on time."

"I don't think so." Meg was disgusted. She wasn't about to be won over by Elv's tricks. "You don't have a car."

"I'll get Dad's."

Meg elbowed Claire. "Come on."

"Seriously," Elv said.

"She's a good driver," Claire told Meg.

Elv sent her a grateful look.

Meg opened the door. "Let's go."

"See you later," Claire called to Elv as they headed for the door.

"Alligator," Elv called back.

They looked at each other and laughed.

MEG AND CLAIRE cut across the lawn, then started down the street. The lawns themselves looked blue, as if the sky had some-how been reversed. There were robins in the trees, on the fences, in the grass. The lawn where Pretzel had always been tied up looked empty. The grass there was ruined.

"She's really not that bad," Claire told Meg.

Meg's book bag was slung over her shoulder. She was wearing a pair of black leather boots, a short denim jacket, and khaki slacks. Her hair was pulled back. "Bad is a relative concept."

There was still a crust of snow and ice on some lawns. They had to walk three miles, but Meg and Claire didn't mind. On their way they sang Beatles songs, their mother's favorites. They sang "Imagine" as high as their voices could go, then exploded into gig-gles. Halfway to the stables, they heard a car behind them. Some-body honked. They turned and saw the Miata. Claire laughed and ran over to the car. The top was down and there was Elv, driving. She looked like a movie star.

"You are so crazy!" Claire said. "You're going to wind up in jail!"

"Dad didn't know last time. He won't know this time. Anyway, I think they went away for the weekend. You said you were late, so hop in. I'll be your chauffeur."

Elv was wearing sunglasses. In the spring sunlight, she looked like Audrey Hepburn in *Two for the Road.* Their mother could watch that movie every night and never get tired of it. It was all about falling in and out of love with the same person.

"Ready, set, go," Elv said brightly. She pushed her sunglasses up.

Claire grabbed Meg's arm. "Let's," she said.

"You've got to help shift," Elv told Claire, who'd already begun climbing into the passenger seat.

"You don't know how to shift?" Meg was standing in a patch of bluebells.

"Two heads are better than one," Elv reflected. "So two drivers are better than one. Come on. Squeeze in. I'm going to get a sports car when I move to Paris."

"You're moving to Paris?" Claire was surprised.

"Maybe. Lorry and I have plans." Elv winked, which was exactly what Audrey Hepburn would have done.

"Come on," Claire said to Meg. "Trust me, it's fun."

Meg got into the back, which was less of a seat than it was a shelf for sacks of groceries. She pulled her legs up under her. She had her book bag on one side and Claire's gym bag on the other. It was only a five-minute ride to the stable. The sky was unbelievably blue.

Elv told Claire when to shift, and after an initial stall-out, they got going. The Miata revved like a racecar every time Claire shifted. They went past the woods, then along the harbor. It was a beautiful stretch of road. Sometimes you could see blue herons glide over the water. There was no traffic, so Elv kept her foot pressed down on the gas. The wind smelled fresh, and the sun was surprisingly strong. When Meg squinted, the light looked green. She could hear her sisters laughing, but she couldn't hear much more. The motor was loud and the wind blew against her ears. She could see bits of the water in the bay and the tall bare trees that would soon be leafing.

They were only going fifty, but it seemed as though they were flying. When Elv lost control they didn't even realize what was happening; they were just flying higher, blue sky, sweet air, the sound of the motor, and then they weren't flying anymore. Elv screamed, but Claire couldn't really hear her. She heard the wind, then a thud and a metal sound. Elv grabbed Claire and pulled her down hard, toward the floor. Claire covered her head with her arms, as she'd been taught to do should she ever fall from a horse. The impact was so hard she bit through her lip. They had leaped from the road into the woods. Everything was dark when they rolled over. It was quiet, but something echoed. Claire couldn't tell if she was blind or if the whole world had turned black.

"Are you there?"

It was Elv's voice. Shaky, unsure. Claire could see shadows: There was the car window, there was the earth covered with leaves and patches of snow, there was a stalk of swamp cabbage.

"Go out the window," Elv told her.

Claire pulled herself through the shape that looked like a window. The car was upside down. There was still a blue sky. Elv was climbing out through the place where the windshield used to be. Broken glass was scattered in the leaves. There was a carpet of diamonds; diamonds were everywhere.

Meg was underneath a big tree. There were pine needles spread out, the color of hay. There was the sound of a siren very far away. It was like something in a dream, but it was coming closer. Elv went to stand beside Claire. Meg's face was cut and she held one arm close to her body, clenched against her abdomen.

She had hit the steering wheel hard. She was covered with glass. Blood was flecked over her skin. Elv stared down at the grass. "Tell her to get up," she said, baffled by what she saw. "Tell her. She'll listen to you."

Claire turned to Elv, sobbing. "Don't you see? Look at what we did to her!"

There were dog violets in the woods. They grew underneath the snow and now the snow was gone. Beneath the tree everything was quiet. The quiet spread out like water in a pond. Elv ran off, but Claire didn't care. She didn't hear the sirens when the police cars drew near. Everything had stopped, even the sky. No clouds moved. No birds perched in the trees. She went to lie down beside her sister. If she really tried, she might be able to imagine they were still safe in bed, hours before this, back when the day was just beginning, when the ice was still melting, when the violets in the woods hadn't yet bloomed.

Part Two

Snow

Twelve girls were missing. One gone for each month of the year. People in town grew used to it. They wondered what beast had done this, and who the next victim would be.

I found a handful of teeth on the ground. My mother said they belonged to a dragon. My father said they had lined the mouth of a wolf. But the teeth were small and white, perfect as pearls. There were twelve all together. I strung them on a chain and wore them around my throat.

That was when people began talking.

There was a town meeting to decide what to do. Everyone said the teeth must be disposed of. They'd bring a curse to me and to my village. But I heard someone whisper "No" in what sounded like my voice.

I ran away. The town council came to my house. They questioned my father and my mother. They

searched for me, but it was too late. I was on the hill-
side, planting the teeth in the ground. When it rained,
twelve girls would grow. They would point to their
murderer before they turned into flowers, each one as
white as snow.

ANNIE HADN'T STARTED HER TOMATO SEEDLINGS THAT SPRING.
She hadn't bothered to weed. The garden was filling with Virginia creeper and thistle. Goldfinches flocked to the weed, trilling
over their good fortune. The weather was lovely, a lamblike
March, nothing like the terrible year when there was a false
spring and the roads were slick with hidden patches of ice. Annie
still wore a coat. She was cold all the time. She sat in a wrought-
iron chair under the hawthorn tree. On the day the accident happened, there had been bluebells. By the following morning,
nearly twelve inches of wet snow had fallen. They had learned
not to trust the weather.

Annie and Claire stayed in the chapel with the body for
twenty-four hours, unable to leave her. At last, the funeral director pleaded with them to go. There were some things for which
family members shouldn't be present. Remember her as she was,
he suggested. But Meg had never been wound up in white, her
face so pale, her eyes closed. They were already remembering her
the way she was in death rather than the way she had been in life.

Claire had to be escorted out. The door was bolted so the body
could be prepared without interruption. When they wouldn't let
her in, she sank to the floor. Mourners had to step around her.
Those who did lean down to try to embrace her were greeted
with stony silence. Just before the service began Natalia insisted

she come into the chapel. "Do this for Meg," she said. Claire sat in the front row, between her mother and grandmother, head bowed. She wore the same clothes she'd had on when the accident occurred. Splinters of glass glittered in the seams.

At the cemetery Claire felt as if she were watching the burial from a great distance. Her head was bare, covered with snow. She didn't feel anything, just a fluttering in her stomach, the same panicky feeling she'd had while waiting on the corner of Nightingale Lane all those years ago, heedless of the mosquitoes and the darkening sky. As she stood between her mother and grandmother, all she knew was that she should be the one being lowered into the ground. She looked up at the falling snow. She couldn't see anything but spots of light. Meg had trusted her. She'd agreed to get into the car because Claire had told her to.

After the funeral, she stopped speaking. Her mother and grandmother thought the muteness would pass with time. It was the immediacy of her grief, the double loss of two sisters—the one gone forever, the other disappeared. Once several weeks had passed, they knew the situation wasn't temporary. When she was forced to communicate, Claire wrote on a small notepad she kept in her pocket. As it turned out, she had very little to say. Sometimes, when it grew late and all the houses in North Point Harbor were dark, she would walk to the end of the street to wait by the stop sign. But no one came to steal her away. No one was there for her at all.

Claire had thought that time would stop, but people went on living, and before long summer had come and gone. Then it was fall. Claire was allowed to have her schoolwork sent home. No one expected her to face her peers. They were all still talking about the accident. Some of the girls who had been in English honors with Meg had set up a shrine on the spot where it happened, where Route 25A turned so quickly it could take you by surprise. A coffee can filled with plastic flowers and several teddy bears of various hues had been arranged on the embankment. Claire went there one night and threw it all into the woods. These girls had never even really known Meg. Claire was breathing hard by the time she was done getting rid of everything. She thought she might be sick right there by the side of the road. Meg had hated teddy bears. She hated false flowers. The local newspaper had a small article about the defacement of the memorial. The authorities never discovered who had done it, but Annie knew. She parked there every day, sometimes for half an hour, sometimes longer. Frankly, it was a relief to be rid of that makeshift shrine, to see only the grass, so plain and tall.

Claire was still an excellent student. Elise came by with her homework twice a week, then took it back to the high school. Mary was away at Yale, and Elise had time on her hands. She didn't mind helping out. She wasn't offended that Annie never invited her in for a cup of coffee or tea. She was a doctor and used to the effects of grief.

"Call me the minute you need something," she told Annie and Claire, but neither one of them could think of a single thing they might need that anyone could possibly give them.

Annie never answered the phone. She didn't want the neighbors' gifts of casseroles or homemade soups. Late one night the phone rang and wouldn't let up. Annie suddenly thought, *What if it's Meg?* Maybe her girl was trying to reach her. Maybe such things really happened, the way they did in horror movies, when the afterlife wasn't as far away as everyone thought, when it was as close as the next room. Annie grabbed the phone, but no one answered. "Meg?" she said tentatively. She heard someone breathing and realized her mistake. "Elv?" she said, but the phone had gone dead.

Leaves piled up in the backyard. Newspapers were delivered

and unread, left to disintegrate on the concrete walkway. The only birds gathering on the lawn were blackbirds that made a racket and wouldn't be chased away. In the mornings, Claire and Annie woke expecting to hear Meg getting ready for school, calling everyone down to breakfast. But there was nothing, only the blackbirds. Meg had always been the one to make sure everyone was on time. Now they overslept, missed entire days. The house was so quiet they could hear crickets that had wandered inside when the weather grew chilly, their calls growing fainter as time went by. Annie and Claire tried their best not to think about Elv or wonder where she might be. Sometimes one went to stand in the doorway of her bedroom, sometimes it was the other. One wept, but the other went through the bureau drawers and destroyed every single thing she could find.

THEY STAYED HOME all winter. They didn't shovel the snow on the walkway. After a while, Elise had to galumph through the drifts to deliver Claire's schoolwork along with basic groceries: bread and milk, coffee and potatoes. Natalia came and turned up the heat, made the beds with clean sheets, replaced the lightbulbs in the darkened rooms. Claire and Annie didn't bother to eat meals. They wandered into the kitchen and grabbed a bite of cheese or a cracker. They didn't trouble to use dishes anymore, only ate standing up, crouched over the sink or using a paper napkin. They reminded Natalia of the dogs one sometimes saw in certain neighborhoods in Paris, wild and uncared for, dangerous to the touch.

"Have you looked for her?" Natalia asked after months had passed and there was still no word from Elv. It was an especially cold night. She and Annie were in the kitchen with cups of steaming tea. Natalia had secretly put ads in all the New York papers begging Elv to phone her. She had informed her doorman that if a young woman happened to show up, even in the company of a dangerous-looking man, she should be let up, no matter the hour. Natalia had been taking taxis to neighborhoods she wasn't familiar with, searching for Elv in Brooklyn and Queens, stopping total strangers to show them the photograph from the Plaza.

"She doesn't want me to look for her." Annie had often thought about the day of her parents' party, when the horse got spooked and Elv knelt down in the grass with blood rimming the hem of her dress. Maybe it had all ended then, on that perfect afternoon when the light was so brilliant and everything had seemed so right.

Natalia banged her hands on the tabletop when she heard her daughter's answer. "Do you think that would stop me if you were missing?" Natalia seemed much older in the past few months. She stayed up nights, gazing out her window. "I would never stop looking."

It was a year before Annie came to a decision. She sat under the hawthorn tree wearing her coat and her gloves. Sparrows and jays came to share the lawn with the blackbirds. On chilly days Annie hated to think of Meg alone in the cemetery. It made her feel colder too. She hated to think of Elv with that man, doing God knows what. And then, before she knew it, it was spring again. That year the garden was so overgrown, a person wouldn't even notice it unless she knew it had been there. By summer, voles had made tunnels through the earth.

Annie had found a detective in the phone book and made an appointment. No references, nothing. Alan would have said she was crazy to put her trust in a stranger, but Alan would never have hired a detective. He was done with the whole situation. He said he had to save his own life, and maybe he was right. He'd come to the funeral and he'd cried for Meg. He'd tried to call Claire, but she wouldn't speak to him, and after a while he'd given up.

Annie herself hadn't believed Smith was the detective's real name—it didn't seem likely to be anyone's real name—but it was. "Prove it," she'd said when she arrived at his office. He'd taken out his driver's license and shown it to her. He'd turned out to be not only a good detective but also a decent man, a retired Nassau County policeman who mostly did divorce cases. He was tall and rangy, in his forties. He didn't talk much, but he had a sense of humor. He hated divorce cases, all the recriminations and vindictiveness, but runaways were even worse. With divorces the story was usually in the same ballpark—infidelity, family and money pressures. But people who disappeared of their own volition had stories that were more difficult to grasp. You never knew which ones wanted to be found, and which ones would do anything to escape; each history was unique and unexpected, with answers you sometimes didn't want to know.

His office was across from the Roosevelt Field shopping center in Westbury, nothing fancy, just a desk and two chairs, a bit bare and depressing. It was Annie's idea to go across the street to a diner. Anyone would have thought they were a good-looking married couple out to lunch, an attractive woman in a Burberry coat rubbing her hands together as though she couldn't get warm, a rough-hewn man who seemed comfortable in his own skin. Smith ordered a Spanish omelet, home fries, and toast. "Let me guess," the waitress said. "No butter." He had the same thing every day. "Creature of habit," he told Annie. Annie had coffee and a grilled cheese and tomato sandwich. It was the meal she and the girls always had whenever they went out for lunch.

"Me too," she admitted.

They began by talking about sports—they were both serious Mets fans and secret admirers of the Red Sox. By the time they'd had their coffee she had told him about her runaway daughter.

"There's one thing you have to understand," Pete said. "If I look for her, I'm probably going to find her."

Annie had left out the part about Meg. She hadn't mentioned the accident or the drugs, but he knew. As soon as she'd called to set up the appointment, he'd started to poke around. He was a detective by instinct. He thought if there was a needle in a haystack, he'd probably find out everything there was to learn about hay before he started searching through it.

"That's what I want," Annie said.

"Just checking."

He'd had a daughter who'd gone wrong too. Rebecca. She had been such a well-behaved child he couldn't believe the way she'd turned out after she was on drugs. He never imagined that after being a cop and witnessing so much pain, one little girl could ruin his life so thoroughly. His marriage had been upended; his career had gone the same route. Rebecca had done everything she could to escape from his love. Love was often the last thing they wanted. If he'd known Annie better, he would have told her that just so she wouldn't think it was all her fault. Love reminded them of everything they'd lost.

"She may not be the same girl she once was," Smith warned.

Annie leaned in. "You don't forget the people you love," she told him. "That's what I've realized. They just get farther away. Like a spyglass turned around."

"All right." Something happened to Smith at that moment. Despite the circumstances, he felt his heart lift. "I'll find her for you."

• ◆ •

FOR HER JUNIOR year, Claire was sent to the Graves Academy, a private girls' school. Natalia and her friend Madame Cohen, who was visiting from Paris, had checked the schools in the area until they found one that met with their approval. "She can't sit home all alone," Madame Cohen told Annie. "She's a quiet girl, but even quiet girls need noise sometimes."

Many of the students at Graves came from overseas and were uncertain about their English, so Claire's silence was not completely out of the ordinary. The fact that she didn't speak didn't impact her grades. She was diligent and completed her studies on time, hunched over her books for hours each day. There was a school uniform: blue pleated skirt, white shirt, blue sweater, maroon sweatshirt. Just as well. Claire paid little attention to her appearance. She closed her eyes whenever she walked past a mirror, hoping to avoid her reflection. At night Annie could hear her fluttering around, like a bird trapped in the attic, where there were still two beds side by side.

Natalia and Madame Cohen had asked Elise to find a therapist for the poor girl. She recommended a Dr. Steiner, whose office was within walking distance. In her sessions with him, Claire communed in writing or not at all. Dr. Steiner suggested Meg's belongings be boxed up and moved. Claire wrote *Fuck you* on her notepad and shoved it across the coffee table toward the doctor. She still carried the piece of paper on which her sister had written *orange*. She had it with her at all times. Meg's books remained arranged alphabetically by author on the shelf. Her clothes filled the closet, the boots and shoes stowed in a neat line. But Dr. Steiner was right. None of these keepsakes kept Meg alive.

The psychiatrist also suggested bringing a dog into the house. In times of trauma a dog could often reach a person in crisis.

Annie decided she didn't have the energy to deal with a floppy, undisciplined puppy. On impulse she bought a fully trained German shepherd. Shiloh had been raised in a kennel on a farm in Connecticut and had spent his days traipsing after boys and girls who did dangerous stunts, diving into ponds, jumping into stacks of straw. When Annie brought him home, he padded right over to Claire, who gazed at him and frowned. She took out her notepad and wrote *Take him back*.

When Claire went upstairs, the dog followed. She kept him locked out for two nights but on the third night, she let him in. Dr. Steiner was soon proven right. Claire seemed less agitated. Annie no longer heard pacing at night. Now it was the dog she heard, keeping watch.

Shiloh proved his worth on the night someone broke in to their house. He immediately began to bark, and whoever had been there fled through the bathroom window, leaving blood on the windowsill. In the morning, Annie found long black hairs on the floor. She swept them up, then called in the glazier to replace the broken glass. She went to examine the footprints crisscrossing the yard. They weren't evidence of anything, but she knew. She went to the back of the garden, then searched the woods behind the house. No one was there. When she called out "Hello" the sound echoed back at her. It made her feel lost even though she had been this way a thousand times or more.

THEY LIVED IN an apartment in a small brick building not far from Astoria Boulevard. The old lady who owned the place rented it to them, and in return, Lorry collected the garbage, shoveled snow, patrolled the laundry room. It was beneath him, but he didn't complain. He knew all the old ladies in the neighborhood. They embraced him and shouted in various languages for him to get a job. They treated him like a grandson, one who attracted trouble. They all saw the girl in the bloody clothes looking for him that night in the spring. They took note of her long dark hair. They observed the way she held on to him when at last he appeared. It was easy for them to spot heartbreak from a third-floor window, despite their bad eyesight and the darkness of the street.

Lorry had taken her to the ER, but they couldn't run any scans because Elv didn't have insurance. She refused to give them her name or apply for Medicaid, even though the intake nurse told her it was possible that her liver had been damaged. Elv came out and told Lorry she was fine. She had pain, but she could cope with it. She deserved any punishment she might get.

When Lorry was forced to leave Elv alone, he worried. She didn't bother to get dressed. Instead she stayed in bed all day. She hadn't been eating. He limited her drug usage, portioning it out for her, but she'd sneak more whenever he went out. She was afraid of the needle, but after a while she got used to it. She fell in love with it a little at a time. She thought Lorry didn't know. She'd be in a dream, naked on the bed, and he'd come to lie down beside her and stroke her hair and tell her it would be all right when it clearly wouldn't be. She knew what she'd done. She had killed her sister.

Lorry told her he'd had a blood brother he'd lost in the otherworld. He'd known tragedy too, and he'd been responsible in a similar way. Elv had heard that those who lived underground were called the Mole People, but Lorry told her never to use that term. It was an insult, another way to reduce them to nonhumans. Kill a mole, and what did it matter? Slit one's throat and who would care?

He'd met Hector when they both were seventeen, soon after the death of his dog. He was a loner to the nth degree, wary at first, but they became fast friends when Hector came to tell him one of the worst offenders living underground had decided he wanted Lorry's platform space. Together they'd waited for their adversary in the dark. The interloper was a man whose wife had left him, moving up into the world. He was out of his mind on drugs. To chase him off they had tied sheets to the metal ladders that led to the world above and set up a fan. When they switched on the fan, the white sheets blew out like apparitions in the dark. Their enemy raced off screaming of ghosts. He'd never returned, and their brotherhood had begun. A friend who had your back in a world of cons and thievery was truly a brother. They had a perfect, easy scam they ran in Penn Station. They helped tourists with their luggage, taking them down a staircase that descended three stories to an abandoned platform. Once the tourist was disoriented, unable to find his way back, they would shake him down, asking for a twenty to lead him back up to the street. It had worked fine until the night when it all went wrong. They were sitting on the floor of the train terminal, drinking cups of black coffee the counter girl at Dunkin' Donuts gave them for free just for being such cute boys, when they spied a confused-looking man.

"You take him." Lorry was feeling lazy, so he stretched out his legs. Let Hector have some fun.

"Back in a flash." Hector grinned, leaped up, and went to the tourist's aid.

Lorry felt a chill. That happened to him sometimes, along his back and neck. He usually knew whom to trust and who was disloyal, who was an easy mark and who was nothing but trouble. On this night he convinced himself that his radar was off. He shook off his fear. He chatted up some girls, hung around with some buddies. An hour later he knew something was wrong. His brother in the world of mayhem still hadn't returned.

He was the one who found Hector's body, sprawled on the platform, his throat cut. A black pool of blood slid beneath him like oil seeping down to the tracks below.

Elv covered her ears, but Lorry made her listen.

In memory of his friend, Lorry set a rosebush on the platform; it bloomed, but the roses were black. He used heroin for the first time that night. He turned to the witch and she brought him comfort. It was easy enough to find in the tunnels; it was another gate, into another world. It didn't mean you forgot those you lost. That was why he had the rose and thorns tattooed on his hands, a memorial that would last. There wasn't a day that went by when he didn't regret sending Hector to do a job he should have done himself. Lorry was bigger, stronger; he could have fought the assailant off. In the end, their intended victim had been the better, more merciless thief. As a final insult, he'd taken Hector's gold ring, the only thing Hector had inherited from his father. Lorry still looked at people's hands, searching for the person who wore that stolen ring. He kept a knife with him at all times in case he found him. But even if he got his revenge, he was the real culprit. He would have to live with the guilt, and so would she.

Elv told him she couldn't. It was too much. He kissed her ardently, but she was listless, a gorgeous rag doll. She saw the accident whenever she closed her eyes, unless she was high. She wouldn't get hooked on anything. She just needed to stop thinking. She roped her arms around Lorry, begging him for it, and although he shook his head, she knew he'd give her whatever she wanted.

After some time, Elv got out of bed. She brushed her hair, washed her face. But she never looked in the mirror and she didn't let Lorry know how much junk she was shooting. Sometimes she went down past Twenty-first Street and bought it herself from a dealer she'd become acquainted with. Life was but a dream, wasn't it? It was the way black roses grew in the dark, searching for sunlight when there wasn't any. The old ladies in the neighborhood clucked their tongues when Elv went by, on her way to score, then to sit on a bench, where she nodded out while the buses roared by.

Once she glanced up to see Lorry walking along. He looked menacing, a man most people would want to avoid. He was carrying a TV and was clearly in a rush. He spied her and for a moment it seemed that he might turn and walk away. Instead he came over, leaned down to kiss her, then wedged the TV between his body and the bench.

"Someone was throwing this away," he said.

There was a price tag still on it. Elv hadn't thought about where their money was coming from. It didn't surprise her that Lorry had schemes. He was cagey and smart; he had to be.

"Okay," Elv said.

"This is what I do," Lorry reluctantly admitted.

People had to live, didn't they? If a lion took a lamb for its supper, did anyone complain or say it was unnatural? She went with him sometimes when he drove out to Long Island, to wealthy neighborhoods where the people were so rich they wouldn't miss a few things. And if they did, all they had to do was phone their insurance companies and everything would be replaced within the week. Elv sat behind the wheel of the car, the engine running, the headlights low, chewing on her lip while Lorry robbed houses. She thought of herself as an accomplice, and she savored the word.

She felt alive in the car as the scent of exhaust filtered in through the window and the sky was so perfect and black. It made her think of Hector and the pool of blood and the black roses. In neighborhoods where people slept through the night, Lorry climbed through windows that were left open. He rattled locks and slipped through doors. He carried a crowbar, but rarely used it. He wanted to be invisible. He often found valuables in unexpected places. In shoes, for instance, in vegetable bins, in kitchen cabinets.

It seemed that Elv too had a knack for crime. They realized this the first time someone came home unexpectedly. Elv got out of the car when a Mercedes pulled into the driveway. She ran over and breathlessly explained that she was searching for her dog, who was old and ill and needed special medication. Elv was in tears, lost in a neighborhood she didn't know. The man was tender-hearted; many men were when faced with a beautiful, distraught young woman. He helped her search the neighborhood, looking through the well-manicured yards. Some had trellises of pale roses, others had large brick patios, swimming pools, greenhouses. In one, a little poodle tied to a tree barked when they entered the yard, then sat and stared at them. Elv had the urge to cut the rope and steal him.

"Bingo," the man exclaimed. "There's your dog."

"That isn't him," Elv said sadly.

When she heard the car horn honk, she knew Lorry was finished and the job was done. She thanked the man who'd tried to help her find her dog, surprising him by kissing his cheek before she took off running. Once she and Lorry were home, they looked through the jewelry. There were some good pieces, diamonds, pearls, 22-karat gold earrings and bracelets. Their victim had been a nice man. Elv thought of how he'd waited for her when she lingered at the gate in the yard where the dog was tied up. He'd buy his wife something far better when all was said and done, maybe rubies this time.

Lorry was delighted with Elv's acumen. She was beautiful and smart and she belonged to him. They went out to dinner to celebrate. They ordered a bottle of wine. They felt lucky and rich, despite their fatal flaws. They went home and got high, then fell into bed, arms around each other, fiercely in love. Lorry told her in no uncertain terms that if she ever saw the police, she was to run. He wasn't about to have her be apprehended. She was an accomplice, that was all. It was fun, a lark. And then, it wasn't.

She was the one who said they should go to her house. She knew where everything was; it would be an easy in-and-out job. It was a time when they needed more cash. Lorry had been questioned when one tenant's savings disappeared from his night table drawer. There was no proof, although it was true that Lorry had a key and had been in the apartment when the tenant was out, checking on a complaint of a ceiling leak from the apartment below. They let him go, but there'd been a lawyer's fee. They needed cash fast, so they drove out to North Point Harbor.

THEY PASSED THE convenience store, the ice cream stand, the high school. Everything looked exactly the same, only smaller, like pieces set up in a child's game. Elv began to feel apprehensive.

"Go the other way," she told Lorry as he was about to turn onto the road that wound along the bay. "Stay on Main Street."

They parked around the corner from Nightingale Lane, near the stop sign. Elv's chest felt heavy. She felt like a stranger in her own life. She told him about what had happened to her. Not the details, just the way she'd stopped that man from taking Claire, how he'd taken Elv to his house and tied her up and done terrible things, and then how she convinced him she wouldn't run away if he brought her a cup of water.

Lorry was enraged. He wanted to go after the horrible man right then and there, but Elv wouldn't tell him any more.

"I want it to be over," she said. "Being here reminds me."

"We can go somewhere else," Lorry said.

Elv shook her head. She knew where her mother kept her jewelry. Where there was a coffee can of cash. When Lorry started to get out of the car, she put her hand on his arm.

"I want to do it."

There was the lawn where the Weinsteins' dog had been tied up. There was the hawthorn tree. She knew this place far better than Lorry did. They argued and at last he gave in. She got out, closed the car door, made her way along the street. Had they even once come to look for her? Had they wondered where she might be? For all her mother and sister knew, she was locked up, the key thrown away, bleeding, falling, waiting for them. In fairy tales, people rescued each other. They made their way through brambles, trickery, witchery, spells.

Elv went through the yard, past the garden. It didn't even look like a garden anymore, just a jumble no one bothered with. There were tufts of spent thistle, tangled black sweet pea vines. The downstairs bathroom window was never locked. It was small, but she could fit through. Elv pulled over a lawn chair, slid open the window, climbed inside. She wondered if time would shift, move backward. Maybe she would be ten again, before the bad thing happened, before everything changed. Elv felt such a deep longing, she was baffled by her own emotions. She dropped down from the window into the tub, then went to open the bathroom door.

She slipped into the hall, then stopped, heart pounding. At first she thought she spied a wolf. She imagined that at last she was to receive the fate she deserved. She would be devoured, piece by piece. The wolf-dog could have bitten her, but he just looked at her, then barked. She ran back into the bathroom, closed the door, crawled through the window, breaking the glass in her hurry. She heard it shatter, but she just kept on. She'd raced down the street so fast she went right past Lorry's parked car. He'd driven after her, and when she threw herself into the passenger's seat, he asked what had happened. She said he was right, it had been a mistake. Her hands were cut up and there was glass in her hair. She was never going there again.

FOR MONTHS ANNIE had been feeling exhausted and out of sorts. Elise insisted she go to the doctor. Tests were run, and she was diagnosed with leukemia, stage four. After her second treatment, her hair began to fall out. She went to a wig shop on Madison Avenue with her mother and cousin and decided to become a blonde. She and Elise and Natalia had laughed so hard everyone in the shop thought they were mad. It was an uncharacteristically wild decision. When Annie came home and presented herself, Claire too had laughed out loud. It was such a delight to hear Claire laugh again in the middle of her great silence that Annie almost felt being bald was worth the price of that glorious sound. Claire raced off to get a magazine. She returned with a photo of a *Vogue* model with the very same hairstyle. Annie laughed too. "Is that what I look like?" They couldn't stop laughing. "Some bombshell," Annie said of herself. Claire wrapped her arms around her mother. "Some blondes are tough, you know. They fight and they win," Annie assured her, even though she knew from the lab reports that that was not likely to be true.

SHE PUT OFF returning Pete Smith's call. When they finally met again for lunch, she tried to pick up the check. After all, she was the employer. Smith wouldn't hear of it. He felt wound up in some foolish way when he was with her. He'd been looking forward to seeing her again and had been strangely determined about calling her even after she canceled several appointments.

"Lunch is on me," he insisted.

They squabbled over the bill, but in the end Annie gave in. It was nice to have someone be concerned about her, even if it was only in regard to a sandwich and a cup of coffee. She didn't kid herself into thinking any man could actually be interested in her. They went outside and he still hadn't said anything, so she knew the news about Elv was bad. He had no choice but to tell her the truth.

Pete Smith drove a Volvo. He liked it because it was dependable, even though it had logged more than a hundred thousand miles. He was a great believer in safety. He believed in keeping his personal life personal, such as it was, or at least he had until recently. But now he had the urge to tell Annie everything about himself. Instead he handed her the address in Astoria. He found out more about the Storys than Annie would have ever imagined. That was what happened once you started digging around.

"She's with him?" Annie asked.

Pete nodded. "You won't like the way she's living."

Annie thanked him and handed him a check. "I didn't expect to," she said.

SHE FOUND THE street in Queens, but first she went to a coffee shop to settle her nerves. The restaurant was grungy, but at least the coffee was hot. The waitress was a young Dominican woman, very businesslike and pretty. Annie left her a five-dollar tip.

Two old woman were sitting on a bench by the bus stop. Annie showed them a photo of Elv. They spoke to each other in Spanish, then one of them patted Annie's arm. Elv lived across the street, in the brick building, first floor. Annie found the apartment, then had a spike of fear. She hadn't thought what she might do if that man was there. He had a hold over Elv she didn't understand. But now Annie had the element of surprise.

She knocked on the door. Nothing. Once more and the door opened wide enough for someone to peek out.

"What do you want?" a woman said.

It was Elv, half in a dreamworld. She had obviously just gotten high. She peered out. The door opened a bit farther, until she realized who it was. "You can't be here," she said, stunned. "You can't just appear."

The apartment was a mess. She wasn't at all prepared. She tried to shut the door, but Annie grabbed it and held on. "Elv, please. Just let me in for a minute."

"You should go away," Elv said. "It's been two years. You never even looked for me."

"I did. I'm here. Just give me five minutes," Annie pleaded. "That's all."

Elv shook her head. "It's too late. You know it is." Her side began throbbing. The ache never went away. Sometimes she curled up in Lorry's arms and pleaded for something to take the pain away.

"Four minutes," Annie offered. "Less time than it takes to boil an egg."

They both laughed.

"Oh, so now I'm an egg," Elv joked.

"Just give me three minutes," Annie urged. "That's a hundred and eighty seconds. You can time me if you want."

Elv opened the door. There were a set of works and some wax paper envelopes on the coffee table. Annie watched as Elv quickly swept it all into a drawer. Elv sat down and lit a cigarette. She felt too much shame to look at her mother. "It's usually cleaner than this."

"I think you should come home. I've thought it over and it will be easy. Just pack up and come with me."

Elv laughed, but her voice broke. "That's why you're here? Come on, Mom. Tell me how I ruined everyone's life. Go on. You know you wish I was the one who had died." She stubbed out her cigarette. "Tell me what a devious bitch I am."

"Elv," Annie said. She hadn't expected to feel this way. "You have to leave him. That's the first step."

"You don't get it. He's not keeping me here against my will. It's nothing like that. *I* don't want to leave him."

"I don't understand—what has that man ever done for you?"

"That man loves me." Elv's fierce gaze met her mother's. "He loves me for who I am." Now that she really looked at her mother she was taken aback. "When did you become a blonde?" When Annie made some corny remark about being a gay divorcée, Elv's heart sank. "It's a wig," she realized. "You're wearing a wig."

"I have leukemia."

"No, you don't." Elv got up from her chair, agitated. She went to perch on the window ledge. She looked like a bird with broken wings. She grabbed another cigarette. She knew she shouldn't have answered the door. "Did I do this to you?"

"Of course not," Annie said, startled. "Elv, I have cancer. No one did it to me."

Elv shook her head. Her eyes were rimmed with tears. She was bad luck. She'd always known that. He'd said that was why he was doing the things he did to her when he took her away in his car. He could tell she was bad and had to be punished. Elv was certain that Claire wasn't bad, and that was why Claire was the one who needed to escape.

It had to be her. It was always her.

"You have to stay away from me," she told her mother.

"Elv," Annie said, distraught.

"This is just going to make you sicker. I can't be who you

want me to be. Claire hates me, and I'll just disappoint you. Don't you see that? You have to let me go."

"I don't think I can."

Elv turned away. "Don't you think I wish it had been me? I can wish it from now until the end of time, but I can't change it. I can't bring Meg back."

Elv was like a flower. She was closing up, the way flowers did at night, petal by petal. She lit her cigarette and exhaled a thin stream of smoke. "Just go."

"Come home," Annie said. She went to hug Elv, but Elv shifted out of her embrace. "You just have to get in the car with me. That's all."

"Walk away, Mom. I mean it. Forget about me." Elv pulled herself together. She could do that when she needed to. She could hurt someone almost as much as she could hurt herself. "I don't want to come back. I don't even want to see you. Get out!" She went to the door and opened it. "If you come here again, I'll call the police. I'll say you're harassing me. I don't want you here. Forget you ever knew me."

Annie went out into the hall. She heard the door close behind her. She'd done everything wrong. Elv was right. She had wished that Meg had been the one to survive. It was her deepest, most shameful secret; at least she had thought it had been a secret. But Elv knew she had been forsaken, and now it was too late. Elv was lost to her.

Annie noticed a figure at the end of the hall, wary, waiting for her to depart. That man had known she was there all along. He hadn't come charging in, demanding she stay away from Elv the way Annie imagined he would. He didn't have to. She belonged to him now.

Annie forgot where she had parked her car. She walked down the street, confused. The two old ladies she'd asked for help were gone. A horn honked and she looked up. Pete Smith was parked on the corner. He signaled her over. Annie went to get into the Volvo. It was a relief to sit down, not to have to drive anywhere or think or be responsible.

"I didn't have any other appointments." Pete pulled into traffic. "I figured I might as well take a ride."

"My car's here," Annie protested when he started to drive away.

"I'll get it for you tomorrow. I'll take the bus in."

"You didn't tell me she was a heroin addict," Annie said accusingly.

"Annie, you knew," Pete said. "You were just hoping you were wrong."

She leaned her head against the seat and closed her eyes. They got off the highway and stopped at the diner. Pete ordered the Spanish omelet. Annie had coffee and grilled cheese, but this time she also ordered apple pie. "What the hell," she said. "I won't be able to eat tomorrow," she explained. "I have chemo."

"Every other Tuesday." Pete Smith was an excellent researcher. He managed to convince people to tell him things they wouldn't dare admit to anyone else. Plus he had learned how to get into hospital records, a fairly simple thing to do once you understood the system.

"Do you have a file on me, too? You seem to know everything. You don't know how much I weigh, do you?"

Pete laughed and shook his head. "No."

"Do you know this is a wig?"

He had to admit that he did.

Annie touched her head. "Is it a bad one?" That would be the kind of thing no one would tell you. But Pete Smith would.

"It's a fine wig," he said.

Annie leaned her elbows on the table. "Do you follow everyone who hires you?"

"Just you," he said, making his intentions clear.

The tables around them were crowded, but they didn't seem to care.

"You must be dumber than you appear," Annie remarked. "Look at my life. It's a disaster."

"I had a daughter too," Pete told her. "Everything went wrong. She overdosed. She was our only child."

Annie looked up at him. "I'm sorry. What was her name?"

"Rebecca."

"That's pretty. I like that."

He insisted on driving her home. Nightingale Lane looked deserted after the traffic in Astoria. Annie invited him in for a drink. Grateful, he followed her inside and asked for a whiskey. She looked around until she found some in a kitchen cabinet. It must have been Alan's a long time ago. She poured herself a glass of Bordeaux. She was glad not to be alone.

The dog hadn't barked when they'd come in, so after Annie brought the drinks into the living room, she excused herself and went to look in on Claire. She stood outside the bedroom door. She could make out the faint murmur of words. Claire was talking to Shiloh. It was the first time Annie had heard her speak since the funeral. Her voice was lovely, quiet and measured.

It had been a horrible day, but Annie was surprised to find that she was glad to be alive. She wanted to be right were she was, in between the moment of hearing Claire's voice and the instant when she went back downstairs, ready for whatever happened next.

PETE WAS THERE more often, helping around the house, driving her to doctor's appointments through the summer and fall, spending more time out in North Point Harbor than he did at his apartment in Westbury. Sometimes he made dinner. He had never cooked for anyone before. When he was married, his wife had done the cooking; and when he was alone, he figured it wasn't worth the time to cook for one person. He was nervous, fearing he'd burn every meal, but as it turned out, he was a natural. He should have been a chef, Annie told him. Even picky Claire would eat the meals he made: lasagna, mushroom soup, his grandmother's recipe for stuffed cabbage, a fragrant old-world dish.

It was there in the kitchen, while Annie cut up a loaf of bread and Claire fixed a salad, the dog stretched out at her feet, that Pete felt he had stumbled into the best part of his life. He didn't know if he deserved it, but he wasn't about to turn it down, despite the fact that there wasn't going to be much time. Maybe that was why it had happened so fast between them. Or maybe he'd been in love with her all along, since that first time she came to his office looking for her daughter.

He started sleeping on the couch when the weather was bad or when their dinner stretched into the late hours. One night Annie came out from her bedroom wearing a robe.

"You can't be comfortable," she said. He was too tall for the couch. His feet hung off the edge.

"I am," he told her. "I'm fine."

"Well, I'm not. I'd be better off with you."

He'd slept with her every night since, waking early to go back to the couch so Claire wouldn't know. Annie laughed at him.

"Do you imagine she'll think we're too young to get serious?"

He was a man used to setting things right, but in this case there was nothing he could fix. He'd done the research, had spent nights searching the Internet. He'd talked to doctors and brought her records to experts in the city for second and third opinions.

Sometimes, when he came to the house, having stopped at the market for groceries on his way, he put off going inside. It was the bright hour of *before*. He wanted to hold on to that for as long as he possibly could. He'd been there once before. He'd lost someone he loved. He knew what happened next. The air was cold; he could feel it in his lungs when he breathed in, little ice crystals. He left the sacks of groceries in the car while he went to the garage for the shovel. He came back and cleared the walk, making a neat path from driveway to back door. His breath billowed into the air. He might have cried if he'd been another man, one who hadn't buried his daughter, lived a solitary life, fallen in love so late in life.

By the time he went inside, the eggs he'd bought at the market had frozen in their shells. The world felt enchanted. Perhaps in this snowstorm they would sleep for a hundred years and wake consoled, young again. Annie was at the kitchen table, drinking tea. She had a scarf tied around her head. She'd been watching him through the window. It was growing late and the snow was turning blue in the darkening light. "I should hire someone to shovel the snow," she said. "You might throw out your back." Pete had a football injury from high school, but he was shy about it. It had happened so long ago he figured he should be completely healed.

"I enjoy doing it." Pete took off his jacket and his gloves, then went to the sink to run his hands under a stream of warm water. He could barely feel his fingers. He still kept an eye on Elv, even though Annie had told him he didn't have to. He didn't like what he saw. She and that boyfriend of hers had gone on a spree of robberies. Pete had followed them out from Astoria to Great Neck one night, then had parked a block down when they pulled over on a quiet street filled with grand houses. Lorry got out, wearing a black coat and cap. He slipped his hands into his pockets and shifted down the lane. Elv watched him from the driver's seat, rapt. The whole time he was gone she barely moved, until at last he came ambling back, a duffel bag swung over his shoulder. They'd sped off, not even noticing the Volvo on the corner, in a world of their own.

Pete decided to make chicken and dumplings, a somewhat complicated recipe. He wanted to take his time, use it for simple things. He tested the dumplings on Claire, who was always so picky. "Delish," she said, then surprised him by asking for more.

It seemed impossible that Pete would know how to make such a dense, homey dish. Nobody cooked like that anymore. Claire fed tidbits to her dog as she studied for a history exam.

"How did you know how to make those?" Annie asked Pete when they sat down to dinner. "Are you sure you're not a gourmet chef posing as a detective in order to sleep with various dying women?"

"It's just flour and water." There was a dusting of flour on his hands. "Annie," he said sadly.

Annie wrapped her arms around him. She couldn't understand how a man like Pete could get involved with a woman in her situation. She hadn't yet told Claire what the doctors had said on her last visit. She wasn't having chemo anymore. There was no further treatment. All she asked was to last until Claire's high school graduation. She didn't think beyond that. As for Pete, he wasn't thinking beyond the current evening.

The snow had slowed down. It was just flurrying. There was a shimmering cast to the drifts, as if sugar had been sprinkled over them. Pete wondered if the endings of things gathered in the corners of a room, hanging down like a spider's web, waiting.

"What?" Annie took note when he grimaced. "You *did* hurt your back!"

Pete insisted that shoveling snow was good exercise, but in fact his back was killing him. That night he couldn't sleep. He thought about Elv in that fast car, about his daughter slamming out of the house the last time he saw her, shouting "Go to hell" when all he'd wanted was to bring her back to life. He thought about the fact that Annie rarely complained or took her pain-killers. She wanted to be in the here and now, she'd told him. She wasn't going anywhere just yet.

Restless, Pete went downstairs for a glass of water. Claire was in the kitchen, submerged in a textbook. Shiloh was stretched out under the table. Claire still spoke infrequently, choosing her words carefully. Although she was a top student, she had decided not to take any college placement tests. She wasn't interested in the future. She dreaded change of any sort and was dismayed when faced with too many choices. Every day after school she went to the cemetery. While other girls were meeting boyfriends, going to dances, working on the school newspaper, Claire was walking through the wrought-iron gates.

She wasn't afraid of the dead. She'd grown accustomed to being there alone. Tall pine trees loomed, and the path was often slippery with mud. Each time she went, she left a stone behind. There was one for every day her sister had been gone. Meg's belongings had been moved out of the bedroom. There was only one bed in the attic now. But Claire had kept a box of her sister's possessions: a collection of Dickens novels, the battered copy of *To the Lighthouse* without its cover, velvet headbands, the boots Meg had been wearing that day. There were shards of glass embedded in the leather, as if sharp slices of the sky had fallen to earth. Claire still carried the piece of paper with the word *orange* written on it. She'd taken it out of Meg's pocket before the hospital disposed of her clothes.

When Pete came into the kitchen that night, Claire looked up, surprised to see him awake at this late hour. She herself got by on five hours of sleep. She was such a light sleeper a single bird settling on the branch of the hawthorn tree could wake her and make her sit up in bed.

"Can't sleep?" Claire's voice, unused for so long, was soft and flat. You had to listen carefully or it faded into empty space.

"Sleep is overrated."

"Couldn't agree more." Claire went back to her reading.

"And my stomach's acting up," Pete explained. He didn't mind how quiet Claire was. He'd lived alone for a very long time. At one point he'd gotten so accustomed to silence that the sound of his own voice startled him. He took some Maalox from the cabinet, then sat at the table and gazed at Claire's notes. "The Russian Revolution. Interesting time."

"People dying for nothing. Isn't that what history is?"

"Nope. History is about love and honor and making mistakes."

Claire smiled. She knew that Pete slept with her mother. The blankets and pillows left on the couch were for her benefit. "You're a romantic," she said.

Pete went to the window. The walk he'd shoveled was already being covered by white drifts. In the morning, he would have to clear it all over again. The truth of it was, despite his bad back, he really didn't mind. Claire was a smart girl. She was absolutely right. He still wanted to believe that people could survive their misfortunes. He believed that was all anyone had.

Thief

I didn't let him in the door until he promised he wouldn't take anything precious. He crossed his heart. He wanted comfort, nothing more. Robbery was tiring work. He slept in a corner, curled up. When he awoke he was famished. I cooked him eggs and toast. I kept an eye on him. He kept his hands to himself. The silver candlesticks were still on the table. The pearl brooch was at my throat.

He made a list of all the things he'd taken. He wanted redemption and faith and I offered him both. When daylight came I asked him to stay. I could see from his face this had happened to him before. Women wanted to rob him of the life he led, the road, the dark night, the open windows, the stars. The whole world belonged to him. When he left he swore he'd be back. It didn't matter. He'd already taken everything I had.

IT WAS A GOOD PLAN, BUT PLANS FALL APART. ONCE ONE THING goes wrong, everything else can easily unwind and there you are, left with nothing but the hole you've fallen into. It was supposed to be safe. They would talk people into handing over their money. Lorry liked to do things that way, use charm rather than force, tell folks what they wanted to hear. People would sign away their savings of their own free will. No more breaking into houses, ferreting around in people's closets, running risks. They'd had several close calls out on Long Island. One had been particularly nerve-racking. Lorry said it was a sign for them to find a new direction. They'd been casing a house in Roslyn for several days, and when the family went out, Lorry got out of the car. He stretched his back, then slipped around to a window left ajar. People were trusting, especially in the suburbs. They wanted to believe they were safe from harm, when it was everywhere, unavoidable, no matter how protected you thought you were. Lorry hoisted himself inside. He was on his way to the bedroom in search of the wife's jewelry when he unexpectedly came upon an eight-year-old boy, left at home. They faced each other in the hall in pure silence. The boy seemed terrified. Then Lorry had said he was there to fix the TV. He said it so matter-of-factly that the boy led him to the den. Lorry told Elv the kid been left home alone as a punishment for bad grades at school. Lorry fixed him a bowl of cereal before he left with the flat-screen TV.

It was Mr. Ortiz who did them in. He was smarter than Elv had guessed. It was almost as if he was a spider spinning his own trap and Elv had dropped right into it. When he notified the authorities, they sent a policewoman who pretended to be his wife. She could have been an actress on Broadway. She was that good. She shrugged and gestured to make it clear she didn't speak English, so Elv didn't mind if she sat with them at the kitchen table. But she understood everything. She was wired to tape the conversation and smiling when Mr. Ortiz signed his bank account over to Elv so she could invest it for him. In earlier meetings Elv had explained how he could double his money and not have to pay taxes. She would handle everything. She would give him an official receipt. *The water there is so blue you'll cry when you see it. All your tears will remind you of your childhood and how free you were before you came to New York and had to navigate the concrete and the dark tunnels and the avenues where nobody cares about you. The banks want to rip you off, taxes are chipping away at all you worked so hard and long to save.*

Lorry had made up the brochure. He'd done a good job. And anyway, people rarely did more than glance at the figures. They looked at the photographs of the condos in the Dominican Republic and they got all excited about getting in on the ground floor. Lorry had successfully used this scam three times. A couple of thousand dollars wasn't going to kill anyone. The old people had seemed so hungry for company it was as if he and Elv were doing them a service, telling a few stories over coffee and cookies. *For you, we'll make an exception. For you, we have a special deal.*

Lorry didn't want Elv to do it, but she pleaded with him. She hated being a burden, never doing her share. She was using every day and that was expensive. She was going to quit as soon as she got all of the bad things out of her head, but that hadn't happened. She remembered precisely the way the car had been flying, the way he'd locked the door and taken off his belt. She thought she was a good judge of character until she picked Mr.

Ortiz. She'd grabbed a few groceries in the market, then walked up to him on line. He looked kindhearted. An easy mark. She ruefully told him she had no cash with her, could she borrow a twenty and return it to him the next day? Her mother was ill and she'd left her purse behind during a visit to her sickbed. The old man didn't mind a pretty girl coming to his apartment, having a cup of coffee with him, bringing him pastries when she returned the twenty she'd borrowed, telling him she knew of a way for a person to double his savings if he was smart enough to answer the door when opportunity knocked. She had just made a similar investment on her mother's behalf. She played it slow and safe, even though Lorry told her to hurry up; give someone time and they'd figure out the con. Even a fool could recognize a lie if you gave him the chance to consider his options.

On the day Mr. Ortiz signed the papers and handed over the check, the woman playing the part of his wife called down to her partner on the street. Elv was arrested as soon as she exited the building. Her natural instinct was to flee, which she tried to do, and to fight when the officer grabbed her. After that, they had her for resisting arrest, which meant no bail. She didn't say anything, just as Lorry had instructed. She didn't even tell them her name. Lorry didn't know where she was for several days. He waited for hours on a bench outside the old man's apartment, panicked when he saw Ortiz going for a walk with his cronies. When Elv didn't show up back at the apartment, he searched Astoria, then went to the Island and drove around North Point Harbor. There were no calls to his cell phone, no messages from Elv's family. At last he received a letter. She'd had to detox at the city jail. She'd been so sick they'd finally taken her to the infirmary. The most they would give her was Tylenol and Valium, finally doling out thorazine to make sure she didn't have seizures. They'd gotten her name out of her, but no address. She said she'd been living on the street.

Don't come here, she wrote. *I don't want you to see me this way.*

The truth of it was, she didn't want suspicion to fall Lorry's way. Did she have a partner? she'd been asked when they took her down to the station. She would never lead them to Lorry. She was familiar with iron, bread, water, ropes. They couldn't scare her. They took her clothes, her ring, her purse. She ignored everyone in the dining hall; those who called her names and those who tried to befriend her were equally invisible. She did what she'd done in Westfield. She behaved. She did as she'd done in that man's basement. She looked for her escape. Waited till she could run.

She wanted Lorry to get out of Astoria, make himself scarce. *I can do this,* she wrote. *I've done it before.*

Lorry packed up the apartment. He threw away anything that could be used as evidence and anything that might tie them together. He got in his car and drove back to North Point Harbor, then parked across from the Weinsteins' house. It was dawn and quiet. It was dead in town. He smoked several cigarettes, considered how stupid people were, including himself as perhaps the biggest idiot of them all, then did what he always did. He came up with a plan. Pete saw the car when he went out to retrieve the newspaper in the morning. He recognized it, so he tucked the paper under his arm. If it was Lorry, he wanted to break his head. If Elv was alone in the car, he wanted to lead her right to her mother, the most precious gift he could give Annie.

He walked down Nightingale Lane in his pajama pants and bathrobe. It was still dark, but the horizon was turning a clear eggshell blue. Birds had begun to call. The car had tinted windows, so he didn't know whether or not Elv was inside. It was a piece of crap car, an Oldsmobile. It probably had a terrible safety record. It was spring, a season Pete had come to hate, just as Claire and Annie hated it. He hated the gnats and the humidity and the birds chirping all the time. He'd hated the way the trees looked so hopeful and green when he drove Annie to the cemetery to visit Meg and then, just the week before, to pick out a plot for herself. She'd been lucky enough to get the one right next to her daughter. She'd actually seemed overjoyed by her good fortune.

Pete had stuck a few spindly tomato plants in the garden this year. Annie was too weak. A real garden was out of the question, even though he'd cleared out all the weeds in the hopes she might rebound. He was carrying her up and down the stairs now. "My hero," she'd whisper when he did this. She meant it, which made it even worse.

Pete went up to the Oldsmobile and tapped on the driver's window. Then he took a step back into the dewy grass. Lorry opened the door, unfolded himself, got out of the car.

"She said her parents were divorced," he said accusingly. He had his hands in his pockets. He'd seen Pete come out of the house for the paper and wondered who the hell he was.

"I'm the new guy," Pete said. He'd told himself to wait and see, not to jump to conclusions because of what had happened to Rebecca, not to try to beat the shit out of this guy, who was younger and stronger—which was not to say Pete couldn't still inflict some damage.

Lorry looked past him. The house down the lane was dark.

"You're not going to talk to her mother if that's what you're thinking," Pete told him. "She's dying."

They stood there at the corner, gazing at the Weinsteins' lawn. It really needed to be reseeded. It was such an eyesore the neighbors were thinking of getting together and lodging a complaint.

"Elv needs a lawyer," Lorry said. "Can you take care of that?"

Pete nodded. He still had friends downtown. He could find out where she was and what she needed.

"Okay. Good. That's all I needed to know." Lorry opened the car door, then hesitated. He took a letter from his coat pocket. "Could you give her this?"

"Because you'll be unavailable?" *Protecting your own ass,* Pete thought, although he didn't say it. He didn't have to.

"Because things are going to be different when she gets out. It's going to be better."

"Yeah, well, I doubt that. But I'll give her the letter."

Lorry lit a cigarette. His hands were shaky. He hadn't slept for a while. He saw the stop sign on the corner. It was a long time before she told him; even then she refused to give any details. "So this is where it happened," he said thoughtfully. "I'd like to kill that fuck."

Pete wished he still smoked. He had wanted to punch Lorry, but that feeling had dropped away into something else. He could tell a man torn apart by love when he saw one.

"Who does that kind of thing to a little girl?" Lorry fumed. "He's considered a model citizen because he was a teacher. She calls him Grimin. If she'd told me his name, he'd be dead by now."

"I'll do everything I can for her," Pete assured him. He kept his thoughts to himself, but his mind started clicking in, the way it always did before he began his research on a particular project.

"Yeah. Well, that's good." Lorry slapped Pete on the back. Pete winced and shifted out of reach. "Bad back?" Lorry asked.

"It would be better if you were out of her life," Pete said. "You know that."

Pete stood on the corner while Lorry got in his car, made a U-turn, and pulled away. He drove slowly, headlights off, a man used to making a getaway. Pete slipped the letter into the pocket of his bathrobe.

He fixed some strong coffee, then phoned Natalia and asked her to come out to North Point Harbor to stay with Annie. As soon as she arrived, he headed into the city. He'd made a few calls and was able to act as the family's representative. Rebecca had been in the holding tank several times, so he had that déjà vu feeling checking in, being taken to the visitors' room. He'd heard that some people had dreams that felt this real, then they woke up in their own beds, safe and sound.

When Elv was led in, her eyes flitted over him. She couldn't conceal her disappointment. They were left alone for ten minutes. They probably wouldn't even need that.

"I don't know you," she said.

"I'm the guy who's going to get you a lawyer. All you have to do is trust me." Pete introduced himself as a good friend of her mother's.

He was a middle-aged guy. Gray hair, worried face, tall. "She sent you?"

"She's not well, Elv. She doesn't know you're here." Pete reached into his coat for the letter. "He sent me."

Elv looked alive for the first time when he handed the letter over. She tore it open, read it, then sat back in her chair, blinking back tears.

"He came to the house?"

Pete nodded.

Elv turned her head. A sob escaped.

"What happened on the corner?" Pete asked.

Elv turned back to him frowning. "Just because you're helping me, don't think you know me."

"Maybe I do," Pete said.

"You'll have to trust me on this one." Elv folded the letter and slipped it into her sleeve. She would read it over again and again until the ink disappeared. "You don't."

◆ ◆ ◆

ON THE DAY of the hearing, Pete claimed a space in the back row of the courtroom. He'd confided in Natalia and she had insisted on attending. A nurse had been hired to spend the morning with Annie. Natalia had taken a taxi downtown to meet Pete. She was flustered. He'd had to help her up the steps to the courthouse.

"I wish I could take her place," Natalia said. She'd never been to court before and was overdressed. She wore her black Chanel coat, high heels, a pearl necklace. She took a handkerchief from her purse.

Pete patted her arm. He wasn't sure if she meant Annie or Elv or both.

"She has an excellent lawyer," he said. "Sam Carlyle." The DA himself had recommended him. "We'll hope for the best."

When the matron walked Elv into the courtroom, Elv noticed Pete in the last row. He was tall and easy to spot. Then she spied her ama. Quickly she turned away, flushed with shame. Elv knew she looked wretched. No wonder her grandmother appeared to be stunned. The detox had been hard. She'd actually wanted to die, but she kept Lorry in her mind, a fierce ray of light, the one thing no one could take away.

Seeing Natalia in court made everything worse. Elv felt a burning inside her chest, behind her eyes. She had begun to dream about the garden at home, the trellis where the sweet peas twined. She longed for the stories her mother would tell. She wanted to go back to a place that didn't exist anymore. Now she scanned the court for Lorry and was relieved to find he wasn't there. He might have tried something foolish, rushed the bench, tried to carry her off. In his letter he'd written he was going out to make his fortune. For every day that she was away, he would be working toward their future together. He would come back for her then. All she had to do was wait and he'd be there.

Elv hung her head while the charges against her were read. Her lawyer pled guilty and asked for leniency on a charge of grand larceny that could potentially carry fifteen years. She was young, he told the judge. Just a girl. She had made a mistake, but she was a worthwhile, intelligent young woman from a good family. Look, Your Honor, there is her grandmother in the last row. Elv turned to glance over her shoulder. Her grandmother stood up. Elv recognized the black cashmere coat as one she had often tried on to model in front of the big gold-framed mirror on Eighty-ninth Street. It was the sort of coat Audrey Hepburn might have worn. When her grandmother waved, Elv waved back. She felt something in her breaking.

"Ama," she called.

The bailiff asked Elv to be quiet and not to speak out of turn. Of course she complied. She turned to face the bench. She never looked at her grandmother again. Everyone could hear Natalia crying, and perhaps that was why the judge said he would consider Elv's attorney's request of leniency.

PETE KEPT IN touch with his old buddies in the system. He checked the newspaper every day. He and Natalia had decided to keep the situation not only from Annie, but from Claire as well. But Claire happened to spy Pete tossing the newspaper in the trash can on the day after the initial hearing. On her way to school, she went to ferret the paper out from the trash. She slipped it into her backpack, then ran for the school bus. Even nice days made Claire think about the cemetery. That's why she usually wore a scarf. She'd visit Meg after school and it always seemed cold there. The trees along the cemetery paths had leaves that curled up and turned black at the edges. The grass was so tall

Claire had the urge to lie down in it and gaze at the world from that position until at last she closed her eyes.

The bus to the Graves Academy stopped on the corner. When it arrived, Claire got on. She nodded to some of the girls she knew, then went to the back, where she always sat. She unfolded the paper and found the small article in the metro section. A suspect had been charged in a scam in Astoria that had tried to bilk people out of their life savings. There was a murky photograph of a woman with long dark hair. Claire had newsprint on her hands. The papers all referred to Elv as Elisabeth Story, so it didn't even seem like the same person.

On the day the sentencing was announced, Claire got up early and went to collect the paper before Pete could. He came downstairs to fix the coffee and saw her out there on the porch, hunched over, reading. It was barely a paragraph; that was all the attention the crime warranted. The weather was warmer by then. It was the sort of spring day Claire hated. Bumblebees rumbled around what was left of the garden.

Pete came out to sit beside her. Annie had taken a turn for the worse, so he hadn't kept up with the case the way he might have. "What did the judge give her?"

"Three to five years." Claire threw the paper in the trash. "Meg's the one who got the death penalty."

"It was an accident," Pete said. "You know that, don't you?"

Claire had to collect herself. She wasn't going to feel sorry for her sister. She wasn't going to think of Elv going to jail, or the way those men had grabbed her at Westfield, or how fast she'd walked along Nightingale Lane on the bad day, as if a demon was right behind her. She'd slowed down once she'd grabbed Claire's hand and they started home. She'd known Claire couldn't keep up.

"Let's make tomato soup," Pete suggested. There were some store-bought tomatoes in the fridge and a container of cream. Annie had all but stopped eating. Maybe soup would bring back her appetite.

Claire nodded. "She'd like that." As they went inside she blurted, "I'm glad you didn't tell Mom about Elv. She would have felt bad for her."

"Love is like a spyglass," Pete said. "Your mom told me that."

"Oh yeah?" Claire said. "Well, I think it's like a pack of lies."

"How do they get lies into a pack? Is there some kind of machine that does it?"

Claire laughed.

"You can look at it from a distance, that's what your mother told me, and maybe it seems far away. But it's still there. It's still the same."

HE BROUGHT LUNCH up on a tray when the soup was ready. Annie had been making a list inside her head of all the tasks that needed to be completed after she was gone. Someone had to sell the house, convince Claire to go to college, make a vet appointment for Shiloh to have his rabies shot. The gutters needed to be cleaned, the mail stopped, the taxes paid. She was too tired to write this all down, but she kept on thinking about all the things she wouldn't have time to do. She thought and thought until she only cared about one last thing.

"I got the good rye bread," Pete said of the toast he'd fixed to go along with the bowl of soup. "The kind you like. With seeds."

Annie took his hand once the tray was set down. Her fierce expression surprised him. "You've already done so much for me. Is it too much if I ask you to keep watch over her?"

"Claire's fine. She's downstairs studying."

"Yes, Claire. But that's not what I mean."

Pete sat on the side of the bed. He knew exactly what she meant. He wished he never had to leave this room and that he and Annie had met years ago. He wished he could somehow let Claire know this was what love was. The ability to ask for something. The desire to give someone what they asked for.

"I intend to," he said. "You don't have to worry about Elv."

CLAIRE WAS GRADUATING from the Graves Academy with high honors. That morning the home health aide said she wasn't certain Annie would make it through the day. Claire had wanted to forgo the whole thing, skip graduation and stay at her mother's side, but her grandmother said absolutely not. Annie wanted to see her in her white cap and gown. She had been living for this day. Claire finally put on her graduation outfit. She went up to her mother's room. The curtains were drawn. On impulse, Claire had thrown up the skirt of her gown, kicking like a Rockette, and they'd all laughed, even Annie. "Oh, hurray!" Annie had cried in a small, delighted voice.

Pete went to graduation with Elise and Mary Fox. He stayed on his cell phone the entire time. Sitting on a chair set up in the soccer field, he felt like one of those commentators in a basketball game, giving the play-by-play. "The headmaster is on the stage," he reported.

"Tell them he's fat and sweaty," Mary Fox chimed in.

"The faculty are all lined up in a row," Elise added. "It's crowded as all get out."

Natalia had been living with them for the past few weeks. Now she was in bed with Annie, holding the phone up so Annie could listen. When the headmaster announced Claire's name, they cheered. They pretended they weren't crying. It had all been so exhausting, holding on for this moment. After a while, Natalia felt as if the air was too close. Annie's breathing was labored. "I think I should get the doctor."

"Don't," Annie murmured. She wanted to close her eyes, but instead, she struggled to listen to the rest of the graduation ceremony. It all poured into the room, the applause and the excitement. They could hear a marching band. Natalia wrapped her arms around her daughter. She sang the lullaby she'd sung a long time ago. Annie was surprised to find that she remembered the words. She remembered her parents' bedroom in Paris, the orange light seeping in around the white window shades. There was the scent of chestnut blossoms and the sound of leaves rustling in a slow, green rhythm. *Sleep, my darling child. Sleep through nights and days. I'll be here to watch over you.*

PETE AND CLAIRE left the school grounds as soon as Claire received her degree. They left Elise and Mary Fox and ran for the parking lot, which was cluttered with cars, many of which had streamers dangling from the bumpers and antennas. *Congratulations. Best of luck.* Claire threw her diploma in the backseat and tore off her cap. Everything was green in the fields surrounding the school. The other students' parents were still in the soccer field, cheering. There was a series of awards, including one meant for Claire from the English Department. Mary would accept on her behalf. The head of the department, Miss Jarrett, read a poem Claire had written during the time she stopped speaking. Claire couldn't have cared less about the award. Her poem was about the sixteenth-century *Golden Book* in Venice, in which all of the maestros of glassmaking were listed by name. She described the ways in which glass could shatter. Rocks, storms, hail, carelessness, slingshots. In the end there'd been too many to list.

Pete broke the speed limit on the way home. As they raced through town, Claire buzzed the window down and leaned outside. Her face was streaming with tears. It made sense for Pete to drive on the bay road, even though they usually avoided the corner where it happened. It was the fastest way home.

Claire's back was to him, but Pete knew she was crying. He reached to pat her shoulder. A soft cry escaped from Claire's mouth.

"She made it till today," Pete reminded her.

When they got to the house, Claire ran inside to see her mother. She hadn't been the smartest or the most beautiful, but she had graduated and that had mattered to Annie. Pete stepped into the kitchen. Natalia had heard the car and had come downstairs so Claire could have some time alone with her mother. She handed Pete a cup of coffee. He and Annie had talked about everything, but they weren't finished.

When Natalia went back to Annie's room, Pete said he would be right up. He stayed in the kitchen with the dog for a while. He covered his face and wept. When he was done, he patted Shiloh's head. This wasn't his house or his family or his dog, but it was his sorrow. The phone rang. It seemed ridiculously loud. The kitchen clock was ticking. It wasn't the sort of day anyone would remember. Just an average June day. Pete blew his nose on a napkin. Maybe it was the ex-husband telephoning. He hadn't been able to attend Claire's graduation because there was also a graduation at his own high school. Just as well; nobody wanted him. Pete didn't care to talk to him either, but when the phone continued to ring he had little choice but to answer, if only to quiet the damned thing.

He grabbed the receiver and said, "Hello," feeling awkward. "Who is this?" A woman's voice.

For a brief alarming moment Pete thought it was his daughter, Rebecca, calling from the beyond. Then he understood.

"It's Pete, Elv."

Elv paused, then went on. "They let me have a phone call. I knew it was graduation day. Claire probably wouldn't want to talk to me."

"She's upstairs with your mother."

"You don't think my mother would want to talk to me, do you?"

Pete gazed out at the tree in the yard. Annie had told him Elv used to sit up there like a nymph, even in the rain. "I think she would. But she's not capable. Do you understand what I'm saying?" Pete asked.

"If I could talk to her once, I could tell her how sorry I am."

Pete said he was going to look in on her mother and that he'd tell her. When he went back up, Claire was curled up in a chair in the corner. Her graduation gown was rolled in a ball, tossed on the carpet. Pete hung it over the back of a chair. He went to the bedside. He didn't know if Annie recognized him or not, but he leaned in close to tell her she didn't have to worry about Elv anymore. She was the way she used to be, the girl in the garden with the long black hair.

The light through the window was changing. It grew oddly bright just before twilight, then faded into bands of blue. By evening it was over. Claire went downstairs and opened the back door. She'd heard that was the way to release a spirit. Her grief poured out in a few wrenching sobs. She pulled herself together and glanced at the clock. This was the hour of her mother's death. Shiloh was staring into the yard, so Claire opened the door wider.

"Go on," she urged.

The dog trotted out to the lawn. The phone rang and Claire ignored it. Speaking had always seemed beside the point for her, now more than ever. What were words but a pack of lies, however you sorted them. There were birds outside, robins. All at once, they flew into the trees.

The phone continued to chime. Claire finally picked up the receiver. When she held it to her ear, a woman's voice said, "Mommy? Is that you?"

Claire felt as though she'd just placed her hand on the burner of the stove. She quickly hung up. The birds were all nesting now. Not a single one sang. It had begun to drizzle and everything was turning gray. Pete came into the room. He'd heard the phone and he'd rushed down to answer it, but he knew he was too late as soon as he saw the expression on Claire's face.

"She called before," he admitted.

"She can go to hell," Claire said.

They didn't need to talk to anyone right now. Instead, they stood at the back door and watched the dog walk the perimeter of the yard. Aside from the spindly tomato plants Pete had planted in a corner, the vegetable garden was filled with stray weeds. Nettle, thistle, jimson weed, nightshade. A few tremulous sweet pea vines had begun to wind along the fence. The tendrils were soft green with luminous pale buds. Natalia came from upstairs. She had covered Annie with the white linen bedspread she'd brought with her from France. It was the one that had been in the guest room, when the girls were young and Annie had slept for seventeen hours and the light was orange. In a little while they would have to call 911 and ask for an ambulance to be sent to the house. But for now they remained at the door, breathing in the evening air. There was really no place else they wanted to go.

Changeling

They said I was just like other children, but I had a tail and claws. They said it made no difference. I would wear a cloak and gloves and I would be just like all the rest. In the dark you couldn't tell that my teeth were sharp.

I went to school and did my chores. I carried water up the hill in buckets. I made the beds and swept the floors. At night I climbed out the window and chased rabbits. I always bathed in a pond before I went home, to wash away the blood. When they served me my breakfast of toast and tea, I said I wasn't hungry. But I was.

What Claire liked most about Paris was that no one noticed her. She could walk for miles without speaking to any-one. Of course there were places she made certain to avoid, the favorite, most-beloved list she and Meg had agreed upon that spring when they'd come here together. The ice cream stand by the Île Saint-Louis. The Rue de Tournon. The bookstore, Shakespeare and Co.

Claire now bought her secondhand books from the stalls along the river. She thumbed through volumes to make certain there were no dedications. She avoided sentiments of love and loyalty. Three years had passed since Claire had moved to Paris with her grandmother. The house had been sold and Natalia had given up the apartment on Eighty-ninth Street. Claire never went to college. She didn't apply. She wanted to go someplace where they'd once been happy. She packed a single bag of possessions and took Shiloh. Sadie, the cat, was still alive, and when the dog arrived, the two agreed to a truce, forced to share close quarters in a small flat. Claire herself despised the cat, and Sadie must have felt her contempt. It disappeared whenever she was around, hiding beneath the couch. Occasionally a claw darted out to strike at a boot or shoe.

Shiloh went everywhere with Claire. He was beside her when she went walking after dark, late at night when the skies were heavy, filled with clouds. The only people out at this hour were the ones who couldn't sleep, those haunted by one thing or another: love thwarted, love lost, love thrown away. They were the sort of people who didn't wish to be noticed, who wanted to slip through shadows, be alone with their despair. Claire wore her hair short and dressed in the worn Burberry jacket her mother had donned while gardening. She had a pair of jeans she'd bought ten years ago and the boots she wore all the way through high school when she had to wait for the bus on the corner of Nightingale Lane. She liked the way the night turned green in Paris, the green air, the slick green sidewalks after a rain. She frequented a café in the Marais near her grandmother's apartment.

Everyone knew her, but acted as if they didn't. Claire appreciated that brusque courtesy. She never looked at the waiters or the proprietor. She didn't wish to make polite conversation about the weather or current events. She didn't want companionship, merely coffee and a quiet table near a window.

Since she'd moved to Paris there had been men who were interested in her, but Claire ignored them. She thought that love ruined people. She kept her distance. Once a man had come up and kissed her as she was searching for shallots in a vegetable bin in the market. He'd grabbed her and pulled her close before she could react, then had blurted out something about her being too beautiful to ignore. Claire abandoned her groceries and left the shop. She'd never returned to that market, although it was the one closest to her grandmother's apartment.

She no longer cared about the many colors of sunlight in Paris. She remembered making lists with Meg about that, too. There were times when the light had been pink or pale lemon, dusty violet or gray as smoke. Then there had been the day when it was orange. Claire preferred the dark. Paris was good for that. People said it was the city of light, but not if you went out on rainy days, coat collar turned up. Not if you waited for twilight before emerging onto the street. There were many things Claire had no interest in anymore besides light. Friendship, food, conversation, men, love, school, work, dreams. She shut herself away in her room and slept most of the day. When she came out for dinner, merely a bowl of soup or some crackers, her face looked crumpled. Sometimes her grandmother feared that Claire was evaporating. What would be left of her if she kept disappearing into a smaller and smaller world of her own? Her shoes, her hat, her coat, nothing more. Claire spoke only when the need arose, but the need for speech is arbitrary. When neighbors greeted her, she looked startled, as though she'd pricked her finger with a pin.

Sometimes she had terrible dreams. That was something even Claire couldn't avoid with sleep. Several times Natalia heard her call out in the gibberish language the Story sisters used to speak.

WHEN CLAIRE WENT on her nighttime walks, she was looking for stones, one for every day she had not visited her sister's and mother's graves. Stones piled up under her bed, in the closet, and in dresser drawers. Her favorites were the glassy ones gathered with a fishing net from the shallows of the Seine, but she also liked the round white ones from the Tuilleries. Her collection grew so large that the apartment rattled on windy days. The downstairs neighbors, unnerved, began to complain. Tenants in the building dreamed of earthquakes and landslides. Before long, such dreams were common even among the littlest children. A young couple moved out, believing the building to be cursed, which was perfectly fine with the landlord, who quickly found new tenants and doubled the rent.

Claire often wondered if she herself was a demon. Long ago, Elv had taught her how to recognize one; she'd whispered the telltale signs as they'd lain side by side in bed. Demons were marked by black stars, pale eyes. When one walked through a room, ice formed on the windowpanes; plants withered. At the moment of disaster, when you turned to them, when you needed them most, they were gone. That was Claire; that was what she'd done.

Meg would have been a grown woman with a life of her own if Claire hadn't called for her to get in the car. She had loved books. Perhaps she would have been a writer by now, living in London or Manhattan. She would have had a lover or a husband. A child, perhaps several. There was no consolation for what Claire had done. The yellow lamplight, the gargoyles with their crooked faces, the cobblestones that clattered as she walked along, the parks ringed with black iron fences were invisible as she walked through Paris in the dark. She no longer cared about human concerns such as love and happiness. She believed in punishments, reprisals, fate. She believed she and Elv were two of a kind. On several occasions she had found herself poised at the edge of the river, boots caked with mud, the gusting wind pushing her onward. What difference would it make if she never returned?

ONE AFTERNOON NATALIA discovered her granddaughter perched on the window ledge gazing down at the white flowers that cluttered the chestnut tree in the courtyard below. It was the terrible season, the one they hated, the time of violets and pollen and green light. It was spring. Time had passed, but in many ways Claire had remained the same. She'd never gone to a university, never held a job or been in love, never cooked a meal for anyone or kissed someone until she was dizzy. She thought it was best for her to be apart from the rest of humanity. Ever since the bad day she thought she might be dangerous.

When Natalia found her swaying on the ledge she called out to her granddaughter, but Claire didn't answer. The world was closing down. Some people might have said it was a nervous breakdown, a mental collapse brought on by trauma and stress. Natalia wondered if it was the philosophy of doom that held Claire in thrall. If you believed in something strongly and gave it enough credence, it could appear right in front of you. Though it had been created in your mind, it would claim a presence in the real world, a monster at your door, a demon pulling at your coat sleeve.

Natalia grabbed her granddaughter back through the window. It was like wresting a sleeper from a dream. She tugged so hard she wrenched her shoulder. She wasn't the sort to let go.

Secretly she wrote to Elv every week, chatty letters about her neighbors, stories about the Marais. She jotted down the histories of local people, how long they'd lived in their apartments, the names of husbands and wives, homey facts—what was eaten for dinner, how it was cooked, what the weather had been. She didn't give up, even though she hadn't heard back. For all she knew, her granddaughter threw her letters away, unread. She didn't realize how much Elv looked forward to these letters until Natalia came down with the flu and missed a few weeks of writing. A letter from the States arrived soon after, the very first she'd received from Elv. *Did Madame Michelle marry the man who'd been courting her? What happened to the Maltese puppy he'd brought her as a gift? Did she ever have the heart to tell him she was allergic to dogs? Did the café around the corner dismiss the waiter everyone loved, but who was so tired from working two jobs, he often fell asleep on his feet, tray in hand? Were the chestnut flowers in bloom? Did the air smell like almonds? What color was the light? When will I hear from you again?*

Natalia refused to let go of her grandchildren. If anything, that was her philosophy. That was the reason she had slapped Claire's face. "Wake up!" she cried.

Claire held a hand to her cheek and looked stunned.

"What did you think you were doing out there? Are you trying to kill yourself?"

Claire shook her head. She didn't seem to know.

Natalia's eyesight was failing, but that night as she made her way to the bathroom she spied something with black wings. She could hear it, trapped like a moth in the narrow hall. She saw a dark haze flit past the gold-framed mirror beside the door. There was no reflection cast, but something was definitely there. She steadied herself. She saw what she believed to be a tiny woman with black wings.

Natalia sat down and had a drink, a good-sized glass of whiskey from a bottle of Johnnie Walker that had belonged to her husband. She always missed Martin, but she especially missed him tonight. She felt quite confused. Had she created the creature in the hallway, imagined it into existence? She wondered if she should see an ophthalmologist, perhaps even a psychiatrist. She had another drink after the first and was considering a third. Madame Cohen had always insisted there were demons in this world. How else would all the troubles that beset humankind come to be? Whatever these creatures were made of, skin and bones, ashes and memory, Natalia was not about to let them get hold of her granddaughter.

SHE WENT TO see Madame Cohen the next day at her shop at the end of the Rue des Rosiers. Each had sorrows she never discussed with anyone else. Their camaraderie was unusual and rare. Friendships were usually based on trivial matters, played out over games of cards and cups of coffee, but theirs was rooted in sterner stuff, catastrophe and survival. They sat in the back room of the shop beside the cabinet of diamonds and onions. They drank steamy cups of Marco Polo tea from the Marriage Frères tea shop on Rue du Bourg Tibourg, where more than four hundred varieties were sold. Good tea was one of Madame Cohen's few indulgences. There was a freshly pressed tablecloth on the small, round table. The linoleum on the floor was peeling, but the spoons they used to stir their sugar were 22-karat gold, brought from Moscow. The family had always been jewelers and goldsmiths; Madame Cohen's grandmother had sewn the spoons into the hem of her coat when she'd fled to France. She had eaten a handful of diamonds meant for a countess's brooch, then shat them out painfully into a bowl. The largest diamond had been set into an engagement ring, which had belonged to Madame Cohen's mother and now belonged to her. It served to remind her of her grandmother's suffering and dedication every single day.

Because Madame Cohen had seen demons before, she was hardly surprised when Natalia reported her vision in the hall. This was not a sign of insanity, but rather a clear-eyed vision of evil in the world. Leah Cohen's sisters, whom she never spoke of because their memory caused her such grief, had disappeared into a hail of ashes, surely a demon's touch. She often thought of a particular summer day when they'd traveled into the country by train for the weekend. It was the last time they were together. They had no idea that demons were already flying into the city of Paris, perching in the trees. At their picnic, the peaches had stained their fingers with juice. They were wearing dresses that were too warm for the season. When no one was looking, they threw off their dresses and lounged in the grass in their slips. Leah Cohen had her watercolors along and she quickly painted her sisters in shades of yellow and wheat and tangerine. Her sisters' names were Hannah and Marlena. Not long after that, they were murdered during the war. The painting of their picnic had been lost during a hurried move when Madame Cohen first married. Things were easily lost back then. But when Madame Cohen closed her eyes, her sisters' faces came back to her, even now. They were beautiful, sitting in the grass in their white slips.

Of course she would help Natalia. She was something of a demon expert, actually. She had learned everything from her grandmother and her mother, who knew tricks few people did. This was reason enough to have a daughter, someone to whom you could tell your secrets.

Madame Cohen suggested setting out saucers of salt at every

window. She told her friend to spray the air with salt water that very evening. Natalia went home and followed her advice. Soon enough the buzzing went away. There were no more creatures flitting about the hallway. This was excellent news, Madame Cohen said when Natalia reported back. But it wasn't enough. Claire was still listless, barely rising from bed.

When Madame Cohen said she must find meaningful work, Natalia suggested that Claire work at the Cohens' jewelry shop, only a few blocks away. She needed a schedule, responsibility, guidance. Madame Cohen would be doing a mitzvah, a good deed, in hiring Claire, who had no work experience and very little to recommend her other than her grandmother's love. Leah Cohen insisted on interviewing Claire first. Charitable actions did not mean stupid, blind faith, after all.

When she came to the apartment on the appointed night, Madame Cohen brought along a cake that was so delicious no one could turn it down, not even a woman who claimed never to be hungry. The batter was a mixture of fresh eggs, flour, sugar, lemon rind. Anise seed was added and dry cherries were mixed in. It was an old recipe, handed down from her grandmother. Some people called it Honesty Cake. No one could eat it and not tell the truth. She'd often made it for her grandsons when they got into mischief to discover who the culprit was. Now it would be a way for Madame Cohen to find out Claire's true nature. This was the job interview.

When Claire was called in to tea, she was surprised to find such a large piece of cake set onto her plate. Her grandmother knew she wasn't a fan of sweets. "I'm really not hungry," she insisted. She was wearing the torn jeans and gray sweatshirt she'd had as a teenager. THE GRAVES ACADEMY was printed in faded maroon letters. She hadn't kept in contact with any of her schoolmates. Her

English teacher, Miss Jarrett, had written to her once, suggesting she reconsider college, but Claire never applied. The only one she ever communicated with was Pete Smith, who phoned on a regular basis.

"You'll be surprised what you'll wind up liking," Madame Cohen told her. "Try a bite."

They sat at the table and ate in silence. The older women took note of how quickly Claire devoured the cake, as though she were starving.

"What recipe was that?" Claire asked when she was done. "I've never tasted anything like it." She was licking the back of her fork, proof that she still had human desires.

"Madame Cohen is here to offer you a job. Would you like that?"

Claire was indeed honest. "Not really."

"But would you show up and be responsible?" Madame Cohen prodded.

"I'm always responsible." Claire said. Everything about herself made her sad, including that. "Even when I don't want to be."

"Why don't you prepare the tea for us," Madame Cohen suggested. This was a part of the interview. People did background checks and extensive questionnaires, but you could tell a great deal more about someone from the way they readied a pot of tea. Madame Cohen had brought along her own tin filled with a green leafy mixture to which she'd added dried violets, sage, licorice root, ginger. The water was already boiling in the kettle. Claire went to pour. As the steam rose she started to cry. That wasn't at all like her. She wasn't a crier; she was empty inside. "I must have gotten a speck of dirt in my eye," she guessed.

After they had their tea, Claire went off to her room.

"What do you think?" Natalia asked her old friend.

A good deed was never as simple as it looked; Madame Cohen

knew that. There were ripples, effects no one expected. Still, after one cup of tea she had made up her mind.

"I'll hire her," she agreed.

BEHIND CLAIRE'S BACK the other employees called her *la fille au chien*—the dog girl. She was never without the wolfish creature, who followed at her heels. Claire didn't mind the shop because she was allowed to bring Shiloh along. As for Madame Cohen, she considered a big dog a good deterrent against robbers and thieves. She had reason to fear intruders. There was the bin of diamonds in the back room kitchenette, right next to the potatoes and onions, and gems scattered about, hidden in drawers, stuffed into pairs of boots, stored in cabinets and closets.

The other employees thought Madame Cohen should be the one to be paid for having agreed to hire such a strange girl. They were kind to Claire nonetheless. The salesgirls, Lucie and Jeanne, befriended her, suggesting style changes that might improve her appearance. Claire seemed wounded, lost, someone to take care of, and she brought out the best in Lucie and Jeanne. They gave her their castoffs, scarves, cashmere sweaters, wool skirts, and dresses. They treated her delicately, explaining the workings of the shop as they would to a child who had never before had a job. *Here is the cash register. Here is the broom. Here is the brass polish and the rags with which to clean the hardware on cabinets and doors.*

It wasn't hard to clean up after misfortune. It was, however, extremely difficult to chase it away for good. Something tapped on the glass windows of the jewelry shop once Claire came to work there. Something was trying to get in. Anyone else would have thought it was a blackbird and ignored it. Perhaps a child throwing stones. Madame Cohen knew better. She set out fly-paper and salt.

Soon enough, she found a huge moth attached to the flypaper. It had managed to get in through the door with the deliveryman. Evil always did that, appeared when you least expected it. That was why a person had to remain alert at all times. Madame Cohen phoned her dear friend Natalia, who already had reasons enough to be grateful. *I think I have caught the problem afflicting your granddaughter.* She had crushed the demon between her fingers and tossed it into the bin with the apple cores and onion skins.

MADAME COHEN HAD taken a special liking to Claire and doled out brusque, worthwhile advice every day. *Don't slump over. Look people in the eye when they speak to you. Brush your hair a hundred times a night. Bathe your face in milk. Sleep with the windows closed.* Madame Cohen had three grown sons and six grandsons. One of them had been so wild as a boy that he'd been banned from the store for his antics after inventing a crude flyswatter using a rubber band and marbles, nothing you'd want tested in a shop filled with glass cases and mirrors. Claire, on the other hand, was a pleasure to have around.

Madame Cohen taught her how to look through a loupe to gauge the clarity and depth of a stone. The best gems had a light inside, as if they were alive. Claire had found several old books on the subject of gemology in the bookstalls along the river. Some of the volumes had jewelers' wax dripped onto the pages. Others were one-of-a-kind editions, handwritten in black ink. When Jeanne and Lucie closed the shop and went home, Claire stayed on, studying. She trained herself to tell the difference between gems with her eyes closed, aware of that inner light of which Madame Cohen had spoken. A ruby gave off heat. An aquamarine was like water in the palm of her hand. Only a few lucky people had such an extraordinary feel for gemstones, Madame

Cohen was proud to say. Her mitzvah had paid off, as good deeds often do. Customers listened to Claire's opinion. Her small sulky voice forced them to lean close in order to catch her advice. In the end they all understood what she was telling them: Stones were the one thing that lasted.

Claire no longer found herself drawn to windows or riverbanks. She didn't sleep her days away. Sometimes she arrived at the shop before it opened, waiting outside on a bench, gazing at the slanted sunlight. *There's a new girl who works in the Cohens' jewelry shop,* Natalia wrote in her letters to Elv. *The other salesgirls have taken her up, taught her what to wear, they drag her along when they go out to lunch, especially on days when the light is orange, when the sky is the color blue it was when you were children, like a china plate, unbroken, luminous if you half-close your eyes.*

ELV READ HER grandmother's letters in the prison library, at a desk by the window. Afterward, she kept them stored in a shoebox beneath her cot, taking them out from time to time, savoring the descriptions of life in the Marais, the stories of the people in the neighborhood. Lorry sent her letters as well, and those she devoured. She read them standing up outside the mail room. He was always on the move, looking for the fortune he assured her he'd find. His letters were brief, but they tore her apart. She destroyed them after they'd been read. She didn't want anyone else to gets their hands on them. They were intimate, erotic, desperate. They weren't something a woman in prison should read while trying to get through each day without feeling anything.

SHE'D HAD THE good fortune to be sent to Bedford Hills but the bad luck of being assigned to the laundry, a job she hated. It was worse than latrine duty at Westfield. It was noisy, with so many inmates working that there was never an end to the chatter and bickering. The room was steamy hot and made her feel faint. The other women called her Missy and made fun of her. They thought she was stuck-up because she kept to herself. They assumed she was well educated when in fact she'd never finished high school. Women who were illiterate secretly came to her to ask if she would read the letters their children wrote. The letters moved her in ways she wouldn't have imagined. She missed her mother. She was glad Annie couldn't see where she'd ended up.

Pete Smith came to visit her sometimes. It was awkward because they didn't know each other and there wasn't much to say. Pete had moved into an apartment on the second floor of a two-family house in North Point Harbor. He'd come to think of the town as his home, the one he'd shared with Annie. He was a fixture at the cemetery, leaving flowers, cutting the tall grass with a scythe. Some kids in town called him Cemetery Man and ran away when they saw him on the street.

"They used to call me a witch," Elv said. "I had long black hair, and I wore a necklace made of bones."

"Gee, I wonder why they thought that," Pete said, and they had both laughed. "Bones?" he remarked.

"To ward off evil."

"I see that worked real well," Pete said dryly.

Most of his neighbors in North Point Harbor were kind; they knew what had happened to Annie. Several had invited him to holiday dinners, but he'd graciously declined. Once in a while a neighbor came to him with concerns over a divorce or a teenager who'd run away. He tried to help, but he never took on their cases. He wasn't in the business anymore. Except for Elv.

"Do you hear from Claire?" she asked him. "How is she?"

Each week Elv began a letter to Claire, and every time she tore it in two. She had even tried writing in Arnish, but she couldn't remember the words, or if she did, she no longer knew what they meant.

Though he wasn't much of a traveler, Pete had recently been for a visit. He'd stayed at a hotel around the corner from the apartment and other than seeing Claire, whom he'd gone to see on the occasion of her most recent birthday, he didn't like anything about France. The food was complicated and expensive. He couldn't speak the language and make himself understood. He sat on a bench across from Notre Dame and thought about Annie and how different Paris would be if she was there with him. In the end Claire had made him a hamburger and dumpling dinner in Natalia's kitchen to celebrate her birthday and they'd all had a grand time. When she showed him all the rocks she'd collected, he bought a suitcase at a shop around the corner, where he'd had to pantomime what he wanted in order to be understood. He paid extra freight so he could bring the suitcase with him to the cemetery. He swore he would come back and visit again and Claire had laughed and said, "When? When hell freezes over?"

"When there are decent hamburgers," he'd joked. Pete had spent an entire day setting down those rocks from Paris, half on Annie's grave, the other half on Meg's.

"She works in a jewelry store. She still has that dog."

"The wolf," Elv remarked, and when Pete seemed puzzled she added, "I just wanted to see my house. I saw the dog in the yard. I'm glad she has someone to protect her."

"Maybe you were the one who needed to be protected," Pete said. He was still trying to find that man Lorry had told him about, the one who had done such unspeakable things. Lorry said it had involved a teacher, and ever since, Pete had been trying to put the pieces together. Elv wasn't much help. She just shook her head and acted as though she didn't know what he was talking about. They were strangers, after all, thrown together because of their attachment to Annie.

"So tell me about your first date with my mother," Elv said. "I want to hear all about it."

"We went to a diner," Pete told her.

"Big spender," Elv joked.

"Actually, she paid."

They laughed again. "That was my mother."

"I was madly in love with her."

Pete turned away. He had stunned Elv with this admission and with his obvious grief. She felt herself soften toward him.

"Well, good," she said. "I'm glad. She deserved that."

AFTER A YEAR of working in the laundry, Elv's hands were chapped and her fingernails were split from hot water and soap. She filled out the application for the canine training class because her arms ached from lifting heavy towels into the driers. She had a true aversion to the scent of bleach. She went to the basement exercise room for the first session thinking she'd managed to pull a scam to get out of real work, as she had at Westfield when she'd been assigned to the stables.

The dog Elv was given was known as Pollo—they'd dubbed him Chicken on the street because he had to be forced to fight. But once provoked, he was a gladiator. If he bit down, he wouldn't let go. He was white with dark scars across his body and face. His legs had been broken when his owner beat him after a loss. Even after surgery he limped. He was hugely bowlegged. Laughable if you didn't know the reason why. He didn't look at Elv when Adrian Bean, the trainer running the program, matched them up. Pollo was the only one with a quiet demeanor, which made him seem even more dangerous. The other dogs stayed away from him, as the women stayed away from Elv. He was the ugliest dog in the bunch. Just her luck. The other women had German shepherds or puppies or fluffy mixed breeds. The dogs had all been abused or abandoned, found wandering on highways or city streets. Most were terrified of thunder, footsteps, cars, human beings. Several were vicious. The slightest provocation could cause them to attack.

Adrian told the women in the class that they were the alpha dogs and their students' futures depended on their success. If rehabilitated, the dogs would be adopted. If not, they would be put down.

"Fuck," Elv muttered. She didn't want to be responsible for some dog's death because she'd failed him somehow. Pollo turned to glance at her when she spoke. He must have recognized the f-word. They looked at each other. For an instant Elv was shocked to see something she recognized. He had yellow-green eyes, like hers.

When the training began everyone clipped a leash on her dog. Pollo refused to move. He wouldn't even accept a biscuit set down on the floor. He ignored it until a hapless puppy approached, then he snarled and gobbled it so fast he began to choke. Without thinking, Elv patted his back. Pollo turned, lips drawn. He was about to bite, but Elv quickly withdrew her hand, more for his sake than hers. If he bit her, he'd be euthanized.

"You are one stupid fuck," she told him.

Pollo looked up. That was the single word he seemed to recognize. Elv saw inside his yellow eyes. He wasn't a chicken. He was broken. She put another biscuit down, even though they weren't supposed to give their dogs treats unless a command was obeyed.

"Don't feel sorry for him," Adrian told her when she spied the breach in training etiquette. "I'm serious, Missy. Anybody ever help you out by feeling sorry for you?"

ELV SPENT SIX months working with Pollo, five hours a day. *He's the smartest of the dogs,* she wrote to Natalia. *When you talk to him, he really listens.* Her loneliness abated when she worked with him. He had emerged from the savagery of his life with great dignity. Elv felt like weeping in his presence. When she looked at his scars, she was ashamed of the human race. She went to the library and found out everything she could about pit bulls and American Staffordshire terriers and bull terriers and the history of dogfighting. She researched wolves and their styles of communicating. She borrowed volumes of psychology, especially methods of behavioral training. She read B. F. Skinner and *My Dog Tulip* and *Lad a Dog* and *Travels with Charlie* and *Lassie.* She hadn't read since Westfield. She'd forgotten how much she'd loved *The Scarlet Letter,* how it had given her such hope in the New Hampshire darkness.

The librarian who came to deliver new books every two weeks began to set aside ones she thought Elv might like.

"You're a serious reader," the librarian observed. Elv had grabbed a copy of *Oliver Twist* because there was a photo of a bull terrier on the cover. She recalled that Meg had read all of Dickens one year.

"My sister was the reader," Elv told the librarian. "Not me."

For the last two months of his training, Pollo slept beside Elv's bunk. Elv's cellmate at the time, who went by the name of Miracle, was in on charges of drug possession, prostitution, and forgery. She wasn't afraid of much, but she had been terrified of Pollo at first.

"You know I hate dogs, Missy," she said to Elv. "I bet he's

going to give us fleas. And what if I step on him in the middle of the night?" Miracle wanted to know. "Maybe he'll freak out and bite me. I don't even know how he can be so ugly."

"I know he looks ugly," Elv agreed. "But he's not. His inside is different from his outside."

Miracle was overweight and had problems with her teeth. She knew what it was like to be called ugly. She gazed at Pollo and reconsidered. "Okay. But the first time he starts scratching, he goes. You know he's just a substitute." Miracle nodded to the wall where Elv had taped up several photos of Lorry.

"No one's a substitute for him," Elv said.

"Yeah. Right. Wait till you start talking baby talk to that dog."

Being together twenty-four hours a day was part of the bonding Adrian insisted was necessary for a dog's rehabilitation. But perhaps it was too much for the human side of the equation. Elv would reach out at night and feel him there. "Hey, baby," she whispered, not wanting to wake Miracle or prove her right. For the first time since she and Lorry had been apart, Elv felt consoled. She'd done such terrible things no one could forgive her, except perhaps for another sorrowful creature who understood the effects of human cruelty, who could lie down beside her and know she hadn't meant any harm.

AFTER EIGHT MONTHS there was an open house to find the dogs new homes. It was held outside in the yard, where the setting seemed more like a park than a prison. *What I really want to do,* Elv had written to her grandmother, *is take him home with me. You can't imagine how smart a dog can be. He senses what I feel before I do. He knows what I think.* Natalia had written back that Claire's dog and the cat Elv had rescued from the river had a strange alliance. When they thought no one was at home, they sat

together on the couch by the window, peering out at the courtyard. As soon as the key turned in the door, they jumped off the
couch so that no one would see their attachment. Dogs and cats
had their secrets too.

People came to watch the inmates put the dogs through their
paces. Elv wanted to show off how clever Pollo was, but she also
wanted him to fail. Some of the younger dogs refused to obey
commands, and one German shepherd barked the entire time,
but Pollo never took his eyes off Elv. The better he was, the more
brokenhearted she became. It was spring and the air was soft.
That made things worse. It was a bad time for Elv. The audience
applauded as though they were watching a real dog show.
"Fuck," Elv said to herself. Something else she would love and
lose. Pollo looked at her, bewildered. She wanted to pluck him
up, run like hell, jump into the back of one of the townspeople's
cars. *Get us out of here,* she would plead. *Get us to Lorry.* But she
didn't even know where he was. She hadn't heard from him in a
month. At this point she probably would just stand outside the
prison door, unsure of which way to go.

After the presentation, inmates and visitors had cookies and
lemonade. Elv figured Pollo was so ugly no one would want him.
She'd already plotted how she could present his case to Adrian.
He could be a useful therapy dog with the inmates, then when
Elv got out, she'd take him with her. But to her distress, a guest
came over right away. He crouched down and petted Pollo as if
he was a regular dog, one that hadn't had his legs broken with a
baseball bat, hadn't experienced the treachery of men.

Pollo tolerated the guy petting his head, keeping one eye fixed
on Elv.

"Nice dog," he said. "Hey, poochie."

"You don't want him," Elv said.

"His scars give him character." The man stood and shook

Elv's hand. He owned a used record store in Ossining. He thought it would be fun to have a dog hanging out with him all day, plus it would be a great deterrent against robberies.

"Want to live with me?" he asked Pollo. "I'll order us a pepperoni pizza. And we'll hang out on the couch."

Adrian Bean had come up behind them. "He'd love it. We'll go over the training rules with you. No sitting on the furniture. No table scraps."

"No pizza? Not even the crusts? What kind of life is that?"

Adrian laughed and ignored Elv's reproachful glances. "We want him to stay the well-behaved gentleman that he is. Right, Missy?" she said to Elv.

The record store owner went with Adrian to fill out all the paperwork, then came back, leash in hand. "I want to thank you for doing such a great job training him," he said to Elv. "Right, Raleigh?" he said to Pollo. When Elv gave him a look, he went on to explain. "I thought he deserved a better name, so I'm naming him after my grandfather. They kind of look alike."

Elv laughed in spite of herself.

"Don't worry. Raleigh's going to love being at the store. He'll be my buddy."

After the leash was clipped on, the dog continued to watch Elv. He didn't move.

"Go with him," she told Pollo.

He kept staring.

"Go on," Elv said. She looked away. "Go."

Pollo did as he was told. That's what she'd trained him to do. Elv went back to her cell. She was sick to her stomach, too anxious to sit still. She picked a fight with Miracle and they didn't speak for weeks, until Elv at last apologized.

"You got attached to that stupid dog," Miracle said with understanding. "That's your whole problem, Missy. You get attached to things." She had heard Elv crying over Lorry in the night. "The dog took the place of your man and now you're back to square one. Brokenhearted."

Elv decided she wasn't going to participate in the training program again. She hadn't even thought she had a heart anymore, but it kept getting broken. She asked to be reassigned to the laundry. But Adrian entered her as a candidate for the next training program without consulting her. Elv went to the first session to tell Adrian to mind her own business, then she saw the dog that was supposed to be hers. Once again, it was the ugliest. A standard poodle that had been scalded with boiling water, tied up in a dark room for months.

"I don't know about this one," Adrian told her. "In all honesty, it might be better to put it out of its misery."

The poodle was hiding under a chair, shaking. Its teeth were chattering.

Elv sat on the chair where the poodle was hiding. She didn't know why she was allowed to be alive. Maybe that was her fate, to know she wasn't worthy of anything and yet be given another chance. "Fine," she said to Adrian. "I'll stay."

It was raining on the day of her release, a bleak November. More than three years had passed and she hadn't seen him—she hadn't even heard from him this past year—but when she spied him it was as if she had seen him the day before. He was outside waiting in the rain. He didn't have an umbrella or that black hat he used to wear. "Hey, baby," he called just when she feared he might not recognize her. Elv felt embarrassed over what she must look like and what she had become. When you worked in the laundry, they made you cut your hair to chin length so it wouldn't get caught in the pressing machines, and hers was still growing out. She was wearing the dumpy clothes they'd given her, a skirt and blouse made of some miserable wrinkly fabric and a light-weight coat. He came to kiss her and didn't stop. He told her he'd tried to get over her, but it had been impossible. All he had to do was think about the first time he'd seen her, the look on her face, the tall grass, her hair flying out behind her and he fell for her all over again.

The rain was coming down harder. They backed away from each other at last and laughed at how drenched they were. They got into the car, a much better one than the one he'd had before, a BMW.

"You're rich," Elv said.

"I keep my promises," he told her. "You know that."

Rain splattered the windshield. He pulled her onto his lap and reached under her skirt, slid off her underwear and fucked her right there, their clothes rain-soaked, the windows of the car foggy. Three years had passed and it was still the same between them. Miracle had warned Elv that he probably wouldn't wait for her, or if he did, she'd be the one to want someone new, but Miracle had been wrong. If Elv believed in friendship, she would have written and said *So there* to Miracle. *Love does exist,* she would have told her. *Believe it or not.* Elv didn't ask where he'd been or if there had been anyone else. She didn't need to know those things. She and Lorry were beyond that.

They drove away quickly. Elv asked how he'd known she was getting out and he grinned. He said, "I called your old friend." When Elv looked puzzled, he added, "Pete Smith. He said he'd look out for you, and he did." Pete had gotten her into Bedford Hills rather than an upstate prison; he'd been the one who had recommended her for the dog training program, plus he'd taken Lorry's calls so that he could report about her situation even though he thought she'd be better off without him. She supposed he had been a friend to her. Her only one. The last time he came to see her, in the week before the release, she'd thanked him for visiting her so faithfully. She hadn't expected him to. He'd enjoyed their visits. And then right out of the blue he said, "She knew it was an accident. Your mother didn't blame you." Elv had been taken aback. He always did that, in the middle of a normal conversation he'd bring up something that had broken your heart. She wondered if he'd done that in the diner, on his first date with her mother, if he'd won her over because he could see through people to their core.

"Yeah, well, Claire does," Elv had reminded him.

"Oh, no," Pete told her. "You couldn't be more wrong. She blames herself."

THEY WENT BACK to Astoria, but Astoria was someplace completely different now that Lorry had made his fortune. "Are you for real?" Elv cried when they went upstairs to his apartment. "You really are rich!"

Two bedrooms, a brand-new kitchen, a terrace. It turned out the entire building was his. He owned it. He was the landlord now. She didn't ask Lorry how he'd managed it. All she knew was that he had traveled all over the country, from California up to Alaska, then back east through Canada and the Midwest looking to make things right. No more scams, no more con games, no robberies. In three years, all he'd done was work at jobs he hated. He'd lived in cheap hotels, talked to no one, went it alone. He got through it by thinking about her. It was funny what stayed with you and what you most remembered: the day she broke the window in her mother's bathroom and he'd taken the slivers of glass out of her hand with tweezers while she told him about the man who had abducted her and the things he'd done; the evening when he came and found her on his stoop, her clothes bloody, after the accident; the time they came upon a pond out in the woods in New Hampshire with water so cold that they screamed after they'd jumped in, then grasped at each other laughing, then found each other, not laughing at all.

Just when it seemed he wouldn't fulfill his promise to set their lives on track, he'd arrived back in New York and his luck had changed. He got off the train from Chicago, where he'd lost what was left of his money gambling on a series of sure things, and there he was at Thirty-third Street. Home sweet home. Exactly where he'd been at the age of ten, on his own. The old routes he and Hector had used had been sealed up. The gates to the lower platforms beneath the subway were mostly unreachable now. The city had decided to block off the entrances because of complaints of drugs and crime from commuters and shop owners. He stood there, jostled by the bustling crowds, dressed in the only clothes he owned. He said a prayer for his old dog and for his best friend, Hector, and for all of the others he'd known who hadn't managed to survive the rigors and grief of a life underground. He had little more than he'd had when he first arrived here. It seemed a cruel joke.

Then he saw the gate near the exit to Eighth Avenue. He had memorized all the entrances and exits long ago. This gateway was entirely new. At that moment he had nothing more to lose.

"But you did," Elv said to him. "You had me." They were in bed, entwined, spent and hot and naked. This was her favorite time to hear his story, when it was late and it seemed the rest of the world had dropped far away.

There was always more to lose, Lorry admitted. But at that moment, surrounded by his own failure, he was convinced otherwise. Three years and nothing to show for it. He should have been the one who'd gone to jail if this was all he'd managed to accomplish. He reached down, fiddled with the grating, then slid open the gate. Without thinking further, he climbed down beneath the train station. He entered that world just as he had when he was a ten-year-old runaway with so little to lay claim to in the world it seemed he had everything to gain.

It had been a long time since he'd been back. It took a while for his eyes to adjust to the dark. He went down the rusty metal rungs of one of the old ladders once used to check the tracks. The trains hadn't run here for many years. The ashy smell of the place came back to him in a rush. He felt like one of the coal miners he'd seen when he passed through Kentucky, men who'd been out in the clear air of the world but who'd never forgotten the cloying depths below.

SOMETIMES WHEN LORRY was asleep Elv lay awake just to watch him. She watched to make certain he wouldn't disappear. He reminded her of the invisible ink she'd once used to make maps of Arnelle. You had to hold it up to the light to see it; otherwise it appeared that you had only a blank page. She still had that one painting she'd done of the Seine, black wash on heavy white paper. She'd kept it all this time, hoping she would one day have a home where she could hang artwork on the walls. Now that time had come. She couldn't believe her luck. She started to think about the future and what it might bring. When she wrote to her ama, she told her they were planning to come to Paris. She would make amends. She had already decided she would never go back to using drugs. It was a different them, but when she woke in the night Elv sometimes feared their old selves were sewn to their skins with black thread, like shadows. Once she found someone's works in the bathroom, in the cabinet under the sink, wrapped in cloth and tied up with a black shoelace. Lorry was in the shower and she waited there in the steamy bathroom till he came out. He grabbed her and pulled her to him. His dark hair was slicked back. He was wet and dripping water onto her clothes. She showed him what she'd found.

"God damn that Michael," Lorry said, disgusted, quickly admitting that he'd let his brother come over one day when Elv was out. Michael had led a life of bouncing in and out of jail, but he was Lorry's brother, after all, flesh and blood. He must have left his works behind. He could tell because Michael always tied them together with a shoelace.

They ran into Michael only a few days later. He was a man now, not some punk kid, and she barely recognized him. She and Lorry were in a bar and Michael waved them over. "Stay here," Lorry told her. "You don't need to spend time with that lowlife." They'd fallen out years ago and now they argued. Lorry grabbed Michael and pulled him off his bar stool. "Don't you ever," Elv had heard him say. When Lorry stalked back to her, Michael put his fingers out and made a shooting motion at his brother's head, then he looked at Elv and grinned.

They decided Michael wouldn't be allowed up to the apartment. Soon after, Elv found some packets of heroin. She was writing a letter, and she went to the kitchen searching for an envelope and found it hidden in a box behind the cans of soup and the sugar. She sat down and looked out the window. The urge to get high rose into her mouth. The desire had a cool, rusty taste. She licked her lips. She felt confused and knotted up. She thought about how easy it would be to set the witch in lines and snort it. She was distraught to think Lorry was lying to her, but she understood. She wanted to get high too. It didn't matter, she couldn't. It was out of her hands. She thought she might be pregnant. She was convinced it had happened the first time they were together, when it was raining and they had been so desperate for each other. She didn't say anything to Lorry right away, but she watched him more carefully. She wondered if this was how Pete Smith observed the world, putting pieces together, seeing everyday life as a puzzle, examining the smallest details.

So she watched and remembered. How he pushed his plate away and wasn't hungry, how he came in exhausted and fell into bed when usually all he'd want to do was fuck her, how he was gone more often, working, he said, although at what she didn't know, how he seemed distracted, how when she wanted to go for a walk or to the movies, he'd say later, baby, as if going to sleep or lying around dreaming on the couch in the middle of the day was perfectly normal. Then he'd go out and she wouldn't know where he was. He said he played poker, had business deals, he said, *Come on, you know it's you and me.* And it was.

She took the home pregnancy test and it was positive. Her grandmother wrote that the only way to be sure was to see a doctor. She went to a nearby clinic and saw a doctor, who congratulated her. Elv took the bus home. She couldn't stop smiling. She stopped on a corner and called her grandmother. "You're going to be a great-*grandmère!*" she cried into the phone. Her ama was overjoyed. They chatted excitedly about names, and whether the child would be a boy or a girl. "Oh, a girl," Elv assured her. "It has to be. The Storys only have girls." When Natalia asked, "And what does Lorry say?" Elv said, "He's over the moon." But she hadn't told him yet. She had a sinking feeling. He was there when she got to the apartment, pacing. She still didn't say anything.

"Where the hell were you?" he said. When he couldn't find her, he flashed back to the day when she was picked up by the police.

"Walking," Elv told him. She felt like a liar even when she told the truth. Suspicion somehow made you an accomplice. "Where were you last night?" He hadn't gotten home till late, then had crawled into bed without even talking to her.

"This isn't about where I was," Lorry said. "Don't try to shift things around."

Elv went into the kitchen and took the heroin out of the cabinet. Lorry had followed, expecting to continue their fight. When he saw he'd been found out, he folded himself into a kitchen chair. He always said that when caught red-handed it was best to come clean. "My fatal flaw," he said sadly.

Elv opened a can of soup and began heating it up in a saucepan. She was starving.

"I'm having a baby," she said.

Lorry stared at her, thinking he'd heard wrong.

"I think it's a girl," Elv told him.

He went to the stove and wrapped his arms around her. "Elv," he said, his voice broken in a way that surprised her.

"I don't want her to have a father with a fatal flaw," Elv said reasonably.

"Got it."

"Seriously."

HE SERIOUSLY TRIED. He stopped going to bars, stopped seeing old friends with whom he had only one thing in common. But one day Elv went down to the laundry room and there he was with his brother. He and Michael had only one thing in common as well. She knew what they were doing down there.

"You're kidding me," she said.

"It's not what you think. I'm just lending him some money because he happens to be broke. Anyway, he's still my brother, right?"

Elv had other things to think about. Natalia had sent two tiny, beautiful sweaters, one white and one yellow, both made of fine merino wool, dotted with mother-of-pearl buttons. Soon after, Natalia sent a blanket she'd knitted out of a marmalade-colored cashmere. She was knitting like a madwoman, out on the bench under the chestnut tree, in the red parlor during a rainy afternoon, in her bedroom late at night. It had been so long since there had been a baby to be overjoyed about. Elv sent photos of herself pregnant and glowing. They wrote back and forth, considering names. Elv wanted a strong name, but something unique. Natalia suggested choosing a name that would work for the rest of a child's life, not too girlish, but not too grown-up. The baby would be born in the summer, and Elv vowed they would come to Paris soon after. Maybe then Claire could forgive her.

Natalia had written in one of her letters that she was worried for Claire. She wrote that she had seen a demon in the hallway hovering near Claire's bedroom and perhaps that was the cause of Claire's great unhappiness. It sounded silly. The superstitions of an old woman with poor eyesight. Other people might have thought she was crazy, but Madame Cohen had believed her, and Elv did as well. She herself had often spied something in her own kitchen when she came for a glass of water in the middle of the night. It was probably a moth, like the onerous thing her grandmother said Madame Cohen had caught with flypaper. These stories made Elv nervous. She feared bad luck might be tapping at her window. She decided to set out salt in the corners of the room, as her grandmother said Madame Cohen advised. She dragged over a chair in order to reach the cabinet above the refrigerator. That was where the salt was kept, but she found more than that. She found everything he was hiding from her. She took it all down the hall to the incinerator.

She heard him rumbling around in the kitchen that night. But he never said a word about what she had done. He took a shower and came to bed. If he was back to his King Kong habit, he'd be sick and she'd know and they'd have to deal with it together.

"You wouldn't lie to me, right?" Elv asked him. It was snowing. All the lights were turned off, but the world outside was bright.

He took up more than his share of the bed, but Elv didn't care.

"Define lie," he said.

They both laughed.

"I'm not stupid," Lorry told her. "I heard what you said."

"Repeat it."

"No fatal flaws."

"And you'll tell me the truth."

"I'm madly in love with you."

"Very good," Elv said. "I knew you were smart."

When she woke the next morning, he was gone. She stayed where she was. She felt her love for him in a place that was so deep she was sure most people wouldn't understand it. By the time it had grown light, he was back. He shook the snow off, took off his clothes, got back in beside her. He had brought her a bunch of roses wrapped in brown paper, the kind they sold outside the market. She told herself that was the reason he had left their bed, to walk through the snow in the pale light, to bring her roses, despite the weather, to come back to her when she needed him most.

HE WAS LATE one Friday night. It was cold, the middle of February, and she was three months pregnant. They had painted the second bedroom a creamy yellow that reminded Elv of the heirloom tomatoes her mother used to have in the garden. She remembered all of their names: Livingston's Golden Queen, Jubilees, yellow Brandywine. Elv had found a cookbook in a junk shop that included the first written recipe for tomato sauce, published in Naples in 1692, a Spanish-style concoction made with thyme. Her mother would have gotten a kick out of that. Elv was fixing the sauce for dinner, to be served with homemade pasta. She had been surprised to discover she could cook; it came to her naturally. She added tomatoes to just about everything. It had become a joke between her and Lorry—her new addiction, her fatal flaw. "Oh no, baby," she teased him and said what she always told him, "that would be you." She thought it was sunny enough on their little terrace to start a container garden in the spring; tomatoes and nothing else. She'd eaten so many already that she wondered if their baby would have red hair, if she'd have a preference for that color and if they'd have to repaint the nursery.

It was 1:00 A.M., then it was 2:00. Elv didn't eat the dinner she'd prepared. Her nerves were shot. She wished she still smoked. She wished she could sleep. She wished he hadn't left in the first place, kissing her, telling her he'd be back for supper. Lorry didn't answer his cell phone, so she bundled up and went down to the closest bar, a place called MacDougal's that was open after hours. No one had seen him, so she went back home. Snow had begun to fall. It was a bleak, cold winter. The sky was always black. The roads were probably bad. She called around and woke up several of his friends, men she didn't like or trust. Most of them didn't answer the phone. The one who did told her not to worry.

At 3:00 A.M. she phoned Pete Smith, hauling him out of bed to answer.

"I was stupid to call. Go back to sleep," she told him.

Pete was already pulling on his clothes, his socks and shoes.

He'd been dreaming about Annie and then all at once her daughter had called.

"Let me check around," he said.

"No, forget it. I'm sure he's fine." Elv had bitten her nails to the quick; rims of blood circled each one. They had both disappointed people, but never each other. He didn't just disappear. But that wasn't true, not really, it was only that he always came back. Elv thought of the three years he'd been gone, and all the things they'd agreed never to talk about. Her dread intensified. Pete phoned after an hour. He'd called around to a couple of people he'd worked with in the department and also to some local hospitals and hadn't found out anything. He was sure to know something soon. Certainly by morning.

But in the morning, there was still no news. Elv went out looking. She asked one of the old ladies on the street who had known Lorry forever and she said, "Try Marguerite's." Elv stared. "You know, Mimi." Elv felt shaken to think there was another woman, until the old lady added, "His grandmother's grave. You know—Our Lady of Sorrow."

Elv walked through the snow. It was a small cemetery behind a churchyard. She asked the caretaker where she could find Lorry's grandmother's grave. It was fairly new; his grandmother had only died the previous winter. There was a holly plant someone had left, the pot wrapped in bright foil. Elv hadn't even known Lorry had a grandmother. She felt undone and confused. She wished she could call her mother, ask her what to do. She had phoned his pals, gone to his haunts, come up with nothing. When she went to the bars, the way the men had looked at her, then glanced away, made her know they wouldn't have told her anything if they had known where he was. Her suspicions were confirmed by their casual replies, their clear desire to be rid of her. So that was it. He'd been using drugs, they all had. Not a single one would have told her the truth.

When Lorry still wasn't home that afternoon, she went out and got on the subway to go to her scheduled doctor's appointment. She went right past her stop, into Manhattan. She felt crazy and lost. She got off at Penn Station. She followed the trail he had told her about, wandering through the crowd, desperate to find him. At last there it was, the grated gate to the otherworld, just beyond the stairs leading up to Eighth Avenue. She went over, leaned hard against it, pushed. It swung open. There was a stair, a metal rung, just as he'd said.

She slipped down onto the rusty ladder. The darkness smelled foul. Soil, shit, ash, flood, mold, smoke. She let her eyes adjust. The bustle of Penn Station was only inches away, but the darkness was endless. A person could slip into it and get lost. She felt a twinge inside her. Her stomach flip-flopped. How could anyone survive this? She held on to the ladder. Anything could be down below, a horde of demons. There might be rats, wild dogs, giants. "Lorry," she called plaintively. Her voice came back to her, mocking her desperation with its echo. "Lorry," she cried until her voice was wrecked.

She went back up aboveground and found the public toilet. People were all but living there. An old woman had made a bed out of newspapers that she'd carefully laid out on the tiles. People stepped over her as though she wasn't there. Elv washed her hands. In the mirror her face looked blotchy. Her eyes were rimmed red. A woman and her child were washing themselves thoroughly, as if the sink was their bathtub. "There you go, baby," the woman said to her little girl as she dunked her face in the water. "Clean as can be."

When Elv got back to their street, she noticed police cars from the 114th Precinct. She went inside, then took the stairs. From the hallway she could see that the door to their apartment had been flung open. Two cops were inside and Michael was there as well, sitting on the couch, his coat thrown down beside him, as if he owned the place. Pete Smith was waiting for her. He took her by the arm before she could go inside and led her down the hall so he could have a word with her. He was still wearing his gray coat and his hat; the same middle-aged sad-looking guy she'd called and woken from a dead sleep even though he didn't owe her a thing.

"What the hell is this?" Elv said. "They can't just be in there."

She couldn't stop thinking about that little girl at Penn Station. She felt choked up and confused. Everything on the surface was flooding away. Everything seemed raw and brutal and immediate.

"He was at an apartment around the corner," Pete said. "His brother found him."

"Good," Elv said. "That sounds close by."

"Elv."

"I'm going to kill him for worrying me. I went all the hell over the city. You wouldn't believe the places I went." She still had rust stains on her hands from the rungs of the ladder to the otherworld. She had ashes on the soles of her boots.

"Are you listening to me, kiddo? It's not good."

Elv looked at Pete, then glanced into the apartment. "He got busted, right? We have to get him out of jail."

Pete embraced her and then she knew what she'd already known last night when he didn't show up, when the snow was falling and he hadn't called to say *Don't worry, baby.* "I'm sorry," Pete said, which was the stupid remark people said when things were irrevocable, when you'd lost the only thing you cared about in this world.

"You're completely wrong," Elv said. Lorry had to be somewhere.

He had his coat on when they found him, Pete told her. He was ready to leave and go home when he overdosed. He had that black cap of his and a sack of groceries from the market and a dozen roses, the kind that were so resistant to cold weather they were often kept on the sidewalk in plastic bins, the kind he'd brought her on the night when she knew the saucers of salt wouldn't protect the two of them from evil. Pete held her while she sobbed. She had never sounded like that. She didn't even know where the noise was coming from if not from the other-world, the scream she would have cried so long ago if she hadn't been tied up with ropes, her mouth stuffed with bread so no one could hear her.

Everyone could hear her now.

Confession

The wolf came to me at midnight and stood below my window. He had chased the innocent, defiled the sacred, run after horses and carriages, caused the snow to turn red with blood. He had an arrow in his side. He was the one bleeding now.

I told him it would hurt, and to shut his eyes. I took out the arrow, cleaned the wound, gave him supper. People in the village said he devoured me then, left only my boots in the snow. They said it would teach the other girls a lesson, and maybe it did. From where I lived in the woods I could hear them calling at night. I wondered what lesson they'd learned.

THE SEASON HAD BEEN COLDER THAN USUAL AND THERE WERE many deaths in the city. The cold crept inside rooms, and Paris filled with people wearing long black coats. Tourists could not believe this was the city they had dreamed of visiting. They locked themselves in their hotel rooms and drank hot coffee, wishing they were back in New Jersey or Idaho. It was a season of grief and broken hearts, and in many apartments the heat gave out altogether. Children were covered with layers of wool blankets at night; in the mornings, they held steaming cups of cocoa to warm their hands. Several sparrows froze solid on the branches of the chestnut tree in Natalia's courtyard and had to be shaken from their perches with the swipe of a broom handle.

Shiloh died in his sleep one morning as the dark was lifting. Claire woke suddenly. Clouds of her breath formed in the chilly air. Nothing felt alive. Usually the birds were chattering at this hour, waking in the dreamy silver light. But now they had all been swept up into a dustpan, deposited in the bin in the courtyard along with potato peelings and newspapers.

Though he'd grown old, Shiloh had insisted on following Claire until the end. When his feet began to drag on the sidewalks, Natalia fashioned boots for him out of leather. For a while he was steadier. People in the neighborhood applauded when he managed to haul himself down the street. Shiloh struggled, but his downfall was imminent. In the end, his hips and legs gave out. It became difficult to wake him in the mornings. His breathing rattled, his eyes were milky. Soon he'd stopped eating his supper. Now he was gone. Claire wrenched herself out of bed and went to lie beside him on the carpet. She had been fifteen when her mother brought him home. She remembered writing *Take him back*.

In the kitchen, where she was fixing a pot of coffee, Natalia heard a plaintive sound. She thought it was a bird, then remembered they were all gone. As she went along the hallway the cry grew louder. She was led to the bedroom door. It was locked. When Claire at last came out, she was wearing boots and the jacket her mother used to wear in the garden. Her face was pale and grim.

"Where are you going?" Natalia followed along behind her granddaughter. She had suspected Claire might do something rash when this time came, something on impulse. She had already phoned Leah to ask her advice. Madame Cohen had assured her that help was on the way.

"I'm going to bury him," Claire told her grandmother.

"We don't have a shovel," Natalia said, hoping to dissuade her. This was what grave diggers were for, to take grief into their capable hands. Surely there was such a service for animals.

"There are shovels in the shed," Claire said.

The landlord kept tools locked up in a little wooden lean-to in the courtyard; tenants were forbidden from using them, but Claire didn't care. She went downstairs, picked up a rock, and smashed the lock on the shed until it yielded. Stringy cobwebs and rusted garden implements greeted her. A few frozen carcasses still littered the courtyard: wren, sparrow, pigeon, dove. Claire grabbed one of the old shovels and slammed the shed door shut. Icicles fell and shattered into blue sparks.

When Claire turned, three young men were standing behind her. They were so unexpected she took a step back. They were tall and all three had shovels. They weren't there by accident. Madame Cohen had sent over her younger grandsons. All were in medical school. The older grandsons were already doctors and unavailable for dog burials, but these three would do. Claire had not seen any of them since they were children, so the eldest introduced himself and his brothers.

"Where do you want it?" Émile, the first grandson, asked. He was known to be the serious one. He said what he meant. People thought he might be a psychiatrist one day.

"Not 'it,' " Claire said. "He."

Claire decided the first grandson was an idiot. She pointed to the chestnut tree. There was a patch of soil between the tree trunk and the cobbled courtyard. Émile and the second brother, Gérald, began to dig. Gérald hummed. People thought he would work in the lab. He was a fool as well. The third of Madame Cohen's grandsons followed Claire upstairs to help bring Shiloh down. He was the youngest, the tallest, and the most awkward. He nodded a hello to Madame Rosen, banging his head on the low kitchen doorway as he followed Claire to the bedroom to retrieve Shiloh. The German shepherd looked crumpled and much smaller than he had in life. It took all of Claire's restraint not to throw herself down beside him.

"I'll take care of this," the third grandson said. This was Philippe, who had once balanced china cups on top of one another in the back room of the shop, carefully constructing a tower, until they'd all come crashing down. He'd made the flyswatter out of a rubber band and marbles. He was full of ideas. People thought he would someday invent a cure for some terrible and debilitating disease. Madame Cohen had specifically told him to carry the dog downstairs for Claire.

The entrance to the room was narrow and Philippe hit his elbows getting in the door. Claire worried that he wouldn't be able to carry the dog downstairs, but he seemed sure of himself. He carefully picked up the body, which he hoisted over his shoulder. His actions were surprisingly tender for someone so uncoordinated.

"You go first," Philippe told Claire, not wanting her to see the way a body looked after death, the hardening of the jaw and limbs. "I'll follow."

The three brothers buried Shiloh. As medical students they'd seen worse and done worse, but it was still a sad business. Claire's tears fell down onto the cobblestones. She seemed fierce and unreachable. When the grandsons were done, they stood there uncomfortably for a while, clothes splattered with dirt. They all had lectures to attend, yet they stared at one another, lingering. Their grandmother had forbidden them to be rude, and because they were rude by nature they didn't know whether or not it was now a proper time to leave. Philippe had been told in no uncertain terms to watch his manners. Natalia came down with glasses and a pitcher of water, which the brothers gulped down, then she discreetly told them they could go.

Philippe went up to Claire, though her silence seemed fearsome. His grandmother had told him not to be tricked by how standoffish she might seem. Claire's hands were stuffed in her pockets. She had slipped on a pair of dark glasses so no one could see that her eyes were red.

"Heart failure doesn't feel like anything," Philippe told her. "Just so you know. He went to sleep and didn't wake up. No sensation. No pain."

Claire nodded, grateful for the explanation. When Madame Cohen's grandsons left, having returned the shovel to the garden shed and repaired the lock, Claire remained in the courtyard. She sat vigil beside the grave until the end of the day, when her grandmother coaxed her back inside.

She returned to work the next day. She didn't speak much, but she did her job. Then she had tea with Madame Cohen in the back room.

"What did you think of my grandsons?" Madame Cohen asked.

"They were helpful."

"A pot holder is helpful," Madame Cohen replied. "Otherwise you'd burn your hand. None of them impressed you?"

"I thought one of them might not manage to carry Shiloh downstairs, but he did."

"Philippe," Madame Cohen said. She was glad that he'd done a good job. "Would you like to see him again?"

"Not really." Claire was always honest with her employer.

Frankly, she didn't wish to see anyone. After Shiloh's death, people in the neighborhood became accustomed to seeing her alone. Even the coldest among them worried for her. In the markets, they offered bargains meant only for the best customers. Vendors sent her home with bunches of flowers for her grandmother. In the spice shop, she was plied with candied fruits. A Monsieur Abetan, who had an antiquities shop filled with knickknacks and junk, gave her an amulet he vowed would bring her luck, but she only stuck the talisman in the top drawer of the bureau in the parlor, where it sat alongside the mints and the toothpicks.

People wondered if Claire had ever fallen in love or walked arm in arm with a friend. She had become a cautionary tale, pitied, whispered about. Some of the older women kept butterfly nets in their shopping bags, ready and able to defend her should a demon happen to appear as she went walking by.

When spring arrived, Claire continued to wear her coat and boots. She was the one person in Paris who dreaded the end of winter. The white flowers blooming on the chestnut tree in her grandmother's courtyard were anathema to her. They made her think of the lost and the dead. They no longer carried the scent of almonds. Instead, when she breathed in there was the stink of bitterroot, sulfur. She wished for snow, rain, turtle-green skies. She had the feeling children sometimes do when they're awakened by a nightmare and desperately yearn for someone to tell them their dreamworld doesn't exist in real life. Claire had always crept into bed with Elv to beg for a story when that happened to her. *Once upon a time there was a little girl who needed to go to sleep,* Elv would begin, no matter how sleepy she herself was. *Nothing could harm her and no one could find her and she was always safe.*

SPRING IN NEW YORK was exceptionally beautiful. The trees in Central Park were a liquid green. When the wind shook the branches, pockets of green showered the ground. There were splotches falling onto the pages of Elv's book, a crisscross of pollen and print. She was sitting on a bench outside the zoo. She was noticeably pregnant by the end of the season. Women going past often stopped to congratulate her. She smiled, thanked them, then returned her attentions to her book. She was reading about children the same way she had once devoured information about dogs. She knew absolutely nothing about them. They were an utter mystery. How had her mother ever managed the three of them, so close in age? How had she known how to cure a fever, a bee sting, a spider's bite? How to make a bed, fix a perfect grilled cheese and tomato sandwich, pour a glass of milk without spilling a drop? *You'll understand everything you need to when your child is born,* Elv's ama had written to her. *Don't worry so much.* But she hadn't understood how to be a daughter or a sister or the beloved of a man who couldn't turn away from his fatal flaw. How could she ever understand a child?

She was in a bad way after Lorry. Her grief was immense, overpowering. It didn't help that she had to leave their apartment. The building Lorry owned turned out to have been an inheritance from his grandmother, and it went directly to his brother upon his death. Michael sent a notarized letter asking Elv to move out, although he allowed her to stay until after the funeral. It was held at Our Lady of Sorrow. There was a surprisingly large crowd, all his hoodlum friends who had done nothing to save him, the old ladies who had adored him when he was a boy, the cousins he'd never mentioned. One of those cousins had looked stunned when Elv mentioned foster homes. "Lorry and Michael were never in foster homes. Their grandmother raised them. I don't know what you're talking about! She was a saint. Their parents were in a house fire, and Mimi took them in. She did a great job. It was this neighborhood that got to them, all the drugs floating around."

She heard another cousin talking about how good Lorry had been to his grandmother. He'd lived with her for the last three years of her life and had taken excellent care of the old lady, shoveling snow, maintaining the building, making certain she got to her doctor's appointments. People said that on the last day of her life Mimi was seen on the street for the first time in months. Lorry had carried her downstairs so she could sit on a bench in the sunlight. She had waved at everyone who passed by. She was a good-natured, friendly woman who had butted into everyone's business and wished everyone well. Lorry had been the light of her life. "Good-bye," she had called in a small voice, until the sunlight began to fade and Lorry took her back to her top-floor apartment.

Elv wore a black coat and high boots and a black scarf to the funeral. The weather was dreadful and the church seemed unheated. She didn't know the priest or the other mourners. Pete Smith had driven her and was waiting in his parked car on the street. She went up to Michael, one of many who waited in a long line to offer him their sympathies. Everyone acted as if Elv was a stranger. There'd been many women before her, and several of Lorry's old flames were in attendance, weeping, gathering in sad little groups.

"I told you he was a mistake," Michael said. "You should have listened."

"I didn't know about your grandmother," Elv said.

"That was Lorry. You never knew what to believe."

"Did he talk to you much about his life underground?" Elv asked.

Michael said something to a friend of Lorry's who was standing nearby and they both laughed. Then Michael took Elv by the arm. It had been a long time since they had both been at Westfield, sneaking cigarettes behind the stable. They walked away from the crowd, stopping beneath one of the pine boughs that was drooping, snow-laden.

"What did he tell you?" Michael wanted to know.

Elv shrugged, suddenly embarrassed. Everything between her and Lorry had been private, a world big enough for two.

"Did he tell you that bullshit about how he lived with the Mole People?"

"No," Elv said, defensive. She had a lump in her throat. Sometimes all of New York City smelled ashy, the way it had been underground below Penn Station. "He just told me some stories."

"Yeah, he was good at that. He liked telling people what they wanted to hear," Michael said fondly. "That was my brother. My grandmother raised us and we paid her back by being wiseasses and getting into trouble. I've gotta say he made up for it at the end. He took good care of her."

"Right," Elv said, dazed.

"One thing that's true. I never saw him with another woman after he got together with you."

"Now you're probably bullshitting me." She glanced up, trying to gauge whether or not she could really believe him. She seriously didn't know what to believe anymore.

"I mean it. It was you, Elv."

She glanced away. She felt burning hot standing there in the snow. "Thank you," she said.

"I wouldn't go that far. If it wasn't for me, you never would have met him, so I guess I'm to blame for the whole thing. The least I can do is be honest with you. Plus, you wrote a good term paper."

Elv tried to smile. "Right," she said again.

SHE OFTEN SPENT time in Central Park after he was gone. She had a ritual of taking the subway in on Sundays after she visited his grave. By now the lilacs in the park were abloom. The air was soft with humidity. Elv read for a while, then closed her book and strolled along the paths. The air smelled like hay and manure, jungle smells wafting up from the zoo. She yearned for the sound of wolves, but in the warm weather they had always hunkered down in the shade of the rocks, silent and wary. It was only in winter that you could hear them howling, the plaintive call sounding like unrequited love. Sometimes she felt Lorry was beside her, walking with her, although he would never be so quiet. He was a talker and she had loved listening to him. She had asked for stories and that was what he'd given her. She missed him so much she couldn't think of anything but him. That's what love was. That's what it had turned out to be. She stopped at the entrance to the underpass where they used to meet during the winter she lived with her grandmother. It was filthy in there, pitch-dark. Elv was afraid to go farther. She saw a bundle of rags. It seemed as if someone was living there. She walked around it, through the green glint of light cast by the trees, past the patch of woods where Lorry said he'd buried his dog. She always stopped there and said a prayer. She wasn't even certain how to pray, but she did her best. Claire was better at it; she'd known what to say, whereas Elv had needed to invent words, she'd needed a whole new language to even begin to get across what she felt.

Not far away was the meadow where the horse had fallen on the runaway day so long ago. Elv had gotten out of the police car and walked across the lawn. She hadn't felt afraid. That was the amazing thing. She'd usually been so scared, but when she was with Claire her fear abated. Her sister had been in the upended carriage, watching, sure of her. Claire had understood why Elv had fallen to her knees. She knew what it was like to carry the past wherever you went, sewn to your skin. Elv wished her sister was with her now, sprawled out in the grass, underneath the lacework pattern of shadows. She was afraid, and she wanted to be with someone who loved her, but since she couldn't think of who that might be, she lay down in the grass by herself and finished reading her book.

THE SUMMER WAS exceedingly hot. Elv still tried to get to the cemetery every day, but her ankles were swelling and the trip was getting more difficult. She had to take two buses from the apartment Pete had found for her in Forest Hills. It was a nice neighborhood. A nice building. Her grandmother helped with the rent, sending a check every month. Elv took photographs of herself pregnant and sent them to Natalia in return. She wrote to her grandmother each week, short, cheerful letters. She didn't let on that she was exhausted or that she suffered from excruciating bouts of loneliness.

At the cemetery there were concrete benches along the narrow paths behind the rectory and very little sunlight. Hostas and ferns grew but not much else. It was the sort of dark garden where there were spiderwebs and peepers in the damp gulleys even though it was in the middle of the city, with buses rumbling by on the other side of the walls. Elv asked the grounds crew if she could pay to have a rosebush planted, but they said it would be a waste of time. There wasn't any sun behind the church, and the high walls wouldn't let in enough light.

Pete Smith had found her a job as well as an apartment, not an easy task to accomplish considering that she was a pregnant woman with no education or skills. She worked at an animal shelter. She did intakes and fed the dogs and took them for walks and checked references and referrals. Elv soon taught herself how to type and use the word processor. But she preferred to spend time with the dogs. She tried some of the training techniques she had learned from Adrian Bean, and several seemingly hopeless cases were adopted after she'd had a hand in their training. It was soothing not to be with people, to accomplish something on the dogs' behalf. They watched her with their dark eyes, waiting patiently for her attention. When they whimpered, Elv crooned to them in a sweet, high voice. She sang to them when she took them out in the shelter's small yard in the evenings before she went home. Sometimes the children who lived in the apartment house behind the shelter swore they heard faeries singing. They opened their windows and leaned their elbows on the sills, but all they could see were brick walls, a crisscross of telephone wires, the darkening sky, a woman tossing a ball for a few dogs.

When Elv thought about Pollo, the first dog she'd trained, she felt a sharp pang of loss. She guessed that if she had to write down the most important quality in a person or a dog, it would be loyalty. All the rest didn't matter. That's what she'd come to believe. It didn't matter at all.

She thought a lot about Meg. She wished she could sit down and talk to her, knowing what she knew now. She wished she could trade places with her, that she could wake the dead, unwind time. One night she dreamed of Meg, who was exactly the same, only she couldn't speak. *Se nom brava gig,* Elv said in the language she'd forgotten in her waking life. Dream talk should have worked in a dream, but Meg disappeared and no one answered her. Elv woke up in a sweat. It occurred to her then that she had invented Arnish because she couldn't speak. She had accused Meg of being jealous, but she'd been the jealous one. She was jealous that Meg didn't know what she knew, that some sins were unspeakable and unpardonable.

Pregnant women have urges, and Elv had the urge to go back to Westfield. She kept thinking about the red leaves, the way the snow had fallen as if she were in a snow globe, the rabbits she would see early in the morning, the hawks that perched in the trees. She took the bus from Forty-second Street one day, only a few weeks before her due date. It was a longer ride than she'd imagined, and once she'd had to ask the bus driver to pull over so she could get out and be sick by the side of the road. The bus was hot and stuffy, and the ride into the mountains was bumpy. She got out in the town, which was still just as small and as dead as it had been when she'd been trapped in New Hampshire. She went to the taxi stand and told the sole driver she wanted to go to the Westfield School. It had been closed for years, he said. Everything had been sold, including the horses; the buildings had been abandoned. There'd been a lawsuit and the state had stepped in, and no one had ever bought the property when it was put up at auction.

Elv walked over to the town hall and the clerk helped her track down the couple who'd taken Jack, the old horse she'd loved. They kept him in a field, and there was a small barn for him in the winter. The wife said it would be fine if she visited and gave her instructions on how to get to their farm. It wasn't a far walk, down the road a mile and a half. When Elv got to the field she was transported back to the day when the grass was so green, when Lorry walked toward her and the rest of the world dropped away. She stood at the fence. There was Jack, his big head bowed, grazing on meadow grass.

"Hey," Elv said. She got up onto the first rung of the fence and clucked her tongue. There were gnats and blackflies in the air. Everything smelled like grass. Jack came shambling over. "Hey there, buddy. It's me. Elv."

The old horse rubbed his big head against her. His back was swayed but he looked beautiful against the sky. The woman who'd bought him waved and came down the driveway. She was an animal lover and couldn't have poor Jack taken away for horsemeat. The other horses had all been sold to riding stables around the state, but no one had wanted Jack because he was so old.

"I think he remembers you," she said to Elv. Jack was eating out of Elv's hands. She'd brought along a package of oatmeal cookies she'd purchased at the general store in town. Claire had said that cookies were what the horses at the stable in North Point Harbor liked best.

"Nah," Elv said. "He wouldn't remember me. My sister was a rider. Not me. I just liked horses. He looks happy here."

The woman gave Elv a lift back to town. She waited in the shade for the bus and thought about the pond where she and Lorry had swam, how he had fucked her in the car and in the water, how she hadn't wanted to go back to school, how she'd been so young and stupid and so unlucky and lucky all at the same time. When the bus came, she got on slowly. Her ankles were enormously swollen, and she was tired. She wouldn't return to this town. She was never going to ride down dirt roads searching for that pond. She was never going to see Jack again, or climb the fence to explore the grounds of the school, or find the bones of the bird necklace she'd made that night when she sat with Claire at the kitchen table. She got a seat and looked out at the trees and thought what a long way it seemed to New York, and how her mother had driven here once in a blinding snowstorm and she had refused to see her. How she'd watched from the window, too prideful to call out to her mother, too young to know how few chances there would be to do so.

SHE SPENT THE Fourth of July going from one hardware store to another in Forest Hills, searching for an air conditioner she might buy on time. Nobody trusted anybody and everything was sold out anyway. She wound up with a lousy fan that merely spread the heat around. She put cold compresses on her head and drank OJ with ice and broke out in a heat rash. Then Pete arrived with an air conditioner in his car. She said he'd done enough, she didn't want to trouble him any more, but he'd said, "That's what kids are for. To cause you trouble." So when the time came, she phoned him. It was embarrassing, but she didn't have anyone else to call. He'd waited in the hallway at Queens County, pacing, as though he were her father rather than a stranger. When they came to tell him the baby was a girl, he shouted "Hurray!" and clapped a few other men waiting in the lounge on the back, then went to phone Natalia.

"Six pounds, six ounces," he told her. "Perfect in every way."

It was the middle of the night in Paris and Natalia had been asleep, but she was grateful for Pete's call. She took out all the photographs Elv had sent her over the years. She especially loved the pregnant ones—there was one in which Elv had lifted up her shirt to show off her enormous belly. She had a beautiful grin on her face. *Tell me it won't stay this way,* she'd written to her ama. *Promise me this baby will come out.*

At first Natalia didn't tell Claire about the baby. If she tried to bring up Elv's name, Claire would shrug off the conversation or make an excuse to leave the room. Natalia hadn't pressed her, but now things had changed. She knocked on the bedroom door and Claire answered wearing a T-shirt and underwear. Her hair was knotted and she looked rumpled, but she hadn't been asleep. She'd been reading Kafka, the master of unhappiness and self-punishment, a genius when it came to revealing the many ways in which people were unable to see the fundamental nature of those closest to them. Just as Claire suspected: human beings were mysterious creatures who hid their true centers, like onions with layer after layer of translucent skin. Claire liked to read the same book over and over again until it was familiar and there were no surprises.

"Sit down," Natalia suggested after Claire had let her into the bedroom.

"I just got up," Claire said. She was pale, out of sorts, a true insomniac. She had grown bored at the shop. She knew the other salesgirls pitied her. Lucie and Jeanne both had boyfriends and social lives. They brought her more and more hand-me-downs, as if that would change her fate. Sometimes she left the bundles of clothes they brought in the bin in the courtyard without even checking to see what was inside.

The fact that her grandmother had come to talk to her now made her anxious. Claire expected bad news. It was the middle of the night, after all. She was convinced to perch at the foot of her bed and listen. Though it was July she kept the windows closed. The room was airless and hot. She didn't mind.

Natalia explained that she hadn't wanted to upset Claire by bringing up her sister's name but there was a time and a place for everything, and this was the time to tell Claire that her sister had had a child.

"She's still with him?" Claire fleetingly thought about the night she'd opened the door to find them in bed when she'd had such a terrible fever. Her face flushed.

Natalia shook her head. No, that man was gone. Dead.

"I pity the child," Claire said.

"Claire!"

"Well, I do! What do you want me to say? That I'm happy for her? That I wish her all the luck in the world?"

"You can say what you want." Natalia's face was ashen. She had never been more concerned about Claire than she was at that moment, or more ashamed. "But Elv knows how to love someone. Can you say the same for yourself?"

ELV'S LITTLE GIRL had black hair, like all the Story sisters. Her eyes, however, were dark, like her father's. Even as a newborn she could easily be comforted as soon as she heard the words *Once upon a time.* The nurses in the maternity ward had been amazed. They all declared her to be the most beautiful child ever seen in a New York City hospital, and her mother couldn't have agreed more. Elv named her Megann, for her mother and sister, but she called her Mimi, which was the name Lorry had favored.

Natalia flew to New York the week after the baby was born. She checked into her hotel in Manhattan, then took a taxi to Queens. She hadn't been back to New York for a long time, and she felt overwhelmed. She stood outside the apartment building in Forest Hills for a while, collecting herself, before she went in. She thought it would perhaps be an awkward meeting after all this time, but when Elv opened the door, she quickly embraced her grandmother. They both blinked back tears and studied each other, then laughed and studied each other again. Elv brought Natalia inside. It was a small apartment, sparsely furnished, but tidy. They went into the room where the baby was sleeping.

"Gorgeous," Natalia breathed.

"This is your ama," Elv said to the baby. She leaned over the crib and stroked Mimi's hair. "She's here to welcome you to the world."

Natalia spent a week entranced by the child. She spent so much time with Mimi that she checked out of her hotel and moved into the apartment, sleeping on the couch. One night they invited Elise and Mary Fox over. Elv was a nervous wreck. The visit went better than she might have expected. Mary worked in the ER at St. Vincent's. She had been such a studious, well-behaved girl, but as an adult she craved the excitement and chaos of the emergency room. She shook Elv's hand and said, "Long time no see," just as corny and smart as ever. Mary's mother, Elise, hugged Elv and told her she couldn't believe how strongly she'd come to resemble her mother.

"Just as pretty. And that's saying a lot."

Elv was flattered. Even when Annie was in the garden, muddy, wearing her old black jacket, she seemed more beautiful than any movie star.

They all oohed and aahed over the baby, who had turned out to be a good sleeper, something Elise assured Elv was the most important attribute of any newborn.

When the time came for Natalia to leave later in the week, it seemed too soon. Pete picked her up at Elv's apartment to drive her to the airport.

"I think our girl's holding her own," Pete said.

When he asked after Claire, who rarely answered his letters, Natalia sadly could not say the same. "She's doing the best she can, considering the circumstances."

As Pete was carrying her suitcase out to the car, Natalia embraced her granddaughter. "Now, you come see us," Natalia said.

She handed Elv an envelope. Elv looked at her quizzically. "Two tickets to Paris."

"Of course," Elv said. She thanked her ama and they both wept, but Elv knew it was unlikely she would come. Every year she planned on going to Paris and every year her plan dissolved. She and Lorry had always talked about it. She'd wanted him to see the Île de la Cité, Berthillon's ice cream shop, the chestnut tree in the courtyard. She had wanted to sit outside Notre Dame with him and let him guess which were the happy families. She wanted to take him down to the riverbank where she'd found the kitten someone had once tried to drown. After her ama left, she gazed out the window, then went to stash the envelope in a dresser drawer, beneath the sweaters that were stored away until winter.

MADAME COHEN NOTICED that something had happened to Claire after Shiloh's death. She seemed wary, like the stray dogs that gathered in the Bois de Boulogne at night. People said they were werewolves, but they were nothing of the sort. They were uncared for and abandoned, dogs left on street corners and in empty lots that gathered in packs deep inside the park. You only saw them at night, if you were foolish enough to walk along the dark paths. Their eyes glinted yellow from behind the lindens.

A year had come and gone, and then another. Claire had begun to drink alone at a café on her way home from work and once or twice had become so inebriated she hadn't been able to find her key and slept in the courtyard, under the chestnut tree.

Madame Cohen had not given up on her. She had plans for Claire even if Claire had none for herself. She still hung long strips of flypaper from the ceiling. So far she had caught forty-two demons. She was watchful, ready for those that might be lingering nearby. She had sent her grandson to the Rosens' several times to complete a series of tasks: He was to change the lightbulbs, open windows that had been shut for the winter and were now stuck, carry Martin's old armchair down for the trashman. But each time he appeared, Claire made herself scarce, hiding out in her room behind her locked door.

"I have a different job for you," Madame Cohen told Claire one day. This was part of her plan. Jeanne and Lucie were shrugging on their coats as they got ready to leave the shop, but Madame Cohen grabbed Claire and told her to wait. She scrawled down an address. "Be there tomorrow at nine."

When Madame Cohen's husband had been alive, he'd designed and crafted the jewelry in the shop, but for the past twenty years his brother, Samuel, who was called the *deuxième* Monsieur Cohen, had taken his place. His were extraordinary pieces, necklaces and rings that looked like gumdrops, or clouds, or slices of tangerine. He could no longer leave his apartment on the top floor of his building. He was eighty-eight and his legs had given out. Although he could get around in his flat with the help of two canes, the steep, circular staircase to the lobby of his apartment building was impossible.

Monsieur Cohen lived on the fringes of the Marais on a street where all his neighbors had three locks on their doors. He had constructed an elaborate alarm system for himself, made of ropes and pulleys that deployed pots and pans that could knock any potential robber unconscious. The whole place rattled when Claire knocked on the door. Monsieur Cohen had a very suspicious nature. But of course, it made sense for him to be paranoid. He had rooms full of gems.

He hadn't wanted an assistant, but Madame Cohen had convinced him he needed one. Claire would do the marketing, make his dinner before she left, sweep the floor. On the first day of her new employment Claire had to show her identification before he let her inside. After that when she knocked three times she would hear the locks being undone and the pots and pans snapping back into place. At last the door would open. The apartment was crowded with very old and beautiful furniture, mohair and velvet couches, gilded tables. The rooms were large and dark and smelled of burning metal. The *deuxième* Monsieur Cohen kept birds that chattered constantly. There was a veneer of feathers over everything, gold canary fluff. Each canary had a name. Each answered to a special whistle, meant for it alone. A crow with a broken wing had landed on the window ledge one rainy morning and Monsieur Cohen had invited it in and fed it bread and milk. It lived atop a cabinet in the kitchen and hopped in and out the window at will now that its wing had mended.

"Hello, hello." Monsieur Cohen pulled Claire inside. He liked Claire even though he was antisocial by nature. He had never been close to anyone. He'd been too busy with his work. Everything in his working life was a mystery, and that mystery had spilled into his everyday life. He never spoke of his methods. He used jewelers' tools in the old way, preferring a small ancient soldering iron that overheated and spat out smoke. He had secrets, as most goldsmiths do.

Claire did the marketing, but she was a terrible cook and she wasn't much better at tidying up. When she swept the floors, all she did was raise dust. Before long Monsieur Cohen allowed her to sit at his worktable exactly as Madame Cohen had presumed he would. In this way Claire became trained in his methods. If there was a difficult piece, she served as his assistant, handing over gold links, citrines, diamonds, clasps. When working with the soldering iron, she wore a pair of battered goggles held together with tape. Through the bubble of the goggles the gold looked green.

Once she saw the shape of a lion in the torchlight; another time it was a butterfly.

At last Claire found herself interested in something. She came to work early, picking up some bread and cheese for their lunch on the way. One day the *deuxième* Monsieur Cohen stunned her by allowing her to make her own piece of jewelry. A little canary had died and he was too depressed to work. "Surprise me," he said. "Show me something that makes life worth living."

It was a tall order for anyone, especially someone new to the craft. Claire spent hours working on a brooch of white gold that resembled the skull of a bird. It was a bit rough around the edges; still, she felt some pride. She recalled the robin's bones Elv had worn, but they had turned to dust, broken apart. Gold would last. It wouldn't scatter in the red leaves or the rain.

She nervously presented her piece to the *deuxième* Monsieur Cohen, who lay almost prone in an armchair. When he saw the brooch, he clapped Claire on the shoulder, pleased. "You have it," he said solemnly, as though diagnosing her with measles or mumps, but referring, in fact, to talent.

As Claire walked home she saw the birds in the gray evening sky. She took note of the budding trees. She felt alive. By chance she stopped at the antiquities shop, where she riffled around in the tangle of junk. There were shells and beads galore. Monsieur Abetan rooted in a drawer, bringing forth an old amulet. A five-pointed star imprinted on thin silver. He handed it to Claire. "Take this."

"Really, I'm not looking for anything," Claire demurred.

"It's this piece that does the looking. It lets you see what's there."

Claire laughed. She took the coin to be polite. She had it in her pocket the next time she went to work. Halfway through the day, she remembered the amulet, and took it out to show Monsieur Cohen. He studied it, then handed it back. "Look what I have at the end of my life," he announced, as if blinders had just been taken from his eyes. "Nothing." His pale blue eyes were watery, swimming with tears.

He was looking hard at what surrounded him. The rooms were dark and the birds were quiet; only one or two chirped as the last of the evening light faded. No children, no wife, not even any photographs. After such a long life, what did he have of any value? Claire was unnerved. She tucked the amulet away. Then she remembered why she had begun to notice things on her way home, why she felt alive. She brought him the soldering iron, the gold, a packet of opals. Monsieur Cohen did indeed have something of value. It was something he'd never expected or wanted, but it was what he had. A student. As for his student, she had even more. She could now see the leaves on the trees, the cobblestone streets, the sky above them, and on some days, when she looked carefully out the window in her grandmother's apartment, she noticed that the light was orange.

WHEN NATALIA AWOKE from her afternoon naps, she often went to her desk to take out the box filled with the photographs Elv had sent her over the years. She loved to look at them, even though they marked how quickly the time was passing and how much she was missing of the child's life. By the age of three Mimi seemed very grown-up. Natalia talked to her on the telephone on a regular basis. "You're my great-grandma," Mimi had said matter-of-factly. "So you're great."

"I am," Natalia agreed.

"You're probably beautiful," the child had announced. "You're like the good witch."

"I am exactly." Natalia had laughed.

Natalia paid for Mimi's day care and ballet lessons. Elv still worked in the animal shelter. She'd been promoted to assistant manager, but she'd made clear what her hours would be. She would not work overtime. She was always out by three, waiting on the corner for Mimi. Elv didn't like to go into the school and tried to avoid it. She felt she'd somehow manage to get herself into trouble. She still didn't trust authority figures. She'd been so nervous about her first parent-teacher conference, even though it was just nursery school, that Pete Smith had gone with her.

"Hey, baby," she would call cheerfully when the preschoolers all came rushing out. You'd never have guessed that she was brokenhearted when her girl came racing over, lunchbox in one hand, pink backpack over her shoulder. Elv had to laugh when she discovered it was her fate to have a daughter who loved pink. Mimi always did extra credit and scored the most stars on her weekly worksheet. "I'm the best," she said quite simply and Elv grinned. She quite agreed. The funny thing was, she reminded Elv of Meg. The serious set to her face, the fact that she worked so hard at every task, how she set her shoes in a neat line: boots, ballet slippers, sneakers. But she reminded her of Claire as well, the way she would reach for Elv's hand when they went to the cemetery in Astoria. *Tell me a story,* she always said, so Elv would sit with her on the bench where the hostas grew. There were starlings in the trees. She wanted to say that she would have done anything to change what had happened, to bring back the people she loved; instead she said that once upon a time, in the heart of New York City, there was a boy who found a secret world, a place where some people were good and some people were bad, and loyalty was the most important trait of all.

"It was Daddy," Mimi would say. She knew the story, word for word, and took great comfort in the fact that it never changed.

It only went forward if she asked *What happened next?* Then Elv would tell her the next section, all about the man who was a giant, and a boy who had a gold ring that could transport him anywhere, and the sisters who could hear tomato plants growing, and the great-grandmother who could sew stars into dresses so that they would glow in the dark, and the little girls who wore them who could never get lost.

SOMETIMES THEY TOOK the train out to North Point Harbor and Pete picked them up at the station. He'd bought the two-family house in which he'd been renting an apartment when the place went up for sale. It was right in the town center; you could walk to everything. Mimi loved the tea shop that served homemade ice cream. She took her doll, Miss Featherstone, with her wherever she went.

"Miss Featherstone is a dancer," Elv told Pete.

"A ballerina," Mimi corrected her.

"I see," Pete said.

They all ordered ice cream. Mimi always ordered vanilla.

"Just like Claire," Pete said.

"Claire, my momma's sister?" Mimi asked.

"That's the one," Pete said.

"Finish up," Elv suggested to the child, who had begun to color on the back of her place mat with the crayons the tea shop provided.

Mimi drew a scoop of ice cream in a silver cup. There were stars all over the ice cream.

"Here," she said, handing it to Pete. "This is for Claire."

Pete looked at Elv, who nodded her okay.

"She lives far away, but I'll mail it to her," Pete said.

"She lives on the other side of the ocean," Elv told Mimi, "where they all speak a different language and the light is a different color every day."

Elv went to North Point Harbor on her own sometimes, when Mimi was at school. She still visited Lorry every Sunday, bringing their daughter along. But she didn't want Mimi to think their world was made up only of the departed, that all there was in this life was something more to lose. She went to the other cemetery with Pete, who had arranged the stones from Paris quite beautifully and who still cut the grass and tended to the lilacs nearby. Elv noticed some spindly green things growing as well.

"Tomato plants!"

"I put them in every year," Pete admitted. "I get different varieties, ones I think your mom would have appreciated. This year I planted Black Krim, from the Ukraine."

Elv ducked her head so Pete wouldn't see that she was crying. Pete handed her a handkerchief and she blew her nose. Before Elv took the train back to Queens, they went to the new diner that had just opened and ordered grilled cheese and tomato sandwiches in honor of Annie. They had strong cups of coffee.

"Remember the Cherokee chocolates?" Elv said. "Those were my favorites. One year I said I was allergic, just to be difficult, but I'd sneak out and eat some when no one was looking."

"I never knew a tomato could be brown and still be edible." Pete chuckled. "Remember the Golden Jubilees? They were huge. They didn't even taste like the same species as what you get in the grocery store."

Pete wanted to say something more, but instead he just started talking about the library project. Annie had left funds for him to oversee a reading room in the new elementary school on Highland Road.

"Is there something else?" Elv asked. "Are you sick of me and Mimi coming out and bothering you?"

"Oh, no," Pete assured her. "I was just thinking of how things used to be."

One day when they were visiting, Mimi went to play in the yard and Pete suggested they have a cup of coffee in the kitchen. They could watch from the window, make sure Mimi was safe.

"I found him," Pete Smith said. He was gazing out at Mimi, thinking how delighted Annie would be if she could see her grandchild dancing around, shoes kicked off. She was picking up leaves, then letting them rain down. Her long black hair was down her back in one neat braid.

"Who's that?" Elv worked hard. She was tired, but she was still beautiful. Not that it mattered. She was far more concerned with the fact that Mimi hated all vegetables. She wouldn't even try broccoli. The only thing she could be coaxed to eat was a tomato, and that was only because Elv had sworn it was actually a fruit.

"The man who was a teacher. The one in the car. He's never going to hurt anyone again."

Elv went to the sink. Mimi had made a bit of a mess while giving Miss Featherstone a bath. Elv took a paper towel and sopped up the spilled water. She felt a shiver inside her, but she kept cleaning up.

"I got rid of him," Pete said.

Elv laughed, then turned from the sink and saw the look on his face.

"That's what Lorry wanted to do," Pete told her. "He told me that the day he came here with the letter. I did it for him."

Elv's eyes were burning. She never cried when there was the slightest chance that Mimi might walk in on her, but Mimi was out in the yard. She'd found a watering can and was pretending to water the garden.

"I wasn't sure I could find the right person. I started to ask around, in town, at the school. I fished around online. I came to think it might be a fellow who had taught at the elementary school years ago. He'd retired suddenly, and there weren't many people who remembered him. But there was one teacher, Ellen Hayward, second grade, who did. She hadn't liked him. She said he'd been fired for some inappropriate actions; children and parents had complained. It had been hushed up. No one would file a legal complaint. Mrs. Hayward said that most children know their parents will be upset if they find out they've been molested. They want to protect them."

Elv sat down at the table. She herself couldn't remember his face, just his voice and what he did to her.

"I went to his house—he lived out past Huntington. He hadn't worked for years. He wasn't well. He had an oxygen tank because of his emphysema. I told him I was researching a book and that his sister suggested I speak to him. He had a sister who lived in New Jersey, but when I called she refused to speak to me. She told me her brother was dead to her."

Perhaps he was lonely, or his interest was piqued in having a writer coming to call. He invited Pete in and gave him a cup of coffee, which Pete didn't drink. It had been cold this past winter. Pete wore his overcoat, his gloves; he brought along a briefcase of what appeared to be notes and, hidden at the bottom, a sealed plastic bag containing two ounces of heroin. Enough to put Grimin away for life. Pete didn't touch anything in the house. When the detectives came later on, he wanted it to be an open-and-shut case.

He said he was gathering stories and that his book was entitled *The Best Advice from the Best Teachers*. Pete was only interviewing the best of the best. The man was flattered. His advice was simple, but vital. Don't think you know the person in front of you. Everyone has their secrets.

For instance? Pete asked. He felt lucky. The guy wanted to impress him. Worst secret you've ever heard?

I've got a good one, the man said. He was ready to talk. Loneliness and flattery did that.

I'll bet you do, Pete answered.

It was a small house and chilly. The heat was turned down low. There were no pets. No family. There was a clock on the mantel, ticking. Pete had parked several blocks away. It was early evening and dark.

The man told his story slowly, with pauses for effect. He said he'd heard it from a friend of a friend. A girl had been on the corner and looked lost. This fellow had pulled up and offered her a ride. He'd wanted the little girl. No one would have expected that of this man—a secret life, just like he'd said. The man had been watching her at her house and now here she was, but another girl had pushed her out of the way and gotten into his car instead. What are you going to do about it, she had said. She was a bad girl, you could see it. That's what the friend of a friend had said. She had green eyes, which was always a sign of evil within, so he took her home and kept her there all day and he'd had to punish her and teach her a lesson. That was the worst story of a secret life he'd ever heard. He'd laughed then. He wasn't even sure whether or not to believe it.

Pete told the fellow he'd heard a story like that too. The world was a small place and stories got around. He thought it had taken place on Nightingale Street.

Lane, the man had said. It was Nightingale Lane.

"Lorry told me you called him Grimin," Pete told Elv. "When I got to his house, I saw why. The letters on his license plate were still the same."

Pete noticed this as he jimmied the lock, then hid the heroin in the trunk. As soon as he drove away, he phoned an old friend in the Suffolk County Police Department. The amount of heroin he'd left behind equaled a life sentence, less for good behavior, but Grimin would be dead by then.

Mimi was putting the watering can away. She dusted off Miss Featherstone, who had leaves in her hair and some dirt on her dress. Miss Featherstone was very persnickety about her appearance. Pete took a sip of coffee. It was cold. He'd gotten rid of Grimin because he'd made a promise to Annie that he'd always take care of Elv. On the way back to the train station, Elv asked Pete if they could stop at Nightingale Lane.

They sat parked there in the Volvo, the engine running.

"Is this where you lived?" Mimi said in a hushed tone when she saw the house. It was a perfectly good house, three stories, white with black shutters and a lovely wide porch. It had two chimneys and hollyhocks by the door. "It's a castle."

There was the hawthorn tree, there was the garden. Another family lived here now. There were lights on in the rooms and they could see inside. Bookshelves, couches, paintings on the wall. There was a cat in the kitchen.

"Which one was your bedroom with your sisters?" Mimi asked.

Elv pointed out the attic windows.

"It was the tower," Mimi said, awed.

"We had the best garden. There were all different-colored tomatoes," Elv told her.

"Tomatoes are red," Mimi said.

"Well, we had pink and yellow and brown and purple and green."

"It's true," Pete said. "They were like candy."

"Unlikely," Mimi said.

Pete and Elv exchanged an amused look over Mimi's head. Claire used to sound like that. So matter-of-fact.

Elv and Mimi got out and stood by the side of the road across from the house. Dusk spread across the lawn in waves of velvet.

So often Elv found herself saying the same things to her daughter that Annie had said to her. She felt a flood of love for the small solemn face upturned in the dark, listening to every word. Here is a story about a boy who had the most loyal dog in the world, about three sisters who danced in the garden, about a mother who would do anything for her child.

Maybe some love was guaranteed. Maybe it fit inside you and around you like skin and bones. This is what she remembered and always would: the sisters who sat with her in the garden, the grandmother who stitched her a dress the color of the sky, the man who spied her in the grass and loved her beyond all measure, the mother who set up a tent in the garden to tell her a story when she was a child, neither good nor bad, selfish nor strong, only a girl who wanted to hear a familiar voice as the dark fell down, and the moths rose, and the night was sure to come.

Faithful

I waited in the place where I last saw you.

It was night and then morning, then night once more.

A decade passed and then a hundred years. Green leaves became red, then green again. The tree that had sheltered me was pushed down by the wind. I saw lightning in the sky, stars that were burning out in the heavens. I saw men tell women they loved them, then turn away. I saw men who were true but were never able to speak their minds. I saw lives begin, graves dug, snow falling. I was there for so long that time went backward. There was the nightingale. There was the hawthorn tree. I was a girl with long black hair watching you come across the grass toward me. When you recognized me, only an hour had passed.

WHENEVER PETE SMITH TOOK THEM SHOPPING HE ALWAYS bought Mimi too much. It didn't matter if the store was Target or Saks Fifth Avenue, by the age of seven Mimi could manage to talk him into whatever she wanted. She called him Gogi, which was her version of Grandpa. She was a big fan of nicknames, and books, and ballet. Her hair was black and her eyes were darker than Lorry's. "She'll be spoiled," Elv would remind Pete, thinking that her daughter's charm was so like Lorry's as well. All the girls at school wanted to sit with her at lunch to hear the stories she told. They hovered around her, wanting to be her best friend. When she came into school wearing pink cowgirl boots, her classmates went home and begged their mothers for the same. Pete didn't think that a few shopping sprees every now and then would have a bad effect. It was nice to spoil someone. He'd been the first person other than Elv and the nurses at the hospital to see Mimi when she'd come into this world, so he reserved the right to be proud.

He'd been around town long enough that people had stopped calling him Cemetery Man, even though he still went every week to cut the grass, trim the lilacs, sit on a bench, bringing along his shovel when the path to the graves was heaped with snow. He was known as Mimi's grandfather now, and even if there was no blood connection, that was who he was. Elv and Mimi had moved into the top-floor apartment in his house in North Point Harbor. Elv worked at another animal shelter in a nearby town, where she was hired as assistant director. Mimi was in third grade at the same school the Story sisters had attended. It had been completely remodeled and the teachers seemed so young. It looked different, but when Elv walked inside, it felt the same. Pete went with her for the first parent-teacher conference. Elv still had trouble with official meetings and authority figures. She got fidgety and self-conscious, all the more so for having to walk down hallways she had taken with her sisters.

Part of the newly remodeled school library was called the Meg Story Reading Room. There had been a celebration when it first opened. Elv shook hands with the mayor and the librarians and the members of the town council. Elise and Mary Fox had come, and Elise cried when Pete got up and said a few words about how books had mattered so much to Meg, and how Annie had wanted to honor her memory by sharing her love of books with the town. When the speakers and the guests were directed to the buffet table set up in the hallway, Elv went to explore the reading room. Meg's name was on a brass plate above the door. Elv drifted over to the fiction section and found the row of Dickens novels, the books by Hawthorne.

"It's beautiful. Perfect," she told Pete later. "It's just what my mother would have wanted for Meg. You did everything right."

On afternoons when Elv got out of work early, she went to the reading room while she waited for the three o'clock bell. If you sat by the window, you could see the bay when the trees were bare. When the trees were in full leaf, all you could see was green. The town felt different to her now that she knew she wouldn't see that bad man again. She had seen his car a second time, long ago, when she was hanging out with the kids who smoked dope under the bridge and that poor Justin Levy was still traipsing after her. It was the same one he'd had when Claire had slipped into the backseat and he was pulling away and Elv had to yank the car door open and jump inside while it was moving so he couldn't take Claire. When she recognized the license plate, she should have called the police, had him arrested, but she was panic-stricken. She remembered that was the day she told Justin he should find someone better, someone who could really love him. But he hadn't known how to do that.

Mimi knew where to look for her mom when school let out. Sometimes Mimi told people the reading room had been named after her, even though she knew it wasn't true. It made for a good story. It made the other girls' mouths drop open, even the ones who were rich and lived in big houses and weren't so sure about Mimi. A couple of the girls whispered that she didn't have a father. Maybe she didn't care what they thought about her or whether or not they believed her when she said the reading room belonged to her family. She had become a fanatical reader, so she felt a special connection to the library anyway, and Story was her name too, so the reading room did belong to her in that way. She liked to think that if her aunt was still alive they would talk about books. Her mother didn't have time to read, although she told the best stories. She'd said that when she was young she had invented an entire world with its own language, although she didn't remember any of it now.

"You should have written it down," Mimi told her. "When you write things down, they're harder to forget."

Mimi had been writing down the stories her mother told her about her father. They weren't true stories; they were better than that. She had a diary full of them in a collection she'd titled *The Most Loyal Dog in the World,* which was all about her father's adventures with his dog named Mother. Mimi thought it was a hilarious name. She had glued a photograph of her father inside the cover. He was smiling. There weren't that many of him like that, when he looked as if he'd take all the time in the world to tell you a story and walk in the woods with you and clomp through the snow in Central Park, which were all things her mother said he loved to do. Mimi liked to study his face. She felt she knew him even though she didn't. It was his grave they visited in Queens, but he was here, too, in her book.

She had been writing to her aunt in Paris. She liked having a pen pal who was so far away. Every time there was a letter for her in the mailbox, it was as if a secret message had been waiting there all day while she'd been in school. She had started out sending her artwork, then had begun to add messages on the back. After a while, she began to get letters back. Her aunt was funny. She sent jokes: Why did the tomato go out with a prune? Because he couldn't get a date! How do you fix a broken tomato? Tomato paste! She drew little sketches of Paris—a streetlight, the pet crow that lived in the workshop where she made jewelry, a bridge over the river with a curlicue railing, a rosebush in the Jardin du Luxembourg.

"What was the name for aunt in your language?" Mimi asked her mother one day as they were headed home from school. They usually took the long way around, but on warm days they went along the bay. Her mother seemed to like to walk there. She would stop in certain places and gaze into the woods and then they would keep going again.

"I don't remember any of the words," her mother said.

Mimi's mother was beautiful and sad. She wasn't friends with any of the other mothers at school. Whenever there was a potluck dinner, Mimi's grandfather Gogi would make a dish for them to bring and he'd go with her because her mother was too nervous about school gatherings. Sometimes their cousin Mary would come over and the two women would sit on the couch and drink wine and laugh and then Elv didn't even sound like Mimi's mother. She sounded like someone who was happy.

"You must remember something," Mimi insisted.

Mimi was the best student in her third-grade class not only because she was a fanatical reader but because she was persistent.

Her mother thought it over. If sister was *gig,* then aunt was most likely *gigi.* That's what she had called Claire when it was just the two of them and the rest of the world had been so far away.

Dear Gigi, Mimi wrote from then on. Mimi's bedroom overlooked the garden, where her mother often worked on warm days. The garden wasn't very sunny, so they'd had to cut down some little willow trees where Miss Featherstone had liked to perch and peer out at the world. Mimi still had Miss Featherstone, the doll who had accompanied her everywhere when she was younger. But now that Mimi was in third grade and would be turning eight in July, Miss Featherstone was left at home most times. She was still a good listener when it came to the stories Mimi told at night before she fell asleep. Her mother's stories always began *Once upon a time,* even though that meant everything in them had already happened and everyone in them was already gone.

Every year her aunt in Paris sent something special on her birthday. It had begun when she was three, the year Mimi sent the first picture. Her aunt had mailed the birthday gifts to Mimi's grandpa, but now his address was their address, too. The presents came in pink boxes, Mimi's favorite color, and were tied with black silk ribbon. She couldn't have been more excited over the charms her aunt made especially for her. Her mother thought they were beautiful, too. She handled them tenderly when Mimi showed her, then gave them back.

The charms were Mimi's favorite things in the world, except for books and Miss Featherstone and her grandparents and her mother and the photograph of her father. She kept them in their pink boxes in her top dresser drawer. Each one had arrived with a message. *So you're always fast.* A gold horse with a moonstone saddle. *So you can fly.* A tiny gold and turquoise robin with a silver beak. *So you never get lost.* A firefly with citrine eyes and an orange opal at its center that glowed like a beacon. That one had looked so real Mimi had taken it to school to show off when the term began. She said it was a real firefly from Paris, and that in France all the insects were made out of gold. Everyone believed her and wanted to touch it for good luck. Then she almost lost the charm when Patti Weinstein dropped it. She quickly wrapped the firefly in a tissue and stuck it in her backpack, and she never brought the charms to school again.

So you are always sheltered. That was the next one, a gold tree with a shower of jade in its branches. "It's a hawthorn tree," her mother had said, and when Mimi asked, "What's a hawthorn?" they walked over to Nightingale Lane. Mimi looked at the big tree on the lawn of the house where the Story sisters used to live and she understood why her mother said she had liked to sit in its branches. She would have loved to have climbed it herself, only it belonged to another family now and she had her own yard in Gogi's house on the other side of town, which was sunny ever since the willow trees had been cut down.

This year's charm had come early from Paris in their ama's suitcase. It was a big occasion to finally have their ama visit and they had spent days fixing up their apartment, making sure there were flowers in her room. They swept away the dust bunnies under the couch and made certain the hall closet wasn't in a shambles with hats and gloves and ice skates and purses falling out when you opened the door. They wanted everything to be perfect. Natalia appreciated it all. She brought along French candies in the shape of violets, silk scarves, cheese for Pete, and the birthday gift from Claire. Mimi hopped around in a circle, clomping in her cowgirl boots, until it was handed over. This one was perhaps the most charming and unusual: *So you never go hungry.* A little tomato plant, with one ruby, one citrine, one brown diamond, and one tiny emerald. Elv laughed when it was unwrapped.

"Are there really truly brown tomatoes?" Mimi asked.

"Cherokee chocolates," her mother told her. "I'll see if I can plant some this year."

Now that she would be turning eight and was responsible, Mimi's grandpa was getting her a gold bracelet so she could attach all the charms and wear them, but only on special occasions. She had learned her lesson about showing off. This year she had made a plan for her birthday. She had already told Miss Featherstone all about it.

Dear Gigi, she wrote. *I know exactly what I'd like this year.*

She knew she shouldn't count on it, because sometimes things didn't turn out the way you expected in this world, or at least that's what her mother always told her. Still, Mimi had a feeling this would turn out just fine. She asked her gigi for what she most wanted for her birthday, and in return she had sent her something special, not her own artwork, but something better—a painting her mother had framed and let her keep in her room, one she had done when she was much younger. It was black and watery and her mother had said it was the river in Paris at night, and that it was called the Seine, and that her sister lived so very close by to it that she probably walked along the banks at night, looking for stones, watching the inky sky fall down like ashes.

CLAIRE HAD BEEN surprised to receive that first crayoned picture that had arrived folded in two, addressed in Pete's blocky hand-writing. The next was of their house on Nightingale Lane. Their bedroom looked like a tower in a castle. On impulse, she went to the workshop and made the little gold horse charm and sent it off. She thought that would be the end of it, a single exchange, but Mimi kept sending pictures, and when she learned how to write there was no stopping her. Printed missives arrived on blue lined paper, chock-full of misspellings. She wrote about her adventures, giving each one a title. *The Day I Started Kindergarten. The Day We Bought a Swing Set. The Day a Sparrow Fell Out of Its Nest and We Had to Take It to Wild Care, Which Rescues Birds.* Once Pete had slipped in a photo of the child and her doll sitting under a willow tree. Claire thought that was unfair. He'd written *Mimi and Miss Featherstone* on the back of the photo, which made Claire smile despite herself. She kept the photo, and sometimes she took it out and gazed at it, the child with long black hair and a serious expression in her eyes, the willow tree, the doll in a white dress, the yard in North Point Harbor.

She began to make other charms, ones for grown-ups, and these had gained her a large following. People were crazy for her one-of-a-kind amulets. There were those who swore they could help to find the lost, heal the sick, help the wearer tell the difference between a liar and an honest man. If you held one in your hand, it would point you toward your future—a decision to be made, a move to a new town, the love of your life. The charms had become a trend—for some, an obsession—and many Parisians owned at least one, while yearning for more. They were swapped at parties and clubs, like expensive and glorious trading cards. The few that had been stolen were said to have found their way back to their rightful owners, returned by post, or simply turned up at the original owner's door, wrapped in brown paper and string.

Many of Claire's charms began with objects found in Monsieur Abetan's antiquities shop, which also sold cigarettes and magazines at the counter. It was just around the corner. Claire and Monsieur Abetan often had tea in the afternoons, after she left Monsieur Cohen's workshop. Sometimes she brought macaroons and dates or a paper bag filled with sugared almonds. She told the *deuxième* Monsieur Cohen all about Monsieur Abetan's collection of relics, hidden beside the drawers of junk, just as she described Monsieur Cohen's fabulous gemstone creations to Monsieur Abetan. In this way the two men became friends without ever meeting. They liked to hear about each other's opinions through Claire, and they often vehemently disagreed, especially when it came to politics. Both, however, were students of human nature; that was what made for a great teacher.

Monsieur Abetan informed Claire that the bells she had just chosen had once been used as love charms for women in Persia.

"Try it yourself," he said knowingly. "You'll see."

Claire went back to the workshop the following day and attached the bells to a strand of lapis lazuli, deep blue stones that shimmered with golden pyrites. Lapis was a primitive, powerful element, one of the first gemstones ever used for jewelry in Egypt and Persia. It was said to be the stone of truth, causing the wearer to be authentic. The *deuxième* Monsieur Cohen said the stone itself had unusual traits. Gem cutters could tell the depth of blue contained within a piece of lapis by the scent it gave off. The deeper the color, the richer the fragrance.

Claire found solace in the *deuxième* Monsieur Cohen's attic. The women in the neighborhood were relieved. The little girls walked past her and whispered that when they were older they would have a dozen of her charms. What others might find in love or faith, she had found in work. She was so intent on her creations that she sometimes seemed to be in another world entirely. When she burned herself with solder, she didn't notice. When she pricked her fingers, she didn't feel the pain. This utter concentration was the mark of a true artist, but Monsieur Cohen worried about his student. Perhaps he was leading her astray? Years were passing, and it occurred to Monsieur Cohen that Claire's youth was being wasted here in his attic apartment. At night when all the birds were quiet and the corners of the rooms were dim, Monsieur Cohen faced a mirror. He saw himself the way he'd been as a younger man. He wanted to slap that young man and tell him to go take a walk in the sunlight. *Go out,* he wanted to shout. *Live.*

He sent a letter to Madame Rosen. *I'm worried about your granddaughter,* he wrote. *Perhaps we should talk.*

Natalia went to visit him soon after. It was a Sunday and she left Claire sleeping. She brought along a cake, some fruit, salted cashews. She struggled to take the many steps up to the attic apartment. There was a great view from the hallway window, but she had to huff and puff to catch her breath. She knocked on the door and called Monsieur Cohen's name, then listened to the strange clanging from within as he moved aside his personal alarm system of pots and pans.

"What a surprise and a pleasure," he said when he opened the door.

They had known each other years ago, when they were much younger, and because of this they saw each other exactly as they had been then. He was a tall man with dark hair and very blue eyes. She was a woman with a gorgeous shape and auburn hair. Flustered, they laughed to see each other this way. Monsieur Cohen excused his bad manners and invited her inside. Natalia made tea and sliced the cake. "So you're worried about my granddaughter."

"I don't want her to wind up like me. Alone in an attic."

Natalia pointed to the cages of birds and to the crow that hopped down from atop the cabinet when it spied cake crumbs on the table. "Hardly alone."

She'd been married when Samuel had met her, and so beautiful he'd been unable to speak to her anyway. He'd been shy, work obsessed. Her husband was an American and she'd soon disappeared, coming back only intermittently. The *deuxième* Monsieur Cohen now took her hand when she served his tea. All at once he was struck with the notion that he was now in his own future. There was no time to waste. He could hardly contain himself.

"It's a little late for that." Natalia laughed, although she was flattered. "Aren't you ninety?"

When Claire came to work the next day, Monsieur Cohen was feeding his birds instead of sitting at his worktable. The next day he was shaving at the kitchen sink. The day after that, he asked if she would fix a simple dinner of salad and cheese and some steamed asparagus. He was having a guest.

Claire hated to leave the piece she was working on—Abetan had found her a heart scarab made of blue Egyptian pottery. Such scarabs were used as a weight on the body after death so the spirit world would assume the wearer's heart was enormous, heavy with goodness, and he would then be judged kindly in the world to come. Claire was fascinated by its shape and purpose. She didn't want to stop and clean up.

"But we always work until dark," she protested, confused.

"Not anymore. A man has to eat." Monsieur Cohen shrugged. "I'm sure my friend Abetan would say the same."

Claire set the table and wished her mentor a good night. She went down the staircase two steps at a time, irritated to have time on her hands. It was still light outside. She had kept the amulet of lapis and Persian bells for herself. They were said to chime and bring the wearer true love, but she had shaken them and shaken them and there hadn't been a sound. She thought of the women who had worn the bells before her, somewhere in a desert, and she wondered if fate had come to them, or if they had chased after fate. As she clattered into the street Claire saw a woman approaching who had auburn hair and a lovely gait. All at once Claire realized it was her grandmother, a woman in her eighties, wearing a black coat and a red scarf, walking through the summer evening on her way to a dinner appointment.

After that, Claire left work at five every day because of a tryst that was meant to be secret, though everyone in the neighborhood seemed to know. "I see your grandmother's keeping busy," the old women would say. "Tell the lovebirds hello," the grocer joked. No matter how intent Claire was on her work, she had to clean up, store away the gems, set the table for supper. As the hour drew near, Monsieur Cohen became agitated, concerned with combing his hair, slipping on a clean shirt. As for Claire, she was becoming a good cook. Excellent, according to the *deuxième* Monsieur Cohen. When she ran out of ideas, she began to collect recipes from the old women in the neighborhood. They were only too happy to put down their heavy purses, in which they stored everything from keys to butterfly nets, and give Claire the secret of their stews, their pot-aux-feu, their potato and cheese tarts. She wrote everything down in one of the faded blue notebooks Meg had left behind. They had all seen Madame Rosen going over to the edge of the neighborhood wearing her red silk scarf. They knew who was being romanced and who ate her dinner all alone, save for the company of the old cat, Sadie. They suggested Claire herself try their recipes, perhaps they could help. Apples for love, rosemary for remembrance, twice-loved pie that melted at first taste. These dishes were clear-eyed; they aided in stamina and steadied the heartbeat, but let the pulse run wild. Old people were smarter about love. They didn't have time to second-guess themselves. "Go on," the neighborhood women urged. "Cook these for yourself." But Claire didn't see the sense in cooking for one. She took her meals standing up, allowing herself a piece of cheese, an apple, sliced tomatoes with vinegar and salt. The cat wound itself around her legs, even though they disliked each other. There was no one else at home.

"Did you know the *deuxième* Monsieur Cohen before?" Claire asked her grandmother one night when Natalia came home from her dinner engagement. Claire's ama was untying the red scarf, humming to herself.

"Who?" Natalia teased.

"Ama! Your boyfriend, or whatever he is at his age. Everyone knows. Even me!"

"Yes, but who said he's the *deuxième?*"

"Well, Madame Cohen calls him that."

"That's because she met his brother first and married him. He's the *premier* Monsieur Cohen to me." Natalia had laughed then. "I knew him but I never saw him. He was like the newspaper stand. You walk by every day, but you never look at who's sitting there, collecting the change."

"My grandmother's in love," Claire told Madame Cohen when she next brought in her collection of jewelry. They were amulets designed in the shape of scarabs carved from semiprecious stones, citrine and turquoise and amethyst. They were snapped up as soon as they were delivered to the shop, as all her charms were. Madame Cohen noticed that Claire was beginning to outsell her teacher.

"Your grandmother's falling, all right." Madame Cohen laughed. "Her knees aren't too good anymore. What about your knees?" she asked.

"They're perfect," Claire assured her. "I could run ten kilometers and not feel a thing."

◆ ◆ ◆

IT WAS THE rainy season in Paris and the weather had turned cold. On the night the thief broke in to the workshop he left icy footprints on the kitchen floor. It was difficult to tell whether he entered through the front door and made his escape through the window and down the fire escape, or vice versa. Either way, he left all the windows wide open. The chilly night air that poured inside killed all the caged birds. Their feathers billowed on the floor and stuck fast to the wet linoleum. Any object of worth had been taken. Gems, bars of gold, envelopes of ancient coins. Everything had been ruined. Even the couch had its pillows ripped open, with more feathers floating about. The alarm system of pots and pans had been left in a heap.

"I thought it was the rainstorm," one of the downstairs neighbors declared when later questioned. "There was so much noise. I was certain someone was dancing," another reported when the officials finally arrived. "He has a woman up there sometimes."

Claire was the one who found Monsieur Cohen. She knew something was wrong as she walked up the stairs. Usually it was possible to hear the canaries singing as soon as she reached the second-floor landing, but on this day there was only silence. When Claire pushed open the door and went inside, there were no pots and pans hanging overhead. The canaries lay at the bottom of their cages, mute, stiff, like little gold statues. Claire surveyed the disaster surrounding her. The cabinets open, the worktable in shambles, the drawers pulled out, the couch cushions slit with a butcher's knife as the thief looked for more, more, more. A few scattered onions rolled across the kitchen floor. Claire had bought them earlier in the week. They'd been meant for a recipe called Love Is Blind Stew. One of the tenants in the building had given Claire the recipe only a few days earlier. They had stood in the hall and the old woman had whispered all of the ingredients for Claire to hastily scrawl into her notebook. A fresh chicken, a handful of apricots, red wine, oregano, a sliced pear. Claire must remember not to add garlic. She must braise, but never boil, cook until tender without overcooking. But Natalia hadn't been feeling well, and Claire hadn't cooked the stew. Monsieur Cohen planned to dine alone, and so he was satisfied with bread and cheese, perhaps a cup of soup.

Claire noticed that the bedroom door was open. She felt her heart drop. She could not remember if she had closed and locked the front door the evening before. She had been preoccupied, thinking about her charms. She was about to make a series of lion amulets, for protection and bravery. She switched the light on to illuminate the bedroom. The *deuxième* Monsieur Cohen was sprawled on the floor. He had a cane in his hand, one he planned to use as a weapon, but he'd had a stroke before he could confront the intruder. Claire sat down on the floor beside him. He had thought to put on his slippers. She moved to close his eyes. She sat there for a long time, on the cold floor beside him. He was her teacher and had taught her everything he'd known.

When the police arrived, Claire went into the kitchen to answer their questions. The neighbors had already been interviewed and the flat had been dusted for fingerprints, although the authorities had admitted that small-time thieves were difficult to track down. Claire found that she kept looking at the onions on the floor. She was plagued with trying to remember whether or not she'd locked the door. She went over her actions, but all she could remember was Monsieur Cohen calling out a good-bye. She picked up an onion, then held it close and began to cry. Onions did that to a person; you could fight it all you wanted, but in the end the onion was more powerful than human will. It forced you to tears.

Madame Cohen's grandsons came to take charge. They summoned an ambulance and made arrangements at the funeral home and the chapel. They were so tall and the attic eaves so sloping that there didn't seem to be any breathing room in the flat. One of them coaxed the crow into a cage. The others were all on their cell phones, calling relatives, making funeral plans. The policemen spoke so quickly among themselves that Claire couldn't understand a word. French wasn't her first language, after all, or even her second. She had a sudden fleeting thought in Arnish: *Nom brava gig. Reuna malin.*

When the police did at last question her, they had to repeat themselves over and over before she fathomed their meaning. Yes, she had worked with the deceased. Yes, he had precious jewels and gold in his possession. And finally: Yes, she might have left the door ajar when she left the evening before. It was possible that she'd forgotten to lock it.

Claire began to hyperventilate then. She grew dizzy and needed to sit down. Anyone would have thought that in a room full of doctors someone might have offered her a paper bag to breathe into, perhaps a Valium. Instead, one of the grandsons brought Claire a glass of vodka, which she gratefully drank.

"Anything else?" the grandson asked. It was Philippe, the one who had carried Shiloh down the stairs. He now had the crow in a cage. When it began to squawk, he tossed a napkin over it and it quieted down.

Claire shook her head no.

When she left, Philippe called after her. She didn't seem to hear, so he followed her down the twisting stairs. In fact, she had heard and had chosen to ignore him. Now she was annoyed. All she wanted was to be left alone. When she turned, Philippe stumbled, then threw up his hands to prove he had no ill intentions. "I thought you might need help getting home."

"Do I look like I need help?"

Philippe had chosen a specialty in oncology, a field many doctors avoided. He was six feet tall, a workaholic. One thing he knew for certain: A diagnosis was always difficult. You could never judge by the first set of presenting facts. "Looks are deceiving," he said.

"I killed him. Can you tell that from looking at me? It's all my fault."

Claire went out and sat in the square across from the building. Being alone felt like something sharp, something that could make a person bleed. She watched the ambulance arrive. Monsieur Cohen was carried out, and then the ambulance and the grandsons set off separately. At last the police dispersed. Sitting there under the darkening sky, Claire was bruised, inconsolable. Nothing could protect the people she loved. She saw a man walking toward her. He had a birdcage under one arm.

"Just go," Claire said.

"I can't. My grandmother insisted I take you home." Philippe Cohen sat down beside her. "And don't be an idiot, Claire. You didn't kill him. He had a stroke caused by a blood clot. Uncle Samuel had been eating badly for ninety years, and he could barely move for the last ten of those years. He had hardening of the arteries. It was bound to happen sooner or later."

"So he would have died today even if I hadn't left the door open?"

"You know as well as I do, he was the sort of man who checked his door. He had a case of paranoia, really. I can't imagine he'd go to bed without doing so, and if he did, well, at least he's out of his misery."

Claire winced. "Is everything so easy for you to explain?"

"No. I can't explain why I took this crow. I hate birds. Come on. You don't even have to thank me for the lift home."

He pointed out his car, which was parked nearby. It was a

Saab that was rusted and in need of washing. Philippe took care of some things, but not others. They both got up and walked toward it. Claire felt unsettled over the fact that he seemed to think he knew her, when he didn't know the first thing about her. "Thank you," she grumbled, without much gratitude, just to prove him wrong since he clearly thought her an ungrateful, spoiled brat.

"You're welcome." He spoke in English to be polite, even though being polite wasn't especially easy for him. He was very blunt and matter-of-fact. That was his nature. It was probably why he didn't mind Claire's bad manners. When they were children, she had once called him a nincompoop at his grandmother's shop, and he'd spent weeks trying to figure out what she'd meant. He still wasn't exactly sure. She was usually so standoffish, he was surprised she let him drive her home.

"Don't bother to get out of the car," she said when he pulled over.

"I didn't intend to," he told her.

"Why? Because your grandmother didn't tell you to?"

"Because one of my assigned patients is dying and I have to go check on him."

"Oh," Claire said, embarrassed. "Well."

"Don't feel bad. We're all dying, but my patient is probably going to do it this afternoon or maybe tomorrow. I may be late to my uncle's funeral."

Claire herself was there early. She asked if she could see Monsieur Cohen one last time before the service. He looked calm, peaceful, far from the world's misery, as Philippe had said. She brought the heart scarab with her, which she tucked beneath his jacket.

The cemetery was small and old with lilacs growing along a stone wall. There wasn't much space, and mourners were forced to edge over graves in order to get to the service, which was held at the grave site. As Monsieur Cohen hadn't left his apartment for more than ten years, he would have been surprised to see how many people attended his funeral and how many tears were shed. Even Monsieur Abetan, who had never met Monsieur Cohen in person, came to pay his respects. Claire's grandmother fainted before the service had begun; it was such a sad day, and there was such a crowd, but there were doctors enough around and she was soon revived with smelling salts and a glass of cold water. Claire went to Natalia and knelt before her. She wanted to tell her she had been responsible for Monsieur Cohen's death, that she had left the door open, but all she said was "I'm so sorry, Ama." Natalia stroked her head. "He was a pleasure for me at the end of our lives. I could never have regrets. And you were like a daughter to him," she said. "Whatever he taught you will stay with you forever."

Natalia sat next to Madame Cohen during the service. One of the grandsons held a black umbrella over the old women's heads. A rabbi said the mourning prayers. Claire was in the last row, wearing the black dress Jeanne had given her when she first started working at the shop. It was wool and scratchy. Philippe came to sit beside her halfway through the service.

"Did your patient die?" Claire whispered.

A woman in the row directly in front of them turned and glared.

"Turn around," Philippe suggested to the woman. "There's a funeral going on." When the woman turned away, Philippe exchanged a look with Claire. There was a glint in his eyes she hadn't noticed before. "Still alive, but on his way. No longer conscious. At this point, he didn't know if I was there or not. And I had to leave to be here with you."

"Let me guess," Claire ventured. "Your grandmother told you to."

Philippe looked at her and didn't answer. Claire glanced away, unsettled. Now it seemed that she was the one who knew nothing of him.

THERE WAS A dinner afterward at Madame Cohen's home. Women from the neighborhood brought their best dishes and soon the table overflowed with food. Claire recognized many of the recipes, the pot-au-feu, the Love Is Blind Stew, the beef with prunes, the crème caramel with pistachio, the meat pies. She had made them all and tried none. She tasted several at the dinner and thought them delicious.

Natalia was staying with Madame Cohen for the night. Everyone insisted Philippe take Claire home. He stood there and shrugged, as if it made no difference to him. "Go on," Claire's ama said. "I don't want you walking home alone." Madame Cohen handed them their coats and pushed them out the door.

"How's the crow?" Claire asked as they took the stairs to the street.

"A pain in the ass. He wakes me up at four A.M."

Philippe had double-parked in a taxi stand. He was always late and always in a rush. As they approached, one of the drivers accosted him and started to yell. Because of Philippe's lousy parking the driver had lost several fares. They both told each other to go to hell, then Philippe gave the driver a few euros to placate him.

"Some people are idiots," Philippe said reasonably.

"Yes," Claire remarked. "I know."

"Or nincompoops, whatever that is. I presume it means idiot."

"More or less," Claire agreed.

It was late and a light rain was falling. Cars were racing by. Philippe opened the door for her because it was rusted. There was a trick to it that involved kicking the door in the right place, just below the handle. The rain was green and quiet and cold. Claire was wearing the lapis necklace. When she bent forward to get into the Saab, she thought she heard the bell chime. Clearly it was nothing. Just to make sure, she took a step back and looked at Madame Cohen's youngest grandson, the one who had been such a problem as a boy, who'd broken windows and made flyswatters and buried dogs and sat with dying men and tried to please his grandmother whenever possible.

"Ready?" he asked.

"Absolutely," she answered.

SOMETIMES MADAME COHEN couldn't recall what had happened the day before, but she remembered the past as if it had happened only moments ago. The color of the dresses she and her sisters used to wear, the dappled peels on the apples set out on her grandmother's table, the recipe for Honesty Cake—three perfect eggs, white flour, cherries, lemon rind, and anise—the scent of the forest in Russia, her first glimpse of Paris, such a stunning sight that even now she sometimes saw it exactly as it had been on that day. Natalia frequently stopped by the shop, even though Madame Cohen was often asleep in her chair in the back room. Madame Cohen's daughters-in-law worked in the shop now; it had become their pet project. Claire spent her days in the *deuxième* Monsieur Cohen's workshop. The jewelry store featured her amulets and talismans exclusively. Lucie and Jeanne joked that perhaps Claire should be called the *troisième* Monsieur Cohen. They were in awe of what she was capable of. Without question, she was the best of the three jewelers. Recently, her work had been exhibited in a gallery on the Rue de Rivoli, with a huge gala to celebrate the opening. Madame Cohen and Madame Rosen had been there and it was all they could talk about for weeks, that and the fact that Philippe was there when his grandmother hadn't even told him about the event, let alone insist that he come.

Madame Rosen had sewn her granddaughter a dress for the occasion, an astonishing creation of pale gray silk and yellow tulle. Claire had framed it afterward and hung it on the wall of the workshop. Under glass, the gown glowed like a firefly. Afterward she had made the firefly charm for Mimi. The two had continued to write on a regular basis. Claire could always tell when one of her letters had been delivered. Mimi used pink stationery and she addressed her letters to *Gigi Story, my aunt.*

THE NEIGHBORHOOD WOMEN no longer worried about Claire. They turned their attentions elsewhere, to Natalia, who was grieving, and to Monsieur Abetan, who they decided must have a wife. Claire was too busy to worry about, plus she was in love. The first time she had slept with Philippe was after their first serious argument. They enjoyed provoking each other, and liked to slyly tease each other, but this was something else entirely. They'd taken Monsieur Cohen's crow to the Bois de Boulogne to set it free. "A crow should be a crow," Philippe had said. "If he dies, then at least he'll have lived a crow's life."

The crow took off and didn't look back, but Claire worried that it wouldn't be able to fend for itself after being babied for so many years in an overheated apartment. All at once, she'd found she was crying, which was completely unlike her. When Philippe asked why, she told him it was because he was an idiot. They'd screamed at each other and called each other names. People in the Bois edged away from them, convinced they were lunatics. Then Philippe kissed her and everything else dropped away. She had never been kissed before and when she told him that, he laughed. "So it turns out you have been waiting for me since we were children."

"Unlikely," Claire had said haughtily, but he kissed her again and she wanted him to and that was that.

Philippe liked to fight, but he also liked to make up. Claire appreciated that. She appreciated everything about him, even his flaws, which were many. He was even more of a workaholic than she'd first suspected, gone on weekends, not returning from the hospital until late in the evening with no excuses. He was a restless sleeper and a picky eater. He still broke dishes when he washed them like the clumsy, curious boy he'd once been. He argued with his coworkers and gave away too much money and cursed the government no matter who was in office. He let her know that he would never have time to take a vacation. None of these flaws were fatal, not even the fact that he gave his patients his home number so that the phone was always ringing in the middle of the night. That was when Claire knew she was in love with him. She didn't need the bells she wore to tell her that. She was sleeping at his place and without thinking had grabbed for the phone when it rang. A woman was crying. Her father was dying and she didn't know what to do for him. Philippe got out of bed. He was on the phone for nearly half an hour.

"What did you tell her?" Claire asked when at last he hung up.

Philippe was so tall he took up more than his half of the bed. He had beautiful long hands and dark hair. He was a very deep sleeper.

"I told her it was an honor to be with someone when they died. I said she should be grateful for her last moments with him. That she should say her good-byes."

"That took half an hour?" Claire asked.

"That takes a lifetime."

"I did something terrible," Claire said suddenly.

More and more often, she found herself wishing she could talk to her sister, the one person who might understand how easy it was to make a terrible mistake when all you thought you were doing was going for a drive on a beautiful blue day, taking the steps two at a time, leaving a door open, stepping on the gas too hard. When you had no intention of harming anyone, not even yourself.

"My uncle? I told you he was going to have a stroke with or without the burglary. Plus I'm convinced you're as paranoid as he was. Claire, you locked the door."

"Not that. Something else. Something unforgivable."

"Is this about telling your sister Meg to get in the car? That was an accident. If every doctor gave up his practice due to some accident he was responsible for, there'd be no doctors. We'd all be dead."

"No. Something worse. Something that ruined someone's life."

"Well, you rescued mine, so that cancels out whatever came before. I've been told I'd be an idiot without you."

"By who?" Claire grinned. "Your grandmother?"

"By you!"

She never told him what she'd done. The only one who knew was Elv.

Elv, who'd turned to look back at her, who'd disappeared into the briars, who'd been taken by an unbreakable spell until nightfall.

BEFORE LONG CLAIRE and Philippe moved in together, to the top floor of Madame Cohen's house. Their grandmothers did them the service of not saying they had told them so. It was a big apartment and they were slowly painting each room white. The woodwork was gold leaf, very old, chipped at the edges, but beautiful.

They decided to keep it as it was. The bedroom overlooked a small garden, nothing as grand as the cobblestone courtyard of Claire's grandmother's building, but still lovely.

When Claire left Monsieur Cohen's workroom at noon, she stopped by the shop to retrieve Madame Cohen and they went home together for lunch. Natalia often joined them. She was recovering from the loss of Samuel Cohen. She seemed more fragile. Her knees were bothering her, and Claire had to help her up the stairs to the apartment. Eighteen years had passed since the anniversary party at the Plaza Hotel, but Natalia still dreamed of that day. She dreamed of Annie and of Meg and of the Story sisters when they were young, wearing the blue dresses she had made for them. Just the night before, she had fallen asleep on the couch in the parlor and in her dream she went to her own party. Everyone was there: her husband, Martin, and Samuel Cohen, and her nieces Elise and Mary Fox. In the kitchen, the staff was hard at work icing petits fours in hues of pink and green and blue. There was the smell of sugar and vanilla. Waves of heat wafted from the huge restaurant stove and made her flush. "Make me something I'll never forget," she told the head chef. "Make sure I remember everything before it gets lost."

When Claire made lunch for Madame Cohen and her grandmother, she used tomatoes whenever possible. She followed the recipe for her mother's gazpacho, she re-created the cream of tomato soup she and Pete had made for Annie when she was so ill, she fixed green tomatoes on toast with olives, so simple and pleasurable, and of course, Madame Cohen's favorite, risotto with yellow tomatoes and thyme. Claire grew her own tomatoes in earthenware containers set on the tiny balcony of their apartment, ordering heirloom seeds from catalogs. In the height of summer, she tossed a net over the plants to keep the birds from pecking at them. When Philippe came home on summer nights, he'd find

Claire on the patio and he'd come to sit beside her, stretching his long legs out beside hers. He had no idea that tomatoes could be green and pink and yellow and gold. He preferred to eat them whole, like apples.

THE FOLLOWING SPRING, the flowers on the chestnut tree were in such abundance that tourists came to take photographs. It was the season the family had always dreaded, but this year was different. When spring arrived, Natalia and Claire welcomed it. They washed the windows in Natalia's apartment, ordered heirloom tomato seeds, went walking by the river in the glassy afternoons. This year upon her return from visiting Mimi and Elv, Natalia was sewing Claire's wedding dress. She had gotten special magnifying glasses in order to see the stitches. She had arthritis in her hands, but she had worked all winter and now she was getting close to completion. She would need to persevere in order to finish by the coming summer. Her fingers bled from the delicacy of the stitches, and she had to soak her hands in warm olive oil, but she felt certain this would be the last dress she would ever attempt, so she put everything into it. She had been in love twice and all that she'd felt went into the dress, with stitches set so close together it was nearly impossible to see them with the naked eye. In Natalia's opinion, that was the way love was, invisible, there whether or not you wanted to see it or admit to it.

On the day the package arrived, Claire was in a hurry to get home. She'd forgotten her umbrella and the rains had begun. She avoided puddles as best she could, leaping across gutters. She had on a raincoat over black jeans and a sweater, but was soon drenched to the skin. She always wore the lapis necklace with the ancient bell, which she half believed had brought Philippe to her. Well, maybe it had and maybe it hadn't, but she wasn't taking any chances. When she got home, she quickly shrugged off her rain-coat, then toweled her sopping hair dry. She slipped off her boots and pulled off her jeans. To her surprise, Madame Cohen and her grandmother were in her kitchen, a pot of tea on the table between them. They glanced up at Claire when she walked in.

"Now what?" Claire only had on underwear and a black sweater. She was pale and long-legged and serious. Love had made her more approachable. People often came up to her on the street and asked for directions or begged a few euros to tide them over until their luck changed.

"Is someone dead?"

"Not at all," her ama assured her.

Though her amulets were more in demand than ever, the only jewelry Claire wore, other than the love talisman, was her engagement ring. Madame Cohen had given Philippe her own ring to present to Claire, the one her grandmother had brought from Russia. Everyone in the family was talking about this. It was something of a scandal. Madame Cohen hadn't offered it to any-one else, and there had been plenty of engagements throughout the years. She'd been waiting for the right person, and that person was Claire. She'd known it when she caught the first demon on the flypaper. She'd known when Claire had cried in the kitchen during her job interview. Madame Cohen had arranged this mar-riage when she sent Philippe to bury the dog. In a world of sor-row, love was an act of will. All you needed were the right ingredients. Not even her own daughters knew the circumstances of how she'd lost her sisters, that's how long ago it had been. She knew that sometimes when you were supposed to feel lucky, all you felt was despair. You were guilty just because you had man-aged to live. For reasons you couldn't understand, that made no sense whatsoever, you were the one left unscathed.

The package that had arrived by post that day had been

addressed in Mimi's girlish handwriting. The postmark was North Point Harbor.

"Open it," Madame Cohen urged.

Inside was a painting in a cheap frame. It was all black. A watercolor. It was a young girl's painting of the Seine with a starless night sky up above. It was the painting Claire had always wanted. She read her niece's note. She thought about girls with long black hair, about the bottle-green leaves of the sweet pea vines and the white-throated squash blooms. She thought about a robin in the grass, and the sprinklers being turned on, and about the hot pavement on the corner where she had waited all day. She thought about the tomatoes in the garden. Cherokee chocolates, Golden Jubilees, Green Zebras, Rainbows. She felt a surge of grief, not for everything she'd lost, but for everything that had never been. She hadn't even known how much she'd missed Elv.

"They want to come to Paris," she said.

THE WEDDING WAS held in the Bois de Boulogne, at the Chalet des Îles, set in the center of the lake. The family had rented out the restaurant and invited sixty people. The Cohens had such a big family and so many friends that several had to be cut from the invitation list to ensure they didn't go over the lucky number of sixty. There were some hard feelings, but there had already been a huge engagement party several months before, at Philippe's brother Émile's house, with too many guests to keep track of. That evened things out a bit.

Sixty was a lucky number, Madame Cohen had decreed, and she had been right too many times for them to ignore her. It would bring them happiness, they would see. Indeed, the weather was perfect, just as she'd predicted. The hot summer's day had faded into a warm blue evening. It would stay light until after ten.

No one worried about the silly rumors about creatures that could be found in the Bois after dark, vicious dogs, wolves, lost souls. This was not the weather or the time for such things. Guests were ferried across the water in little boats, disembarking on a dock strung with white lights. A trio played in the garden and music drifted across the island. The bees were moving slowly through the thin blue light, drawn by the sweet glasses of champagne and kir, making themselves drunk with the scent and the taste.

The dress Natalia made was stunning—white tulle and silk. Every seam was perfect. There were sixty pink pearls sewn into the bodice. When she'd presented the dress to her granddaughter, Claire had cried and said it was far too beautiful for her. She was afraid she might ruin it.

"Wear it and be happy," Natalia told her.

Now Claire was standing near a bank of wild ferns that grew beside the restaurant. Bullfrogs were calling in the reeds. The heat had settled on Claire's skin and she looked flushed. She was drinking a glass of vodka and soda. She was a nervous wreck. She didn't know if happiness would suit her. She wasn't prepared for it. Philippe wasn't supposed to see her in her wedding dress until the ceremony, but he went right over. He didn't care about rules. He never had. That was why Madame Cohen had kept him out of the shop when he was a boy. He was nothing but trouble back then. But a boy who is trouble is something entirely different as a man. He was leaning in close, whispering. Claire laughed and let him have a sip of her drink.

Peter Smith had come from New York to give the bride away. They had teased him that hell must have frozen over because here he was back in Paris, staying with Philippe's parents, who didn't speak a word of English. Pete was surprised to find that this time around everything was better than he'd remembered, especially the food. He was becoming an expert on cheese and thought he might open a shop in North Point Harbor, right on Main Street. Elise and Mary Fox were there as well, splurging on the Ritz. Mary was delighted to find that so many of the guests were doctors, even if she couldn't speak the language. She'd discovered that one of Madame Cohen's grandson's friends was working at NYU Medical Center. She and Claire had already discussed catching the bouquet; Claire was to throw toward the right, where Mary would be standing, arms outstretched.

But the wedding gown wasn't the last dress Natalia had sewn. She had made a pink silk and tulle dress for her great-granddaughter. It arrived in North Point Harbor in a huge white box tied with string. The package was so special that Mimi had to run upstairs and get her mother to come out to the porch and sign for it before the postman would hand it over. They carried it up to Mimi's room, then sat it on the bed and stared at it, wondering what on earth it might be, before Elv went to get the scissors to cut the string.

"It's definitely something French," Mimi said solemnly.

"Definitely," Elv agreed.

There was a huge amount of tissue paper, and then the dress. Elv looked at it, then turned away, overcome. Mimi was too excited to notice; she grabbed the dress and raced down to her grandpa's apartment to show it off. It was by far the most beautiful dress in the world. Elv stayed behind and took up the envelope inside the cardboard box that had been addressed to Miss M. Story. It was an invitation to Claire's wedding. Elv opened it. She shouldn't have, but she did. She couldn't believe how much time had passed. It was low tide in the bay. The birds were swooping over lawns and through the tall marsh grass beyond the yard. *Bring your mother,* Claire had written.

• • •

NATALIA PAID FOR the tickets, as she'd always said she would. But of course Elv and Mimi were too excited to sleep on the plane. Elv whispered how every year the Story sisters would notice a new shade of light in Paris. The sisters were in love with French milk and French bread; they all practiced tying their scarves the way French women did, but could never get it right. Every spring the chestnut tree in the courtyard bloomed. The river was green in the daytime, and black as evening approached. One night Elv had rescued a cat that had fallen into the water. Their ama had named it Sadie, and it was still alive, only now the cat was very old and cranky.

Mimi did not find Sadie cranky in the least. It sat on her lap and purred and she sneaked it bits of her dinner. She loved being in Paris in her great-grandmother's house. They stayed in the guest bedroom, the room that had been Claire's before she'd moved in with Philippe. The parlor was still painted red, lacquered so that it gleamed when the lamps were turned on. The light was still a thousand different colors, changing with the weather and the hour of the day.

"It's the color of lemons!" Mimi declared when she woke to her first morning in Paris. "Now it's the color of peaches!" she said as she and her ama later fixed a pot of tea in the kitchen. Mimi had seen photographs of her gigi on the mantel, but Claire still hadn't been by after two days.

"She doesn't want to see me," Elv said to her grandmother while Mimi was doing her best to watch French television.

"She wouldn't have told Mimi to bring you if she didn't want you here," Natalia assured her.

But Elv got herself so worked up the night before the wedding that she came down with a fever. In the morning she dressed, then went to splash water on her face. She was burning up. She told Natalia she couldn't possibly go, but then she saw Mimi in her frothy pink dress. She wished Lorry were there to see how beautiful his daughter was. *Oh, baby,* he would have said. *How did you get to be so grown-up?*

Mimi talked her mother into going with them to the park. "Maybe you'll feel better once you get there," she said reasonably. "You don't have to go any farther if you don't want to." She was practical, the way Meg had been. Plus she had Lorry's talent for talking you into nearly anything.

"Sure," Elv said, catching up her daughter's hand. "Will do."

Pete was there with a taxi, which they took to the Bois; the driver went wickedly fast. Pete had second thoughts about Paris all over again.

When the taxi parked, they could see the lake and the island. Mimi was utterly enchanted. "It's the fairyland you invented," she said to her mother.

"Go on," Elv said, sending her off with her ama. "I'll watch from here. This is fine."

Mimi was too smart. She came to her mother and gestured so that Elv would lean close and she could whisper. "Is it because they all hated Daddy?"

"Oh, no," Elv said. "Everyone loved him. He told people stories and they just sat and listened and they didn't want to be anywhere but right there with him. Believe me, I know."

"Your mom doesn't like crowds," Pete said. He had come up behind them. Elv threw him a grateful look. "Like at the school dinners. She has a good view from here."

Elv waved to Mimi when she got on the little boat and Mimi waved back. She had a sense of loss just seeing her daughter float away. The boat was indeed like a faerie boat, leaving water lilies in its wake. Once it had drawn up to the dock, everyone got off and was greeted by the Cohen family. Music drifted across the water in bits and bursts. Every now and then Elv spied Mimi on the other side, exploring the island, and then she couldn't see her anymore. Mimi caught sight of the bride standing by the reeds with a tall, handsome man. She ran right up to her gigi, and when Claire turned she knew Mimi immediately. She recognized the long black hair, the way she smiled. She was wearing the charm bracelet and she held up her arm for Claire to see. She shook it and there was the sound of bells. Mimi's eighth birthday had just passed. She was exactly the same age Claire had been when she did the unpardonable, horrible thing for which she could never be forgiven.

She had gotten out of the car.

Claire glanced around and spied a woman on the other side of the lake. She asked Mimi if she would take care of her bouquet for her. It was made up of a hundred roses, all white. Each rose was small and perfect. Mimi nodded. She took her duties very seriously.

Claire could hear the birds in the linden trees; they always called when it was growing dark. The nature of love had totally escaped her until now. She had thought that if you lost it, you could never get it back, like a stone thrown down a well. But it was like the water at the bottom of the well, there when you can't even see it, shifting in the dark. She remembered everything. The violets and the blood, the day when Elv hunkered down in the garden after refusing to cut her hair, the bird they had found with its tiny white bones, the charm Elv had strung together to protect them against evil. When they were in the garden looking up through the leaves, the whole world turned green. Elv thought she saw her sister walking toward the dock in her white dress. She had been waiting for her and she'd wait for her for as long as she was gone, and there she was, in the falling dark; she hadn't gone anywhere at all.

Madame Cohen sat in an armchair that the waiters had carried out to place under one of the lindens. The air was still sultry. The last of the day's light filtered through the shadows. It was lemon colored, exactly as Mimi had noted. Madame Cohen had been brought a kir *pêche* that reminded her of the peaches she and her sisters had once eaten on a picnic out in the countryside. Natalia pulled a chair next to her friend's. She could see her great-granddaughter holding a bouquet of white roses, spinning in a circle on the dance floor that would later be crowded with couples. She and Madame Cohen had worked side by side in this world of grief. Today their grandchildren were happy. That was gratifying.

They could hear frogs splashing in the shallow water. There were white lights everywhere, as if the stars were falling down. It was twilight. The light would soon be turning to ink, another color for Mimi to write in her diary. Philippe shouted out and waved his arms, calling the two grandmothers over.

"They need us," Natalia said.

"Let's let them think so," her friend suggested.

As they walked across the grass, Madame Cohen saw a small black shadow in the shape of a moth. It hovered above her glass of kir, drawn like the bees to the sugar and fruit, then it flitted away. She didn't worry about it in the least. It was summer, and hot, and everything was just beginning.

Acknowledgments

MANY THANKS TO MY FIRST READERS—Maggie Stern Terris, Pamela Painter, Tom Martin, Gary Johnson, Elaine Markson, and John Glusman.

Thanks to Camille McDuffie. Much gratitude to Shaye Areheart.

And many thanks to Sandra Hoffman-Nickels and Max Hoffman for sharing Paris.

The Story Sisters

Reading Group Guide

The Story Sisters charts the lives of three sisters—Elv, Claire, and Meg—whose close bond and seemingly charmed lives in a small Long Island town are altered forever when Elv and Claire encounter an evil man who changes their future. The two sisters swear themselves to secrecy and attempt to overcome the trauma they've endured with their own brand of fairy tales and lies. But their secret, imaginary world sets them apart from all others. Their mother is unaware of what has happened and fails to see her eldest daughter's downward spiral until it is too late. Elv is sent to a special school in New Hampshire and Claire and Meg become more sharply divided over their allegiance to her. The Story sisters are no longer united.

As the girls grow into young women, they are haunted by the events of the past and by choices they've made. They turn to their beloved grandmother, Natalia —known as Ama—who lives in Paris, for help time and time again. The beauty of Paris, the idea of true love, and Elv's redemption through her love for the man who has always stood by her, despite his flaws, and for her own young daughter—offer salvation for the Story family.

Questions for Discussion

1. When Elv and Claire set out to rescue the horse at the beginning of the novel, what do you learn about the family dynamics and the personalities of the three sisters? How do they relate to one another and to their mother, Annie? Which sister is most like Annie? What does Annie mean when she says, "People who said daughters were easy had never had girls of their own" [p. 4]?

2. The importance of storytelling is a central theme of this novel. What purpose do stories serve—for the individual and for society? Do you see any parallels between the Story sisters and other literary sisters, such as the Brontë sisters or the March sisters in Louisa May Alcott's *Little Women*? Can imagined worlds be both positive and destructive? What is the thin line between storytelling and deception/denial, and how does it come into play in the novel?

3. After her abduction, Elv begins to invent the world of Arnelle. It's a way for her to escape reality, but her fairy-tale world becomes a trap of its own. Discuss the otherworld that Elv creates and how it functions. What are the rules of Arnelle and how do

they relate to Elv's abduction? Why does Elv later decide to change the story by "going over to the other side" [p. 69] and joining with the "demon world"? Can you understand and have compassion for her when she turns her back on the "human world"?

4. Fairy tales typically include common mythic elements, including the battle between good and evil, the idea of "the quest," and the notion that sacrifices must be made in order for an individual to earn wisdom and faith. How are the qualities of fairy tales incorporated into the novel?

5. Each chapter begins with a "fairy tale" from Elv's *Black Book of Fairy Tales*, the stories she tells to her sisters. If you read them in order, what do they tell you about Elv's inner life? Are fairy tales often a psychological map, a way to get to truth via mythic and symbolic references? If so, how?

6. On the day of Elv's abduction Meg is reading the Charles Dickens novel *Great Expectations*. Why is this significant? Meg also reads *Oliver Twist* and Virginia Woolf's *To the Lighthouse*. Why might these novels appeal to her? Which author does Claire read in Paris, and why do you think this novelist would appeal to her considering her unique vision of the world? Are there novels that you feel affected you greatly at certain points in your life? If so, which ones and why?

7. Why does Elv keep her abduction a secret? Whom is she trying to protect? Why does Claire go along with her decision? Is keeping another person's secret a sign of loyalty or does it—as Meg asserts—make you an accomplice? How did your vision of Elv change as you learned more details about her abduction?

8. When Elv's family brings her to Westfield, she feels betrayed. Why does Elv place such a high premium on loyalty, and how do you think she defines it? How does each family member react to the intervention? Are there situations where it's necessary to deceive loved ones in order to save them? Have you ever faced such a situation with a loved one?

9. First at the Westfield School and later in prison, Elv strongly identifies with Hester Prynne in Hawthorne's *The Scarlet Letter*. What parallels do you see between Elv and Hester? In what ways does Elv imagine herself to be "marked" and set apart from others? Have you known people who have made a youthful mistake that has haunted them?

10. What stories does Lorry tell Elv about his past, and how do they mirror her own tales of Arnelle? Why doesn't she feel betrayed when she learns that Lorry's "true-life" stories about living below Penn Station with the mole people are in fact fiction? What is the distinction between a story and a lie? Do you think Lorry gave Elv what she wanted or needed? How do you view the love they had for each other?

11. When Annie hires Pete to track down Elv, the two strike up a friendship that leads to romance. What do you make of Pete's decision to stay with Annie and pursue a relationship with her even though he knows he doesn't have much time left with her? What does that decision say about his character?

12. After Meg dies, her sisters are emotionally lost, shattered by the tragic circumstance of her death. Elv disappears and Claire withdraws deep inside herself, refusing to speak or relate to others. Why does Elv run away from the scene of the accident? Does

she want to be found? Whom does Claire blame for Meg's death and why? Why does it take an outsider such as Pete to understand and try to assuage the sisters' guilt?

13. While in prison, Elv works with abused and abandoned dogs and later takes a job with an animal shelter. After Meg dies, Claire's constant companion is her dog, Shiloh. Lorry's stories revolve around a heroic dog as well. How does the relationship between human and dog relate to the theme of loyalty? What impact do the dogs have on the sisters and why?

14. As a detective, Pete is in the business of uncovering secrets. But he is also a keeper of secrets when he feels it's necessary to protect those he loves. Why does he pose as an author when he visits the man who abused Elv? Is this man correct when he says people are unknowable and that "everyone has their secrets" [p. 286]? Do you feel Pete has made a moral decision when he frames the man who is responsible for so much of the damage in the Story sisters' lives?

15. In Paris, Claire leads a solitary life and speaks only when necessary. She avoids love and relationships and suffers from intense guilt. What does Claire mean when she says that "she and Elv were two of a kind" [p. 227]? Do you see the similarities between the sisters, even though their lives take such different arcs? What role does art play in reconnecting Claire to the world?

16. How does motherhood change Elv, and what does she discover about the nature of maternal love? Do you think we often understand our parents best only after we ourselves become parents? What stories does Elv pass down to Mimi? How does the telling of family stories help Elv and connect her to the past?

What role does Mimi play in bringing Elv and Claire together again? Do you see a future for the Story sisters? If you were to write the next five years in the sisters' lives, how do you imagine Claire and Elv's relationship will progress? Would you agree that the major theme of *The Story Sisters* is the possibility of redemption and forgiveness?

About the Author

ALICE HOFFMAN is the author of twenty-five works of fiction. *Here on Earth* was an Oprah Book Club selection. *Practical Magic* and *Aquamarine* were both bestsellers and Hollywood movies. Her novels have been ranked as notable books of the year by the *New York Times, Entertainment Weekly,* the *Los Angeles Times,* and *People,* while her short fiction and nonfiction have appeared in the *New York Times, The Boston Globe Magazine,* the *Kenyon Review, Redbook, Architectural Digest, Harvard Review,* and *Ploughshares.* She divides her time between Boston and New York City.

About the Type

THIS BOOK WAS set in Granjon, an oldstyle typeface designed by George William Jones in 1928 for the Mergenthaler Linotype Company. It was modeled after sixteenth-century letterforms of Claude Garamond and was named for Garamond's contemporary, Robert Granjon, who was known for his italic types.

Also by Alice Hoffman

In *The Third Angel*, Hoffman weaves a magical and stunningly original story that charts the lives of three women in love with the wrong men: Headstrong Madeleine Heller finds herself hopelessly attracted to her sister's fiancé. Frieda Lewis, a doctor's daughter and a runaway, becomes the muse of an ill-fated rock star. And beautiful Bryn Evans is set to marry an Englishman while secretly obsessed with her ex-husband. At the heart of the novel is Lucy Green, who blames herself for a tragic accident she witnessed at the age of twelve, and who spends four decades searching for the Third Angel—the angel on earth who will renew her faith.

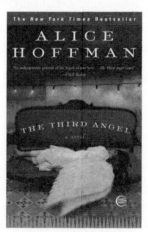

The Third Angel
$14.95 paperback (Canada: $16.95)
978-0-307-40595-1

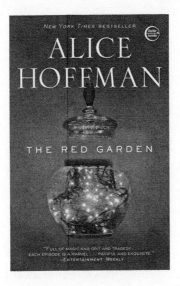